THIS SIDE OF
MURDER

THIS SIDE OF
MURDER

ANNA LEE
HUBER

KENSINGTON BOOKS
www.kensingtonbooks.com

KENSINGTON BOOKS are published by

Kensington Publishing Corp.
119 West 40th Street
New York, NY 10018

All Kensington titles, imprints, and distributed lines are available at special quantity discounts for bulk purchases for sales promotion, premiums, fund-raising, educational, or institutional use.

Special book excerpts or customized printings can also be created to fit specific needs. For details, write or phone the office of the Kensington Sales Manager: Kensington Publishing Corp., 119 West 40th Street, New York, NY 10018. Attn. Sales Department. Phone: 1-800-221-2647.

Kensington and the K logo Reg. U.S. Pat. & TM Off.

eISBN-13: 978-1-4967-1316-2
eISBN-10: 1-4967-1316-8
First Kensington Electronic Edition: October 2017

ISBN-13: 978-1-4967-1315-5
ISBN-10: 1-4967-1315-X
First Kensington Trade Paperback Printing: October 2017

10 9 8 7 6

Printed in the United States of America

For my second daughter, my darling little chipmunk. You were growing inside of me while I wrote this book, and undoubtedly influenced it. May you always shine your light on places bright and dim, and may you always know how deeply you are loved and cherished.

ACKNOWLEDGMENTS

There are always so many people I want to thank who contribute to the creation of each of my books. First and foremost, I want to express my gratitude to my agent, Kevan Lyon, who encouraged me to pursue this idea and helped me bring it to fruition. Her enthusiasm and wisdom are boundless.

Second, I want to thank my editor, Wendy McCurdy, and the entire team at Kensington for welcoming me with such open arms, and lending their skills and expertise to bring this book into existence. I look forward to a long and fulfilling relationship with all of you.

Third, I must thank my amazing family and support team. My husband, who is always there for me through thick and thin. My children, who make everything in life sweeter. My mother, who enables me to find the time to write. And all my friends and family who offer me unending love and encouragement.

I also wish to thank my readers. Without your enthusiasm and excitement, none of these stories would be possible. Thank you for allowing my stories into your lives.

"I'm not sentimental—I'm as romantic as you are. The idea, you know, is that the sentimental person thinks things will last—the romantic person has a desperate confidence that they won't."

—F. Scott Fitzgerald, *This Side of Paradise*

CHAPTER 1

You might question whether this is all
a ruse, whether I truly have anything
to reveal. But I know what kind of work
you really did during the war. I know
the secrets you hide. Why shouldn't I
also know your husband's?

June 1919
England

They say when you believe you're about to die your entire life passes before your eyes in a flurry of poignant images, but all I could think of, rather absurdly, was that I should have worn the blue hat. Well, that and that my sister would never forgive me for proving our mother right.

Mother had never approved of Sidney teaching me how to drive his motorcar that last glorious summer before the war. Or of my gadding about London and the English countryside in his prized Pierce-Arrow while he was fighting in France. Or of my decision to keep the sleek little Runabout instead of selling it after a German bullet so callously snatched him from me. In my mother's world of rules and privilege, women—even wealthy widows—did not own motorcars, and they certainly didn't drive them. She'd declared it would be the death of me. And so it might have been, had it not been for the other driver's bizarre bonnet ornament.

Once my motorcar had squealed to a stop, a bare two inches from the fender of the other vehicle, and I'd peeled open my eyes, I could see that the ornament was some sort of pompon. Tassels of bright orange streamers affixed to the Rolls-Royce's more traditional silver lady. When racing down the country roads, I supposed they trailed out behind her like ribbons of flame, but at a standstill they drooped across the grille rather like limp seagrass.

I heard the other driver open his door, and decided it was time to stop ogling his peculiar taste in adornment and apologize. For there was no denying our near collision was my fault. I had been driving much too fast for the winding, shrubbery-lined roads. I was tempted to blame Pinky, but I was the dolt who'd chosen to follow his directions even though I'd known they would be rubbish.

When my childhood friend Beatrice had invited me to visit her and her husband, Pinky, at their home in Winchester, I'd thought it a godsend, sparing me the long drive from London to Poole in one shot. I hadn't seen either of them since before the war, other than a swift bussing of Pinky's cheek as I passed him at the train station one morning, headed back to the front. All in all, it had been a lovely visit despite the evident awkwardness we all felt at Sidney's absence.

In any case, although Pinky was a capital fellow, he'd always been a bit of a dodo. I couldn't help but wonder if he'd survived the war simply by walking in circles—as he'd had me driving—never actually making it to the front.

I adjusted my rather uninspired cream short-brimmed hat over my auburn castle-bobbed tresses and stepped down into the dirt and gravel lane, hoping the mud wouldn't damage my blue kid leather pumps. My gaze traveled over the beautiful pale yellow body of the Rolls-Royce and came to rest on the equally attractive man rounding her bonnet. Dark blond hair curled against the brim of his hat, and when his eyes lifted from the spot where our motorcars nearly touched, I could see they were a soft gray. I was relieved to see they weren't bright with anger. Charming a man out of a high dudgeon had never been my favorite pastime.

One corner of his mouth curled upward in a wry grin. "Well, that was a near thing."

"Only if you're not accustomed to driving in London." I offered him my most disarming smile as I leaned forward to see just how close it had been. "But I do apologize. Clearly, I shouldn't have been in such a rush."

"Oh, I'd say these hedgerows hold some of the blame." He lifted aside his gray tweed coat to slide his hands into his trouser pockets as he nodded toward the offending shrubbery. "It's almost impossible to see around them. Otherwise, I would have seen you coming. It's hard to miss a Pierce-Arrow," he declared, studying the currant-red paint and brass fittings of my motorcar.

"Yes, well, that's very good of you to say so."

"Nonsense. And in any case, there's no harm done."

"Thanks to your colorful bonnet ornament."

He followed my pointed stare to the pompon attached to his silver lady, his wry grin widening in furtive amusement.

"There must be a story behind it."

"It just seemed like it should be there."

"And that's all there is to it?"

He shrugged. "Does there need to be more?"

I tilted my head, trying to read his expression. "I suppose not. Though, I'll own I'm curious where you purchased such a bold piece of frippery."

"Oh, I didn't." His eyes sparkled with mischief. "My niece kindly let me borrow it. Just for this occasion."

I couldn't help but laugh. Had he been one of my London friends I would have accused him of having a jest, but with this man I wasn't certain, and told him so. "I'm not sure if you're quite serious or simply having a pull at me."

"Good." He rocked back on his heels, clearly having enjoyed our exchange.

I shook my head at this teasing remark. He truly was a rather appealing fellow, though there was something in his features— perhaps the knife-blade sharpness of his nose—that kept him from being far too handsome for any woman's good. Which was a blessing, for combined with his artless charm and arresting smile he might have had quite a devastating effect. He still might, given a more susceptible female. Unfortunately, I had far too much experience with charming, attractive men to ever fold so quickly.

I pegged him at being just shy of thirty, and from his manner of speech and cut of clothes, undoubtedly a gentleman. From old money, if I wagered a guess. A well-bred lady can always tell these things. After all, we're taught to sniff out the imposters from the cradle, though it had begun to matter less and less, no matter what my mother and her like said about the nouveau riche.

He pulled a cigarette case from his pocket and offered me one, which I declined, before lighting one for himself. "If I may be so bold . . ." he remarked after taking a drag. "Where precisely were you rushing to?"

"Poole Harbor. There's a boat I'm supposed to meet." I sighed. "And I very much fear I've missed it."

"To Umbersea Island?"

I blinked in surprise. "Why, yes." I paused, considering him. "Are you also . . ."

"On my way to Walter Ponsonby's house party?" He finished for me. "I am. But don't worry. They won't leave without us." He lifted his arm to glance at his wristwatch. "And if they do, we'll make our own way over."

"Well, that's a relief," I replied, feeling anything but. Some of the sparkle from our encounter had dimmed at this discovery. Still, I couldn't let him know that. "Then I suppose if we're going to be spending the weekend together we should introduce ourselves." I extended my hand across the small gap separating our motorcars. "Mrs. Verity Kent."

His grip was warm, even through my cream leather glove, as he clasped my hand for a moment longer than was necessary. "Max Westfield, Earl of Ryde. But, please, call me Ryde. Or Max, even. None of that Lord business." Something flickered in his eyes, and I could tell he was debating whether to say something else. "You wouldn't by chance be Sidney Kent's widow?"

I'm not sure why I was startled. There was no reason to be. After all, I'd just discovered we were both making our way to the same house party. A party thrown by one of Sidney's old war chums. There were bound to be one or two of Sidney's fellow officers attending. Why shouldn't Lord Ryde be one of them?

My eyes dipped briefly to the glow at the end of the fag clasped between Ryde's fingers, before returning to his face. "You knew him?" I remarked as casually as I could manage, determined not to show he'd unsettled me.

"I was his commanding officer." He exhaled a long stream of smoke. "For a short time, anyway." His eyes tightened at the corners. "I'm sorry for your loss. He was a good man," he added gently.

I tried to respond, but found alarmingly that I had to clear my throat before I could get the words out. "Thank you."

It was the standard litany. The standard offer of condolences and expression of gratitude that had been repeated dozens of times since Sidney's death. I'd developed a sort of callus from hearing the words over and over. It prevented them from overly affecting me, from making me remember.

Except, this time was different.

"Did you know Sidney before the war?" I managed to say with what I thought was an admirable amount of aplomb. They were of an age with each other, and both being gentlemen it seemed a safe assumption.

"Yes, Kent was a year behind me at Eton and Oxford. Same as your brother, if I recall. They were chums."

I nodded. "Yes, that's how we met. Sidney came home with Freddy to Yorkshire one school holiday."

"Love at first sight?"

"Goodness, no. At least, not for him. I was all of eleven to his sixteen. And a rather coltish eleven, at that. All elbows and knees."

He grinned. "Well, that didn't last."

I dimpled cheekily. "Why, thank you for noticing. No, Sidney didn't return to Upper Wensleydale for six more years. But by then, of course, things had changed."

My chest tightened at the bittersweet memories, and I turned to stare at the bonnet of my motorcar—Sidney's motorcar—gleaming in the sunshine. I'd known this weekend was going to be difficult. I'd been preparing myself for it as best I could. Truth be told, that's why I'd nearly collided with Lord Ryde. I'd been distracted by my recollections. The ones I'd been ducking since the telegram arrived to inform me of Sidney's death.

I'd gotten rather good at avoiding them. At calculating just how many rags I needed to dance, and how much gin I needed to drink so I could forget, and yet not be too incapacitated to perform my job the following morning. And when I was released from my position after the war, well, then it didn't matter anymore, did it?

But this weekend I couldn't afford the luxury of forgetfulness.

As if sensing the maudlin turn of my thoughts, Ryde reached out to touch my motorcar's rather plain bonnet ornament, at least compared to his. "Kent used to talk about his Pierce-Arrow. Claimed it was the fastest thing on four wheels."

"Yes, he was rather proud of it." I recognized the turn in subject for the kindness it was. He'd sensed my discomfort and was trying to find a gracious way to extricate ourselves from this awkwardness. I should have felt grateful, but I only felt troubled.

I lifted my gaze to meet his, trying to read something in his eyes. "I suppose there wasn't much to talk about in the trenches."

His expression turned guarded. "No, not that we wanted to. Motorcars were just about the safest topic we could find."

I nodded, understanding far more than he was saying. Though, I also couldn't help but wonder if that was a dodge.

Almost reflexively, I found myself searching Ryde for any visible signs of injury. I'd learned swiftly that those soldiers fortunate enough to survive the war still returned wounded in some way, whether it be in body or mind. The unluckiest suffered both.

As if he knew what I was doing, he rolled his left shoulder self-consciously before flicking his fag into the dirt. He ground it out before glancing down the road toward Poole. "I suppose we should be on our way then, lest our fellow guests truly leave us behind to shrift for ourselves."

"It does seem rude to keep them waiting longer than necessary," I admitted, suddenly wishing very much to be away, but not wanting to appear overeager. "Is it much farther?"

"Just over the next rise or two, you should be able to see the town laid out before you."

"That close?"

"Yes, and as I said, I suspect Ponsonby will have told them to wait for us all before departing. He was always considerate about such things."

"You know him well then?" I asked in genuine curiosity.

He shrugged, narrowing his eyes against the glare of the midday sun. "As well as one can know another man serving beside him during war." It was rather an obscure answer. And yet Ponsonby had thought them friendly enough to invite him to his house party to celebrate his recent engagement to be married. Of course, the man had also invited me, a woman he hardly knew, though I assumed that was because of Sidney.

As if sensing my interest and wishing to deflect it from himself, he added, "I know he and Kent were great friends."

"Yes, since Eton. I met Walter once or twice before the war. And, of course, he attended our wedding." One of the numerous hasty ceremonies performed throughout Britain during the months at the start of the war, between Sidney's training and his orders to report to France as a fresh-faced lieutenant. I'd only just turned eighteen and hadn't the slightest idea what was to come. None of us had.

I looked up to find Ryde watching me steadily, as if he knew what I was thinking, for it was what he was thinking, too. It was an odd moment of solidarity under the brilliant June sky, and I would remember it many times in the days to come.

Because who of us ever really knows what's coming? Or what secrets will come back to haunt us in the end? The war might be over, but it still echoed through our lives like an endless roll of thunder.

CHAPTER 2

True to Ryde's assurances, we crested the second hill and the city of Poole appeared before us, spreading out along the rounded shoreline. The water of the natural harbor sparkled in the midday sun as flocks of birds dipped and wheeled over its surface. I breathed deeply, invigorated by the rush of the wind against my cheeks as the motorcar raced downward. The thrill of its gathering speed sang in my blood. The concentration required to drive the speeding vehicle steadied me, allowing me to regain control of the nerves that had been frazzled by my first encounter with a fellow guest.

A glance in the wing mirror revealed I hadn't left Ryde in the dust. Though whether he was enjoying himself or merely determined to keep up was difficult to tell. I didn't peg him as the reckless sort. Not like Sidney, anyway, whose devil-may-care driving had been somewhat legendary. But even the chariest can be seduced by the power of a good engine. In any case, I forced myself to ease the Pierce-Arrow down to a more reasonable pace, lest I actually cause a collision.

Poole was larger than I'd expected, but still easily navigable when one's destination was the harbor lined with tall-sailed yachts and large Channel-crossing ships. We skirted the shore of a lake and passed the train station, where most of our fellow guests had disembarked from their journeys down from London or elsewhere in England. I could have taken the train as well. After all, there were stops in both Winchester and Epsom, where I'd attended the Derby before driving on to Beatrice's. But I'd wanted the freedom of being able to come and go as I pleased, of flight should it become necessary.

My hands tightened around the driving wheel. Though, how that would be possible when we were all about to be ferried out to an island I didn't know.

I shook the worrying thought aside, slowing the motorcar as we approached the quay. I wasn't at all certain we would be able to pick out Walter's boat among all of the ships lining the waterfront, but true to his assurances I spotted the brilliant scarlet and yellow checked flag flying above the yacht's sails. The sight of the boat and its fellow passengers standing along the rails with drinks in their hands relieved me far more than it should have. I'd had mixed emotions about attending the house party, but apparently missing it was no longer to be borne.

Ryde insisted on hefting my larger case as we made our way down the dock toward the waiting boat while I carried my valise and hatbox. But I was relieved of even those burdens as a dark-haired man smartly dressed in a brown pin-striped suit descended the gangway to take them from me.

"Here you are," he proclaimed, passing my parcels up to one of the sailors. Taking my hand, he grinned broadly and insisted on helping me aboard. "We were just about to leave without you."

"Then it's lucky we arrived when we did. I would so have hated to have to swim across."

His eyes gleamed with interest as he scoured my features at a closer proximity.

Deciding it would be best not to overly encourage his forward behavior, *if* that was all it was, I extracted my hand from his and glanced over my shoulder at Ryde. "What about you, Max?"

His lips quirked, not having missed my deliberate use of his given name when I hadn't done so earlier. "I don't know. A dip in the water might be quite refreshing. Of course, then we would be battling pneumonia. So perhaps it's for the best we won't need to."

The man in the pin-striped suit smiled, but I also noted the tightening of his brow as he studied Max. "You and Westfield know each other, I see."

"Oh, yes. For all of three quarters of an hour now," I drawled. "I'm afraid I nearly ran him down in my motorcar."

"Really?" A smirk tightened his mouth. "I think a number of us would have quite cheerfully saluted you for that but a year ago."

It was spoken in jest, but I sensed there was something behind the words that wasn't altogether in good fun. I could tell Max did, too, though he didn't even flicker an eyelash at the barbed comment.

"That's what comes of allowing females to drive motorcars," another man muttered from his chair nearby.

I stifled a sigh, far too familiar with this narrow-minded opinion. However, I could hardly chide the man when I'd practically prompted him by announcing I'd almost crashed. Though I did turn a weary glare his way.

An effort that was wasted as he wasn't even looking at me. He was too busy glowering at the deck for some unapparent offense. The right sleeve of his coat was folded and pinned, hanging just below the bicep of the arm he'd lost from the elbow down. "And he's Lord Ryde now, remember?" the seated man snapped, turning icy blue eyes on the smartly dressed man who had helped me board the boat. "Heaven forbid, you should read the papers."

"Not if I can bloody well help it," he sneered.

I glanced at Max, who was sparing far too much effort conferring with the steward. I suspected so that he wouldn't have to address the topic at hand. His father, the previous Earl of Ryde, had been quite a prominent figure in politics until his death seven months ago, just weeks before the armistice he'd fought so hard to help secure. The newspapers had speculated endlessly on whether the late earl's son and heir would attempt to step into the void left by his father or accept a quieter role in Parliament.

"Gentlemen," he chided the other men as he swiveled to pass me a flute of champagne he'd taken from the steward's tray.

"Perhaps, rather than bickering, you'll allow me to introduce Mrs. Verity Kent." His eyes twinkled with mischief. "And these two sorry souls are Felix Halbert"—he dipped his head toward the man in the pin-striped suit and then the man in the chair—"and Jimmy Tufton."

"Charmed, I'm sure," I murmured, seeing the curiosity in their gazes as I sipped my champagne.

Apparently, Max had, too, for he confirmed all our suspicions. "They served in the Thirtieth with your husband as well."

I nodded at both men. How many of the guests had fought alongside Sidney in France? First Walter and Max, and now Felix and Jimmy. Surely Walter's friends were not all veterans of the Thirtieth?

Or had so many of his friends from before the war died that these men were all that was left? I'd met a man one evening at a nightclub who'd confided in me while we were dancing and both half bosky that he was the only man from his circle of eight friends who had survived the war. A few weeks later, I'd read in the paper that he'd shot himself.

As if in answer to my unspoken query, a voice called out behind me. "Verity?"

I swiveled around, delighted by the sight of a familiar face. "Tom!" I hurried forward, grateful in more ways than one to see my childhood friend and neighbor. He wrapped me in a fierce hug. "I didn't know you were going to be here," I gasped as he released me.

"I could say the same to you."

There were fine lines around his eyes that hadn't been there the last time I'd seen him. The same fine lines I'd been surprised to see marked my brother Freddy's face when he'd stepped onto the train platform in London after the war ended. But in this case at least, they only seemed to emphasize Tom's happiness.

His hands held me away from him so that his gaze could sweep up and down my figure. "You are a sight for sore eyes, Pip," he proclaimed, using the shortened form of Pipsqueak, the nickname my older brothers and their friends had taken to calling me long ago. "I'm glad to see you're all in one piece." His smile dimmed. "Though I was sorry to hear about Sidney. Rotten luck, my girl. He was a dashed fine fellow. We all thought so."

I pressed a reassuring hand to his chest, feeling the same emotion I'd choked down in front of Max fist in my throat. "Thank you."

His lips curled in a reflexive grimace of commiseration; then he turned, draping his arm around my shoulders as we walked toward the opposite side of the deck. Until he'd done so I hadn't noted his limp, but with every step I felt the jolt of his body compensating for the weakness in his left leg.

"So who is it you're friendly with? Ponsonby or his fiancée?" he asked.

"Walter stood up with Sidney at our wedding."

He nodded. "Of course. I think your brother mentioned that. Once upon a time."

"But what of you? I didn't think you served in the Thirtieth?"

Tom's eyes cut sideways at me. "Noticed that, did you?"

"It's hard to miss."

"Yes, well, Ponsonby seems to have gotten along with his fellow officers rather better than most, if this sampling of the weekend's guest list is anything to judge by. For my part, when the war ended I was more than happy to never have to see the sullen, puppy faces of a couple of lieutenants and the ugly mug of one Welsh corporal ever again." Then he added as almost an afterthought, "It was always the good ones who clicked it."

I had no response for that. Everything I could think to say sounded too trite.

In any case, he wasn't waiting for a reply. "But to answer your question, no. It's Nellie who received the invite." He glanced up, drawing my attention to his wife standing beside the rail. "The fiancée, Helen Crawford, is her cousin."

I'd forgotten Tom had married. A rather rushed affair in the midst of the war. When a few months later my brother wrote to tell me Tom had a newborn son, I'd suddenly understood the haste. Not that I blamed them. After all, I remembered how feverish Sidney's and my couplings were when he was home on leave.

Even so, Tom's choice in a wife smarted.

"Nellie, darling," I murmured, stepping forward to embrace her loosely. "You look well."

"Thank you. Likewise."

If Tom noticed the stiltedness between us, he was intelligent enough not to comment.

Nellie and I had been friends when we were younger, though admittedly, never very close ones. However, she'd never gotten over the fact that Sidney had chosen me over her, quite without my interference. The last time we'd spoken we'd both said a number of nasty things to each other, but there was one thing she'd shrieked that time had only hardened within me. One thing I wasn't certain I would ever be able to forgive.

Her eyes drifted toward the opposite side of the deck, where the trio of men who had served in the Thirtieth had been joined by a fourth man. They all looked on as the gangway was removed and the anchor lifted by a pair of sailors.

"I'm sorry about Sidney."

I glanced over at Nellie, trying to tell if she was sincere, but she refused to meet my eyes, and her porcelain features remained as smooth as stone. Ignoring her, I turned back toward Tom, taking another sip from my glass. "Where is Walter? Didn't he come to meet us?"

"No, I imagine he's waiting to greet us on the island. From what I gather, some of the other guests will have already arrived."

"It's his leg," Nellie interjected, turning to stare out into the harbor as the boat moved away from the quay. "He can't get around as well as Tom. Has to use a cane. And Helen says on bad days, he doesn't even try to leave his chair." Something in her tone made it sound as if it was a competition. One that Tom was winning.

But Nellie had always been like that.

"Yes, well, it will get better," Tom replied. "It's only been nine months since his injury. I've had the better part of two years to reach this point."

Nellie lifted one shoulder negligently.

"What of Umbersea Island?" I asked, deciding it was time to change the subject. "What do you know of it?"

"It's just there." Tom pointed toward a large landmass, rather closer to shore than I had expected, though still too far away for anyone but the strongest to swim out to, even in calm weather.

The larger part of Poole Harbor formed a sort of diamond, with Poole at the top tip, and the passage into the English Channel lying at the middle of the bottom right side. Umbersea Island sat more or less at the very center. From this vantage, it appeared thick with trees and vegetation, more a haven for animals than the opulent country retreat of a wealthy businessman, as I knew Walter's father to have been.

"From what I understand, it was fortified in Henry the Eighth's time and then largely used as a pirates' haunt until some well-heeled gentleman bought it and fixed up the island as his country estate. There was a pottery business based there for a short time in the nineteenth century"—Tom shook his head—"but not much else to tell."

"Helen says it doesn't look like much from Poole. That the quay and all the buildings and beaches of any note lay on the far shore." Nellie sighed. "I certainly hope so. Because I did not come here intending to rusticate."

I had to agree with her, though I would never have been so rude to say so out loud. Out of the corner of my eye, I could see Tom's brow furrowed with displeasure, and I decided it would be best to excuse myself. For some reason, Nellie was apparently indulging in a fit of the sulks—something she had done as a child, but should have long since grown out of—and I felt absolutely no compulsion to charm her out of them.

I strolled down the deck in the direction I'd seen the gentleman I'd yet to meet disappear. Ostensibly this was done to introduce myself, but in truth I wanted a few moments alone.

I sipped the last of my glass of champagne, which had begun to grow warm in the sun, and paused to lean against the railing, staring out across the harbor encircling us. The white sails of other yachts dotted the water in the distance, far removed from the line we now cruised toward the far side of Umbersea Island. Beyond them I could see sandy beaches and cottages peppering the bluffs of tall grass. The air was thick with the scent of the sea and the lemon wax the deckhands must have used to polish the wood beneath my fingers to a gleam.

"Did Tom Ashley and his wife point out Umbersea to you?" Max asked, approaching to stand next to me.

I swung my gaze in the direction we were sailing, watching as the island loomed larger before us. "They did."

"I suppose he also gave you a brief accounting of its history."

Hearing the amusement in his voice, I glanced back at him, curious how he knew that.

"Ashley was stationed as a town major in a village near the Somme during the middle of the war, acting as liaison between the locals and the British troops. Used to use any opportunity he could to expound on his vast knowledge of the area's history to any officer passing through."

I smiled. "Yes, Tom took a first in history at Cambridge." I glanced upward at him through my lashes. "As I'm sure he let you know."

"Of course."

"As a boy he was forever yammering on about Romans and Saxons, and what have you. Though, I admit, I think I learned more from him about Britain's noble history than any of my governesses. But, heavens! Don't tell him that."

"Your secret is safe with me." He drank the last finger worth of brandy from his glass before plucking my empty flute from my hand and passing them to the steward. "Speaking of scholars, have you met Montague yet?"

I turned to see he was hailing the man I'd intended to introduce myself to, a fair-haired fellow who appeared far too young to have served any time at the front. He looked so hesitant to approach, I almost told Max to leave the poor boy alone. But he called his name again louder, forcing the chap to either join us or blatantly snub us.

"Charlie Montague, allow me to introduce Mrs. Verity Kent," Max declared, performing the introductions.

I suspected he already knew who I was, for he displayed no shock or uncertainty upon hearing my name. Though when he took hold of my proffered hand, ever so briefly, I noticed how his hand shook.

"Very nice to meet you." His lips pressed together for a moment; then he blurted, "Sorry about your husband."

"Thank you. That's very kind."

He clasped his hands behind his back, rocking back on his heels.

Seemingly accustomed to the other man's fretful demeanor, Max offered us both a reassuring smile. "Montague plans to attend Cambridge in the autumn."

"How marvelous," I said, trying to set Charlie at ease. "Then you'll want to talk to Tom." I glanced toward the man in question, still standing with his wife a dozen meters away. "He studied there before the war."

"Thank you. I shall," the young man replied, then astonished me by striding off to do so.

I stared wide-eyed after him.

"Sorry about that," Max murmured resignedly. "Charlie always was a bit peculiar, but I'm afraid the war has only made it worse. Some of the men have a more difficult time readjusting than others."

Shell shock. I could read between the lines.

I watched as he clumsily introduced himself to Tom and Nellie, the latter of whom turned away, almost as if he had leprosy.

Yes, I supposed that would explain it. He wasn't the first man I'd met whom I'd suspected of having it. And sadly I knew he wouldn't be the last.

I couldn't stop my thoughts from straying to memories of Sidney's last leave. The few short days he'd been allowed to spend with me in London, he'd been jumpy, fidgety, as if he couldn't settle. After the first night when he'd frightened us both awake, yelling and thrashing from a nightmare, I would wake in the middle of the night to find he'd slipped out of our bed and down the hall to sleep on the sofa. Sometimes he wouldn't even be trying to sleep, just sitting there wide-eyed in the dark, staring into the shadows.

I hadn't said anything. There wasn't anything *to* say. I'd heard enough talk at the office about the "poor sods whose minds cracked under the strain of the war." Sidney didn't need to know his actions made my chest clench with worry and dread. Not when he had to return to the front and face it all again.

But now I wondered if there might have been other factors at play. Other reasons he was so flighty and furtive, answering all of my questions with queries of his own. Other reasons he had returned to the front two days before he had to report back. I wondered if I'd been too quick to fear it was shell shock when there were other possibilities to consider. Ones that, at the time, I'd never dreamed of contemplating.

CHAPTER 3

"There." Max pointed over my shoulder. "You can see the top of the castle."

I shook away my troubled musings and turned to follow his finger. Rising over the dark treetops on the opposite side of the island stood the solid stone block of Umbersea Castle. However, to reach it we had to round the eastern tip of the island, the northern part of which appeared to be a large lagoon bounded by a thin breakwater. Assorted large waterfowl floated across its surface, and I even caught sight of some woodland creature darting into the forest on the far side.

At the southern edge of this cove, a short block of stone buildings lined the beach, perhaps the old customs house and a few assorted homes or businesses. A small pier protruded from the far end of these structures, but it was not to this dock that the yacht sailed, but farther along to a far grander landing nearer to the castle. I blinked in bemusement at the gleaming white pier topped with castellated watchtowers on either end. No one entering or leaving Poole Harbor could miss it.

We disembarked and slowly made our way up the long wooden dock, each of us trying to catch our first glimpse of the castle proper. Regrettably, a wall and a series of tall elm trees blocked our view, making it difficult to see much more than the redbrick tower with its Union Jack flying proudly atop. That is, until we stepped through a portal and up the walk into a small garden. Then the castle loomed before us, as if sprouting from the forest.

The façade facing us was constructed from gray limestone and lined with numerous tall, Georgian-style windows, winking in the afternoon sun. At each corner the castle projected outward like a turret, but without the presumptuous pointed roofs that some buildings of newer construction tried to adopt with dubious success. Though apparently Walter, or his father before him, hadn't been able to resist stamping their family's coat of arms above the door.

Even so, it was certainly nothing to sniff at, as Nellie was doing, wrinkling her nose. I'd never known her to be such a high-hat, but our lives had taken very different courses since the autumn of 1914.

As we neared the arched door, it suddenly burst open and a lovely woman in a yellow dress of georgette crepe hurried out to greet us. "Oh, marvelous! You're here. We were just discussing whether we should alert the lifeboat crew." She beamed brightly at us and then at her fiancé as he emerged from the building to stand beside her, enjoying her own joke.

"I'm afraid that's my fault," Max told her. His lips quirked upward. "Ran into some trouble north of Poole."

"Not you, Ryde," Walter teased. He shifted his weight with his cane, then obliged him by inquiring, "What sort of trouble?"

"Me," I stepped forward to proclaim, stealing Max's punch line.

He smirked. "You said it, not me."

Several of the men chuckled, a bass accompaniment to our hostess's trilling laughter.

"Verity," Walter said, reaching for my hand. I allowed him to pull me closer, leaning in to kiss the air next to his cheek. "It's good to see you."

His smile was warm. The same soothing countenance I remembered grinning at me from over Sidney's shoulder the day we were wed. The same expression I imagined had calmed and bolstered hundreds of soldiers before they went over the top into battle. And yet it did not quite reach his eyes, not completely. I sensed some wariness there, some hesitance. Whether it was recognition of our mutual loss or something more, I didn't know. But it chilled me more than I would have thought possible.

"You too," I managed to reply before glancing into the eager eyes of the woman beside him. "And this must be your fiancée."

Walter's posture straightened proudly. "She is. Helen, meet Mrs. Verity Kent."

"Oh, Verity . . ." She grabbed hold of my hands. "May I call you Verity?"

"Of course," I answered, bowled over by her enthusiasm.

If possible, her face beamed brighter. "And you must call me Helen. In fact, I insist we *all* use our given names," she declared. "It's *much* too tedious otherwise."

Everyone else seemed too stunned, or too enchanted, to answer, so I responded for them. "Frightfully tedious."

She squeezed my hands where she still gripped them. "I'm so glad you could come after all. I *knew* we were going to be fast friends." She laughed. "Isn't this too grand?"

"Too."

She released my fingers and I wiggled them inside my gloves, trying to get feeling back into them as she turned to the next person.

It was impossible not to note how young Helen was. Barely twenty, if I were to wager. To think, I had been two years younger than her when I'd wed Sidney and then watched him march off to war, utterly ignorant of the horrors he would face. As ignorant as Helen appeared to be about what Walter had come back from?

I wanted to believe she was more discerning, more understanding than I had been. After all, she couldn't be completely blind to the pain Walter had endured as he recovered from his bullet wound. She must have lost friends and loved ones in the fighting. No one in Britain had been untouched by the massive casualties. But I had my doubts.

And yet they said youth was resilient. If it lived long enough. I was only two years older, but I didn't feel so buoyant. Even when I was frantically dancing a tarantella with a handsome chap, thoroughly embalmed with gin, I knew what really lay beneath it all, even if I didn't particularly want to take it out and air it.

At least, they seemed happy together. I only hoped Walter's fond smiles indicated something more than indulgence. Otherwise they were swiftly going to grow disenchanted with each other once the initial whirl of attraction wound down.

"I expect you would all like to refresh yourselves," Helen said, leading us through the doors and down a short corridor to what must have been the main foyer. "But after you've done so, I do hope you'll join the rest of us on the lawn for tennis. There will be chairs and refreshments, of course, for those who have no wish to play."

A pair of grand staircases curled around the edges of the round chamber, drawing one's eyes upward to the massive crystal chandelier glittering overhead. The room was swathed completely in white, from the walls and moldings to the marble tile on the floor and the crisp white runners on the stairs, making the room appear massive, but also cold. The only spots of color to alleviate this blank canvas were the black wrought iron of the staircase railings and the round black table topped by an arrangement of crisp white flowers.

Next to this sparse coloring, Helen appeared even more bright and vivid, and her blond bob and buttery spring gown only accentuated that fact. I thought I began to better understand her appeal to Walter. She was directing the men to follow the butler when Felix sidled closer.

"I suspect you're a woman who's good with a racket."

I eyed him askance. "Why, yes, Mr. Halbert. In more ways than one."

His smirk widened. "Felix, please," he reminded me. "We mustn't disappoint our hostess." He tipped his head forward, making a single dark curl from his slicked-back hair flop over his forehead—a calculated gesture I was certain.

He was an attractive enough fellow. I was sure plenty of women noticed when he entered a room. But regrettably for him, his antics did nothing but amuse me.

"Can I count on you to partner with me for doubles?" he asked.

I crossed my arms over my chest and swiveled to observe him more closely, narrowing my eyes in mock consideration. I didn't particularly wish to encourage this flirtation of his, but I also realized it might prove to be quite useful. In any case, he seemed to find my deliberation entertaining, taking the opportunity to sweep his eyes up and down my form. Cheeky bounder.

"I'm game," I told him. "But I warn you, I play for keeps. So if you prove to be a hayburner . . ."

He'd begun to walk away, following the other single men toward the stairs, but he glanced over his shoulder and winked. "Oh, I'm not."

I shook my head at his unabashed conceit and turned to find out who was to guide me to my room. Helen was busy reassuring Nellie about the accommodations in her and Tom's chamber. Accommodations Nellie had yet to see, and so could not possibly have found fault with. Yet. Even so, I noted a small furrow between our hostess's eyes. The first sign of any strain I'd seen her exhibit.

While Helen was distracted, I took the opportunity to cross the room toward the main entrance. The large, oaken doors were propped open, allowing a delicious sea breeze to sweep through the house. It blew softly against my flushed cheeks and feathered the hairs against my temples. I could see now that the castle was oriented so that the front faced the sea. The wall separating the house from the pier stopped short of here. One could stride down the broad set of stairs and across a thin strip of pale sand, and dip their toes in the vibrant blue water in a matter of three dozen steps. It was a tempting thought, but for the fact that I knew the water would be icy cold, and certain to freeze my toes in a handful of seconds. Certainly not worth the effort to fumble with stockings and garters.

Sidney would have done it.

The thought struck me before I even knew it had formed, and I found myself smiling at the image of him hopping on one leg across the sand as he removed his shoe and stocking from the other, all the while calling over his shoulder, taunting me to join him. He would roll his trousers legs up to the knee and wade in, grimacing from the cold, but determined to coax me in. And I probably would have gone. I'd been eager enough to follow along that summer of 1914 when he'd returned to visit Freddy at my parent's house. At least, until the autumn, when I couldn't follow him anymore. Not across the Channel to the fighting in France.

I couldn't follow him now either.

The image of Sidney faded, scattering in the breeze, and I wrapped my arms around myself, suddenly chilled. The knife blade of grief once more cut into my breast, making me hold my breath to try to blunt the pain. I was constantly deluding myself into thinking I'd moved past this, when all I'd done was dull the point occasionally with gin and dancing and vigilance. Then something would strike me from nowhere—a whisper of a resemblance in a stranger passing on the street or the smell of his cologne—and I would find myself right back here. Trying to catch my breath.

We hadn't been married long enough before he went to war for me to miss the normal domestic things. Like his razor beside the sink, or his clothes scattered on the floor, or his warmth beside me in bed at night. And at times I'd counted myself lucky not to miss that.

But conversely, I'd spent our entire marriage waiting for him to come home, and sometimes it felt like I still was. Like the war had never ended. He'd been dead fifteen months, but I would still find myself wondering when he would have leave next, or noting something I should tell him in my next letter. Those were the moments that were most agonizing, as if I were reliving the initial shock of his loss over and over again.

"Verity, I almost forgot. This arrived. . . ."

I turned back to meet Walter, who had returned to the foyer through a doorway on the left, his cane tapping on the marble floor. But something in my face must have given away my distress, for he stopped abruptly.

"What is it?" he asked in concern. "Is something wrong?"

"No." I forced a smile to my face. "No, just . . . my shoe pinching my foot."

The excuse was clumsy, but he was kind enough not to say so. I could see in his eyes he'd guessed the real cause of my sorrow, for he seemed to feel it, too. It was etched in the lines at the corners of his eyes, the sadness pleating his brow. Apparently, I wasn't the only one who was finding this weekend difficult.

Then why invite me?

His gaze dropped from mine to the item held in his hand. "Of course." He cleared his throat. "Well, this came for you earlier."

His arm extended and I stiffened. It was a letter.

For a moment, I couldn't make myself reach out and take it, too wary of what I would find. But when Walter glanced up at me again curiously, I forced myself to accept it.

"Thank you." My fingers brushed over the handwriting on the cream envelope and I exhaled in relief. It was from a friend in London. I would know her distinctive swirls and flourishes anywhere. She'd asked me to run an errand for her on my way through Ringwood, and was undoubtedly anxious to remind me of it.

I could feel Walter's eyes still watching me, and I attempted to laugh off my earlier misgivings. "Just a friend reminding me of an obligation. Again."

"Rather persistent."

"You have no idea." Daphne didn't understand the meaning of the word *pester*.

Having seen Nellie and Tom off with the housekeeper to show them to their rooms, Helen rushed over to us. "Verity! I'm so terribly sorry. You must've believed I'd forgotten you."

"Not at all," I assured her. "I was just admiring the view."

She followed my glance toward the open door. "Oh, yes. Isn't it heavenly? And to think, Walter almost sold this place." His expression tightened at the reminder, but her blue eyes gleamed at him with undaunted affection. "I'm so glad he didn't."

Some unspoken communication seemed to pass between

them, though I couldn't read it. A command or request given, and the other acquiesced.

Then Helen reached out to take my hand. "Come with me. I'll show you to your room myself."

I allowed myself to be towed along, listening with only half an ear as she burbled on about the other guests and her plans for the party. The other half of my mind was diverted by the evidence of recent refurbishments and the sheer opulence of our surroundings. From the carpets to the furnishings to the sculptures and artwork adorning the walls—everything was fashioned of the highest quality one could buy.

I was slightly taken aback by it all, as I remembered Sidney mentioning early in the war how low Walter's coffers were running. But between the castle and the gleaming new yacht, it was evident that wasn't the case now. I couldn't help but wonder if some of that was courtesy of Helen's inheritance. After all, her father had been a wealthy and well-connected man, and rumor was he'd left it all to her. Perhaps cynically, I pondered whether that was part of Helen's appeal.

Not that she wasn't beautiful and effervescent enough to capture most men's notice on her own. I knew she'd been popular among the London set during the war. I'd never met her, but I'd certainly heard of her.

As she seemed to have heard of me. "I can't imagine how we've never crossed paths before now. I've been hearing your name and that of your darling husband for years." Her expression arrested in horror. "Oh, I'm so sorry. That was rather thoughtless of me." She pressed a hand to my arm. "You must forgive me. Walter is always chiding me for the way I chatter on. It really is frightfully annoying of me to do so."

"There's nothing to forgive," I replied, trying to stem the flow of her words. "I can't expect everyone to act as if Sidney never existed. Nor would I want them to."

"I suppose you're right." She smiled gratefully and resumed her stride down the hall. "In any case, it's been over a year now, hasn't it? You must be learning to get on without him."

The words were spoken carelessly, and though I knew she meant well, they still lodged in my chest like a splinter. As if one could quantify the exact period of mourning one should endure. As if the pain automatically lessened once enough time had passed.

"Yes," I murmured. "Is there any other choice?"

She stopped at a door on the right, opening it as she pivoted to face me, displaying no evidence she'd heard the slight edge to my voice. "Here we are. You'll let me know if anything isn't to your approval. I *do* so want you to be comfortable."

For a moment I thought I detected a hint of sarcasm in those words, but nothing in her expression or demeanor supported that notion. I brushed it aside, deciding I'd imagined it. Easily done, as I was drained and somewhat oversensitive after the long drive that morning and my vigilance when confronted with the other guests.

And now I had to change clothes and join them on the lawn for tennis, as Helen reminded me before leaving me to explore my chamber on my own. I closed the door with a decisive click and turned to survey my assigned accommodations.

This room had plainly been treated to the same refurbishments as other parts of the house. Mallard blue toile wallpaper covered the walls, and gold satin drapes flanked the windows, already pulled to allow warm sunlight to flood the room. A four-poster bed with caramel and ecru striped hangings, and a soft gold coverlet dominated the space. I crossed the medallion-patterned carpet, feeling the heels of my pumps sink into the plush texture as I pulled my gloves from my hands. My luggage had been brought up for me; the large case was propped on a bench next to the wardrobe, while the valise and hat box rested on the dresser.

I had turned my steps toward the suitcase to search for my tennis whites when something resting in the middle of the counterpane caught my eye. It was a book. A rather plain volume of moderate thickness, and yet my heart quickened in dread. Somehow I knew the presence of this work of literature was no accident, nor was it a simple courtesy of our host. If he or Helen had meant to leave books in our room, they would be placed on the escritoire by the window, not the bed.

I glanced around me stupidly, as if the person who had left it might still be there watching me, waiting for me to pick it up. Inching closer, I sank down on the edge of the mattress to reach over and lift it into my hands. I could feel how worn and dented the cover was, my fingers finding the sunken divot where something had either struck or been dropped onto it. A sense of déjà vu swept over me, a feeling that I had somehow already done this before. And when I cracked open the book I understood why.

There, at the top of the first page, read my inscription: *To my dearest Sidney. With all my love, Verity.*

I hadn't seen the book in three years. It had not been among the few effects Walter and the other men in Sidney's battalion had been able to send home to me. I'd never even missed it. And yet, there was no denying this was the copy of *The Pilgrim's Progress* I had given my husband after he'd mentioned in one of his letters that he wished he had a copy. At the time I'd thought it an odd book to request, but I'd wanted to do what little I could for him, so I'd hurried out and bought a copy. Nothing fancy. I knew it had to stand up to the mud and marching. And it had. Remarkably.

But what was it doing here now? Where had it come from? And why had someone placed it on my bed?

Loosening my grip on the book, I feathered through the pages. Surely there would be something. . . . There. Tucked between the pages was a plain white slip of paper. I turned the book to read the short, typewritten note.

                    And so it begins.

My heart dipped into my stomach. The beginning? The beginning of what?

Rising from the bed, I hurried to my valise and began rifling through its contents until I found the letter that had arrived at my London flat a week before. The letter that had lured me to this house party when initially I'd declined the invitation.

I yanked it from its envelope and swiftly unfolded it, holding it up to compare it to the typeface of the note in the book.

I know the secrets you hide.

It was the same.

Part of me wanted to hurl the offending book and letters across the room, but I knew that would be both childish and useless. At any rate, another part of me wanted to clutch the book to my chest knowing Sidney had held it, had sweat and bled on it. Maybe that wasn't what the dark stain seeped along the edges of the pages truly was, but it looked too rusty to be simple mud, even from the Somme.

I blinked against the sudden burn of emotion at the backs of my eyes and reached up to swipe angrily at the offending tear that had rolled down my cheek. Who was doing this to me? And why? What purpose did it serve other than to hurt me?

The letter I'd received had claimed they had information to share with me about my late husband. Information that implied he'd gotten himself involved with some sort of treasonous activity. But they wouldn't tell me more until we met in person at Walter Ponsonby's house party.

My first instinct had been to burn the letter filled with all of its preposterous assertions. I knew Sidney. I knew he wasn't capable of anything so disloyal, so duplicitous.

But then they'd mentioned my war work, my position with the Secret Service—an organization no one was supposed to even know existed, something I'd never even made my husband aware of. How had the letter writer known about it? Had I given myself away? Had I unwittingly betrayed sensitive information to Sidney? Was that the treasonous activity they referred to? And how was it all connected to this battered copy of *The Pilgrim's Progress*?

I flung the open book down on the bed and stalked away from it, tugging harshly at the navy-blue sash around my waist. The belt tightened into a knot, and I grumbled in aggravation. Plop-ping back down on the bed, I leaned over to remove my shoes before attempting to unsnarl it. The book slid down the satin counterpane toward me and I reached out to shove it back, but my fingers caught on the edge of the binding. I glanced down to see that it had come loose, buckling the shape of the book.

I dropped my shoe on the floor next to the first one and then lifted the book into my lap, curiosity overriding my irritation. By pushing the outer covers inward, I discovered I could create a space between the bound pages and the outer board of the book. And tucked down inside this tiny well was a folded piece of paper. My fingers were slim and I was able to wriggle them down inside and extract it.

With a disquieting certainty that this was what I was sup-posed to find, not just the typewritten note, I slowly set the book aside and began to unfold the paper. It was slightly faded and showed evidence of some water spots, but the handwriting was still clear and concise. And obviously penned in some sort of code.

In my official capacity with the Secret Service, as a secretary and translator, I'd not dealt much with ciphers. But they'd been part and parcel with the clandestine assignments I'd taken on later in the war, traveling into war-torn Belgium and France. Then I'd routinely been called upon to write and decrypt codes. However, this was not a cipher I was immediately familiar with. Nor was it formulated like any of the traditional trench codes I'd ever seen. It was much too long and complex.

Which was all to the point, what in blazes had Sidney been doing with this coded missive? Why was it concealed in the binding of his book? And why was my anonymous correspon-dent giving it to me now?

CHAPTER 4

"There you are," exclaimed Helen as I strode across the lawn. Her voice barely reached me above the din of the rag music blaring from a gramophone issuing through one of the castle's windows. The tinny melody gave a sort of festive atmosphere to the gathering.

Three tables had been set out under the shade of the tall elm trees bordering the perimeter of the back garden nearest the sea. This garden was much larger than the one we had passed through upon our arrival, and boasted a wide, green expanse of lawn, one corner of which had been converted into a tennis court.

I forced a smile to my lips. Even if it did feel a shade too brittle, I suspected no one would notice. After all, I'd gotten very good at hiding my true thoughts and feelings during the war, sometimes knowing I risked certain death if I let them slip. Feigning delight in a social gathering was a cakewalk compared to that.

"My apologies. I'm afraid I put my feet up for a moment and found I was simply too comfortable to rouse myself with any speed," I replied, allowing the lie to trip off my tongue. The truth was, the discovery of Sidney's book and the coded missive concealed within had shaken me, and it had taken me far longer to settle my nerves and change into my tennis whites than it should have. I still felt a slight tremble in my abdomen, and sought to squash it. "Is that lemonade?"

"It is," confirmed a brunette seated next to the pitcher of soft yellow liquid I was eyeing, its surface slick with condensation. Her dark eyes beneath the wide brim of her hat returned my smile. "That is, lemonade with a little extra kick."

"Perfect," I proclaimed, plopping down into the empty chair next to her.

As the other woman poured me a glass, Helen draped an arm over her shoulders. "This is my cousin Mabel." Her lips curled into an impish grin. "She's a funny old bird. But she mixes the most divine cocktails. And for that I could forgive her just about anything."

"Yes, well, we all have our talents," Mabel responded affably as she passed me my drink, though I didn't miss the fleeting glance she cast her younger cousin's way. It was rather sharp with insinuation, but Helen didn't seem to notice.

"Then are you Nellie Ashley's cousin as well?" I asked, searching for my childhood friend among those lounging in the dappled shade. Although I could see some resemblance between Helen and Nellie, Mabel couldn't have appeared more different. Where they were all blond and lightness, Mabel was sloe-eyed and olive complexioned.

"Good heavens, no," Mabel replied with such vehemence I nearly choked on my lemonade.

Helen grinned. "Mabel is the daughter of my mother's sister, while Nellie is some distant cousin through my father. I can't recall the exact connection."

Mabel arched her eyebrows. "Then why on earth did you invite her?"

"I know she can be a bit of a Mrs. Grundy, but I felt I *had* to invite *someone* to represent my father's side. And believe me, she's by far the most tolerable." Her eyes slid toward the tennis court and narrowed in consideration on Tom, who appeared to be doing a rather admirable job returning his sandy-haired opponent's shots, even with his weak leg. "At least her husband seems to be a darb."

"Yes, Tom's a capital fellow," I assured them.

Helen glanced at me in surprise. "You're acquainted?"

I took another sip of the sweet liquid, attempting to gauge how much liquor had been added to the beverage, and nodded. Much as I would have loved to down my glass in one swallow and ask for another, I knew I had to keep my wits about me. "We were raised in Yorkshire not far from each other, and he and my oldest brother were great friends."

"And you kept in touch?"

I met her curious gaze, finding her interest a bit odd. "Well, Freddy did. I haven't seen Tom since early in the war. We happened to cross paths fleetingly one morning outside St George's while he was on leave." Much of my warmth at the memory fled as I recalled why I had been there in the first place. It had been shortly after my middle brother, Rob, was killed, shot down over France. "We shared a cup of coffee and then he was off again."

I still remembered as I watched Tom walk away how terrified I'd been for him, for all the boys from back home. By then the grim reality of war had sunk in, and I knew each meeting with any soldier might be the last. My mother kept me updated about all the families who lived near us in the Dales, and oh, how I had dreaded those letters. Each one seemed to relay news of another death, another tragedy. Sometimes I set them aside for weeks until I felt capable of reading them. That usually meant I was a trifle corked, so that when I woke the next morning, their contents seemed almost like they'd been nothing but a bad dream.

I could feel Mabel studying me, so I shook aside the memory and gestured toward Tom's sandy-haired opponent. "Who's that fellow?"

"That's Sam Gerard." Helen peered coyly over her shoulder at her cousin. "Mabel's beau."

I smiled at Mabel, wondering if Sam had also served in the Thirtieth or if he was solely here because of her.

A gasp from one of the other women returned our attention to the court, where Tom had crumpled to his knees, his weakened leg evidently having given out as he dashed to return a serve. I stiffened in alarm, but knew from long experience not to rush forward. All the males of my acquaintance tended to become rather waspish when you fussed over them or offered them unwanted insistence, viewing it as an insult to their manly pride. My male colleagues at the Secret Service, some of whom had been invalided out of service at the front lines because of serious injuries, had been the worst.

In any case, Tom was already pushing himself to his feet to test the strength of his left leg by the time Nellie reached him, chastising him like a schoolboy. "I *told* you not to play. I knew your leg wasn't strong enough yet. What were you thinking?"

"My leg is perfectly fine," he snapped back.

But Nellie wasn't listening. Instead she'd turned to admonish Helen, who cautiously approached the pair. "Why on earth did you decide we should play tennis? You can see that half these men aren't capable of it. Even your fiancé is hiding inside because he can't play."

My eyes widened in shock at her insensitive words. As if these men needed to have their infirmities thrown in their faces. My eyes strayed toward Charlie, who fidgeted in his chair. Next to him, Jimmy's thunderous expression darkened as he rolled the shoulder of the arm he was missing below the elbow.

It was true, I had also noted Walter's absence. However, I had not leapt to the assumption it had anything whatsoever to do with tennis. In fact, I'd been wondering whether it had anything to do with that look he and Helen had shared earlier in the entrance hall. Or if it was in any way connected to the gift that had been left on my bed.

It was quite possible Walter had been the person to place Sidney's book in my room, but then logistically it could have been any one of the people present. Several of the guests—including Mabel, Sam, and two young women to whom I'd yet to be introduced—as well as our hosts, had arrived at the castle earlier than the rest of us. The gentlemen on the boat at midday had all been shown up to their rooms close to ten minutes before I had, giving them plenty of time to discover where I was staying so they could slip in and leave the book. Though Tom and

Nellie were the least likely culprits, having gone up only minutes before I had, even one of them feasibly could have accomplished the task.

But why? Why go to such trouble to send me that letter and convince me to attend this house party only to leave Sidney's book with that coded missive tucked inside the binding on my bed? There had been no further explanation of what I was supposed to do with it. Was it simply meant to be proof of their initial accusations of treason? Did they think that cryptic note alone would convince me of Sidney's guilt?

It was absurd. For one thing, how could they expect me to believe that they had, in fact, found that message concealed inside Sidney's book? My mysterious letter writer could have placed it there themselves. And for another, the code wasn't even written in Sidney's handwriting. It was messy enough that I supposed it was possible he could have written it with his left hand to disguise his script, but that seemed rather far-fetched.

No. Surely my correspondent wouldn't think me so foolish as to believe I wouldn't require further proof. It was all too ridiculous to be believed.

Whatever Helen responded to Nellie's accusation, we couldn't hear for she did not raise her voice. But it seemed to give Tom some sort of grim satisfaction. He smiled tightly at his hostess and then gripped Nellie's arm, propelling her off the lawn court as he limped beside her, his stride growing stronger with each step.

He guided her toward one of the chairs, but rather than take a seat, she pulled her arm free of his grasp and stamped off toward the house. His shoulders drooped wearily as he watched her go, clearly debating whether to follow her or not.

"It's time to let some of the rest of us have a go anyway, old chap," Felix declared, rising to slap Tom heartily on the shoulder.

This seemed to catalyze Tom into motion. "Excuse me."

Mabel shook her head. "That man needs to rest his leg, not go running off after his wife."

"I couldn't agree more." I tilted my head in consideration. "But then apparently his injury has healed remarkably well. So maybe chasing after his wife has done him a world of good."

She laughed, a pleasant, hearty sound, nothing at all like the tinkling twitters most women made.

"Verity, what say you?" Felix moved closer to stand over me, smirking confidently. "Are you still up for a match?"

"I'm here, aren't I?" I replied pertly, disliking his smug tone.

"Well, then." He flipped his racket toward the court. "Ladies first."

Felix proved to be an able, if vainglorious partner. I quite lost count of the number of times he reached over or darted in front of me to return a ball I was quite capable of hitting. It was all rather tedious. And to make matters worse, he refused all my attempts to gain information from him, either ignoring my questions or turning the subject so that it was about something he wished to talk about, usually himself. I couldn't decide if he was as hesitant to discuss the war as most men who had returned from the front, or just incredibly self-centered and shallow.

I suspected I would have found the match much more pleasant and enlightening had I been paired with our opponent, Max. He had teamed up with one of Helen's friends, a woman named Elsie. She had an annoying tendency to titter, particularly when she missed the ball, which was sadly quite often. When she did manage to make her racket connect with it, it had a tendency to sail off in every direction but the lawn court.

After one of these wild shots, which had narrowly missed striking one of the guests lounging in the shade some fifty feet away, I stood near the net fanning myself as we waited for someone to collect the ball and return it to us. While not overly warm, the sun still shone bright, and I was grateful for the cool breeze blowing in from the sea.

Max pointed his racket at me. "You have a wicked serve. Don't tell me old Sidney taught you how to do that. He never mentioned what an ace he was."

I smiled. "No, that would be my brothers."

"A rowdy lot, were you?"

"Maybe," I teased.

"Looks like you could have used some of those lessons, West-field," Felix called out to Max as he moved closer to the tables to get the ball.

Max shrugged off this dig as he had all the others, though the truth was he was playing quite well, all things considered. It wasn't his fault Elsie wasn't much of a player. In any case, this was supposed to be a friendly match. But Felix, whatever his reasons, seemed determined to best Max, and his antagonistic behavior had only grown worse as the match continued.

I was accustomed to most men's competitive natures, and the good-natured ribbing that went along with them. I'd grown up with three brothers, after all. But this was something different. There was a nastiness underlying Felix's words, and the sharp glint in his eyes said it was personal.

I frowned after Felix, wondering at his harsh animosity and the cause for it.

As if sensing my frustration at my partner, Max lowered his voice to explain. "He simply feels the need to get his licks in now since he couldn't during the war since I was his command-ing officer. That eats at some men's pride." But despite his ca-sual tone of voice and his willingness to defend the man, I could see he was troubled.

"Perhaps," I replied. "But that doesn't make his actions any more pleasant."

"True."

I tilted my head, trying to understand what he wasn't saying. Something evidently concerned him, but I wasn't sure whether it was Felix's hostility or something else.

"Hurry up, will you," Felix barked at someone.

We glanced over to see Charlie striding forward with the ball. His head was lowered, almost as if he was ducking whatever words or expression Felix might aim at him next as he handed him the ball. However, Felix was paying him little heed, his attention having shifted to Jimmy, who sat hunched in his chair staring rather forlornly out at the tennis court, as he'd done for much of the match.

"Oh, cheer up, Tufton," Felix jeered. "You aren't missing much. You were never very good anyway, even when you had two arms."

Jimmy glared at him, but Felix only seemed to find the other man's anger amusing. A few of the ladies giggled nervously, but no one else seemed to find his jest particularly funny. He jogged back toward the court, where Max shook his head.

"That was rather poorly done, Halbert."

Felix rolled his eyes. "Oh, sod off, Westfield. It was a joke. Just because you red caps all lost your sense of humor doesn't mean the rest of us have."

I turned to study Max with new eyes. I hadn't realized he'd been a staff officer. One of the lucky men who were stationed well behind the front lines in commandeered manors and chateaus shuffling papers about and issuing orders. Orders that could potentially see thousands of the soldiers under their command injured or killed. They were called red caps by the men in the trenches because of the red band they wore on their hats, and they were largely derided for being heartless and out of touch with those doing the actual fighting.

During my work for the Secret Service, I'd encountered several staff officers, and found them to be much more of a mixed breed than I was led to believe by the sharp commentary of my colleagues back in London. Some of the staff officers were quite scrupulous and well-informed, while others had infuriated me with their incompetence and callousness. But regardless of their natures, it took a certain amount of detachment for them to be able to effectively perform their work, regularly making decisions to send men into harm's way. As a result, most of them were a bit aloof.

I hadn't pegged Max as such an officer. He simply didn't exude the qualities I'd learned to expect from a man of such rank. But perhaps he hadn't always been a red cap. After all, he'd mentioned serving alongside Sidney in the trenches, and the shoulder wound I suspected he'd sustained also suggested he'd taken part in combat in some capacity. Nevertheless, this knowledge gave me a new insight into why Felix and the others were not necessarily pleased by his company, and fair or not, it made me look at him a bit differently as well.

As if Max sensed this, he dipped his head in agreement. "Now you understand. I can hardly blame them for their dislike." He sighed. "And these men have more reason to hate me than most."

"Why is that?" I asked, surprised by his admission.

His expression turned guarded, as if unwilling to face the memories my question evoked. "Let's just say, the Thirtieth was rather unlucky, particularly during the Somme."

Any mention of that long, bloody battle caused pain in every British heart. Scarcely a soul in all the country didn't know of at least one man, if not dozens, who had been killed in that struggle. Having worked in the offices of the Secret Service at the time, I knew better than most civilians the toll it had taken. I had spent that entire summer and well into autumn feeling cold all over with fear, half-certain that I would read Sidney's name on the daily list of casualties. I don't think I'd ever been the same since, as if from that moment forward I'd known the inevitable would happen, and I was merely bracing for it.

I rubbed my arms, suddenly chilled by the sea breeze rustling the leaves overhead. Goose flesh had raised on my skin, and I glanced behind me, suddenly feeling as if I was being watched. But from where?

There were the other guests, of course, but most of them were distracted by Helen, who appeared to be trying to salvage everyone's good spirits after Felix's nasty jest. Servants came and went, carrying trays of refreshments, and a few gardeners were at work behind the shrubs in the far corner, quietly pruning, but none of them seemed to pay me the least mind.

"It's my serve. Who's receiving?" Felix called out impatiently from the back of the court.

I shuffled into position, scanning my surroundings one last time, though the feeling had lifted. I decided it must have been caused by my own uneasiness at not knowing who among the guests had sent me those letters. Given the circumstances, it was only natural that I should feel a bit hounded.

We resumed our match in much the same manner as before, though with slightly less enthusiasm on my part. In the end it didn't matter, for we still trounced our opponents. Even though this was not Max's fault and he was too gentlemanly to point it out and wound Elsie's feelings, Felix seemed happy to overlook this fact so that he could gloat and preen for Helen and her other friend Gladys.

Distancing myself from his rude antics, I poured myself another glass of cold lemonade and flopped into an empty chair at the edge of the party next to Jimmy. Adjusting my white skirt around my legs, I leaned back to sip the sweet liquid. My mouth puckered at the strength of the alcohol, noting this pitcher seemed more potent than the last. Whether that was wise given the hostility and animosity exhibited between some of the guests remained to be seen.

"Felix is a bounder," I declared, narrowing my eyes at the man in question as he gestured broadly, reenacting one of his returns.

Jimmy scoffed in agreement before muttering, "Well, don't dislike him on my account."

I turned to look at him, arching one eyebrow in annoyance. "Who said I was?"

It was quite evident to me that the last thing Jimmy wanted or needed was my compassion, which out of necessity had become a rationed emotion over the past four and a half years. His surly demeanor made it all too easy to withhold.

"I know how soldiers joke with one another. Granted, they usually don't do so in mixed company. But I'm sure his crude jest wasn't the first time you've had a comrade make light of your injury." I dipped my head at his other hand, which cradled a half-empty glass of brandy. "Besides, you seem to be getting along just fine."

He lifted the cup to his lips, grimacing as he took another drink. "Better than some, right?"

I studied his profile—the crook in his nose, the sunken hollows of his cheeks—trying to decide how much of my private pain to reveal. "If you're referring to Sidney, then yes." I looked away. "I would very much rather have him here with me bereft of one arm than buried somewhere in France."

We sat silently for several moments, watching Felix retake the court across from Mabel's beau, Sam, while I inhaled past the tightness in my chest.

I was surprised when Jimmy next spoke that his voice had not only gentled, but also contained a slight lilt. "I liked Captain Kent. He was one o' the good ones." His blue eyes lifted to meet mine. "Makes me glad to know his wife is mournin' him, as she should be."

There was a kindness in his words I hadn't expected from such a bitter man, but also a sharp condemnation of others. Perhaps of this entire house party. I turned to watch the antics of the other guests. Helen's friends Gladys and Elsie were linked arm in arm, laughing as they rather ineffectually demonstrated some sort of dance to Max and Charlie, who looked on with amusement. Mabel slumped low in her chair, her lips curled contentedly from the edge the lemonade had given her. While Helen flitted about between them all, the pristine white of her skirt belling out with each twirl. It was evident she was in her element as hostess.

"I suspect everyone deals with their losses in their own way," I murmured.

"You could have fooled me," he sneered derisively, never taking his gaze from where it was narrowed on the tennis court.

"You do realize they're not *all* insensitive," I tried to explain, thinking of the somewhat manic nature of my own social life in London. "The drinking, the dancing, the gambling, the forced joviality of it all. They're just trying to deal with the pain, or drown it out, however they can. The same as those who retreat into silence or anger are doing, just in a different way."

He didn't reply, so I decided to venture another comment. "The truth is, I would probably be as tipsy as the rest of them, except . . ."

I stopped myself before I said any more, choking down the words I didn't dare reveal. *Except someone has accused my husband of treason, and I don't yet know who or why.*

Jimmy's eyes lifted to meet mine, curiosity shining in their depths. He seemed oblivious to my turmoil, and I was tempted to explain, but I knew that would be imprudent. Especially when I strongly suspected the missive and the book had been sent by one of these men who had served alongside Sidney in the muck and mud of the trenches, sharing a cigarette and their confidences. Until I knew more, it was best to keep my own counsel.

When it became evident I was not going to say more, the light in his eyes dimmed and his expression resumed its customary scowl. "Well, you're all fools deluding yourselves."

I took another long drink, feeling the sting of his words. "Perhaps. But what if we prefer the distraction. What if it's the only thing that keeps us moving? What if lucidity and silence only leaves us with a head filled with memories we wish to avoid." I twirled the ice in my glass. "Perhaps we prefer to keep spinning. Perhaps it's better than having to face what all that movement blurs."

Jimmy's eyebrows arched. "Yes, but you can't spin forever. Eventually you crash."

As if I needed the reminder.

"True," I admitted, but couldn't resist challenging him in return. "But you also can't stay angry at the world forever, or you won't be long in it."

His lips actually curled into the semblance of a smile, and I liked him all the better for it. "Are you threatening me, Mrs. Kent?"

I sat back, rearranging my skirts. "I wouldn't dream of doing such a thing." I peered up at him through my lashes. "But that doesn't stop me from contemplating it."

He gave a sudden bark of laughter, making some of the others swivel to look our way in disbelief. It was evident Jimmy wasn't often inclined toward mirth, so their reactions were only to be expected. But Jimmy seemed to find it all vexing, smothering his humor and excusing himself to retreat to the house before his cantankerous reputation could be damaged further.

I watched him go, wondering whether the loss of his arm was truly the source of his determined anger, or if it was something else. Something he'd decided was far easier to reveal in writing than confront directly.

CHAPTER 5

I joined the others, accepting Helen's good-natured razzing about my charming Jimmy out of his dudgeon. Most of the guests seemed to be in high spirits, undoubtedly helped along by the spiked lemonade. Even Felix and Sam seemed to be more interested in attempting impossible shots than actually playing a match.

Ordinarily, I would have been at the heart of the fun, pulling one of the men to his feet and demanding he dance with me. But my lack of inebriation and current apprehensions made the scene before me seem far more annoying than amusing. So as soon as I could, I slipped away, deciding my time was better spent gathering my thoughts than trying to gain information from any of these people in their current state.

Passing through the French doors into the room where the grammy was blazing, I found my way out to the hall and then the cool white foyer where we'd gathered earlier. I'd climbed more than halfway up the stairs twisting around to the right when I heard raised voices below me. My steps faltered, as I easily recognized them as belonging to Jimmy and our host, Walter, who had yet to make an appearance in the garden.

"Why is he here?" Jimmy demanded to know, filling the space between his words with colorful cursing.

"Not that it's any of your affair," Walter snapped back, "but I had to invite him."

Invite who? I couldn't skulk away now. Not without knowing whom they were talking about. I leaned closer to the railing, peering down at the tops of their heads just visible below me. I hadn't noticed Walter was going bald before, but there was definitely a thinning of his brown hair on top.

"Why?!" Then Jimmy paused, considering something before he leaned forward into Walter's space to snarl. "If you brought him here to tell him . . ."

Walter sliced his hand through the air. "No! Are you mad?"

"No, but I'm questioning if *you* are."

Huffing an exasperated breath, Walter glanced around him, before lowering his voice to a more moderate level. "I had to invite him because he's dashed near engaged to Helen's cousin. *She* wanted him here. And I could hardly tell her why *I* didn't."

"Rather a rotten coincidence, don't you think?" Jimmy's voice was laced with suspicion.

Walter's response was terse. "Yes, but there it is."

A trill of laughter coming from the back of the house made both men jump and turn. I padded quickly up the last few stairs and out of sight.

They obviously had been talking about Mabel's sandy-haired beau, Sam. I'd yet had an opportunity to speak with the fellow, but he'd seemed rather bland and average. Certainly no one to be alarmed about. But Walter and Jimmy were anxious about him for some reason.

I dropped into the pale ecru upholstered wing chair beside the window in my room and lifted aside the curtain to peer out at the cloud-strewn sky. My window looked out on the harbor, giving me a clear view of both island's piers, and the ships coming and going through Poole Harbor. On this warm, sunny day there was no shortage of traffic.

Releasing the gold drapes, I sank my head back against the chair's cushion, pondering again the oddity of the guest list. The female guests seemed natural enough, being comprised mostly of Helen's friends and cousins. I was the only peculiarity there, but I supposed that was explained easily enough by my late husband's friendship with Walter.

The male guests, on the other hand, made little sense to me.

None of them seemed to like one another, nor had I observed any of them being particularly close to Walter. I'd considered the possibility that Sam was, but after overhearing Walter's conversation with Jimmy that was unlikely. Why invite any of them then? Had it been done to make up numbers? There must be other men Walter was friendlier with still living. Even cousins or distant relatives, as Nellie was to Helen. The only thing that seemed to connect most of the men here was the war. And the fact they'd all been part of the unlucky Thirtieth.

Or was that the real reason they were here? Was that the real reason I was here in Sidney's stead? Was the letter and its accusations of treason simply pretext to lure me here for some other purpose?

I considered the possibility and then discarded it, rising to my feet to lock my door. Whatever the reasons for the others being here, that decrypted missive had looked real. Opening my valise, I pulled out Sidney's battered copy of *The Pilgrim's Progress* and perched on the edge of the bed before removing the worn paper scrawled in code.

I brushed my fingers gently over the impressions, not wanting to damage the document, but also wary of its contents. Though I could already feel my mind stirring with possible permutations, practically itching to attempt to crack the code, I firmly shut them down. Not now. Not yet. Not until I knew more about what this letter might contain.

It seemed all too evident that the only reason my mystery correspondent had shared this with me was so that I could decrypt it. Why else would they have passed along such a valuable piece of evidence? How they knew I was even capable of such a thing, I didn't know, but somehow they'd discovered I worked for the Secret Service during the war. Why shouldn't they also know, or at least have guessed, which skills I possessed?

Regardless, I was justifiably hesitant to try. How was I to know exactly what information this missive contained, whether decrypting it would make the situation better or worse? I couldn't know for certain whether my correspondent was friend or foe. For all I knew, they could be traitors themselves, and the faded letter held secrets they wished to sell to Britain's enemies. They'd provided me with no qualification; only wild accusations they'd yet to prove.

I tucked the letter back into the spine of the book, telling myself I was merely being sensible. However, I was too honest with myself not to recognize a part of me was also terrified and as yet unwilling to face the possibility that the coded missive would confirm everything the letter writer had claimed and implied was true. That Sidney had committed treason. That I had been blindly duped.

I gripped the book between my hands, as everything within me rebelled against the notion that my late husband had been capable of such a thing. But I knew all too well how war could make people do things they would never have done otherwise. Terrible things. Things that did not vanish with the rising of the sun, or the coming of peace.

Suddenly feeling exposed in such a large chamber, I stood to scan the room. I didn't know precisely what or whom I was dealing with. Consequently, it seemed best not to leave anything to chance, including leaving the book and its dubious contents lying about for anyone to find. While working for the Secret Service, I'd learned very quickly never to commit anything to writing, and in those instances when I had to, that I'd better find a good hiding place for it. A midwife I'd worked with in Belgium, whose job enabled her to regularly cross military lines and secretly record her observations of the enemy while she did so, had taught me how to conceal my missives and reports by wrapping them around the whale bones of my corset. However, I rarely wore a corset these days, and a book was much too large to conceal in such a manner.

Crossing to the large oak wardrobe, I knelt to pull out the lowest of the large drawers fashioned at the bottom. Reaching inside, I discovered, just as I'd suspected, that there was a shallow well between the underside of the drawer and the bottom of the wardrobe. I carefully placed the book inside and slid the drawer closed over top of it.

If only I could just as easily shut away my apprehensions.

*   *   *

By the time I descended the stairs a short while later, I'd regained some of my equilibrium. It certainly helped that I was wearing my favorite evening frock of black satin with a lightweight net over-layer decorated in seed pearls with a scrolling acanthus leaf pattern on the bodice and skirt. Sheer turquoise fabric draped over each sleeve, and a wide turquoise sash circled my waist, tying at the side before trailing to the hem. A long necklace of ivory pearls and my black pumps completed the ensemble.

Given the guest list and the nature of the questions I needed to ask, I must accept that comments were bound to be made about Sidney. I would simply have to face them and whatever emotions they wrought as calmly and graciously as I could. Pretending his loss no longer impacted me was foolish. I should have realized that long ago.

In any case, mercifully he was not the first person someone asked after.

"Verity, whatever happened to that termagant of yours?" Tom's voice boomed across the parlor, where everyone had gathered before dinner.

Several of the guests were clustered near the sideboard, where Mabel held sway, mixing together one of her famous cocktails, I presumed. As I made my way toward where Tom stood next to his wife perched on a cream Weston sofa, I couldn't help but note his red cheeks and bright eyes. Coupled with his boisterous manner and the slight slurring of his speech, it was not difficult to deduce the glass cradled in his hand was not his first.

"What was her name again?" he muttered as Nellie shot him a quelling look beneath her lashes. Evidently, she was the one who had noted that my maid was missing, likely voicing her disapproval in the same breath.

"Matilda?"

"Right-o! She's the one." His eyes sparkled with mischief. "Don't tell me you convinced her to ride in that motorcar of yours?"

I smirked. "Not on her life. No, she's returned to the Dales."

He gasped in amusement. "You mean you finally sacked the old gal?"

"I didn't sack her," I protested, sweeping aside my sash to settle into one of the bergère chairs flanking the sofa. "I simply sent her back to my parents."

My mother was the only person to whom she was loyal anyway. She might as well resume her proper place in their employ, considering the fact she'd never actually left it.

A small furrow formed between my brows at the thought of the woman's duplicity. Despite my reservations, I'd allowed my mother to convince me to take her long-time retainer, Matilda, with me to London when I married. It had been a compromise of sorts when I refused to remain in the Dales with my parents since Sidney was marching off to the front. I hadn't wanted my husband to waste any more of his precious time on leave traveling to see me in the north than was necessary. Not to mention the fact that, as a headstrong eighteen-year-old newlywed, I was more than eager to escape my parents' strict supervision and strident disapproval of all things modern.

It wasn't long before I'd begun to suspect the truth. Matilda hadn't been sent along with me so much to look after me as to spy for my mother. She had always been rather disapproving of me, something I had strained against as a child and adolescent, and came to positively loathe as a young soldier's wife making her way in the city, doing her own important part for the war effort. Under the circumstances, I had kept her with me far longer than I should have, possibly in some misguided attempt to please my difficult mother. But after Sidney was killed and Matilda had taken to openly chastising me for behavior she deemed inappropriate for a widow, I could no longer tolerate her presence. Especially when I was already berating myself enough without the maid's help.

Tom raised his glass to me. "Good for you, Pip. She always was the worst sort of fire extinguisher."

"Who are we talking about?" Helen asked, looking rather dashing in her powder blue satin tunic gown with shell pink tulle. She took a sip from her glass and then tipped it toward me. "It's a martini. You simply *must* ask Mabel to make one for you."

"Verity sacked her nursemaid," Tom replied with a grin, recapturing her attention.

I narrowed my eyes at his teasing. "She was not my nursemaid. And I didn't sack her." I glanced up at Helen to explain. "She returned to work for my parents." Likely plaguing my sixteen-year-old sister. I felt a twinge of guilt at the thought.

"But who cares for your clothes?" Nellie leaned forward to ask. Her wide eyes roamed over my form. "Who dresses you?"

I smiled at her horrified disapproval. "I *do* have a maid." Another soldier's widow, who had been rather desperate for work. "But there's no need for her to travel with me." Especially on this trip. "I can dress myself, after all." I flipped my bobbed hair in illustration. "There are some decided advantages to short hair."

"But . . . it's so boyish."

It was a rather rash statement to make, as three of the six women at the house party had bobbed hair, and I suspected it was only a matter of time before Elsie and Gladys lopped off their tresses as well.

Walter chuckled as he joined our group, wrapping a possessive arm around Helen's trim waist. "I doubt anyone would mistake Helen or Verity for a boy. But it's understandable that you should be so attached to such beautiful tresses, Mrs. Ashley," he added, smoothing any ruffled feathers.

Nellie flushed in pleasure at his polite praise. "Well, thank you, Mr. Ponsonby."

Helen pressed a hand to her husband's chest. "Darling, everyone agreed to use our given names, remember."

From the manner in which Walter flicked a glance at Nellie it was evident he was aware that not everyone had happily accepted this decree, but he didn't argue. "Yes, of course."

"We missed you this afternoon," I told Walter.

The corners of his eyes tightened as he drew on his cigarette, exhaling a long stream of smoke before answering, and even then his reply was stilted. "Yes, well, with the ongoing renovations there always seems to be something to attend to."

Helen gazed up at him fondly, shaking her head as he seemed to search the room for something.

"Ah, there's old Chumley. Dinner must be ready," he said, spying the butler standing in the doorway.

Helen closed her mouth, refraining from voicing whatever she had been about to say. I couldn't help but be curious what that was, and why he'd stopped her from doing so.

In any case, the moment passed as we were ushered into a sumptuous dining room wallpapered in forest green Romany damask. Large windows spanned the length of one wall, providing a view of the front garden in the fading light, while the opposite wall was completely covered in floor-to-ceiling mirrors. The effect was rather dazzling, and a shade overwhelming, what with all the candles and reflected light, as well as the crystal and silver cutlery. I suspected there was more glass and gilding than I'd seen at one table since before the war.

And that wasn't the only excess. The rationing that still affected those of us in London didn't seem to apply here, for there was no shortage of butter, flour, sugar, milk, and meat. Consommé Olga, baked haddock with sharp sauce, Filet Mignons Lili, chateau potatoes and creamed carrots, and clafouti; it was all so rich and delicious. I couldn't recall the last time I'd eaten so decadently, and that was saying something, considering the fact that the circles I ran in hadn't exactly been living a deprived existence. I would have to take care, or my already unfashionably rounded figure would become downright voluptuous. Sport kept my waist trim and my legs shapely, but no amount of effort was going to shrink my bosom or hips.

There seemed to be endless bottles of champagne to be uncorked, and decanters overflowing with brandy for the gentlemen who preferred less bubbles in their libations. All of which was quite lovely, but did not seem to be helping the general mood of the party. Some of the guests were quite merry, namely Helen and her two young girlfriends, but many of the others brooded behind their glasses or darted uncertain glances around the table.

It was such an odd gathering for an engagement party. Here we were supposed to be celebrating Walter and Helen's impending nuptials, and yet a more edgy, mistrustful get-together I'd never experienced. And I'd sat through my share of tense meetings during my time with the Secret Service.

I wasn't the only one who sensed it. Seated across from Max as I was, I could see how he observed everyone, weighing their actions and expressions, much as I was doing. He also seemed to be moderating his alcohol intake—at least more so than anyone else at the table—and when our eyes met over the gleaming spread I could sense he was in agreement with me. Something was definitely peculiar about this party.

From the manner in which Walter continued to attempt to make jokes—each one more forced than the last—and gulped his brandy, it was clear he was also conscious of the strain, even if his fiancée seemed oblivious.

When the contrived laughter at his latest jest faded, I leaned toward Helen. "So tell us how the two of you met." I gestured between her and Walter with my champagne glass before taking another sip. "I haven't heard the tale yet."

"Oh, it's a lovely story," Helen cooed, casting doe eyes at her fiancé. "Why don't you tell it, darling?"

Walter nodded, distractedly refilling his glass once more. "We met through a Lonely Soldier column."

When he failed to elaborate further, Helen gave a trill of laughter. "Oh, Walter, you fussy thing. That's not how you tell it!" Her eyes sparkled as she turned toward me. "I was in London, *desperately* trying to find a way to fill my time and help our soldiers, since my father wouldn't allow me to assist in the canteens or any of the charitable associations all the other ladies were contributing to." She wrinkled her nose in remembered frustration. "When one day I stumbled across a Lonely Soldier's column in one of the newspapers." From the manner in which she glanced at Walter, it was clear the advert had been his, and also just as clear from the way he was so absorbed in the food on his plate that he was somewhat embarrassed by it. "It was the most heartbreaking thing I'd ever read, and I simply *had* to respond."

"As did six or seven other women," Felix muttered under his breath, making Charlie snort a laugh into his drink.

Walter shot him a deadly look, but Helen's smile was undimmed.

"Did you think I didn't know that? But, of course, other ladies wrote him. And sent him gifts, I'm sure." She arched her eyebrows and her fiancé flushed. "But that didn't last along. Especially after we met in London on his next leave." The warmth behind her words and the look in her eyes left no doubt as to what she was implying.

This wasn't a new story. I'd known about the Lonely Soldier columns and their Lonely Stabs, the nickname the soldiers had dubbed the girls who replied. Though I would never have mistaken Helen for one. Nor had I ever heard of such a relationship resulting in marriage.

Sidney had spoken of them in passing as being somewhat of a joke among the men at the front. One corporal in his company had contrived to receive two to three parcels a week from different women by this method, sharing the spoils among his fellow soldiers. From the reactions of the other officers in his battalion, I couldn't help but wonder if Walter's post in the Lonely Soldiers column had begun with the same intention.

Was that why some of the men seemed so uncomfortable? Were they aware that the happy couple's relationship had begun with less than honorable intentions, at least on the groom's part? If so, they were a far more scrupulous lot than most of the gentlemen I knew.

I knew without looking at Nellie that she disapproved of this courtship tale on principle, even if her own was nothing to sigh over, and in many ways far less romantic, as it was quite possible Tom had felt compelled to marry her because of her unexpected pregnancy. It seemed Gladys and Elsie, on the other hand, could not have found Helen's story more idealistic, cooing over their friend's evident happiness. None of these reactions surprised me.

However, the look Mabel shared with her beau, Sam, suggested to me that all might not be as Helen wished it to appear. If anyone knew more about the details surrounding the pair's courtship, I suspected it was Mabel. Not only was she Helen's cousin, but she was also older and more experienced. And far more likely to notice the things Helen's young, giggling friends would overlook.

I wondered what Sidney would have thought of all this. Whether he would have been able to read more from his friend's strained expression than I could.

Forcing myself to affect good cheer, I lifted my champagne flute. "How positively charming. To the happy couple."

Helen beamed at me as the others reached for their glasses to join me in my toast.

"Hear, hear."

Then she blew a playful kiss at Walter across the expanse of the table, who had recovered himself enough to feign it hitting him like one of Cupid's arrows. We all laughed delightedly at their antics, glad to see them behaving as a betrothed couple should at their engagement party.

Happily resettling to our meals, we fussed over the chocolate soufflés being set before us. I closed my eyes as the chocolate melted on my tongue. Sugar had also been in short supply, so to taste something so sweet and delicious was quite a treat.

Max must have shared my sweet tooth, for he was the first to finish his dessert, relaxing back in his chair contentedly with his glass of brandy. "What of the peace talks in Paris? I'm afraid I haven't seen the papers today. Has Germany agreed to the terms?"

"Not a word, ole chap," Jimmy replied, narrowing his eyes at the center of the table. His heavy drinking made his lilt more pronounced. "Makes ye wonder what's takin' 'em so long."

"Well, the terms were somewhat harsh."

"No more than they deserve," Tom declared, echoing a popular sentiment bandied about London, usually by the people who knew the least about the situation. Most ex-soldiers I knew remained mute on the subject. Many of them having spent years opposite the Germans in the filthy trenches, I wondered if they actually held the most sympathy for their former opponents, even if they never voiced it. Or perhaps it was more a matter of comradery. If anyone understood what they'd been through, it was their adversaries on the other side of No Man's Land, not the people back home.

Walter shook his head in answer before lifting his glass toward me, sloshing the contents inside. "Maybe you should ask Verity. With her contacts in London, she probably knows more than the lot o' us."

Stunned by his comment, I fumbled to form a response as everyone's heads swiveled toward me. "Whatever do you mean?"

He opened his mouth to respond, but his fiancée cut him off.

"Walter, you know I expressly forbade any talk of war or politics." Her mouth had tightened into a tiny moue. "That was all my father ever spoke of, and I've been bored enough for one lifetime."

"My apologies," Max told her, flushing with guilt since he'd started the conversation.

She offered him one of her charming smiles. "It's quite all right. You didn't know any better." She leaned toward him. "But tell us about your estate on the Isle of Wight. I hear it's frightfully spectacular."

I listened with only half an ear to Max's reply, my mind still absorbed by the question of whom Walter had been referring to when he mentioned my contacts. I couldn't imagine who that would be.

Unless he meant my colleagues among the Secret Service. But how could he possibly know such a thing?

No one was supposed to even know of its existence, let alone who had worked for it. I'd been forbidden from even telling my husband. To the rest of the world, my official job had been a secretary to an import-export business. And a rather liberal one at that, as they'd been one of the few places who hired married women.

I glanced over at Walter, hoping to catch his eye, but he seemed determined to avoid it. I couldn't help but note that my anonymous letter writer had also known about my work with the Secret Service. Were he and Walter one and the same?

CHAPTER 6

It was a beautiful night—warm and cloudless, with just the whisper of a breeze to ruffle the turquoise sleeves of my gown. I stood leaning against the balustrade of the terrace, where we had adjourned after dinner, nursing my drink and watching the last bit of sunlight bleed from the western sky over the garden. The air was delicately scented with the alstroemeria, freesia, and peonies growing in the flower beds below and the sea just beyond the elms.

I stared out at the deepening shadows, wondering why I felt that curious sensation of being watched again, and why it should so intrigue me. It was almost certainly just a servant or an estate worker, interested in seeing what antics we Londoners got up to while wearing our glad rags. After all, Walter's father's parties had been quite notorious, but it had doubtless been years since anything so disreputable had happened here.

Before I could give the matter much more serious consideration, Gladys and Elsie rushed over to join me.

"Walter is winding up the grammy so we can dance," Gladys said, her dark eyes shining with eagerness. I supposed as one of the women currently unattached, they had decided to include me in their bonhomie.

"How delightful," I declared, swiveling to survey the gentlemen gathered around the terrace lit by oil lamps. "And who are each of you eyeing?"

"I think the earl is simply divine," Elsie sighed.

"So handsome," Gladys agreed with a giggle. "But Felix is rather dashing as well."

I smiled, wondering if Max realized what a flock of admirers he was gathering.

"What of Jimmy?" Elsie asked, having tilted her head in consideration of the man slumped against the wall of the house. "He's not so bad looking. Do you think he can dance?"

Gladys sniffed. "I don't know, but *I'm* not dancing with him."

It was difficult to tell what exactly the pert blonde found distasteful—his brusque manner or his missing arm—and I didn't know enough about her to judge.

Elsie, on the other hand, seemed remarkably unpretentious. "He is rather surly, isn't he?"

"*I* heard he has pockets to let," Gladys informed us. "Did you smell those stinkers he was smoking earlier? No one buys those horrid American fags if they can afford anything else." Leaning back against the balustrade in her slinky silver gown, an elaborate corsage of pink silk roses nodding on her shoulder, she turned her gaze toward one of the other gentlemen. "However, Felix, it seems, is quite flush. Came into some sort of inheritance shortly after the war. What luck!"

She glanced fleetingly at me. "Verity, I realize you don't have to concern yourself with such things since your husband was decent enough to leave you with a pile of money when he died. You'll have no trouble whatsoever attracting a second husband. But my father wasn't so fortunate. I'm all but dowry-less."

I stiffened, uncertain how to respond to such an insensitive remark. I would have traded all that money in a heartbeat just to have Sidney return to me. But I also understood what a strained situation many in the upper classes had found themselves in since the war. There was rather a large number of poor aristocrats wandering about London nowadays. Property taxes and death duties—sometimes owed double- and triple-fold because of the war—had crippled any number of wealthy noblemen, forcing some of them to sell land and property that had been in their family for dozens of generations.

Regardless, Gladys seemed completely oblivious to how rude her comments had been. She tilted her head to the side in consideration. "I wonder how loaded the earl is."

I couldn't answer this question, nor was I going to help her size up our fellow guests' financial situations. At any rate, music suddenly blared forth from the French doors to our right, saving me from having to reply. Gladys and Elsie leapt forward to coax the men into dancing.

"Aren't you coming?" Elsie paused to ask.

"In a moment."

She smiled and returned to her quest, her kindness allowing Gladys to snag Max first.

I slowly crossed the terrace toward where several of the other guests clustered around a wrought-iron table fashioned with delicate tracery. Large potted plants that looked like they'd been grown in a hothouse were positioned to one side in order to form an arc that screened the terrace behind them from our view. However, the area in front of the table had been cleared to form a dance floor. Along the wall of the castle stood a large table weighted down with chilled buckets of champagne and vodka, and decanters of brandy, ready for our indulgence. I also noted a platter filled with sweet strawberries and pineapple slices—my favorite.

However, before I could make my way over to the table to sample them, Mabel beckoned me over. "Verity, have you met Sam yet?" she asked, blowing out a plume of cigarette smoke.

"No, I can't say I've had the pleasure."

Sam rose to his feet to take my hand. "The pleasure is all mine, I'm sure." His broad grin revealed a charming little gap between his front teeth. "Mabel tells me you're from London. Is that where you met Helen?" He glanced over his shoulder toward our hostess, who was coaxing Charlie out onto the dance floor.

"No, I'd actually never met her until today. My husband was great friends with Walter," I explained. "I suppose you could say I'm here in his stead."

"Oh, yes," he replied with a grimace. "My apologies."

I nodded, tipping my head toward the dancers to cover my discomfort. "Aren't you two going to join them?"

Sam offered a hand to his sweetheart. "A marvelous suggestion."

Mabel's lips curled in a teasing smile. "Why, darling, I thought you'd never ask." Stubbing out her fag, she allowed him to pull her to her feet.

I grinned at the sight of them fox-trotting across the terrace. But I wasn't allowed to remain an observer for long. An arm slid around my waist from behind, guiding me toward the other dancers.

"Come on, Pip. It's been a long time since I've gotten to dance with you."

I laughed as Tom spun me into his arms. "What about Nellie? Didn't she want to dance?"

His eyebrows arched, telling me he knew very well that I was aware of Nellie's distaste for ragtime. "No, claimed she had a megrim." He shrugged one shoulder. "Whether that's true or not . . ."

He didn't have to finish that sentence. I was familiar with Nellie's frequent ailments, some of which were genuine, while others, not so much. At least, that's what I and the other children from Upper Wensleydale had always suspected, given the fact they seemed to come and go whenever she wanted to get out of doing something she didn't wish to do.

"Well, her loss is my gain," I told him, and was glad to see the twinkle return to his eyes. Tom had always been a splendid dancer. Not as good as Sidney, but still quite keen, even while half bosky on brandy.

Our steps slowed as the song on the gramophone changed before resuming our quickstep. Gladys and Elsie swiftly switched partners, while Walter looked on indulgently as Helen continued to hold Charlie in her sway. Which left only Jimmy to brood at the edges of the party. The look on his face was forbidding, but I suspected before the war he'd liked to dance as much as the rest of us. He still might, though I knew better than to ask. He would never admit it.

Noticing the direction of my gaze, Tom swung me in a tight spin. "I know that look," he cautioned.

"What look?"

He shook his head. "Don't spare much sympathy for Tufton, Verity. He did it to himself."

"What? His injury?"

His face was grim.

I frowned in aggravation. "How? Did he shoot himself in his arm?"

"No, but he charged that machine-gun post alone for one sole purpose, and he didn't achieve it. Though he sure tried."

I opened my mouth to argue, but then comprehension dawned. My eyes widened in shock, and I darted another glance toward Jimmy. "You mean . . ."

Tom nodded.

Like so many others, I'd read Siegfried Sassoon's poem "Suicide in the Trenches," and felt my throat close up with the pain and horror it represented. By then I'd known not to cheer when soldiers marched off to war, but I'd also refused to let myself contemplate the desperation a man must feel to commit the ultimate act of self-destruction.

"Do you know why?"

Tom's expression shuttered. "Who knows?"

It had been a dumb question, for, of course, he knew. All the soldiers did. There were a thousand reasons why, even if one didn't know the exact event that had ultimately broken them.

I smiled tightly in apology and tried to concentrate on losing myself in the steps of the dance and the larks of the other guests. But I couldn't stop thinking of Jimmy's reckless charge, wondering if it had anything to do with the tension between the men or the letter I'd received. And what of Max's comments earlier about the Thirtieth battalion's bad luck?

I studied Tom's face, knowing that if I could convince anyone to explain about the Thirtieth, it would be my childhood friend.

So when the dance ended, I tugged him toward the balustrade, snagging him another glass of brandy along the way. When I turned to face him, shoving the drink into his hand, he eyed me warily.

"What's this for?"

I hesitated, comprehending that what I was about to request of him was not an easy thing. "I need to ask you a question."

His jaw hardened and he turned aside, gazing out into the dark lawn.

"Please, Tom. I need to understand, and you're the only one I can ask."

He tipped the glass back, taking a swift drink. "I'm not going to tell you about the war."

"I know. That's not what I want."

He glanced at me out of the corner of his eye.

"Not really," I hastened to explain. "I . . . I just need to understand why the Thirtieth was so unlucky at the Somme."

"Who told you that?"

"Max."

Tom's brow furrowed.

"Why? Is it not true?"

For a moment I wasn't sure he would answer me. Instead he continued to stare out into the darkness, wrestling with his own thoughts. Whatever they were, I knew they weren't happy. His eyes had taken on the same bleak cast I'd sometimes witnessed in Sidney during his last few short leaves of absence.

I hugged myself, hating that my questions had put that look in Tom's eyes. Hating that I had to contemplate any of this at all. But how else was I to learn the truth? To uncover just what it was my mysterious correspondent wanted?

When Tom spoke, his voice had lost all inflection. "They were decimated. At the Somme. Cut down to almost nothing."

My chest tightened at his words, thinking of all those dead soldiers, and of the men left behind to try to struggle on without them. No wonder Jimmy had found it too much to bear. I shook my head. "Sidney never told me—"

"He wouldn't have," Tom said, cutting me off.

I nodded my understanding. How did one put such loss into words?

But Tom's next remark stole the breath from my lungs.

"Because he blamed himself."

I stood there blinking, trying to grasp what he was saying. "What do you mean?" I finally managed to ask.

Tom exhaled and his hand shook, jostling the liquid in his glass. He stared down at it as if he'd forgotten it was there. "His company got separated from the others because the map they'd been given was rubbish. And to make matters worse, the artillery shells had gone astray, blowing a crater in the middle of their path. At least, that's what the official report found. But the fact of the matter is, Sidney's company was supposed to flank some of the others, and when Sidney couldn't get his men into position in time, the Germans overran them." Tom lifted his glass to his lips, but before drinking added, "He never forgave himself for that."

I watched as he downed the rest of the contents of his glass while my heart ached with the knowledge that Sidney had been carrying around that guilt and grief alone. I knew better than to question why he hadn't told me. Our fighting men simply didn't discuss such things with those at home. They couldn't. Not without exposing us to the horrors they were trying so hard to keep us from finding out about.

I had often wondered if it would have been different if Sidney had known about my work with the Secret Service. Would he have shared more with me knowing I'd already seen and heard so many terrible things? I suspected not.

"Thank you for telling me," I murmured.

Tom nodded.

"Do you know if the others blamed him?" I asked, daring one last question.

He shrugged, glancing over his shoulder. "I honestly don't know."

I followed his gaze toward where Felix now stood talking with Charlie. Or rather, talking at him. Then he threw his head back and laughed, nearly toppling backward.

"Hey, everyone! Listen to this," he slurred, grasping the other man's shoulder. "Charlie is . . . Charlie is going to become a vicar!"

Charlie's cheeks flushed a fiery red as Gladys and Elsie began to giggle and some of the others snorted.

"Really, Charlie? A Holy Joe, hey," Walter quipped. "If you'd chosen your calling sooner, you could have led the cushy life at the front."

"Could've had your own dugout and everything," Sam chimed in, making everyone chuckle.

Gladys reached out to loop her arm through the shy fellow's. "Maybe you can marry Helen and Walter."

"I'm not waiting that long," Helen protested with a mischievous smile. "But you can christen our first child."

As the laughter began to subside, Max stepped forward to slap Charlie on the back. "Well, there's no shame in becoming a clergyman," he remarked reassuringly, displaying some of the commanding presence that had likely gotten him promoted up the ranks. "It's a respectable profession."

"No, it's not." A voice from behind them snapped. "They're all liars! And cowards!"

Max turned to face Jimmy as he rose to his feet a bit unsteadily. "Now, Jimmy . . ."

"Oh, stuff it, Westfield," he cursed, using stronger language than that.

Elsie gasped, pressing a hand to her mouth.

It was a testament to how furious and drunk Jimmy was that he'd forgotten to call Max by his new title after correcting Felix earlier that day.

"Ye don't have to step in and try and smooth everyone's feathers, or save them from disaster. 'Cause yer a bloody sap at it."

Max blanched.

"And ye know as well as I do." He swiveled to point angrily at all the men, ending on Charlie, who he shoved backward. "There is no God! Or if there ever was one, he abandoned us long ago. Left us all to die in those bloody pits." With one last scornful stare, he stormed off into the house, slamming the door behind him.

We all stood silently, none of us knowing what to say after facing such fury and vehemence. Gladys wrapped an arm around Elsie, who had begun to silently cry. Charlie looked as if he'd been punched in the gut. I didn't know how strong his faith was, but if he was determined to become a vicar, he would have to find a way to respond to such angry rebuttals. For I knew Jimmy wasn't the only British soldier who'd lost his faith in God somewhere in the trenches, though few would tell you so in such strident terms.

Unsurprisingly it was Felix who spoke first. "He's barmy," he proclaimed derisively. "Come on, Elsie." He reached for her hand. "Dry your tears. Don't let him ruin our fun."

Elsie gave him a bleary smile and allowed him to pull her into his arms. After this display of heroics, I suspected Max would be losing one of his admirers. Possibly two.

"Charlie, dance with Gladys," Felix ordered.

The others began to gather themselves, rejoining the dancing or pouring themselves another drink. But though they attempted to carry on, much of the gaiety had drained from the evening. Unable to paste on another fake smile, I refreshed my glass of champagne and retreated to the shadows at the far end of the terrace, needing a few moments to myself.

The music grew softer and the hushed sounds of night reached my ears again—the hum of crickets and the rustle of the wind trailing its fingers through the leaves. On this side of the castle, away from the sea, the trees grew thicker, for I could smell them and the faint perfume of London Pride in the bushes bordering this end of the terrace. I paused to lean against the balustrade, tipping back my glass to drain it, in need of the fortification. I probably shouldn't have taken this latest glass. I'd already consumed far too much, and drinking this one so fast would only make me tipsier than I wished, but having a clear head suddenly seemed intolerable.

I'd been more unsettled by Jimmy's outburst than I wanted

to admit, especially as it had followed so swiftly on the heels of Tom's revelations. All I could think of was Sidney during his final leave. I kept picturing him sitting there alone in the dark, his head cradled in his hands. Should I have gone to him? Should I have asked? Would it have made any difference?

I tensed at the sound of footsteps. Glancing over my shoulder, I forced a taut smile, thankful the shadows that cloaked this end of the terrace also hid much of my expression.

Even so, the man before me seemed to sense I was less than pleased by his intrusion, for he paused. "May I join you?" he asked.

Hearing the pleasing timbre of Max's voice and not one of the other gentlemen's, my shoulders relaxed. "If one of those glasses you're holding is for me." I'd meant for the comment to sound flippant, but my words rang all too hollow.

"But, of course." Max joined me at the balustrade, passing me one of the flutes filled with bubbling champagne. Already feeling the effects of my last glass dampening the sharpness of my thoughts, I sipped this one more slowly. I'd been considering making a flirtatious remark to break the stilted silence that surrounded us and redirect both of our attentions to something more pleasant, but he beat me to the punch.

"I'm sorry Jimmy's comments upset you."

I set my glass down on the stone with a hard clink, wishing I had spoken first. I could hardly deny my distress, for it was obvious. "Well, my maternal grandfather was a rector. And I adored him," I mumbled in response, knowing perfectly well that didn't actually explain anything.

But Max just nodded. "From my experience, some of the men became overzealous to deal with the war and all the horrors they'd witnessed, while others . . ." He sighed. "A lot of others—like Jimmy—lost their faith altogether. It's how they coped."

I turned to look up at Max's handsome profile in the dim light, amazed by how at ease he seemed discussing these things when most of the former soldiers I knew would rather be sent back to the trenches. I could say almost anything to him and he wouldn't flinch. He wouldn't shy away. The last time I had felt the same comfort, the same connection with anyone, had been with Sidney. But that had been before the war. Before all the secrets that had torn us away from each other.

"And what do you think?" I asked, curious whether I was right. Whether he would answer me.

His brow furrowed, and I could see he was giving the matter his serious consideration. "I saw so much . . . too much . . . not to make me doubt." He paused. "But the idea of there being no God . . . well, somehow it seems untenable."

Gripping the edge of the balustrade under my hands, I swallowed the lump that had formed in my throat and dared to ask the question I really wanted to know. "What about Sidney?" Max's gaze lifted to meet mine. "What do you think he believed?"

It was too dark to read the expression in his eyes, but from the manner in which he had stilled, I knew I had managed to unsettle him.

When he didn't answer, I hastened to explain. "I wondered, that's all. Because I've had similar doubts." I gave a huff of laughter. "And wouldn't my mother be horrified to hear that. She would find a way to drag me back to Upper Wensleydale. Not that she hasn't already tried."

Max smiled. "I don't know. But . . . I'm certain you would know better than I what your husband was thinking."

"But that's just the thing." I narrowed my eyes, trying to peer into the darkness as if it were my own murky memories. "I don't think I would. We married so swiftly, you see, just as the war broke out, as soon as I turned eighteen. And then he was gone." I pressed my lips together, wondering if I would dare to say the thought that had been eating at me for weeks. "Sometimes . . . sometimes I wonder if I ever really knew him at all."

If I could have looked my anonymous correspondent in the face that very moment, I knew I would have slapped him. I had never doubted Sidney before. Never questioned his love or loyalty. But now all I could do was ask myself whether he was the noble man I'd believed I married, or the lying traitor they implied. And if so, how had I missed it?

I glanced up as Max's warm hand covered mine where it rested on the cold stone. He was close enough now that I could see the compassion reflected in his eyes.

"Verity, I don't know everything Sidney was thinking or feeling. But I *do* know he cared for you very much. That couldn't have been plainer to see."

I blinked against a sudden wash of tears and nodded before turning to stare out again at the shadowed garden. While I struggled to regain control of myself—cursing those last two glasses of champagne I'd allowed myself to drink that had made me maudlin—he stood quietly next to me, sipping from his own flute. Fortunately, I'd had four and a half long years of practice at stuffing my emotions back deep down inside me. With one last sniff, I tucked away my handkerchief and turned to look at Max.

"So tell me, how does an officer in the trenches manage to distinguish himself enough to be promoted to a staff officer?" I knew the change in topic was abrupt, but at the moment I couldn't manage anything smoother.

Max grimaced. "My father."

This wasn't entirely surprising, as the previous Earl of Ryde had been a rather influential and powerful politician, but Max's tone of voice made it clear he hadn't been pleased by his father's actions.

"I was injured in my shoulder. A *minor* injury," he emphasized. "I was ready to resume my command in a matter of weeks. But by the time I was preparing to return to the front, my father had already had me promoted away from the trenches."

"And you didn't want that."

"Sounds cracked, doesn't it? What officer doesn't wish to be promoted? And to a safer position well behind the heavy fighting?" He inhaled, as if remembering the burden he'd carried. The burden he plainly still carried. "But if I wasn't there, who would look after my men? Not all the officers were conscientious, you know."

I did. I'd heard the complaints often enough from the men I worked alongside at the Secret Service. Usually from the soldiers who had been invalided home from the front, but sometimes even the Chief had chimed in, lamenting the fact that one man or another had been given a command.

But my agreement would not ease the guilt and frustration I still sensed vibrating through Max at his inability to protect his men. Though, I couldn't help but wonder if his promotion had occurred before or after the devastation of the Thirtieth on the Somme.

"I'm sorry," he said. "I'm sure that's more than you wanted to know. It's just this house party." He glanced over his shoulder at the couples still dancing near the middle of the terrace. Walter now held Helen in his arms, castle-walking with her. "It baffles me why Walter invited all of the surviving officers from his battalion to his engagement party." His voice lowered as if he was speaking to himself more than to me. "Most men want to forget the war when they come home, not be forced to relive their memories of it. Especially in front of their young fiancée."

His words echoed the same thoughts I had been turning over and over in my head since I arrived, and it was reassuring to hear I wasn't the only one to note the oddity of the guest list. However, it didn't explain Max's presence here.

"Perhaps this is an impertinent question, but why did you come then? I mean, you and Walter don't exactly seem to be bosom buddies."

His mouth creased into a humorless smile. "We aren't. To be honest, I was shocked when I received my invitation. And I almost declined, but . . . I suppose I felt I owed it to him to attend. I wondered . . . I wondered if perhaps there just wasn't anyone else for him to ask in order to fill the numbers."

Because of the war. Because of all the thousands and thousands of young men who'd died. Some of whom would have been under his command. He didn't say the words, but I could read between the lines.

"And . . ." He broke off, as if he wasn't sure he wanted to say more.

"And what?" I prodded, somehow knowing whatever he said next would be important.

His eyes were troubled. "I know this will sound mad, but for some reason the entire thing seemed strange to me. Everything about it is just a little off." He shook his head. "Though I can't put my finger on the exact reason why."

My gaze drifted toward the other couples dancing, noting that our separation from the others had not continued to go unnoticed. We wouldn't be left undisturbed much longer.

"Does that make any sense at all?" he asked, seeming genuinely baffled by it all.

"It does," I murmured. "Because I sensed it, too."

His eyes studied me intently, as if trying to divine my thoughts, but I wasn't yet ready to give them up. "So you didn't come just because of Sidney?"

I knew he meant because of Sidney's friendship with Walter, but ironically he couldn't have been more right. "On the contrary, he's entirely the reason I came."

CHAPTER 7

By the time I'd managed to extricate myself from the drinking and dancing on the terrace, it was well past midnight. Normally, I would have dived wholeheartedly into such frivolity, but underlying it all there had been a tense, almost desperateness to the fun. It lurked underneath everything about this party.

My first inclination upon returning to my room was to pack my bags and leave at first light, to abandon this entire charade. But then I thought of Sidney, of living with the letter writer's accusations about him hanging over me, making me doubt everything I knew about the man I still loved. I couldn't merely brush them aside and leave them here like an old coat I no longer wanted. Even if I burned the coded missive and whatever secrets it held, they would still haunt me, probably for the rest of my life.

Besides, what would I be returning to? An empty flat. I had no job, no obligations. Only endless swathes of time to be filled with endless rounds of parties and meaningless social engagements. And far too much time to think. The alternative was to return to Yorkshire, and I simply couldn't do that. Then I wouldn't have to just face Sidney's loss, but also my brother Rob's, and all the other boys I'd grown up with who had never returned from the war.

No, I couldn't leave.

So there was nothing for it then but to move forward, confront the truth head-on. I planted my hands on my hips and turned to face the wardrobe. No more dodging and hedging. If I was ever to begin to understand exactly what this was all about, it seemed I would have to decrypt that message. And the sooner it was done, the better.

I removed my shoes and crossed the soft carpet to kneel down and extract Sidney's book from its hiding place. I considered curling up with it on the bed, but I knew the temptation to doze off would be too great. So instead I settled down at the desk and scrutinized the items before me.

The fact that the coded missive had been tucked inside a book—a book Sidney had specifically requested—made me wonder whether it was a book cipher of some kind. If that were true, then it would mean my husband might have been committing treason for quite some time, and that without my knowledge he had involved me in his duplicity by asking me to send him the book. The idea made me want to retch, but I swallowed my dismay and did my best to push such thoughts from my mind. If I was to succeed, I must stay objective and focused.

Picking up the battered copy of *The Pilgrim's Progress,* I flipped through the pages, searching for stray marks or particularly well-thumbed pages, and examined the spine for other hiding places. When nothing leapt out at me, I turned to the coded missive itself, trying to tell whether it had any tell-tale patterns or markings linking it to the book. However, I rapidly deduced that if the book could be used to decode it, then I was missing the key. Whether the missive itself somehow contained the key or it was a separate document I did not hold in my possession, I didn't know, but if so, I hoped it was the former. Otherwise deducing it was going to be infinitely harder.

Lifting the letter to my nose, I sniffed the paper, curious whether some sort of invisible ink might have been used. At the Secret Service, invisible ink had been its stock in trade, and the agency was always looking for better substances that could be used for such a purpose. Though, as a woman, I wasn't supposed to know anything about it, I recalled how excited C had become when one of the staff had discovered semen could be used in such a manner, particularly as it didn't respond to iodine vapor. Though adopted by some, not all of the agents had employed this method.

Waving the paper under my nose, I could smell any number of scents, but none that indicated a particular material I knew to have been utilized for invisible ink. I did not have any iodine solution or lemon juice at hand, but I cautiously lifted the page toward the lamp, curious whether heat would render anything visible. When after a few minutes no reactions occurred, except a singeing of my fingertips, I abandoned the effort. There was always the possibility that the book contained the invisible key, but searching through its hundreds of pages individually would take far too long, and I had only ten fingers.

With a determined frown, I pulled out a few pieces of the blank stationery stocked in one of the drawers and began the painstaking work of considering one of the more analytically intensive ciphers. Despite the divergence in word and sentence length, I strongly suspected this was a transposition cipher, for they were much more common and had a far greater capacity for variation and difficulty. However, I knew there was also the chance it had been written in a much simpler Caesar Shift cipher, and if I didn't spend the relatively short, but tedious amount of time needed to check, only to later discover it had been something so mundane, I would be furious with myself. So I bent over the scratch paper and began my examination.

It didn't take long for me to realize this cipher was anything but simple. I wasn't even sure whether the plaintext of the code would be written in English, German, or French, though fortunately I was fluent in all three. Tapping my pencil against my paper, I considered the possibility that rather than a monoalphabetic cipher like the Caesar Shift, the missive might be coded in a polyalphabetic cipher, like the Vigenère or the Beaufort variant, methods that were nearly unbreakable without a cipher disk. At least for someone with my limited skills. If so, I could spend months attempting to crack the code without ever making a dent.

Such a realization was incredibly discouraging. I sighed. Then there was nothing for it but to focus on what I could do in such a restricted amount of time. That meant turning my efforts to what I deemed to be the far more likely transposition cipher and all its variations. Which in and of itself was no mean feat. Examining just one technique from all angles could take hours.

Nonetheless, I dived in. And for a moment, I thought I'd caught a lucky break and stumbled on to something, but I soon discovered it was a false lead. Perhaps even an intentional one.

Sometime later, I was staring bleary-eyed at my piece of foolscap, trying hopelessly to concentrate, when I heard a man cry out. The harsh exclamation, which sounded as if it had been pulled from the depths of his soul, sent a chill down my spine. I pressed a hand to my wildly beating heart and listened for more, but all had fallen silent.

It wasn't the first time I'd been woken in the middle of the night by an ex-soldier having a nightmare. But, at least, in this instance, I couldn't tell exactly who it was. At home, I knew all too well it was my hollow-eyed neighbor. Inevitably, it seemed, we would meet in the hall the following morning. He would keep his gaze lowered in shame while I would try to treat him as if nothing had happened, as if I hadn't heard his anguish. I sometimes wondered if our determination not to acknowledge his torment made it better or worse.

Setting down my pencil, I rubbed my eyes and glanced at the clock. It was nearly half past two in the morning, and I still hadn't found the correct variation. I blinked down at the paper before me, wondering if I should continue this last attempt, even as the letters swam before my eyes. Sighing in dejection, I stuffed the letter and the pages filled with my scribblings inside the book and returned it to its hiding place.

Flopping down on my bed, still wearing my evening gown, I moaned. If only I could telephone my friend George. An absolute whiz at mathematics, he had been one of the foremost codebreakers in all of Britain during the war, and had taught me the little bit I knew about decryption before I was sent on my first assignment in the field. If anyone could decrypt the missive, it would be him, and far faster than I ever could. But I knew it would be foolish to even think of contacting him until I knew more.

George was a good man, but his rationale was also very black and white. If whatever we found in that message indicated treason or misconduct of any kind, he would report it to the authorities, regardless of who was involved. If it pointed to Sidney, and consequently me, if it turned out I'd unwittingly betrayed sensitive information to my husband, I knew George would hesitate. But in the end, neither our friendship nor my demurrals would secure his silence.

At any rate, it seemed best not to drag him into this mess. Not yet. Not when I didn't know what I would find. If there was something in that letter that pointed to Sidney and traitorous activity, I wanted to be the first to know.

At the very least, I owed it to the man I loved, to his memory, to keep quiet until I knew for certain. If the worst came to be . . . Well, then, I supposed I would have to deal with the ramifications then. For now, all I really had was the word of an anonymous letter writer that Sidney had done anything wrong.

I tried to comfort myself with that thought as I turned off the light and tried to settle into slumber, but I already knew his memory would haunt my dreams. As it had every night since that blasted German bullet had taken him from me.

I wasn't surprised to discover I was one of the first people to stumble downstairs for breakfast the following morning. Had my mind not been consumed by that coded missive and my own misgivings, I would have still been in bed, too. As it was, I'd barely slept, and what slumber I *had* gotten had been filled with dark figures and lurking shadows.

Sam and Mabel greeted me as I entered the sun-filled room, and pointed me toward the sideboard, where a large selection of food had been laid out for us to serve ourselves.

"Coffee or tea," Sam asked as I settled into a chair next to him.

"Oh, thank heavens. Coffee, please."

I hadn't indulged as much as I often did, but the quantity of champagne I had consumed along with the late night and intense concentration on the code had left me with a mild throbbing in my temples.

Sam passed me a cup as well as the cream and sugar so that I could prepare it as I liked. I was relieved to taste it was a dark Turkish roast and sighed contentedly.

Mabel's eyes danced with amusement. "Like nectar from the gods."

"Mmm, yes," I agreed.

"Is that coffee I smell?" a deep voice pleaded from the doorway.

I glanced over my shoulder to watch as Max staggered forward. "Yes. Have some?"

"Please."

It was my turn to smile as Max accepted his cup and promptly put the hot brew to his lips, drinking half the contents.

"Do you have any remaining taste buds?" I teased him.

"No, they were blistered off long ago by that terrible swill they used to give us in the trenches," he responded good-naturedly. "My batman could only ever serve it boiling lava hot or freezing cold."

Sam leaned back in his chair. "I think it was a requirement for their position."

"Listen to them complain." Mabel leaned toward me. "I heard the officers had the best of everything. Including dugouts that flooded only twice a week, and boxes and crates to sit on instead of dirt." She shook her head, tsking. "Cushy."

Sam had opened his mouth to quip back when Charlie came rushing into the room. His gaze darted over his shoulder, almost as if he was afraid of being followed. "Have any of you seen Tufton this morning?" he demanded without preamble, lurching to a halt next to our table.

"Good morning to you, too, Charlie," Max replied.

This seemed to prompt the man to remember his manners. "Oh, yes, good morning."

"Now, to answer your question. No, I haven't seen Jimmy."

Max glanced at the rest of us with raised eyebrows, and we all shook our heads. "He's probably still in bed," he added, addressing the distress that had sprung anew into Charlie's eyes.

"No. No, I . . . I checked. He's not there."

"Well, then, maybe he's gone for a morning stroll."

I glanced toward the bright sunshine outside the windows, having a difficult time imagining anyone who had been as scrooched as Jimmy was last night willingly going out at such an early hour. It was more likely he'd passed out in some dark corner somewhere and was sleeping off the night's excess.

"I'm sure he'll turn up," Max assured him.

Charlie nodded, but I could tell he wasn't convinced.

"If we see him, should we tell him you're looking for him?"

"Yes. Yes, please." Then without a word good-bye, he scurried off.

Mabel shook her head. "If that young man ever hopes to become a vicar, he's going to have to learn not to be so dashed awkward, or those parish women are going to eat him alive."

I knew what my mother and her friends would have said about him. And the war would not have passed for an excuse.

We passed a quarter of an hour pleasantly as we each drank another cup of java and finished our breakfasts. When we still didn't hear the sounds of anyone else stirring, Mabel pushed back from the table.

"Well, I'm not going to sit about gathering dust while I wait for everyone else to rise from their beds." She turned to me and Max. "Have either of you had a chance to see the rest of the island?"

We both said we hadn't.

"Then why don't Sam and I take you on a bicycle tour." She grinned in challenge. "If you're up for it?"

"I would love that," I declared, eager to escape the house and stretch my legs. Plus this provided me with a chance to engage Sam in conversation. I hadn't yet learned much about the sandy-haired man. This would be the perfect opportunity to find out more about him, and perhaps give me a hint as to why Jimmy had been so unhappy about his presence here.

The morning was already warm, so I elected not to throw on a coat over my slate blue voile blouse and charcoal gray serge skirt with buttons down my right hip. Mabel seemed to agree, looking lovely in a white blouse of silk georgette crepe with black banding on the collar and down the front of the placket.

After collecting our bicycles, we set off through a small gate on the north side of the castle grounds and turned left down what appeared to be the main dirt road leading across the island. One of the estate's hounds decided to join us, happily trotting alongside our bicycles with his tongue lolling out. Any glimpse of the castle was quickly swallowed up by the lush greenery and tall pines and elms overarching the road. If not for the salty scent of the sea on the breeze, it would have been easy to forget we were even on an island and not driving through the heart of the English countryside. No wonder King George IV, when still acting as Prince Regent, had declared Umbersea Island one of the most delightful spots in his kingdom.

At an intersection in the road, we came upon the charming pale stone edifice of a church.

"It was built here by the island's owner in the mid-nineteenth century to serve the needs of the workers and their families who moved to Umbersea Island to work for his clay and pottery company," Mabel explained, as we paused to look up at the castellated tower. "Though the business failed a few years later, and now the church is mainly for show."

It seemed to me the neo-Gothic structure of St. Mary the Virgin might be a lovely spot for a wedding, and I said so. "Do Walter and Helen plan to be married here?"

Mabel shrugged one shoulder. "Maybe. But I doubt it. It's not nearly swank enough for my cousin's taste. I suspect they'll be wed in London."

And yet they'd decided to host their engagement party here with only a select number of guests in attendance. It seemed an odd choice. From what I knew of Helen, I would have expected her to throw a large party in a townhouse in Mayfair or Belgravia, and open the doors to any who cared to join in the celebration. So why the quiet, intimate gathering? Was she conceding to Walter's wishes in this so that she could insist upon her grand affair for the wedding?

We pedaled on, taking the turning by the church to follow an even narrower road south toward the sea, but after passing a cluster of farm buildings, all of which were visibly still in use, the road swung west again. From time to time we caught glimpses through the trees and over the stone walls bordering the road into fields planted with assorted crops, mostly corn, barley, and oats. Though one large field appeared to lie dormant.

"Daffodils grow there in the spring," Mabel called over her shoulder. "Acres and acres of them, as far as the eye can see."

"Oh, how lovely," I exclaimed.

"It's truly a sight."

We detoured down a small road to the left so that they could show us one of the prettiest vantage points looking out over the sea toward the Studland Peninsula and beyond to the Channel. I hadn't even realized we'd been climbing in elevation, but the cliffs there were steep, dropping precipitously down a forested slope to a wide stretch of sandy beach. Red squirrels chattered over our heads, leaping from branch to branch. I laughed at the antics of one particularly daring fellow, who scurried along the branches, determined to get a closer look at us.

Sam clicked his tongue merrily at the little chap and he fled up the tree. "This is one of the only places in Britain where you'll find them. Most everyplace else, the gray squirrels have driven them out."

"The poor dears," I commiserated.

"Here at least they have free rein."

"Did Walter tell you all this?" I asked as we set off back up the road to resume our ride west toward the far side of the island. "Or do you just happen to know it?"

"I read it in a magazine somewhere," he admitted, tilting his head to consider the matter. "Though I can't recall which one." He smiled. "I simply find such things fascinating."

"Nature and science, and whatnot?"

"Yes."

I returned his grin, breathing deeply of the fresh air. "Sidney would have loved this," I said, conjuring his ghost. Partly because he was already on my mind, and partly because I wanted to draw Sam out. "He was always trying to convince me we should travel down to our cottage in Sussex. But then . . . his leaves were always so short."

I turned to gaze over the heathland to our right, its shrubs and gorse studded with purple and yellow flowers. I wished now I'd allowed him to persuade me. Just once. The Secret Service office could have done without me for a few more days than what I was traditionally given off whenever Sidney returned to London. But I had always found the cottage to be too close to the Channel, to France and the Western Front. The few times I had traveled there myself to get away from everything I had not stayed long, for I could hear the large guns. I would lie awake on clear nights and count the pounding artillery shells.

I'd almost forgotten I was baiting Sam for a response when he spoke up, consciously or not, giving me the exact information I sought.

"I knew Sidney," he said softly.

I looked up in surprise, though I didn't know why I was so astonished. "You did?"

He nodded. "I served in his company later in the war."

This news was not altogether welcome. It answered two of my questions, but it also added another suspect to my list. I'd already decided my mystery correspondent was likely one of the men who had fought alongside Sidney at the front, for how else could they have gotten their hands on Sidney's dented copy of *The Pilgrim's Progress*. But that left me with six potential letter writers—all the men in attendance except Tom.

"I learned later that he'd specifically requested me," Sam told me, then anticipated my next question. "He knew my brother. Ben had also served in the Thirtieth battalion. Though not under Sidney."

A sick feeling of dread filled me, and I wondered if I already knew what he was going to say next. "Was he killed at the Somme?" I asked as gently as I could.

It was Sam's turn to appear startled. "No, about six months later. During a trench raid."

"Oh," I replied lamely before remembering to offer my condolences. "I'm sorry for your loss." After everything I'd learned from Tom the night before, I'd assumed Ben's death must be connected to the disaster that befell the Thirtieth at the Somme, but apparently not. It would have connected Sam to that tragedy, but now I couldn't see how he had anything to do with it.

"I'm sorry for your loss as well." A heavy sadness filled Sam's eyes. "Sidney was a good man. He looked out for us all. As best he could." His voice trailed away at the end, making me wonder if he was thinking of something specific. But before I could find the words to ask, he turned to me with a determined smile. "Would you like to see one of the old pottery kilns?"

Max glanced over his shoulder from his position riding down the lane in front of me. "I would."

"We'll take them to the one near the Maryland pier," Mabel suggested. "I wanted to show them the abandoned village anyway."

"Good choice," Sam answered with forced cheer. Whether he actually believed he was fooling me, I didn't know, but I could see the tension in his smile, the haunted look in his eyes. I had seen it too many times in the faces of the men who had returned from the war. Which meant I had no way of knowing whether Sam's troubles were in any way remarkable, or even connected to me, or if they were merely a result of the typical soldier's experience.

The abandoned village Mabel spoke of had once been populated by the pottery workers and their families. Now the wood and stone buildings sat empty in their orderly rows, as the forest crept back in to reclaim them. By and large the buildings still appeared sound, though two of the cottages had seen their roofs cave in. We climbed off our bicycles to walk them between the solemn old cottages. Here and there a door stood open—either left that way by the inhabitants who'd moved away or by a curious stranger who'd taken little care—and leaves and debris littered the floors inside to be used as nesting material for woodland creatures.

Overall the village had a lost and woebegone quality to it. It was a ghost town, long forgotten and long neglected. Being in the heart of it, surrounded by the deserted buildings that seemed to yawn with longing for the joyful memories of the past, a chill settled around my shoulders. It was almost as if the village was watching us, waiting to see what we would do.

No one spoke until we reached the far end of the village, where it met the waters of the bay, as if we all felt the same unsettling sensation. Even the dog stayed close to our heels, refusing to venture into the buildings or even sniff around their foundations. But once we returned to the bright sunshine blazing down on the beach, chasing away the shadows behind us, I wondered if I hadn't imagined it all. Shaking my head firmly, I decided it was this deuced house party, and all of the unnecessary intrigue my mysterious correspondent had forced upon me.

A short distance to the left stood the old pottery pier, jutting out into deeper water. It was warped in places, and in need of some maintenance, but not so dilapidated that we were afraid to leave our bicycles behind and walk to its end for a better view of the island behind us. Farther south along the shore stood the abandoned pottery, its tall smoke stack still soaring into the air. Though having been neglected so long, I would not have trusted its stability.

Max and Sam were determined to get a closer look, so Mabel and I followed them down the beach, smiling at their boyish enthusiasm. Here the sand gave way to rocks in some places, forcing us to pick our way carefully around them. The hound happily sniffed his way through them, following some sea creature's scent. Then suddenly he stood straight, flaring his nostrils, and took off at a trot toward the old pottery. Max called after the dog, trying to get him to return, but whatever smell he'd picked up was far more alluring than Max's voice.

"Dash it all," Max exclaimed. "What's the hound's name? Does anyone know?"

Mabel and Sam shook their heads.

"Come here, boy!" he called again as the dog disappeared into the pottery. He sighed. "If he's anything like my hounds, he's probably picked up the scent of some moldering animal's corpse and has to go stick his nose into it."

None of us looked forward to following the dog into the darkened interior of the pottery, but we couldn't leave him behind. After all, we'd allowed him to trail after us. Fortunately, he decided to bark, alerting us to his location. We inched our way around stacks of abandoned crates, some still packed with pottery, as our eyes adjusted to the light. Near the back of the building, we discovered what had so intrigued the canine.

Appallingly, Max had been right. It was a corpse. But it hadn't yet begun to molder, nor was it an animal.

Jimmy stared sightlessly down at us, dangling from a chain flung over the rafters. Whatever pain he'd felt at the prospect of continuing to live was now drained from his eyes.

CHAPTER 8

"Get him down," I gasped in horror, as the hound continued to bark.

Max and Sam hastened to comply, fumbling with the stack of wooden crates toppled over beneath where Jimmy's body swayed overhead. The chain wrapped around his neck creaked.

Mabel draped a comforting arm around my shoulders. "He can't feel anything now," she said gently.

"I know," I replied, lowering my hand from over my mouth. "But he still doesn't deserve to be left up there."

It took a great deal of effort, but Max and Sam were eventually able to extract Jimmy from the chain and lower him to the floor. I didn't need to move closer to see the wounds. It was obvious he'd hung himself.

Or that someone had wanted us to think he had.

Perhaps having a similar thought, Max knelt down beside the body, still panting from exertion, and closed Jimmy's eyes. The hound moved closer to sniff at Jimmy, and Max shooed him away. Then he lifted Jimmy's only hand to examine it before leaning over to look at his neck.

"What are you doing?" Sam asked, staring over Max's shoulder.

"I just wanted to see if he had any defensive wounds," he replied calmly before rising to his feet once again.

Sam's brow furrowed. "Defensive wounds? Why? Don't you think this is a suicide?"

"It certainly seems that way." He shrugged. "But it doesn't hurt to be thorough."

"Were there any?" I queried.

Max looked at me with troubled eyes.

"Were there any defensive wounds?" I repeated, perhaps a bit more forcefully than necessary, for Mabel glanced at me in surprise.

But Max seemed to understand my insistence on an answer. "If there were, it's impossible to tell now." He stared down at Jimmy. "His fingers are damaged from his scrabbling at the chain. Whether he committed the deed himself or not, it's evident he regretted it before it was over. Which isn't altogether surprising." His voice turned grim. "It's a difficult way to go. Especially if the weight of the fall doesn't snap your neck."

I flinched at the bluntness of his words, but recovered myself quickly lest they start treating me like some fainting female. In any case, something that was sticking out of Jimmy's pocket had caught my eye. Stepping closer, I bent down to retrieve what appeared to be a piece of paper of some sort. My first assumption was that it must be a suicide note. As I pulled the letter free, something tumbled out of his pocket after it. It rolled toward Max's feet, and he picked it up to examine it.

I wasn't certain. It could have been a trick of the murky light shining through the dirty windows at the top of the building, but Max's complexion seemed to pale.

"What is it?" I asked.

He swallowed, opening his palm so we could see what was cradled within. "A piece of burnt cork."

"Burnt cork," I echoed in puzzlement. Whatever it meant, it seemed to affect Sam in much the same way as it had Max. I decided to give them both a moment to compose themselves while I unfolded the piece of paper to read what it said.

However, I quickly discovered it wasn't a letter, but a Field Service Postcard. One of the preprinted forms used by the soldiers to write home to their loved ones during the war. Each card was printed with remarks that the soldier could circle if they were applicable or cross out if they were not, and then lines for them to sign and date before posting it. Nothing else was allowed to be written on the postcard or else it would not be dispatched.

I had received my fair share of them during the war, usually from Sidney or one of my three brothers. Most everyone had. Particularly during times when the fighting was fierce. It was the fastest way for soldiers to let their families know they were still alive, or if they had been wounded and sent to the hospital.

However, this postcard did not follow regulations. In fact, a quick glance at the back where the address would have been written showed me it was blank. The words "I have been wounded" had been circled, but then "stabbed in the back" had been scribbled after. The name scrawled on the signature line was that of a Ben Gerard.

My gaze lifted to Sam, recalling the conversation we'd had just a short while ago. Sam's last name was Gerard, and he'd mentioned his deceased brother was Ben. What would be the chances that a different Ben Gerard was meant to have sent this? Miniscule, I imagined.

"What?" Sam asked uncertainly, glancing back and forth between the Field Service Postcard and me. "What is it?"

Mabel gasped behind me, having moved close enough to read over my shoulder.

I passed Sam the postcard, watching as all the blood drained from his face.

"But . . . but that's impossible!" he gulped. "Ben . . . Ben . . ." He shook his head, unable to finish that thought.

"'Letter will follow at first opportunity,'" Max read, taking the postcard from Sam's hands. His eyebrows arched, obviously finding the last comment circled as disturbing as I did. He turned to look at Sam, who still seemed to be grappling with this news. "Are you certain your brother is dead?"

"I . . . well, yes. As certain as a person can be when their brother was killed during a trench raid and their body was never able to be properly identified," he snapped. "But they found his identification discs." He clenched his hands into fists as anger began to overcome some of his shock and dismay. "This must be someone's idea of a cruel joke. It's sickening, I tell you. To use Ben's memory in such a way . . . Just sick!"

"Darling," Mabel murmured, wrapping her arms around him to comfort him. He stood rigidly in her arms, but as she continued to croon in his ear, the tension in his shoulders slowly began to loosen.

Trying to give the lovers a moment of privacy, I turned to Max, who was still examining the postcard with one hand and restraining the curious dog with the other. His gray eyes had turned stormy with grief, and I recalled what he had shared with me the night before. I knew what thoughts flitted through his head. He'd failed yet another of his men. The war might be over, but I knew he still considered them that way.

I pressed a hand to his forearm, trying to offer what reassurance I could. His lips flattened in a tight smile before his eyes dipped to Jimmy's supine form.

"I'm sorry you had to see all this," he remarked politely, trying to regain his footing.

I allowed my gaze to drift down toward Jimmy one last time. "I've seen worse."

Max's eyes flared with curiosity, but before he could speak, I turned back toward Mabel, and Sam, who seemed more in control of himself.

"I apologize," Sam said. "I suppose I'm just shocked." His sandy eyebrows drew together. "And confused."

"Understandably," I remarked. "But if I may, what does the burnt cork mean?" I looked between him and Max. "You both seem to know."

Max cleared his throat and stepped forward, saving Sam from having to answer. "We used burnt cork to blacken our faces whenever we went over the top for a trench raid. It was supposed to make it more difficult for the enemy to spot us in the darkness."

And as we already knew, Ben Gerard had been killed during a trench raid, presumably by a German bullet. However, the message on the Field Service Postcard seemed to suggest otherwise, if the words "stabbed in the back" were any indication.

"But what does any of that have to do with Jimmy?"

Sam and Max shared a pained look.

This time Sam was the first one to find his voice. "He was part of the raiding party who went out into No Man's Land with my brother. And one of the men who reported back that Ben had been killed."

We were all silent during our bicycle ride back to the castle, and made certain the hound followed us. For my part, I had no desire to share my morose ponderings, or the fact that I couldn't help but wonder if Sam had played a part in Jimmy's death. I already knew from overhearing Jimmy's heated conversation with Walter that Sam's presence here had upset him. Was it because he'd felt guilty about how Sam's brother had died during that trench raid? If so, I could hardly lay any blame at Sam's door.

Unless Sam had prodded him over the edge.

Though his shock at seeing them had appeared genuine, he seemed the likeliest person to have sent that Field Service Postcard and piece of burnt cork to Jimmy. But why? Had he suspected Jimmy of foul play? Is that what the card meant when it said Ben had been stabbed in the back?

I frowned in frustration. I couldn't possibly know what had really happened during that trench raid.

My gaze slid toward the man pedaling beside me. But Max might know.

If he had been these men's commanding officer at the time, or even if he'd already been promoted on to HQ, he might have heard something about the incident. From the manner in which he'd behaved inside that pottery, I suspected he wasn't taking Jimmy's apparent suicide at face value either. Perhaps he would be progressive enough to share his thoughts with me.

Having taken the most direct route down the main road that sliced through the center of the island, we reached the castle faster than I'd anticipated. However, more than an hour had still passed since we'd set out from the house. The morning was well advanced, and a number of people were seated outside under the shade of the terrace sipping coffee and nursing cigarettes.

We hadn't discussed how the situation should be handled, but we all seemed to be in silent agreement that Walter should be told first, so that a telephone call could be placed to the proper authorities on the mainland. So when Helen reached a hand up to shade her eyes to observe us as we crossed the lawn toward the terrace steps, we all pasted on fake smiles.

"Now where have the four of you been at such an ungodly hour?" she demanded to know, her eyes smiling as if at a jest.

"Just out for a bicycle tour of the island," Mabel replied, patting her arm as we passed.

Helen's eyes dipped to examine each of us in our dusty attire. "How industrious of you."

"Yes, well, I'm certain I positively reek for my trouble. I simply must go change before I rejoin you, darling," Mabel declared, pulling her blouse away from her neck to waft air down it.

She waved us off. "Of course."

The four of us trailed into the house, moving toward the breakfast room, where we thought to find Walter. However, we intercepted him only just coming down the stairs. His slow, methodical plod and the rap of his cane were immediately identifiable.

"Hullo, there," he greeted us. "Chumley told me you'd taken some of the bicycles out. Did you enjoy your ride?"

"Walter, we need to speak with you," Max told him. "Privately."

The seriousness of his tone and the somber expressions on each of our faces must have communicated our earnestness, for Walter's good cheer vanished. "Of course. How about my study?"

We followed him into a room not far from the main foyer. Unlike the rest of the castle, this room had not seen any recent refurbishments. Faded Chinese silk wallpaper hung on the walls next to heavy Victorian drapes and overlarge pieces of oak furniture. The air smelled strongly of old cigar smoke and worn leather. It didn't take much deductive skill to recognize that was because this room was Walter's domain, and so Helen had not been allowed to put her stamp on it. Yet. But I had little faith in his ability to keep her from making changes here once she was finished elsewhere.

Mabel and I settled into the two shabby, but comfortable chairs across from Walter's desk while Max fetched a pair of wooden ladder-back chairs from the corner. Sam ignored his proffered chair in favor of leaning against the sideboard, where he poured himself a generous drink and then downed it.

Walter eyed him warily. "Now, what's this all about?"

"Walter, you should have a seat," Max suggested, taking the lead of the conversation.

I was content to let him do so, for it allowed me to focus on Walter's reaction, as well as the fidgeting of the others. Our host appeared sincerely stunned by the news of Jimmy's death. With each detail, he seemed to sink deeper into the chair behind his desk, as if the weight of our news was too heavy for him to remain upright. But when Max showed him the Field Service Postcard and the piece of burnt cork we'd found in Jimmy's pocket, he abruptly straightened and his expression turned stony.

"But this makes little sense," he remarked, almost woodenly. His eyes flicked toward Sam. "Your brother was killed by enemy fire. Taken out by a sniper when he was caught under the flare of the very lights the Germans sent up. I was there when the raiding party returned to the trenches. I remember how shaken up several of the men were. We had to give them an extra ration of rum."

"How many men did they lose?" I asked in sympathy.

"Well . . . er . . . just the one," Walter stammered. "Lieutenant Gerard. But they were pinned down by sniper fire for some time. I gathered it was quite a hellish ordeal. It's a miracle that more of the men weren't hit."

"What's to be done about Jimmy, then?" Sam interjected, undoubtedly not wanting to hear any more about the night his brother had died. I supposed he'd heard all the particulars before.

Walter glanced almost regretfully toward the telephone sitting on a table in the corner. "Well, I suppose we must contact the authorities. And I'll dispatch some servants down to the old pottery to handle the body." His gaze turned to me and Mabel. "I must ask. Have you told anyone else about this yet?"

Mabel and I shared a look of mutual feminine annoyance that he should assume we would be the ones to blab about our gruesome discovery.

"No, we haven't," she replied flatly.

Walter regarded each of us anxiously. "Then may I ask that you all keep this matter quiet for the time being?"

I frowned, having difficulty accepting the insensitivity of his request. And from the silence of the others, I suspected they felt the same.

"You think me callous." Our host grimaced. "And perhaps you're correct. But Helen has so been looking forward to hosting this party. It's her first as mistress here. I don't want Jimmy's suicide, sad though it may be, to overshadow the festivities." When still no one replied, Walter's brow furrowed as he reached out and began to roll a fountain pen back and forth over the blotter on his desk. "I mean, it's not as if this is any great shock to those of us who knew him. It was only a matter of time before he tried again."

That might have been true, but I couldn't help but feel uneasy. Another attempt might have been imminent, but why on earth had he chosen to end it all at a house party? Even if that postcard and cork had prompted him to do it—prodding at a secret or a failing he just couldn't live with—why not wait until he had returned home? Had it truly been so unbearable?

Or had he been afraid that at home no one would find him? That no one would even notice he was gone?

I realized I knew almost nothing about what Jimmy's life had been like, whether he'd lived alone or with some sort of family. Perhaps there had been nothing and no one to fill his days. Nothing but the bitterness I had sensed festering in him. Though, in truth, if he'd been determined to kill himself at this house party, I would have expected him to do it in a more conspicuous place. One final effort to make us all feel guilty for our determined frivolity. But that's not what he'd done. Instead, he'd taken himself to a remote part of the island, where none of us might have thought to look, before ending it all.

We all reluctantly agreed to keep Jimmy's death a secret, though my reasoning for doing so did not align with Walter's. I was far more interested in seeing how the others behaved now that he was gone, and whether any of them would display a guilty conscience.

I was contemplating this as we departed Walter's study to return to our rooms to change when Chumley, the butler, approached me.

"Miss Kent," he inquired. "This arrived for you in the post."

I stared down at the pale white letter resting on the silver tray he held out toward me, feeling a sense of dread overtake me. I knew it was too much to hope that my friend Daphne had written to pester me about her errand a second time, and I could think of no one else who would post a message to me here. Which meant it was probably from my mysterious correspondent.

Swallowing my trepidation, I forced myself to take the letter from the tray. "Thank you."

My voice and movements were stiff and tense, but I couldn't seem to disguise them as I should. Looking up, I found Max observing me. But before he could comment, I hurried away, scurrying up the staircase to my assigned chamber.

Once the door was safely shut behind me, only then did I dare to tear open the envelope and extract the simple typewritten card.

Trust no one.

CHAPTER 9

The day being so sunny and warm, Helen declared we should all go out on Walter's yacht for a picnic and a dip in the sea. So we set out across the harbor and around the headland out into the English Channel, sailing along the coast to some sheltered cove that our hostess assured us was absolutely charming.

Having eaten little for breakfast and taken that long bicycle tour of the island, I soon followed my stomach's rumblings inside to the galley, where the food had been laid out for us to serve ourselves whenever we wished. But rather than fill a plate and rejoin the others above deck, I elected to stand at the table, popping crudités into my mouth and enjoying a moment of solitude.

Anger had always made me hungry. There was nothing like a righteous fury to send me straight to the pantry to devour everything in sight. And I was definitely irate now. If my mystery correspondent had stood before me at the moment, I would have given him a piece of my mind, and thrown in a few curse words for good measure. Words so foul, Sidney had never even heard me use them.

How dare he . . . whoever he was! He'd dragged me to this party on the pretense he had information to share with me in person, in private, and then instead proceeded to leave me obscure little notes and a coded missive I was supposed to decipher. He expected me to trust his word, and yet he refused to reveal himself.

I was fed up with this little game! "And so it begins." "Trust no one." What on earth did any of that even mean? Was he worried I would confide in someone else and ruin his amusement?!

I shoved another Canapés à l'Amiral in my mouth, chewing while I stewed.

For a brief moment, I'd considered pleading a thick head and remaining behind. The prospect of affecting a carefree attitude after everything that had happened this morning—after receiving that blasted note—had simply seemed too daunting. I also wanted to search the house for any typewriters that might possibly have been used to compose these messages, but even had I found one, there were no distinguishing marks on the cards or in the type to tell me whether it had been the one used. Plus, there was no telling how long the yacht would be gone, and I would miss a prime opportunity to chat with and observe the other guests, and perhaps find out once and for all who was tormenting me and why.

So I'd reluctantly joined the party aboard the boat, hoping to regain my good humor. But everyone's false cheer only irritated me further. *That one may smile, and smile, and be a villain.* Only Charlie seemed at all troubled, and that was out of concern for Jimmy's absence. We'd been forced to lie and tell everyone he was feeling ill. Seeing the worry in Charlie's eyes, I'd felt rotten for not telling him the truth, little comfort though that might have given him.

I had just selected another vol-au-vent, this one filled with savory chicken, when Walter strolled into the galley. His limp seemed less pronounced, but that might have been because of the morphia I suspected he had dosed himself with since our revelation in his study. His pupils were dilated and the brackets of pain around his mouth had all but disappeared.

"Ah, Verity," he proclaimed. "Enjoying our cook's delicacies, I see."

"Yes, they're quite good," I remarked, taking another bite.

Walter sank down on one of the benches. "Yes, he's a Frenchman. And you know how serious they are about their food."

I smiled tightly, dropping my gaze to examine the rest of the selections. I'd expected Walter to demur his wife's suggestion that we take the yacht out, but apparently he wasn't concerned about keeping the authorities waiting when they came to retrieve Jimmy's body. They were certain to have questions for us, or at least for the men. In my experience, they tended to think females needed to be shielded from such sordid matters as much as possible.

"That reminds me," Walter suddenly declared. "I *do* believe I owe you an apology."

My ears perked up, and I found myself holding my breath, wondering if my mystery correspondent was about to reveal himself. "Oh?"

He grimaced sheepishly. "Yes, I was quite indiscreet about your wartime service at dinner last night, wasn't I?"

I exhaled in disappointment and then rallied myself, anxious to hear more. "Yes, I wondered about that." I frowned, trying to deduce how much he knew without revealing more. "How did you know?"

He reached out to pick up one of the little tea sandwiches. "Sidney let it slip one evening while we were both deep in our cups."

"Sidney told you?" I repeated, trying to come to terms with this revelation.

Walter nodded, chewing a bite of his sandwich. "But I'm sure"—he swallowed—"he regretted it as soon as he did. Told me to keep it close to the vest, and all that."

I watched as he took another bite of his food, sorting through the implications, wondering how Sidney had known . . . whatever he had known. Had I slipped up? Had I inadvertently given myself away? I couldn't recall ever doing or saying anything that would reveal the true nature of my wartime work. I'd been so careful. But then, this *was* Sidney. He'd had the rather potent ability to make me forget myself at times.

So perhaps I *had* betrayed myself. But when? How long had Sidney known?

"Do you remember when this was that he told you?" I remarked as casually as I could manage while reaching out to select a warm grape.

But something in my voice must have given me away, for Walter glanced up from his absorption with the spread of food before him. His eyes softened with understanding. "You never told him, did you?"

I considered denying it, but it seemed silly to do so when it seemed he already knew. So I shook my head.

He reached across the table to pat my hand. "I wouldn't let it trouble you, Ver. Sidney could flush out anything. That's why the men all called him 'the ferret.' They quickly learned they couldn't gas Ole Captain Kent. Chances were he already knew the truth." His eyes turned to the side, as if seeing something I couldn't see. "Nothing got past him," he murmured almost to himself.

"And yet he couldn't see ahead to know that his company would be separated from the rest of the battalion on the Somme," I risked mentioning, curious whether Walter could tell me more about that day.

His gaze lifted to meet mine, but I wasn't sure he was actually seeing me. "Yes, well, that wasn't his fault. No one expected him to be a soothsayer. Though, he seemed to think so."

"What of the others? Maybe there were some who blamed him."

"No, no," Walter muttered forcefully, shaking his head. "None of the men blamed him. We all knew he'd done what he could to relieve us."

But as adamant as he insisted this was true, I wasn't so sure. And I didn't think he was as certain as he wished me to believe either. I was Sidney's widow after all. He wasn't likely to tell me the truth, especially if it wasn't complimentary.

Tom chose that rather inopportune moment to enter the galley, preventing me from asking Walter about the odd guest list. His strident voice told me he'd already indulged in a number of cocktails above deck. "There you two are. Keeping all the food to yourselves?" He draped an arm lazily around my shoulders and scooped up a pair of Lobster Rissoles with his other hand before popping them one by one into his mouth.

Max followed more sedately, his gaze immediately searching mine out. From the hesitancy of his movements I suspected he'd guessed their interruption wasn't exactly welcome.

"We're about to drop anchor," Tom told us around his mouthful of food. "And Helen wants us all to go for a swim."

I arched one eyebrow. "Even Nellie?"

"Well, no." He smirked. "As usual, she's refusing." A mischievous glimmer entered his eyes. "But *you* might be able to convince her. After all, you were the one who coaxed her into climbing Hardraw Scar."

I crossed my arms over my chest and swiveled to stare at him in incredulity. "Where she got stuck and had to be carried down on Rob's back? She complained for weeks that I had been trying to kill her."

"Yes, well, she still listened." He studied the spread of food, carefully selecting another canapé. "Never liked to be shown up by you."

That wasn't how I remembered it, but I didn't debate the issue. Instead, I joined the others up on deck, doing my best to help cajole Nellie into joining us, though I knew she would decline, if for no other reason than just to be contrary.

Walter's crew had sailed us into a sun-drenched cove surrounded by tall white cliffs. The water there lapped gently against the rock face, where it had worn away at the smooth surface for centuries, if not millennia. A short distance out to sea stood a pillar of the same white stone, which at some point had broken away from the rest of the coastline. The men promptly made it a challenge to swim out to it and back. Even Walter and Tom struck out at first, but they pulled up short a few hundred yards out, perhaps recognizing their wounded legs might not withstand the strain of going so far.

For my part, I had never been a very strong swimmer, and the water was positively frigid. So I soon elected to return to the boat, settling onto one of the deck chairs with a large towel snuggled around me. Mabel eagerly followed, and we lay reclined side by side, soaking up the warmth of the sun. The crew obligingly brought us drinks and Mabel her cigarette case, and I was quite content to have abandoned the others to their splashing and laughter.

"I hate to admit it, but she may have had the right of it from the start," Mabel remarked, nodding toward Nellie, where she lounged a few chairs away, her eyes closed in what appeared to be slumber. "But one has to humor Helen and her schemes."

"She seems very lively," I remarked.

Mabel nodded, taking a drag on her fag. "Always has been. Even when she was under her father's thumb. He wasn't the sort to appreciate a spirited daughter."

"I can imagine." My mother was much the same sort of parent, always chiding me for my vibrant nature. Some of that exuberance had been diminished by the war, but I was still far too animated for her liking.

She shrugged. "But I suppose it doesn't matter now. He's gone, and she can pretty much do as she likes." She tilted her head toward me conspiratorially. "Her trustees are rather easily persuaded to her side of things, particularly now that she's engaged to a war hero." She closed her eyes, turning her face up toward the sun. "I think that's the real reason why she didn't invite any of her father's family except Nellie. She didn't want to risk them voicing their disapproval and cutting off her purse strings before she was wed."

"And she doesn't think Nellie will do the same thing?"

"Oh, she knows she will. But Nellie's reputation is already tarnished amongst that august clan, and so her words aren't likely to be heeded."

I glanced at my childhood friend, curious whether she could hear us, but her expression remained unruffled, her body in repose. I felt a slight pulse of sympathy for her, knowing how little she must like being considered the black sheep of her family. Rebellion had never been in her nature. It was one of the reasons we had clashed so often as children.

"It's silly, isn't it?" I said. "As if thousands of unwed women didn't find themselves compromised during the war, courtesy of one of our soldiers home on leave. A simple seeking and giving of comfort to one another. I'm sure had Sidney and I not already wed, given the opportunity, we would have behaved likewise."

"It didn't just happen at home," Mabel interjected, reaching over to tap the ash off the end of her cigarette into the tray set on the table between our chairs. "More than one of my fellow nurses found herself in a delicate situation. And we were watched like a hawk by the sisters." She shook her head. "I still don't know how they managed it."

Having witnessed her cool head earlier in the day when confronted with Jimmy's body, I wasn't surprised to hear she had served as a nurse during the war. She seemed to possess the perfect temperament for it—calm, efficient, no-nonsense. "Where were you assigned?" I couldn't help asking, curious whether she might have cared for any of the men in the Thirtieth.

"For most of the war I was at a field hospital near Albert." She lifted her glass to her mouth, but then paused before taking a drink, as if considering something. "I was familiar with your husband, actually."

I blinked in surprise, not having expected such a thing. Was everyone at this benighted party acquainted with my husband?

"He would stop by the hospital from time to time when at rest to check on his men and their injuries." Mabel grimaced as she swallowed the remainder of her drink and then set it aside. "And I helped stitch up his leg after it was gouged by that shrapnel."

"What do you mean?" I asked in confusion.

She turned to look at me, her brow furrowed. "Did he not explain? A shell landed near where he was stationed in the trenches. Ripped that hole in his leg and nicked him a few other places. But all in all, he was rather lucky."

I continued to stare at her in bewilderment, for I had never seen any wounds on Sidney's legs. At least, none as significant as those that would have been inflicted if he'd been hit by shrapnel. "When was this?"

"I . . . I can't recall exactly," she answered hesitantly, and I could tell from her expression that she wished she'd never said anything. "It must have been sometime after the Battle of Cambrai in late 1917." She studied the end of her cigarette. "But before spring. I remember it was bitter cold that week. We had difficulty keeping anything warm. A few of the taps even froze." Her dark eyes lifted to meet mine expectantly. "I believe he was sent home for a short leave after he'd healed enough that the doctors weren't afraid his wound would reopen."

"Oh. Then it must have happened just before the holidays," I replied in some relief, for that had been the last time Sidney had been given leave before his death. The last time I'd seen him. Though I still didn't recall any shrapnel wounds, and I was certain I would have. Sidney had never felt any shame when it came to his body, rather justifiably. And he was always quite thorough and energetic when it came to matters of the boudoir, even right up until the end. If he had suffered from any physical pain or twinges, I would have noticed.

But maybe that was one of the reasons he'd been acting so strangely. Maybe I hadn't recognized his wound for what it was. His body had been riddled with any number of cuts, insect bites, and bruises. Perhaps somehow I had overlooked it, and not wanting to alarm me he hadn't mentioned it.

However, Mabel extinguished that small bit of hope. "No, it couldn't have been then. I was on leave for a few weeks in December myself. This occurred about a month later."

A hollow space began to open up inside me. "You're certain?"

"Yes."

"You couldn't have mixed up Sidney with another soldier?" I asked, wanting to find some way to refute what she was saying.

"No, I'm certain it was him." Her gaze was concerned. "Why?"

I shook my head. "I . . . I'm just surprised I missed it, that's all."

Mabel was perceptive enough not to pry further, even though it must have been obvious I was lying. I stared forlornly out at the seagulls wheeling across the sky as I tried to come to grips with the implication of what she'd just told me.

For if Sidney had been given leave a short time before he was killed, he had not come home to me. But why? Where could he have gone? And did it have anything to do with the allegations my mysterious letter writer had made against him?

My stomach pitched. Or had my husband simply not cared to see me?

I turned my head to the side, wanting to hide my heartbreak. Which was how I caught sight of the vicious little smirk curling Nellie's mouth even as she continued to feign sleep.

CHAPTER 10

"Verity, come join us," Helen called across the lawn from where she wielded a croquet mallet. Dressed in a frock of ivory georgette crepe with two deep bands of peach seif and a matching hat tipped jauntily on her head, she looked fresh and lovely.

I descended the terrace steps, my own mauve taffeta dress with ivory lace swishing about my legs. A handful of other guests had congregated about her to try their hand at the game. The heavy clouds we had noticed earlier gathering in the west, their ominous appearance having chased the yacht back to the island, now completely blotted out the sun. But it appeared as if the rain would continue to hold for at least a bit longer.

Still smarting from Mabel's revelation and feeling troubled by all the other events of the day, I'd thought to remain in my room until dinner, determined to decode the hidden missive inside Sidney's book. However, frustration had overtaken me, and it had become evident I was in no frame of mind to concentrate on such an intense and fraught task. So instead I'd gone in search of distraction, hoping I might learn something helpful from the others, as well as avoid some of the more uncomfortable emotions swirling about inside me.

For the truth was, discovering that Sidney had not come home during his last leave had made me doubt his innocence more than ever. I wanted to persuade myself that Mabel could have been mistaken, that she'd mixed up the dates or her patients, but the little I knew of her told me that was unlikely. Instead, I must face the fact he'd chosen to spend his leave elsewhere. And that elsewhere could have something to do with my mysterious correspondent's allegations against him of treason.

I didn't *want* to believe it was possible, but it was becoming harder and harder to dismiss the fact that my husband had been behaving oddly those last few months before he died. Even his letters hadn't sounded like him. It was almost as if he worried I would notice this, because he'd begun sending me more Field Service Postcards than actual letters to keep me apprised of his status. At the time, I'd convinced myself he must be involved in heavy fighting, and too exhausted between engagements to write letters. Or that he had been privately battling a bout of frazzled nerves, or worse, shell shock. But now I wasn't so sure.

Clutching my cream short-brimmed hat to my head against a sudden gust of wind, I leapt over a small divot in the otherwise immaculate lawn and took stock of the other players. Max was present, along with Felix and Charlie, and Helen's friend Elsie, who flitted around the gentlemen like a bee gathering nectar. Despite the gentlemen present, I wasn't surprised to find Gladys missing. She had looked a little rather worse for wear when we returned to the castle, and I suspected the choppy sea, as well as the large quantity of gin she'd consumed, had disagreed with her.

"You are a godsend," Helen proclaimed. "We need six players, or else one of us shall be forced to sit out. So you see you simply *must* join in."

"Well, who am I to naysay our hostess," I replied, accepting the mallet Felix passed to me.

Helen dimpled and swiveled to glance at the others, making her skirt flare outward. "Hear that, everyone. You should all take notes."

We laughed.

"Well, then. Whose team am I on?" I asked.

Felix smirked, leaning on his mallet. "How about ladies versus gentlemen?"

Helen and I exchanged an arch look, for it was clear that Felix didn't think we would be much of a challenge.

"Suits me," she declared flippantly.

"Me, as well," I chimed in, fed up with being Felix's teammate after our tennis match the day before.

The men won the coin toss and elected to go first. It swiftly became apparent that Felix and Max were skilled players, if a bit rusty. I couldn't help but wonder whether either of them had played since before the war. Charlie, on the other hand, was not so adept. Though, given Elsie's ineptness, that only meant the teams were more evenly matched.

But to Charlie's credit, he did seem rather distracted. His gaze scoured the gardens or stared up at the windows on the upper floors of the castle, as if seeing something the rest of could not. I tried to score shots off of his ball whenever I could, hoping to distract him from whatever was troubling him and draw him out. It was evident he was still concerned about Jimmy's absence, and I felt another prick of guilt that we had not revealed the truth to him. Perhaps it would be best to pull him aside later and tell him about Jimmy's apparent suicide. I would ask Max his opinion on the matter, for he also seemed to be going out of his way to be kind to the younger man. Or maybe it just seemed so when compared to Felix's sly insults.

Regardless, Charlie didn't seem to notice much of what either of them said. However, whenever I attempted to speak with him it was a different matter.

"I wonder how long it will rain," I murmured, gazing up at the clouds as we waited for Elsie to take her next shot.

"I . . . I don't know." His eyes shifted from side to side as if looking for escape while his hands twisted round and round the handle of his mallet.

"Where I grew up, in the Dales, it would sometimes rain for days and days. Oh, I do hope that's not the case here. I should hate for Helen and Walter's party to be washed out. But I suppose we're lucky it has held off this long."

I turned toward Charlie, whose mouth had curled into a strained smile. Clearly my presence unsettled him, but why?

Tilting my head, I gestured toward him with my mallet. "And where do you hail from, Mr. Montague."

He swallowed. "Faversham."

"Near Canterbury?"

"Yes."

"I believe Sidney had a great-aunt who lived near there," I remarked, knowing full well his only great-aunt resided in Wales.

Charlie fidgeted, tapping his mallet awkwardly against the side of his shoe.

"But I'm sure he doubtless mentioned her to you."

He shook his head.

"No? Well, I imagine the matter never came up. You must have certainly had better things to talk about," I remarked breezily, pivoting to watch as Max tapped his ball through a hoop.

"We didn't talk much," Charlie retorted, his words snapping from his lips in that peculiar monotone he used. I couldn't tell if he was lying or he was always this fretful.

"You're playing dirty, Verity," Felix called out playfully, though the look in his eyes was far from jovial. "Quit trying to rattle ole Charlie."

"I'm only making conversation," I replied. "There is no 'rattling' of any kind going on."

But Charlie belied my words, mumbling something breathlessly to himself that I only partially heard, though I leaned toward him to try to catch it.

"What was that, Charlie?"

"'. . . resist the devil, and he will flee from you.'"

Then he dropped his mallet and strode off toward the castle.

"Charlie?" I called after him in concern, then when it became apparent he wasn't coming back, in astonishment. "Charlie, wait. Where are you going?"

I hardly knew what to say to the others. I hadn't meant to send him running from me. And what on earth did those last few words mean? Was he referring to *me* as the devil? But why?

"No rattling, indeed," Felix accused, crossing his arms over his chest.

"Oh, leave her be," Max told him with a frown. "You know she didn't do anything to upset him. Charlie's always been a bit . . . erratic."

Felix's eyes narrowed as he watched Charlie disappear inside the castle. "And I suppose being forced to talk to the widow of the man you practically worshipped doesn't help either."

I stiffened as his gaze swiveled to meet mine.

"Not that Sidney ever returned any of those feelings," he hastened to add, though the malicious glint in his eyes never faded.

Max stepped forward, his brow thunderous. "Halbert, that's quite uncalled for."

"Oh, stuff it," Felix scoffed. "I didn't insult her husband. It's not his fault the young pup believed the sun rose and set with him, even though it was clear he was besotted with his wife. That's what comes of having German blood. You know his grandparents were Huns."

"What utter nonsense," Helen interjected cuttingly. "My stepfather was a German, and the best man I've ever known." She paused, pushing a strand of blond hair behind her ear. "Save Walter, of course."

I noted her snapping eyes and high color, surprised by her defense of those with German blood despite the fact that most of society derided it. Even the king had changed their surname from Saxe-Coburg-Gotha to Windsor in order to distance himself from his German ancestors and cousins. I also had German relatives, in particular a great-aunt whom I adored, and second cousins who had fought and died for the Kaiser, so I didn't share in the general public's disgust of all things Germanic either. Perhaps Helen wasn't such a naïve match for Walter after all.

But Felix was not so impressed. "Yes, Walter." He glanced about him. "Where is he, by the way? He's missing all the fun yet again." His voice lowered in mock concern. "Is his leg giving him a spot of trouble?"

Helen lifted one perfectly arched eyebrow in disdain. "Actually, he's allergic to bee stings, so he rarely ventures into the gardens. None of us would fault him for that, now would we?"

This was news to me, though as his close friend I expected Sidney must have known. I'd simply assumed Walter was dealing with the authorities and their inquiry into Jimmy's suicide. After all, his butler had been waiting for him when we returned to the pier, conferring with him on some matter before they set off toward the quay, where the authorities had most likely docked.

Felix rolled his eyes and turned away, swinging his mallet at one of the croquet balls and sending it careening off toward a stand of flowering bushes. Then he dropped his mallet and went striding off toward the sea.

Elsie's feet shuffled sideways toward the house. "I . . . I think I should go look in on Gladys."

Helen sighed. "It's all right, darling. I believe our match is at a standstill." She glanced up at the leaden sky. "Perhaps we'll have time to finish tomorrow."

Before the house party ended and we all left Umbersea Island to return home.

I frowned. And yet, my anonymous letter writer had still not stepped forward to explain why exactly I had been lured here.

Almost as if he'd read my thoughts, Max moved to my side. "It looks as if the storm will hold off a little while longer," he murmured softly, with his eyes on the horizon beyond the trees. "Would you care to stroll with me?"

He turned his head to meet my probing gaze and my heart kicked in my chest. Was this it, then? Was he my shadowy correspondent?

"Yes, I would like that," I somehow managed to say.

He dipped his head once in acknowledgment.

We followed the path we had taken earlier in the day to collect our bicycles for the tour of the island, but rather than head west, deeper into the island, we turned our steps eastward. A tall Tudor-style gatehouse marked the edge of the castle's property, through which we could see a dusty track leading down toward the small cluster of buildings along the island's main quay. Max asked if I would like to see them, but I shook my head, sensing that this conversation required privacy, and I wasn't certain we would find it on the quay.

A tall brick wall extended past the gatehouse, acting as the boundary to the castle's smaller east garden, through which we'd passed upon our initial arrival to the island. We followed the wall into the sheltered space, which operated as a sort of a breakwind against the increasingly stronger gusts that threatened to rip my hat from my head. However, the trees above us still whipped about, their leaves slapping together like sharp applause, reminding us that rain was not far off. The air was thick with anticipation and the scent of the sea and the coming storm.

"You know that what Felix said back there was utter claptrap," he insisted. His eyes were soft with concern. "Charlie might have idolized Sidney to some extent, but he never—"

I pressed a hand to his arm, halting his flow of words. "I know. There's no need to explain," I assured him with a tight smile. "Felix likes to stir up trouble." My brow furrowed. "I think he just wants everyone to be as frustrated and miserable as he is."

Of course, that didn't make his words any less true. Maybe Charlie *had* had strong feelings for Sidney, inappropriate or otherwise, but I knew Sidney better than to believe he'd ever returned them. I was fairly certain he'd always been faithful to me. I had never questioned the truth of our physical intimacy. But even if he hadn't, I couldn't believe it would have been with a man, and certainly not with a subordinate. I had overheard some of the crude comments made by my colleagues in the Secret Service. I was not ignorant of the existence of men who preferred the company of men. But Sidney was not one of them.

Max sighed heavily. "You've described Felix to a T. It's why he was never promoted beyond first lieutenant. We couldn't risk having him destroy the morale of an entire company."

"I'm surprised he was promoted beyond second lieutenant."

He cleared his throat. "Yes, well, by the end we were running rather short of experienced officers."

I nodded, feeling thoughtless for even remarking on it.

Max lifted aside the branch of a holly tree that had dipped low over the path, letting me pass through first. I noticed that his eyes cut behind us as he did so. Checking to be certain we hadn't been followed?

"I hope I'm not being too forward," he murmured, lowering his voice so that it was just audible above the crunch of the dirt beneath our feet and the rustle of the wind through the trees above us. "But I couldn't help but notice your reaction to the letter the butler passed you earlier, and I wondered . . . Well, I suppose I'm curious whether we've both found ourselves in the same predicament."

I looked up at him expectantly, refusing to react, to give any indication that I faced any particular dilemma until he explained his. My time with the Secret Service had taught me too well that it was better to play dumb than risk revealing yourself unless you were absolutely certain of the other person's loyalties. And sometimes not even then.

He offered me a strained smile. "I received a rather . . . unsettling letter a few weeks ago. It urged me to attend this house party."

My back straightened at his admission.

"You see, I wasn't going to come. In fact, I couldn't figure out why I'd even been invited. Walter and I had always rubbed along quite fine, but we certainly weren't any sort of chums. Definitely not close enough for him to have invited me to his engagement party." He frowned down at his feet. "And then this letter arrived, and after reading it, I suppose I felt I had to come."

"What did it say?"

His soft gray eyes were troubled. "That the sender—whoever he is—has information about Ben Gerard's death."

"Sam's brother?"

He nodded.

"But what information?"

He raked his hand back through his hair in obvious frustration. "I don't know. I admit I was suspicious of Ben's death from the beginning, but I couldn't find any evidence to prove it didn't happen exactly as it was reported. That it wasn't just another senseless casualty among the hundreds of thousands of other senseless casualties."

I inhaled sharply, trying to breathe past the band tightening around my chest. The same band that had seemed to press down on me, making it impossible to breathe deeply throughout the entire war.

"Why were you suspicious, then?" I turned to study his furrowed brow, remembering what Sam and Max had revealed this morning. "Was there something odd about that trench raid?"

"No, not really," he admitted. But then he hesitated, as if weighing how much he wished to say. His mouth twisted in scorn. "Unless you count Ben's being ordered to take part, when he'd led another stunt into No Man's Land just five days earlier. Generally, the men, particularly the officers, rotated that duty."

"Because it was so dangerous?" I guessed.

"Yes."

I scowled at the bushes bordering the path. Then why had Ben been ordered to go again so soon?

"*And* Ben came to see me shortly before he was killed."

Hearing the graveness of Max's voice, I looked up to meet his eyes, knowing what he had to reveal next was important.

"He confided in me that he had some misgivings about the death of two soldiers from his battalion who had been convicted of desertion and killed by firing squad a few months prior."

My eyes widened. A serious offense indeed.

"Ben was convinced the two men were framed, and that the entire matter was orchestrated by one or more of his fellow officers."

My head spun at the implication, and my heart clutched in dread. "Did he say who?" I finally managed to push from my dry throat.

"No, he was hesitant to name names. Not without proof." Max's brow lowered thunderously. "But, by Jove, I wish he had."

"Why on earth would someone do that to two innocent men? Men they commanded?"

But I was really thinking of Sidney. Why would he do such a thing? Was this the crime that my mysterious correspondent had alluded to as being traitorous?

Max clasped his hands behind his back, staring at the path before us. "To cover up their own crimes. Out of pure spite. Who knows?"

"But aren't you at least familiar with the deaths he was referring to? I mean, wouldn't the paperwork for such a court-martial have passed through your HQ? And since it was a capital offense, wouldn't the convictions have needed to be approved?"

He seemed astonished I knew this. "Yes. But, following protocol, the matter was presided over by officers from another division. I only saw the paperwork later because I wanted to understand what had happened."

His eyes were dark with shadows, and I realized what he wasn't saying. He'd studied the case because he felt responsible. Yet another failure he heaped on his plate.

"So you know which officers were at least involved? Who his accusers were?" I pressed.

"I do. But I don't know if Gerard was suspicious of all of them. I don't actually have any proof of wrongdoing on any of their parts, only Ben's vague remarks that he had uncovered discrepancies between some of the officers' stories and what some of his men had confessed to him about the matter. So you understand why I find Ben's being ordered to take part in that raiding party—a mission from which he never returned—to be a little too coincidental for my liking?"

"I do," I replied calmly, though my insides were tied in knots. "And now Jimmy is dead—one of the men who reported that Ben had been killed."

"Exactly." I could hear the satisfaction in his voice that I had worked out that implication on my own. That he hadn't had to put it into words. "Jimmy was also one of the officers who testified at that court-martial."

"So Jimmy's apparent suicide might not be so apparent after all," I added, finishing both of our thoughts.

I wished I could feel as relieved as he seemed to be to have shared all of this with me, but the truth was his confession had only made me more wary. Yes, I now had more information than before about what my anonymous letter writer may have been hinting at. I had another potential angle to pursue. But I had no way of knowing if Max was being completely honest with me.

Maybe Max truly had received a letter from a mystery correspondent. Maybe he *had* been lured here the same as I had. However, I also couldn't dismiss the possibility that Max himself could actually be my anonymous letter writer. That this sudden revelation wasn't merely a way to share information with me without giving himself away directly.

As angry as that last message had made me, I couldn't dismiss the warning it had contained from my mind. The truth was, I *didn't* know who I could trust. And if I chose the wrong person to confide in, it could end in dire consequences—for me, for Sidney's memory, and possibly for another guest if Jimmy's death was not as straightforward as it had been made to appear.

Crossing my arms over my chest against a sudden chill, I cupped my elbows with my hands and glanced sideways up at Max where he continued to stroll beside me. The thorny thing was that I *wanted* to trust him. I wanted to take someone into my confidence, and he seemed the natural choice.

For reasons I didn't fully understand, I felt drawn to him. I could already feel the seeds of attachment beginning to grow inside me, stirring something within my breast. It was comforting, and yet somehow terrifying all at once. And I wasn't sure I wanted to name this feeling or examine it too closely. Not now. Not yet. Maybe not ever.

I exhaled a ragged breath. "And you have no idea who sent the letter?" I could hear my anxiety and wished I'd taken the time to temper my tone.

Fortunately, Max seemed too preoccupied by his own thoughts to notice. "To be honest, at first I wondered if it might be you."

"Me?"

"Yes." His gaze held mine steadily. "There was something in

your eyes when we chatted on that road north of Poole after our near collision. Something that made me think you knew something. You seemed . . . uncertain."

"Uncertain?"

"Like you weren't sure how to proceed after you discovered who I was. I thought maybe you hadn't been prepared to meet me so soon."

Thinking back on those few snatched moments, I supposed I could see how he had interpreted my reactions as such. Except, he had my motivations turned around. I wasn't hesitant to share information. I was wary of receiving it.

"But how would I have known anything about Ben Gerard's death?" I asked.

"That I wasn't sure about, though I supposed there was always the chance, however unlikely, that Sidney had shared something with you. But then Walter made his ill-advised comments at dinner." His eyebrows arched in expectation. "And I realized you weren't exactly who you portrayed yourself to be."

"Whatever do you mean," I replied in feigned bewilderment.

The skepticism stamped across his features told me he wasn't fooled, but he didn't press the matter. "Well, regardless, your reaction to that letter you received this morning made me change my mind."

I considered lying. Telling him the message had come from my mother, or a friend in London, or a creditor pestering me to pay a bill. Anything but the truth. But whether he was my unknown letter writer or another recipient of that mysterious person's correspondence, I knew he wouldn't believe me. Not to mention that it seemed an ill use of the faith he had shown me if he *was* merely another pawn lured here. I needed to tell him something, even if it wasn't the strict truth.

"You're right," I admitted. "I also received a letter from an anonymous sender."

The manner in which Max's head perked up, as if he was almost shocked to discover his suspicions were correct, gave me more confidence in what I was about to share.

"Like you, I never intended to attend this house party. Though

I was less shocked than you seem to have been to receive an invitation. Sidney and Walter had been the closest of friends, after all. And with Sidney . . . gone, it seemed they were extending a courtesy to invite me in his stead."

I inhaled, buying myself some time as I debated how much to share. "But then I received a letter urging me to attend. That the letter writer had information about Sidney's death I needed to know." I frowned. "Naturally, I was mistrustful. But the way they spoke about my life, about Sidney's life before he died. Well, I thought if there was any chance they were being truthful, I should come, or else I should never forgive myself for not hearing what they had to say."

Max's steps halted as we reached the arched doorway through which we had entered the castle's east garden when we first arrived on the island. I stood farther back, still sheltered by the wall, away from the worst of the wind now buffeting the island. But in the distance I could see the waves of gray water being whipped up to foaming white.

When he turned to look back at me, his eyes were dark with apprehension. "Did they give you any hint as to what information about Sidney's death they wished to share?" he asked, forced to raise his voice to be heard over the gusts of wind.

"None."

He did not respond immediately, but I could see his mind was chewing on something unpleasant. When next he spoke, I wondered if it would not have been better had I told him the complete truth.

"Then maybe Sidney's death is also not so straightforward."

I stiffened. "What do you mean?"

He moved back into the garden, away from the arch, taking hold of my arm to draw me closer. "I'm not sure how much was disclosed to you about your husband's death. I suspect not much. Commanding officers tend to be rather circumspect in that regard. But your husband was killed during a time of great chaos. The Germans bombarded our trenches for days and then overran our front lines, and some of our commanders"—his voice hardened in frustration—"being too stubborn to accept when withdrawal with the chance to regroup was necessary, failed to call the retreat until far too late. At some point during that turmoil, your husband was shot and killed."

I stared up at the grim set of Max's jaw, trying to breathe, struggling to maintain my composure. I hadn't known any of the details of Sidney's death, only the date, the name of the battle, and the possible location where he was buried. And yet I sensed Max was trying to tell me something more, something I hadn't yet grasped.

"I wasn't there, but I read enough of the reports to comprehend it was absolute madness. If anyone were going to choose a moment to silence your husband, Verity, it would have been the perfect opportunity."

CHAPTER 11

I was so stunned I had trouble finding my words. "Are you saying . . ." I crushed the mauve taffeta of my skirt in my hands. "Do you mean . . ."

"I don't know anything," Max replied. "Not for certain. But I do know that I wasn't the only person to whom Ben Gerard voiced his doubts. He told me he'd also confided in Sidney. And while your husband's death was many months later, I don't think he'd forgotten about it. Not if the fact that he requested Sam Gerard join his company is any indication."

I spun away to press my hand to the rough bark of an oak tree, trying to remind myself that this was all just supposition born of my lie.

But was it?

None of the facts and implications Max was relaying had been changed. They were still true no matter what my mystery correspondent had written. Could Sidney have been killed by friendly fire? Or was the crucial bit of knowledge contained in Max's words that Sidney had also known about Ben's suspicions? And knowing what Ben suspected, had Sidney then chosen to silence him?

Max stood behind me, silently offering me his sympathy. I was grateful he didn't try to touch me or offer me any hollow words of comfort. Had he been more demonstrative, I'm not sure I could have remained composed.

I lifted my gaze from the point I stared at unseeing, and a blur of movement in the distance caught my eye. Standing straighter, I tried to peer through the curtain of trees and flowering shrubs to catch another glimpse of what I thought I'd seen. But whoever the person was—if they had even been there at all—had vanished.

I swiveled toward Max to ask if he'd seen anything, but his gaze was still considerably averted from me. When he turned to face me, I could see no trace of alarm, only weary compassion.

Maybe it had only been a trick of the light. Some illusion created by the wind-beaten trees and the growing gloom. As if to emphasize that explanation, I felt the first splatter of rain against my cheek and glanced up at the forbidding sky.

Max stepped forward to pull my arm through his and hastened me down the path toward the house. But just at that moment Felix came bustling through the archway, which led down toward Umbersea Castle's grandiose pier, almost colliding with us. Both men pulled up short, glaring at each other.

Though Max had always been careful to mask his true feelings about Felix in the past, he did not bother to do so now, eyeing him with naked hostility and distrust. "What are you doing out here, Halbert?"

"Not that it's any business of yours," Felix mocked, "but I've been catching a bit of fresh air before the deluge starts." His sharp eyes raked over the sight of me clinging to Max's steadying arm. His lips curled into a nasty sneer. "I think the more pertinent question is, what are you doing out here?" He turned his feet toward the castle, but not before adding one last parting shot. "I would have thought you'd find one of the chambers in the castle far more comfortable."

The muscles in Max's arm flexed beneath mine, making me suspect he would have liked nothing better than to slug the other man. But another splatter of rain reminded us of the urgency of returning to the castle. He started forward again, tossing one last glance over his shoulder through the open arch. I followed his gaze down toward the pier where Walter's yacht was securely docked, wondering what he was contemplating.

However, before I could ask, the sky opened in earnest,

pouring down rain. I lifted the hem of my dress and we dashed toward the house.

By the time we reached the castle, the taffeta of my dress was speckled with water spots. So I hastened up to my room to remove it, hoping one of the maids might have a remedy to salvage the delicate fabric. It was nearly time for dinner anyway, so I changed into my sleeveless sage green evening frock with its draped V-neck, an embroidered brassiere peeking out at my cleavage. It was rather daringly short, hitting my legs just above mid-calf, but given the day's events I decided I needed to feel a little audacious or I might never make it through the evening. In any case, my legs were one of my best features, and it always gave me a surge of confidence to catch gentlemen admiring them.

I repaired the rest of my appearance, including my deflated hair, and elected to descend the staircase a bit early. Most of the others would still be upstairs attending their own ablutions, which might give me the opportunity to catch one particular individual alone.

I'd noticed that Charlie gravitated toward the library, seeming to prefer the company of Walter's books over that of the other guests. Honestly, I couldn't blame him. Not with all the tense unpleasantness that seemed to bubble under the surface of everyone's interactions. I'd also noted his predilection for punctiliousness, and trusted this evening would be no exception.

After my conversation with Max, I'd decided I needed to try harder to convince Charlie to talk to me, as he seemed the officer, still living, who was likeliest to be persuaded to share what he knew. I wasn't above using his regard for my late husband and his memory to induce him to confide in me, but I hoped it wouldn't come to that. However, I did want to catch the man alone, not wishing to expose Sidney's potential part in Ben's death or any other nefarious plot until I knew what I faced.

Unfortunately, Max seemed to have had a similar idea.

My steps faltered at the sight of him in his dark evening attire rounding a corner in the corridor just outside the library door.

His dark blond hair was slicked back, making it appear a soft brown in the dim lighting of the corridor where the gas sconces had yet to be lit. He seemed equally startled to see me, though not the least dismayed, as I was feeling, for the corners of his mouth lifted in amusement.

"I should have known we would be thinking the same thing."

I laughed lightly, hoping he could not sense my apprehension.

"After you." He bowed, indicating I should precede him into the library.

I had yet to enter this particular chamber, but was not altogether taken aback by how unremarkable it was. Walter had never struck me as a particularly studious man, and from what I'd gathered about his family, they were much the same. It appeared Helen followed in the same vein, for here was another room that had remained untouched by her renovations, despite the rather large water stain spreading across the ceiling in one corner.

The room was no larger than my bedchamber and lacked any sort of charm. Overlarge furniture upholstered in heavy brocades crowded the space, but failed to hide the worn appearance of the rug or lend the room any sort of air of comfort. The drapes had been drawn against the rain now falling steadily outside the tall windows, but a fire had been lit to beat back the shadows that clung to the dark wood paneling and yawning bookshelves.

Charlie was perched somewhat awkwardly in a chair before the fire. The cushions seemed to almost swallow him, forcing his shoulders forward at what looked like an uncomfortable angle. At first he didn't hear us enter, being so absorbed in the book he read. It gave me an opportunity to study his fair boyish features in the firelight. He really did look young, and yet having served in the war for several years, he must be at least twenty-one. At repose, it seemed impossible to imagine him holding a gun or commanding men almost two decades older than himself, but he had. And survived. I must remember that.

When he did look up, I was nearly standing over him, and his contemplative expression froze into something akin to panic.

"Hullo, Charlie." I perched on the edge of the chair across from him, nearly toppling backward myself into the mound of cushions. "What are you reading?"

"This?" He looked down almost in confusion at the book he seemed to have forgotten was resting in his lap. "Oh, just a history of the island. Tom Ashley suggested it."

Hands in his pockets, Max leaned against the bulky, rounded arm of my chair. "Tom was always good for that sort of thing. Did you ever have occasion to visit the village of Suzanne on the Somme where he was stationed for a time as the town major?"

In spite of the awkward position he was seated in, Charlie's already rigid posture somehow stiffened further, as if someone had thrust a hot fireplace poker down his back. He shook his head.

"No? Well, you would have received an earful then." Max pulled his cigarette case from his pocket, offering us each one, but we both declined.

While Max lit his fag, Charlie stared at some spot along the hem of my dress, fretfully ruffling the pages of his book. During the lull in our conversation, I tried to think of what to say. How could I ask Charlie what I needed to know without the risk of him saying something about my late husband in front of Max that I would rather he not hear? The soft shush of the paper the younger man continued to rustle did not help, setting my already frayed nerves on edge.

Before I could decide on the right tact, Max blew out a plume of smoke and leaned toward the other man conspiratorially. "Charlie, we need your help."

His wide eyes blinked back at him. "My help?"

"Yes."

Charlie's gaze darted toward me and then back to Max. "But I've never been to Suzanne. I . . . I don't know anything about it."

I couldn't stop myself from frowning in confusion. I knew Charlie's brain worked differently from mine, whether because of shell shock or normal predisposition, but I could not figure out why he had latched on to Suzanne as the subject of our questions, or why he should be so nervous about it. Max, on the other hand, while momentarily stunned, seemed to take it in stride. But, then again, he was much more accustomed to the younger man and his quirks.

"No, no. This has nothing to do with Suzanne." He reached over to tap a fall of ash into the dish on the table next to him. "I want to speak to you about Ben Gerard."

Charlie's face whitened.

"I hate to bring this up. Heaven knows, we'd all like to forget that sodding war. But as I'm sure you're aware, our fellow guest Sam is Gerard's brother."

Charlie sat rigidly, giving no indication whether he had known this or not.

"And that has gotten me thinking again. There's something about Gerard's death that has always bothered me."

Once again, he shook his head. "I wasn't there. I don't know anything about it."

"I . . . I know." Max seemed startled by his stringent denial. "But perhaps you heard something. From Walter? Or Jimmy?"

"Nobody told me anything."

Max and I shared a glance.

"What about Sidney?" I ventured to ask. "Did he . . . mention anything?"

Charlie looked as if he might be sick. His hands shook as he closed the book in his lap and clumsily set it on the table next to him. "I . . . I don't know anything. I wish you would stop asking me."

Stubbing out his cigarette, Max leaned forward, propping his elbows on his knees. "Charlie, look at me," he ordered gently, but sternly, and waited for the trembling man to comply. He arched his eyebrows. "It's evident you do."

Charlie started to shake his head, but Max would have none of it.

"You do. Now, why don't you just tell us what you know."

But the young man had fallen mute. His eyes dropped to the floor, as if searching for the answers there. His hands gripped the arms of his chair, their tips turning white. He was plainly conflicted, and if I wasn't mistaken, also terrified. But of what? Of whom? What did he know that he was so afraid of revealing?

My stomach churned at the possibility he was hesitating because he didn't wish to divulge Sidney's perfidy to his wife.

When no words were forthcoming, Max decided to prod him again. "What about the two men in your company who were convicted of desertion?"

Charlie's feet began to bounce.

"I know you gave evidence at their hearing."

At first, I thought he would refuse to answer this, too, but then his hand darted up, rubbing the back of his neck. "All I knew about that was that they were sent on an errand, and they never returned. They . . . they were given a letter, and it was never delivered, and then they were found out of uniform, miles away from where they were supposed to be. That's it."

I wanted to reach out and comfort the young man, to soothe his distress, but I knew he would only flinch away. Max nodded, but then out of the corner of my eye, I saw his body still.

"Wait. They were delivering a letter?" His brow furrowed. "I don't remember that from the inquiry."

Charlie's expression contorted into something almost painful. "Then maybe I misspoke."

"No. No, I don't think you did. What letter? And to whom were they supposed to deliver it? They weren't runners, after all."

"I don't know!" he exploded, rising up from his chair. "I . . . I don't know."

"Well, then whom was the letter from?"

Charlie turned toward the hearth. His breathing was fast and frantic, and his right hand scrabbled at the tie around his neck. For a moment I was worried he was going to do himself some harm, or strike out at us. Clearly having the same thought, Max rose to his feet, shielding me.

"Charlie," I murmured softly, wishing I knew what to do, how to calm him. Perhaps Mabel would know.

I glanced toward the door, preparing to stand and go look

for her, when Charlie began to mumble. "Submit. Confess." He repeated the two words twice and then fell silent.

Max's eyes met mine, reflecting the same bewilderment I felt.

"There you are!" a voice behind me exclaimed. "I was wondering where everyone had run off to." Tom strode into the room, once again choosing abominable timing to make his entrance. "I knew I couldn't have been the first person to make an appearance downstairs." His brow furrowed as he finally seemed to take note of the scene before him. "I say, is everything quite all right? Charlie, old chap, are you unwell?"

Charlie inhaled sharply. "I . . . excuse me." Then he beat a hasty retreat, sliding past Tom and out the door.

Tom stared after him, shaking his head. "It's too bad. Seems a nice enough fellow. Hate to see when it happens to them."

That he was referring to shell shock was obvious, but I was no longer certain that was what was wrong with Charlie. I began to suspect he might actually be plagued by a guilty conscience. Add to that the fact that he was religious, and it wasn't difficult to imagine how tormented he was, especially if whatever he was hiding was also not good for his soul.

Max paced toward the fireplace, reaching up to fidget with some small object on the mantel before turning to face us. Though he did a good job of masking it, I was beginning to read him well enough to discern his apprehension. I wasn't the only one who believed there must be something about that letter that was worth concealing; otherwise, Charlie would not have become flustered when he realized he'd slipped up by mentioning it. And why hadn't it been cited during the hearing?

Dinner that evening was much more subdued than the night before, which was not unexpected given the manner in which the wind howled and buffeted the castle outside. Rain pinged sharply against the windows concealed behind their drapes like pebbles being flung by a child, and the candles overhead periodically flickered as if disturbed by a stray draft. I'd risked a glance outside the window in the foyer earlier as we'd passed through and been alarmed by the size of the waves crashing against the lowest steps of the castle leading down toward the beach.

Despite all this, or perhaps because of it, the drinks continued to flow. Even Gladys, despite her wan complexion and the dark circles under her eyes, claimed to have recovered from her queasiness that afternoon and joined in the effort to embalm herself once again. She and Elsie bemoaned the impossibility of us dancing on the terrace that evening, but Helen was not without a solution.

"Then we shall just have to push some of the furniture in the parlor out of the way to make room for dancing."

Elsie clapped. "Oh, splendid!"

"Darling, don't forget we're a bit short-staffed at the moment," Walter interjected before turning to the rest of us to explain. "I decided it was best to allow some of the servants who do not live on the island to return home early because of the weather. So we only have our small contingent of live-in servants at our disposal until tomorrow."

"Well, then our gentlemen guests will have to do it," Helen replied sharply, then softened the sting of her words to her fiancé by offering the rest of us a smile. "I'm sure they would be only too happy to oblige."

"Of course," Max answered.

Helen beamed at Walter in triumph. "You see."

He nodded curtly and turned back to his conversation with Nellie seated next to him.

It was impossible not to notice the strain that seemed to be growing between the happy couple, for these weren't the first cutting retorts and snapping glances they'd exchanged. Something had noticeably upset their joy, and I couldn't help but wonder if Walter had told her about Jimmy's suicide.

My gaze swept around the table, again noting Charlie's absence. I felt guilty for upsetting him with our questions, though they had been necessary, and even more so for not telling him about Jimmy's death. I couldn't help but wonder if he would have been more or less willing to confide in us after learning of his fellow officer's suspicious passing.

I met Max's eyes over the glittering table spread. From the tightening at their corners, it was evident he, too, was bothered by Charlie's empty seat. I suspected we would not see him again tonight, not that he would readily converse with either of us again anyway. So it seemed best if we turned to someone else for possible answers.

I had absolutely no desire to draw Felix aside, and highly doubted he would share anything worthwhile beyond his snarky opinions. Walter might be able to answer our questions, but somehow I didn't trust him to be honest. There had been something in his eyes when we told him about Jimmy's death and later on his yacht that made me wary of tipping our hand to him, especially about our suspicions. We needed more concrete information first, not guesses and suppositions.

Mabel's throaty laugh pulled my attention toward the opposite end of the table, where she was once again seated next to Sam. I wondered if Sam knew any more details about his brother's death than Max or I. Whether he held any misgivings about the official report. I would hate to plant any seeds of doubt in his head if they weren't already there. But after finding the burnt cork and that Field Service Postcard supposedly written by Ben tucked into Jimmy's pocket, marked with the words "stabbed in the back," I didn't know how he couldn't be questioning what had truly happened out in No Man's Land during that raid.

When the meal was finished, we all rose as one to cross over to the parlor, but rather than enter the room, I paused to fidget with an imaginary snag near the hem of my dress. Having trusted Max to see through this ruse, I was gratified when his hand solicitously cupped my elbow and helped me straighten back up to my full height.

"I think we should speak with Sam," I murmured.

Max nodded, understanding without words what I intended. Then he stepped to the side to softly hail the man in question. Sam whirled about at the doorway, his eyebrows arched in query as he moved to the side to allow Mabel to precede him into the parlor.

"Could we have a word?" Max requested in a lowered voice.
"Of course."

Max gestured us into a small alcove a few paces away from the parlor door, though if Sam found such a maneuver odd, he didn't remark on it.

"What can I do for you?" he asked with a warm smile.

I hesitated, hating to lower his mood, but the question had to be asked. "We have been discussing this morning's events."

His expression sobered. "I see."

I glanced at Max. "Most particularly that Field Service Postcard we found and . . . Well, I wondered if since you've had some more time to think, whether it holds any more significance for you."

Sam met my gaze steadily. "I'm guessing that you refer to my brother's death."

I cringed. When phrased so bluntly, my inquiry did sound terribly gauche and insensitive. "Yes, I'm sorry. Perhaps I shouldn't have said anything. . . ."

"No, no." He waved it off. "It's a legitimate question." His brow furrowed and he glanced over his shoulder as if to be certain no one was listening. "And the truth is, I have been thinking about it. Though I hope you're not about to propose that my brother is alive."

My eyes widened at the suggestion, which until this moment I hadn't really considered. But now that he'd mentioned it. . . . "Do you?"

He shook his head. "No, Ben is dead." His gaze slid to the side as a pained expression crossed his features. "If he were alive, I would know it. Maybe that makes little sense, but . . ." He shrugged his shoulders.

When his eyes lifted to meet mine, I nodded, even though I didn't understand. Not really. Whenever I thought of Sidney there was only a yawning hole, an emptiness that went unfilled. But it had been that way for much of our short marriage, with him away at war and me in London always waiting. Waiting for the war to end and our lives together to finally begin. Each leave he came home was merely a bittersweet interlude, a snatch of stolen time. And as the war stretched on year after year, imagining a time when it was over, when we could truly be together, became harder and harder to do, until it almost seemed impossible. Our life *was* the war. All the hopes and dreams we had for afterward were only pretend.

And then suddenly it was over. A telegram in a brown envelope was delivered by one of the boys on their blood-red bicycles, telling me Sidney was dead. That was the only closure I'd been given. No body. No funeral. No sensation of some inexplicable earthly tether between us being severed. Just . . . emptiness. Never-ending emptiness.

Unaware of the confusion that reigned inside me, Sam cut straight to the heart of the matter. "Then what you're really wondering is if I'm suspicious about Ben's death." His brow furrowed as he stared at the painting above my head, but somehow I knew he wasn't focused on the seascape, but on something in the past. "And the answer is, yes."

Max and I shared a look filled with both dread and a sort of vindication. For suddenly this was not our own little theory, but one shared by others.

"I've been suspicious for some time," Sam added.

"Why?" Max asked. "Did Ben write to you or say something about any misgivings he was having?"

Sam's eyes slowly lowered from the wall, and it was clear he knew what Max was talking about. "Not to me." His gaze shifted to meet mine, and I knew what he was about to say. "But he did tell Sidney."

My stomach clenched.

"About the two men who were executed for desertion? About his doubts that they were guilty?" Max attempted to clarify.

"Yes," Sam replied, though he never broke eye contact with me. "That's why Sidney requested I be assigned to his company. He wanted my help to uncover the truth."

All I could do was stand there mutely, trying to reconcile it all. Those certainly didn't sound like the actions of a guilty man. If he'd been responsible for Ben's death, wouldn't he have wanted to keep Sam as far away as possible?

"Because he didn't trust the others?" Max guessed.

Sam's dark eyes flicked toward Max, unpinning me from his stare. "Yes, he said he didn't know who was involved, and he couldn't risk exposing his interest."

"Not even to me." His voice rang hollow.

Sam didn't attempt to deny it. "He . . ." His words faltered and he shifted his feet, glancing over his shoulder again. "He said he had a lead, and he intended to look into it during that last leave he took in February of 'eighteen."

"And did he uncover anything?" I lowered my voice to ask, following Sam's cue.

He shook his head in frustration. "I don't know. By the time he returned, I was laid up in the field hospital with a severe case of bronchitis. I resumed my command at the front just two days before the bombardment and our disastrous retreat. There was never time for him to divulge what he'd found out."

Disappointment trickled through me, but it did not last long, for Sam inhaled a shaky breath to continue.

"Which, in the end, may have saved my life." His eyes pinned me again with compassion. "Because I don't think Sidney was killed by a German bullet. I think it was one of our own."

CHAPTER 12

Hearing this pronouncement a second time shouldn't have had as great an impact on me, but it did. Max's earlier suggestion that Sidney might have been killed by one of his fellow officers had been disturbing, but it had been nothing but a guess. One I had led him to by not revealing the true contents of the letter my anonymous correspondent sent to coax me into attending the house party.

But Sam's assertion had not been influenced by anything I had said or done. He had come to it all on his own. Having served beside Sidney as his subaltern and been privy to the doubts and suspicions he was weighing, Sam almost certainly knew the facts of the matter better than anyone. So his supposition shook me to the core.

I reached out a hand to steady myself, and this time Max latched on to it, pulling me closer. He wrapped his arm around my back, lending me his support as I forced a breath into my lungs.

"I'm sorry," Sam said in alarm. "Perhaps I shouldn't have said anything. . . ."

"No, I'll be all right," I assured him in a wobbly voice. "It's just . . . not an easy thing to hear."

The corners of Sam's mouth curled in a humorless smile, letting me know he understood. After all, he'd had a similar conversation about his brother with my late husband.

I leaned into Max, focusing on breathing in and out as he asked the question I hadn't yet been able to form.

"Why do you think Sidney was killed by a Tommy? Did you witness something?"

"Not directly," Sam replied. "But Sidney was . . . on edge. He was usually so astoundingly calm during engagements. While the rest of us were struggling to keep our nerve, he seemed so dashed assured and steady. It's one of things that made him such a fine officer." He frowned. "But that time was different. He seemed wary, mistrusting. Constantly scanning his surroundings. Checking his back."

"Couldn't his resolve have just been shaken?" Max asked. "He *had* recently been injured, and that can rattle even the bravest of men."

I straightened, not certain I liked hearing such a thing suggested about my husband, even if he was only playing devil's advocate.

Sam shook his head. "No, he wasn't windy. Just attentive, cautious. And when the retreat was sounded, he hustled all the men down the communication trench toward the rear before him, including me." His brow tightened with distress. "I wish he'd let me stay behind with him, but I couldn't disobey a direct order." He looked to Max for reassurance.

"No, you couldn't," he answered, not ungently.

Feeling stronger, I stepped away from his supportive arm. "Who reported that Sidney had been shot by the Germans?"

"Walter," Sam said. "But he didn't say who the shot came from. He didn't see it. Everyone just assumed with the Jerries swarming the area that it must be one of them."

Which meant that either Walter had fired the bullet or he had been nearby when it happened.

I crossed my arms over my chest against the sudden chill of the hallway. I hated to think of Walter as a suspect. He had been one of Sidney's closest friends. They'd known each other since they were practically babes. And yet, I couldn't quite dismiss the possibility. I'd already observed Walter's strange behavior more than once during this interminable weekend.

"Did anyone else see anything?" I asked.

Sam sighed heavily. "If they did, they didn't report it. But I've done a great deal of thinking about this, and I've figured that the only people who could have been directly involved with all aspects of this are Walter, Felix, Charlie, and Jimmy." He ticked the chilling events off on his fingers. "They each gave testimony at the deserters' court-martial or submitted reports that held bearing on the matter. They each either took part in or were stationed within the front-line trench during the night raid when my brother was killed. And they were some of the last officers to escape from the trenches after our retreat."

"And all four of them are here," I pointed out. "Or *were* here," I revised, recalling Jimmy's timely suicide.

"Yes," Max murmured. "It does all seem rather convenient."

I arched a single eyebrow cynically. "Which part? Their all being invited to his house party or Jimmy choosing to end it all and carry whatever secrets he held to the grave?"

"Both."

A blast of music from the gramophone spilled out of the parlor, recalling our attention to the fact that the others might miss our presence at any moment and come looking for us. Especially since Max had all but promised to help move the furniture for Helen so that we could dance.

"I think we could use some more information about all three of those incidents," Max declared, staring over Sam's shoulder at the entrance to the parlor. "And the men involved. I have a friend in the War Office who might be able to help us." He glanced at his wristwatch. "It's a bit late, but if you two can keep the others occupied, I'll go telephone him and see if he might be able to dig up some records for us tomorrow."

We agreed this was a sound plan. After all, none of us had seen the official reports in entirety on any of those incidents. As a staff officer, I knew Max had tried to keep abreast of the events concerning his old battalion, but naturally he had only had access to those files that crossed his desk or that colleagues had been willing to consult with him on.

I watched Max as he strolled down the hall and disappeared

around the corner, half hoping his friend would also stumble across some indication as to why my mystery correspondent had accused Sidney of treason.

Or was their allegation all a ruse? Perhaps they'd only written that in order to lure me here, knowing I would never be able to dismiss such a horrid assertion about my late husband without discovering who had made it and why.

The more I uncovered, the less likely it seemed to me that Sidney had been a traitor. There was still that coded missive hidden inside his book to be considered, but as I'd already recognized, someone else could have slipped that message inside the binding. It might not have had anything to do with Sidney at all. And even if it did, the contents of the letter need not indicate treason. Perhaps they were written in cipher for another reason. Perhaps they were notes about his own investigation into the framed deserters and Ben Gerard's death.

Somehow I needed to decrypt that message. Whatever it was, it must hold some answers as to what was going on here, and why Walter and Helen had invited such a contentious collection of guests to their engagement party.

But before I could retire to my chamber, I had a task to accomplish. It certainly wouldn't do to have one of our suspects overhear Max on the telephone. So I took Sam's proffered arm and strolled nonchalantly into the parlor.

But rather than the dancing I expected, we found the guests ranged around the room on various chairs and settees while the ladies indulged in some sort of feverish debate. Walter, Tom, and Felix seemed content to sit back, sipping their chosen libations and smoking. From the looks on their faces, I gathered they found the ongoing discussion quite entertaining. A cursory glance around the room told me Charlie was still absent.

A tingle of unease swept through me. The last time someone had been absent for so long, we'd found him dead in the old pottery warehouse.

Taking a firm hold of myself, I dismissed the wayward thought as nonsense. There was no reason to think anything was amiss. Charlie had visibly been upset by my and Max's questions. As such, he was almost certainly in his room upstairs, hiding from us. And just for my peace of mind, I was sure Max could be prevailed upon to look in on him before he retired.

Though I'd entered the parlor twice before as we gathered for dinner both nights, I was struck anew by the bold sumptuousness. With its deep red Romany damask wallpaper, black marble fireplace, Japanese lacquer chest, and silvered bronze chandelier, it somehow seemed suited to the evening. Most parlors and drawing rooms were decorated in soothing feminine tones and gilded elegance. Not so with this room. Helen seemed to have deliberately eschewed such standards, instead opting for brazen and ostentatious.

"Verity, we need you to break the tie," she exclaimed to be heard over the gramophone. The fire crackling in the hearth behind her seemed to create almost a halo around her blond bob and creamy white dress. "Nellie and Mabel wish to play a humdrum game of charades, while Gladys and I think Wink, Murder would be more amusing."

I stiffened at the jollity of her suggestion, and couldn't stop myself from darting a glance at Mabel. She arched her eyebrows high, acknowledging the macabre nature of such a proposal less than twelve hours after we'd found Jimmy's body. Clearly, Walter had *not* informed Helen of this morning's misadventure.

"No dancing?" I questioned, confused by the change in plans after Helen had seemed so set on it earlier.

"We're short of gentlemen who are up to the task." She arched her eyebrows pointedly. "Charlie has gone off to who knows where, and Jimmy is likely still in bed nursing whatever illness he's mysteriously come down with. And now even Max has seen fit to abandon us all. Six women can hardly share three eager men and one who's quite reluctant." She glared at her fiancé.

"A bit like France, ay, chums?" Tom remarked, cackling at his own jest. "'Cept 'twas the other way around. Not enough pretty French girls." He elbowed Walter, who leaned against the Bombe chest that served as a sideboard, sloshing the drink in his glass. "Though you always seemed to have the luck. What was that blonde's name?"

Walter's face had gone conspicuously blank. "I don't know what you're talking about, ole chap."

"Sure ye do," Tom insisted. "She used to hang round the estaminet in that slinky mink."

"Sorry. You must have me confused with someone else." He turned a black scowl on Tom, who finally seemed to realize this wasn't a topic his host wished to discuss, particularly in front of his fiancée.

"Max will be rejoining us shortly," I hastened to reply to Helen's unspoken query, hoping to shift some of the attention away from Tom's ill-advised comments.

However, Helen's eyes remained narrowed on the two men, and I couldn't decide whom she was angrier with—her faithless intended or bumbling Tom.

I'd visited an estaminet once. I'd seen the relatively harmless merriment that went on inside those cafés, some of which were real establishments in the French villages a few miles from the front, and others that were scarcely more than barns or shacks filled with bales of hay and a makeshift bar from which to dispense the liquor. But I'd also been aware of the activities that went on just upstairs or next door. Services that could be bought by a lonely, desperate soldier for five francs.

I'd realized then it would be naïve to think that most soldiers hadn't employed these women at one point or another during the war, maybe even Sidney. Though it churned my stomach to think of him in another woman's arms, I also found I couldn't totally begrudge him for seeking some sort of solace. Though I was certain he would have been horrified to discover I even suspected such a thing went on, let alone had witnessed other men behaving this way and fended off a few unwanted advances of my own.

However, I was aware that most women hadn't the slightest inkling what went on while their men were at ease during their rotation back from the trenches. Just as they'd had no clue how dreadful the conditions were at the front, or the horrors their men had faced almost daily. The press never told the truth; propaganda at its finest. And the men didn't want their loved ones back home to know it anyway, even though it caused countless divides and misunderstandings. They didn't want the terrors they'd confronted to touch those they'd loved and gone to war to protect and preserve.

That I'd walked in both places as a Secret Service agent had set me apart from the larger part of the civilian population. It had marked and scarred me, even with as little as I'd experienced. And yet, I wasn't a soldier. I wouldn't dare to claim their wounds.

I wasn't certain how Helen would react to the news that her husband might have taken a French lover. In one sense, she'd seemed more worldly than most, having so easily accepted the fact that she wasn't the only woman to respond to Walter's Lonely Soldier advert. But on the other, she still seemed so naïve and immature, blind to the realities of war. Whatever she felt, she'd been trained well, for she masked the vehemence burning in her eyes and resumed her role as hostess.

"Well, regardless, I decided a parlor game might be more to everyone's liking," she said, explaining away her whim with a flick of her wrist.

"And what of Elsie?" I asked.

The pretty brunette sat to the side, almost pouting. Couldn't she have broken the tie?

"Oh, she wants to play Hot Cockles." Helen rolled her eyes. "And we're *not* doing that."

"Unless you want to play it," Elsie interjected, narrowing her eyes at her friend in challenge before tossing me a hopeful look.

Despite Elsie's wheedling, there was no contest as to which game I preferred. Given the events of the day, Wink, Murder sounded far too ghoulish. And I was not about to lay my head in anyone's lap to play Hot Cockles. But I suspected if I chose charades, Helen would be very put out with me. She clearly wanted to indulge in something a bit outrageous, and Tom's tactless remarks would only spur on that desire.

It was on the tip of my tongue to suggest poker, but witnessing how much spirits had already been consumed that night, I thought that might not be such a good idea, lest one of these ladies or gentlemen gamble away a fortune. "Why don't we play both," I hedged. "Surely there's time for more than one game."

"Hmmm, yes. I suppose," she murmured, turning to stare out the two long windows looking out on the garden. Their drapes had yet to be pulled and we could see the rain sluicing down them in rivers. "Though, with this weather, I did think Wink, Murder would be more atmospheric."

"Then we shall play that first," I suggested, only to be interrupted by a gasp from Helen.

"I have it!" She grinned with delight. "I have the perfect parlor game for us." She rushed forward to tug at the bell rope to summon a servant. Then she swiveled to face the room, gesturing to the men. "Help me arrange the chairs around this table."

I stepped back as they followed her instructions, shifting the furniture so that it surrounded the low, circular tea table.

"Helen, what are you on about?" Gladys asked, shifting forward in her seat. "What are we playing?"

Her eyes lit with mischief, as she clasped her hands before her. "We're going to do a bit of table-turning."

Her words made my stomach drop. If Wink, Murder had seemed somewhat ghoulish, a séance was in downright poor taste, especially with the number of ex-soldiers present. And I could tell I wasn't the only one who thought so, even if Elsie and Gladys seemed keen on the plan, jumping up from their seats in excitement. Sam's shoulders stiffened, and Mabel actually gave a start.

But it was Walter who stepped forward to protest. "Helen, dear, do you really think that's such a good idea?"

"Oh, hush! It'll be fun." She spoke lightly, but there was an unmistakable bite underpinning her tone. When a maid appeared in the doorway, she ordered her to fetch her Ouija board.

I reluctantly joined the others in the chairs forming our circle, uncomfortable with this entire scheme. It wasn't that I actually believed *we* could summon someone from the dead. The notion was preposterous. But the very act of attempting to do so, all as a bit of a lark, seemed dreadfully wrong.

Collectively, how many loved ones had we lost? How many

friends, cousins, brothers, lovers, and husbands had perished in the war? How many of us nursed wounds that were too recent to have healed? And yet we were going to make a game of contacting one of them beyond the grave?

My mouth filled with the acrid taste of revulsion. Had I not promised Max I would keep the others occupied while he telephoned his friend, I would have pled a headache and retired rather than endure this nonsense. From the faces of many of those present, I suspected some of them were considering the same thing.

The servant returned with the Ouija board, and Helen set it up while she ordered the maid to lower the lights in the room to a dim glow and turn off the rag music blazing from the gramophone. "All the better to create the proper atmosphere," she proclaimed.

I crossed my arms over my chest against the chill silence that suddenly seemed to fill the room. Had I not known better, I would have believed there was something to this table-turning bit, but rationally I knew it was nothing but the loss of light and a draft from one of the windows. Though Nellie and Sam, on either side of me, seemed not to feel any difference in temperature.

"This is ridiculous," Sam grumbled under his breath, but Mabel hushed him where she sat on his other side.

"Just play along," she whispered. "She'll tire of it soon enough."

Sam shifted uneasily in his seat, but fell quiet.

"Now, everyone, breathe deeply," Helen directed us as she herself inhaled and then closed her eyes. "We must be calm and focused. The spirits do not like distraction." Her voice had taken on an airy tone that, far from relaxing me, set my teeth on edge.

I had never visited a spiritualist myself, despite their rampant popularity in London, but I suspected Helen had. She seemed to almost be adopting another persona of otherworldly serenity, and there was definitely an air of showmanship to her actions.

Lifting her hands as she filled her lungs with one last deep breath, she rested her fingers against the planchette. "Spirit, this is a safe place. Speak with us. Tell us your name."

The rain outside gusted against the windows, tightening my nerves, as Helen slowly began to move the pointer across the board.

"*J*," she intoned as the pointer stopped. Then it slid a fraction to the left. "*I*."

The air in my chest constricted, as my mind automatically began to sort through the possibilities. The only names I could think of that started with "JI" were Jim or Jimmy. Our Jimmy? But how did Helen know he was dead? I thought Walter hadn't told her.

Or was she not moving it on her own? Was Jimmy actually trying to speak to us? To tell us what had happened to him?

It seemed an eternity before the planchette stopped on another letter.

"*N*."

I blinked. *N*? Had she made a mistake? Perhaps she'd misread. After all, the *N was* next to the *M*.

But then the planchette swung across the board.

"*G*," Helen continued reciting.

So it wasn't Jimmy.

I shook myself.

Of course it wasn't Jimmy. What had I been thinking to even consider the possibility? It was fake. All of it. If Helen had revealed the spirit to be Jimmy, then all that would have meant was that she knew something about Jimmy's death. But she hadn't. Instead she called out three more letters.

"*L. E. S.* Oh!" she gasped. "Are you that little boy who used to sell newspapers on the corner near my father's house?"

The planchette jerked upward to the left, pointing to the word *yes*.

"Oh, poor dear. He got run over by a cart several years ago," she explained, then frowned. "I wonder why he's contacting us."

I barely restrained myself from rolling my eyes. *Because you decided he would.* Sam snorted, obviously having a similar thought.

I only half listened as Helen asked "Jingles" a series of questions, much of my attention being fixed on the door over Sam's shoulder, curious whether Max would be able to uncover anything from his friend tonight.

When Helen had exhausted her questions, she thanked Jingles's "spirit" and told him good-bye, before sitting back with a pleased smile. There seemed to be no cunning or duplicity in her expression. I couldn't decide whether she actually believed she'd spoken to a spirit or she was simply that good of an actress.

"Can I try next?" Gladys asked eagerly, her words slightly slurring.

"Of course." Helen shifted the board to her left and passed Gladys the wooden planchette.

Gladys rested the signaling device reverently against the board. Her eyes darted around the circle as she lowered her voice to a sharp whisper. "Who should we summon now?"

We all glanced at each other, no one seeming willing to put forth a suggestion.

"It's best to let the spirits come as they will," Helen informed her friend. "I doubt we have the psychic ability among us to call forth a specific spirit."

Gladys's mouth twisted. It was evident she didn't like being told she lacked the talent for such a thing. But nonetheless, she obeyed. Her gaze swept around the circle one last time, resting momentarily on Nellie. Her lips curled into a swift smile before flattening into seriousness as she inhaled and lowered her gaze to the board.

I flicked a glance at Nellie out of the corner of my eye, wondering what Gladys had seen when she was looking at her. As little as I liked Nellie, I didn't wish to see her hurt. If Gladys had decided it would be great fun to conjure up someone close to Nellie—perhaps her brother or her father—I knew Nellie would be upset. Rightfully so.

"Oh, spirit, speak to us," Gladys chanted, imitating Helen's voice. "Do you have a message for someone here tonight?"

The planchette moved upward to hover over the word *yes*.

"Whom is it for?"

The pointer dropped to the number 4 and then shifted to the letter *V* before stopping.

Everyone looked up at me, for I was the only one present with a name that began with the letter *V*. I struggled not to react, though a trickle of unease slid down my spine.

Gladys paused dramatically, as if I should say something, but when I didn't, she resumed her questioning. "Tell us your name. Who are you?"

The planchette glided toward the *S*.

My heartbeat quickened, and my breathing grew shallow.

Then the *I*.

I struggled to maintain my composure, forcing myself to wait to see where it would land next. After all, I had been wrong about the name of Helen's "spirit."

But when the pointer landed on the letter *D,* I could remain silent no longer.

"Stop it!" I shouted at Gladys, leaping to my feet. "Stop it now!"

CHAPTER 13

Gladys and several of the others stared up at me in shock.

"That's not funny! That's not funny at all." I whirled away, moving beyond the circle. That they should use Sidney in such a way for this stupid, childish game. It . . . it was unforgivable!

"No, Verity," Helen's voice called after me frantically. "Please come back to the circle. We need to close it."

I turned back to face her. "Is this your idea of a joke?!" I didn't care that I was yelling. I was beyond furious. My gaze swung to Gladys. "You have no right to toy with his memory in this way. No right!" Feeling that I was perilously close to tears, I spun away again.

"Poor form," Walter's voice trembled with anger.

"For shame," Mabel agreed.

"You're absolutely right, Verity," Helen said. "But, please. Please, come back to the circle. Just for a minute. It must be closed properly or Sidney's spirit will linger with us. He won't be at rest."

I swung back to glare daggers at her. I was so incensed that I could not think straight. Words failed me. They bottled up behind my teeth with such force that I thought if I opened my mouth I might actually shriek.

Such was the force of my stare that she startled back a step, her knees bumping into the settee behind her and causing her to sit.

That she could even suggest such a thing! Sidney's spirit wasn't here. He was *not* with us. His body was somewhere in

France, and his spirit, God willing, was in Heaven. It was the only comfort I had. To think that he could be called back here, into this foolishness . . .

I spun around to flee the room, only to run smack into a man's chest.

I choked on a scream, pushing away from the form before me. But the man's hands came up to grasp my upper arms and I fought harder.

"Hold on. What's this?"

I inhaled a ragged breath at the realization that it was Max's voice, and sank against his warm, solid frame.

"Why are the lights so low?" he asked in confusion.

One of the sconces on the wall suddenly flared brighter, and I realized Max had reached out to turn the gas up.

"No!" Helen protested, but he ignored her, instead gazing down at me in concern.

I felt ridiculous now that for even a moment I'd actually believed the form I'd collided with was Sidney's spirit. Given all the theatrics and my own distress, I supposed it was inevitable that would be the first thing to cross my mind. But to have strained against Max that way . . .

I couldn't lift my eyes to meet his. Ripples of panic still coursed through me, making me tremble as I struggled to regain my composure.

"Mabel," Helen huffed.

"Helen decided we needed to do a bit of table-turning," Mabel explained in a mocking low voice, having come to stand just behind me. "And Gladys thought it would be jolly fun to summon Sidney."

Max's hands tightened around my arms where he still gripped them, and I felt the intensity of his glower pulsing through him as he lifted it to look at the others.

"I . . . I'm calm now," I stammered, not wanting to rehash the whole thing. It had been bad enough to live it once, and now I was feeling faintly ashamed of my outburst. I had always prided myself on my self-possession, but rather than remaining composed and simply walking away, I had lashed out.

"It wasn't my idea," Gladys protested almost pettishly.

"Of course, it wasn't," Helen replied. "You can't help which spirits choose to contact us."

It took everything within me not to stomp across the room and slap Helen for her gullibility. As if sensing it, Max's hands rubbed up and down my arms to soothe me.

But I wasn't the only one who'd lost their patience with our hostess.

"For goodness' sake, Helen!" Mabel snapped, tossing in a curse word for emphasis. "Sidney's spirit didn't choose to contact us. Gladys was pretending."

"Is it true?" Helen gasped in outrage.

"Nellie told me to do it," Gladys said.

I stiffened, finally turning in Max's arms to look back at the rest of the group still clustered around the Ouija board.

Nellie sat perfectly poised in her bergère chair, blinking at the others innocently. "I did no such thing."

"You tipped your head at her," Gladys said.

"Yes, but only because I thought Verity might like to speak to her *dearly* departed husband." Her voice dripped with sarcasm. "I didn't know you were going to fake it."

"But why? Why would you suggest such a thing?" Tom scolded his wife.

Nellie's eyes flashed. "I thought she might have some questions she'd like to ask him. Like where he went on his last leave instead of coming home to her." Her gaze shifted to meet mine, sharp with malice.

My face heated. So she *had* overheard my and Mabel's conversation on the boat. And now she sought to throw it in my face in the most public way possible. Well, she'd succeeded.

Rather than answer her as I would have liked, I turned and walked away. Perhaps that was exactly what she wanted, but I just couldn't engage with her then. Her callous behavior stung too much. That I, at one time, had called her my friend seemed unbelievable.

I should have expected nothing less from her. After all, she was the one who had never been able to accept the fact that

Sidney had fallen in love with me over her. Rather than wish us well that last time I'd seen her a few days before my and Sidney's wedding, she'd instead told me she hoped I got what I deserved—a cold bed and a cold womb when my husband never returned from France.

That her cruel taunt had come true had only made things worse. But apparently that wasn't enough for her. Nothing was ever enough for Nellie.

I paused before the right staircase in the foyer, not yet ready to return to the ringing silence of my room, where I would only have my own thoughts for company. But where else could I go? Rain still tapped against the windows, and though it had slackened somewhat, combined with the wind it still made the terrace an imprudent choice. Perhaps the library, but I suspected all I would be able to think of there was Charlie.

The sound of footsteps striding down the hall toward me brought my spinning thoughts to a standstill. Had they been the light patter of a female's shoes, I would have fled up the stairs, but the heaviness of the tread alerted me that it was a man. I could easily guess which one.

Brushing behind my ear the heavy locks of curling auburn hair that had fallen forward over my right eye in my haste to escape, I turned to look at Max. His steps faltered as our eyes met, but he continued coming until he stood before me, the space of a single person separating our bodies.

He studied my face, searching for something that I was both helpless to either give or conceal. I felt almost as if I stood naked before him, and while it terrified me to reveal so much of myself, it was also somehow comforting that it should be him.

"Do you wish to be alone?" he murmured.

I shook my head, hesitantly at first and then with more certainty. "Not particularly."

His mouth creased into a humorless smile of commiseration. He reached for my hand. "Then come with me."

I allowed him to pull me down the corridor past Walter's study and into a smaller antechamber. It looked like a cozy little parlor for two, naught but two chairs and a rectangular table holding a few decanters and glasses between them. The tiny hearth behind the chairs was not lit, but the room was warm enough without it. The drapes over its single window had been pulled tight. A single gas lamp provided enough light for me to read the gilded titles tucked into the bookcases along the opposite wall.

I settled into one of the chairs and accepted the cut crystal glass of brandy Max poured for me. Sipping gingerly from its contents, I welcomed its warmth as it spread through my stomach and into my limbs. The not unpleasant scent of cigars and cheroots clung to the leather, mixing with the smell of gentlemen's cologne.

Max sat next to me, savoring his own brandy as he allowed me to gather my scattered thoughts. If I'd wished, I suspected we could have sat there all evening without his prying, such was the undemanding nature of his presence. I could have simply derived what ease I wished from his companionship and moved on without revealing a thing. But I found that the longer we sat there, the more I wanted to speak. To tell someone the thoughts that had occupied me for so long.

"I thought it would be easy, you know." I spoke softly, gazing into the warm amber depths of the brandy inside my glass. "I thought it would be a simple thing to send Sidney off to war. That I would miss him, but that in a matter of months he would return to me for good—safe and whole. And then our lives could actually begin in truth." I inhaled a ragged breath. "But as it turns out, I was rather hopelessly naïve."

"No more than most of the population of Britain," Max replied.

"My mother wanted me to return home with them to the Dales, but I couldn't bear the thought of going back there as if nothing had happened. As if I wasn't a married woman who had just sent her husband off to war." My gaze lifted to drift over the finely wrought leather of the books on the shelves to my right. "So I moved into Sidney's flat and waited there for him to return. Except I didn't anticipate how long and lonely and *intolerable* that wait would be.

"I needed something to fill my hours, so I began searching for work, a way to contribute to the war effort. I couldn't just sit there twiddling my thumbs. And a friend of mine found me a position that was actually quite perfect, quite well-suited to my abilities." I found I was too well-trained, too accustomed to hiding my association with the Secret Service to speak of it in anything but innuendo. "But even though I went to bed every night exhausted in mind and body, I still could not stop the worrying. The dread."

I set my cup down on the table between us, expecting Max to say something, but he didn't. He just sat very still, waiting for me to finish.

"And then . . ." I exhaled. "And then it was over. The telegram I'd so feared arrived, and Sidney was dead." I was somewhat amazed by how calmly I could speak of it, almost as if I were outside myself, listening to someone else utter these words. "Of course, I was wild with grief, but I had work I had to be able to perform. I was needed elsewhere." I swallowed. "So I got on with it, the best I could, just like everyone else. I did my job during the day and I drank to forget at night. Sometimes I went dancing. Sometimes I let my dance partners kiss me. Once, I even . . ." But I stopped myself in time, shaking my head, unwilling to say the words.

"Did you ever try morphia?" There was no judgment in his voice, only restrained curiosity.

I could only feel relieved that was what he'd suspected I was hesitant to admit and not the truth. "Once," I admitted. "But it made me so ill, I never sampled it again. Or cocaine. I had a friend who was rather infatuated with morphia. I saw what it was doing to her, and I had no desire to become a morphineuse."

Max nodded. "I'm glad."

I ignored him, pressing my palms together in my lap to keep them from shaking. "I'm quite certain if Sidney were alive to see me, he would be ashamed of my behavior. He never could abide maudlin emotions." A self-deprecating huff of laughter escaped from me. "And I have been quite desperately maudlin."

"Is that why you were so upset by their decision to pretend to summon Sidney? Beyond the fact that it was cruel of them to do so in the first place," he hastened to add.

"Partly, I suppose." I wasn't entirely certain myself of the reasoning behind my reaction, other than that I didn't want to think of Sidney haunting this world rather than at peace. Truthfully, I wasn't entirely certain *what* I was trying to tell Max, except that speaking to him made me feel better.

I looked up to find him watching me, his eyes warm with some emotion.

"For what it's worth, I don't think Sidney would be disappointed in you in the least," he murmured. "On the contrary, I suspect he would be the first to understand."

I pushed to my feet, turning my back to him to examine the bookshelf as I dismissed his sympathy. "Oh, well, that's kind of you to say—"

"It's not kind," he insisted, standing and taking hold of my wrist to make me look at him. "I think you're being too hard on yourself *and* Sidney to think he would not have been able to appreciate the pain you've endured. Whenever he spoke of you it was with pride and love. Feelings like that do not diminish because you show yourself to be less than perfect in your grief."

I stared up at him in astonishment. I so wanted to believe that, and yet my battered heart wouldn't quite let me.

My eyes dropped to where his warm fingers rested against the delicate skin on the inside of my wrist, thinking he must be able to feel how my pulse raced. "Thank you," I whispered, before turning away.

I crossed to the other side of the room and lifted aside the drapes covering the window, staring out at the rain that now fitfully fell, only to be gusted against the glass in abstract splatters. I couldn't help but think how fitting it was to my mood. To the entire mood of this house.

"What of your telephone call?" I asked, recalling the reason I had willingly taken part in Helen's séance.

Max heaved a disgruntled sigh, sinking into the chair I'd vacated. "I wasn't able to place it."

I turned in surprise. "What do you mean?"

"The telephone in Walter's study wouldn't connect. Presumably because of the storm."

I frowned, not having considered that. We were rather isolated here on the island. The lines need not be severed for them not to work. "What of the other connections? Are there any others throughout the house?"

He shook his head. "They aren't working either. But the butler informed me a second line had been installed at the church for the farm workers and the few locals who still live on the island. I was coming to tell you and Sam when I heard you shouting."

I cringed. "Yes. Well, do you still wish to contact your friend?"

Max considered the matter for a moment and then nodded. "Yes, I think that's our best hope of gaining any useful information." His mouth twisted cynically. "Unless you think tonight's excitement will have convinced any of our suspects to share what they know."

If I had been confronted with the possibility of meeting the spirit of the man I had killed, I would certainly have had my nerves shaken, but I doubted it would have convinced me to confess. "No, we need to reach that telephone."

It was Max's turn to be surprised. "You want to come with me?"

"I don't want to stay here."

Thankfully, he didn't argue with this logic, merely flicked his gaze up and down the rather delicate material of my dress. "Do you wish to change?"

"Give me ten minutes. Tell me where I should meet you."

True to my word, ten minutes later I appeared outside the conservatory dressed in a wool serge skirt; my sturdiest shoes; and my dowdy, but faithful mackintosh, which by some stroke of luck my maid had packed. Max was still dressed in his black trousers, but had changed shoes and thrown his own wartime khaki trench coat over his evening kit. For a moment, it brought me up short, for if he had been wearing his officer's cap and high-polished boots, he would have looked very like Sidney had that cold December morning when I had seen him off at the train platform, headed back to the front for the last time. I had seen hundreds, thousands of men dressed thusly, but it was Sidney's image that fixed in my mind.

"Are you ready?"

I shook the troubling thought aside and nodded.

"Then let's go before anyone sees us. I should hate to have to explain why the devil we're venturing out in this."

I followed him into the darkened conservatory filled with the perfume of flowers and through the winding aisles to the French doors at the far northwest corner of the castle.

After unlocking them at the top and bottom, he reached back to grasp my hand. "Ready?"

We plunged out into the storm, keeping our heads bowed against the wind as it whipped rain into our faces. Fortunately, the butler had not questioned Max's urgency to use a telephone, or seen fit to confer with his employer on the matter. Being an earl did have its advantages, particularly when it came to upper servants and their rather snobbish tendencies. Chumley had been only too happy to inform Max that he could have the use of the estate's lorry. He'd offered to have one of the footmen drive him over, but Max had declined, telling him he could manage quite well on his own.

We had seen it earlier when collecting the bicycles from the adjoining shed, and hastened across the short distance between the castle and the old carriage house. Max opened the passenger door and boosted me up inside before rounding the hood to crank the engine. The interior smelled musty, but it was otherwise unobjectionable, especially since it was dry.

Max carefully drove the lorry through the wooden doors and swung it around to the narrow road leading into the center of the island. We bumped along down the muddy track, neither of us speaking as he strained forward, trying to see through the splatters of rain. As I remembered, the church had not been more than a mile or two from the castle gardens, and traveling along in the lorry we swiftly reached the corner on which it sat.

Turning left, Max followed the lane bordered by the low stone wall marking the boundary of the churchyard straight up to the gate. In the storm's gloom, I could barely make out the outline of St. Mary's as an even darker shape against the already black night.

"Climb out on my side," he suggested, throwing the lorry into park.

I followed his suggestion, allowing him to lift me down, and then took his hand as we dashed across the short stone walk between the road and the church. The arched wooden door opened, letting us into a small vestibule. I exhaled in relief as Max closed the door behind us, shutting out the swirling wind and rain.

In the darkness, I couldn't see anything, but I could sense how confined the space was. When Max opened the interior door to the sanctuary proper, a rush of cold air swept over me, but I still couldn't see anything. Not even Max, who hovered at my shoulder. I heard him patting his hands along the wall, searching for a light source. He grunted in satisfaction when he found it, but despite the clicks and taps I heard, no illumination appeared.

"The lights are out," he groused, moving back toward me. "Or, at least this one is. Wait here."

His footsteps shuffled back into the vestibule, leaving me alone in the gloom. The smoke from extinguished candles seemed to linger in the air, as well as the must of a room not often opened. My eyes gradually began to adjust, and I could see that the arched roof was framed of a darker material than the paler walls and floor. Pews in the shape of dusky hulks marched up the aisle to my right.

I started to move forward, to try to feel my way along the pews toward where the altar candles must be stored, but something made me hesitate. Some nameless dread seemed to steal over me, holding me immobile. Most churches emanated a sense of peace, of stillness, of refuge. Not so here. I stared wide-eyed into the darkness, somehow knowing something was terribly wrong here. Something I wasn't certain I wanted to see.

I slowly backed up a step, even though my limbs pulsed with the urge to flee. "Max," I murmured.

I could hear him muttering to himself as he rummaged through the items stored in the vestibule, oblivious to my distress.

"Max."

"Ah! Here it is."

Light suddenly flared and I flinched away from the brightness.

"I knew there must be an electric torch somewhere," he declared as he rejoined me.

I blinked, trying to adjust my vision, peering around me as he swept the torch's beam left and right, continuing to chatter amicably.

"Now, I suppose the telephone will be in the vestry or the narthex."

"Max!"

This time my choked cry caught his attention. Especially when I pointed down the aisle toward the body crumpled facedown halfway up the nave.

CHAPTER 14

He hurried toward the lifeless form, dropping down on his knees next to him. Reaching out, he carefully turned the man over so that we could see his face.

I gasped in recognition as Charlie's sightless eyes stared back up at me. Covering my mouth with both hands, I stifled a sob as I took in the sight of the blood splattering his chest. The front of his once-crisp white shirt was soaked with it, and a pool of the bright crimson liquid covered the floor where he'd lain.

Max passed his hand over Charlie's eyes to close them, and slowly inched backward to lay him on the floor.

"Wh-what?" I stammered.

"He's been shot," he stated.

I swallowed and forced myself to take a steadying breath. "Yes. Yes, I can see that."

It would be difficult to miss the hole blasted through Charlie's shirt and deep into his heart. Evidently, this death had not been a suicide, but I glanced about us, searching for the gun, just to be certain.

Max rose to his feet and looped his arm through mine. I latched on to the support he offered, allowing him to pull me away from Charlie. I could feel now that I was trembling, though I didn't know if it was from shock or the chill of the room.

"Do you need to sit?"

"Maybe for a moment," I admitted. Much as I wanted to escape the building, it wouldn't do for my legs to give way before we even reached the door.

He guided me into a pew and sat down beside me, blocking my view of the dead body on the floor.

Staring blindly toward the altar at the front of the church, I focused on breathing in and out. I reminded myself I had seen corpses before, many in worse shape than this one. But never in so intimate a setting, or so soon after speaking to the person in question.

Poor Charlie. He had been so young, so innocent-seeming, despite the heavy secrets he obviously carried.

Is that why he had been killed? To keep those secrets? Had Max and I pried too closely to the dark truths someone had wanted kept, and fearful that Charlie would betray them they'd decided to silence him?

I could think of no other reason why someone would wish the young man dead. And we *had* been pushing him for answers before dinner. Anyone could have overheard us questioning him, not just Tom. In fact, anyone could have snuck down to the church to kill him after that silly séance in the parlor. Max and I had been closeted in that antechamber for at least half an hour.

I pushed a hand through my damp hair, wishing I hadn't lost my head. Maybe then I wouldn't have stormed out and kept Max from venturing to the church sooner. I glanced up at his handsome profile. He might have made it here before the killer struck. He might have been able to stop it.

Or he might have been shot as well. There was really no way of knowing.

Regardless, it was pointless to be sitting here speculating when there were things to be done. I opened my mouth to tell Max I was recovered now, when a prickling sensation began along the back of my neck. Shifting in my seat, I turned to search the darkness behind us.

"What is it?" Max asked, instantly alert.

"I . . . I don't know," I admitted in a hushed voice. "But are we certain the killer isn't still here?"

Max met my gaze in understanding. "Stay here," he ordered before rising to his feet with the torch.

I watched as he swung the torch around the building, shining it into every corner. Then he retreated down the aisle, pointing it between the pews and even opening the door to peer into the narthex. My muscles tensed, waiting for someone to spring out of the shadows.

But then, just as suddenly as the sensation had begun, it vanished. I looked around me, faintly dazed. If we had been watched, we weren't any longer.

Max strode back up the aisle, his gaze still searching the shadows at the front of the church. "There's no telephone in the narthex. Come. Let's search the vestry and then get out of here."

I could hear the worry in his voice, even though he was commanding me like a soldier. Plainly this was not an optimal place to take cover. Too many nooks for the enemy to hide in.

I allowed him to take my hand, pulling me up from the pew. But rather than hurrying past Charlie as he urged me, I asked him to wait.

"I've had a thought," I explained, stooping down next to Charlie's body. Keeping my gaze carefully averted from his face, I lifted the edges of his coat to search through his pockets. After all, Jimmy's pockets had contained that Field Service Postcard and a piece of burnt cork. If Charlie had been killed by the same person, then perhaps his pockets also held some sort of note or clue.

I stilled as my fingers brushed against something in his left coat pocket.

"What is it?" Max asked.

I slowly extracted a piece of paper wrapped around a long, rectangular object. Rising to my feet, I unfolded the note to find a battered harmonica. I stared at it in confusion before passing it to Max and then focused on the words typed on the paper.

"If we confess our sins, He is
faithful and just to forgive us
our sins and to cleanse us from
all unrighteousness." 1 John 1:9

"Submit yourselves therefore to
God. Resist the devil, and he
will flee from you." James 4:7

A chill swept through me reading these Scriptures over a dead body. Words that in the Bible had been intended to be a comfort. This way they sounded less like a benediction and more like a threat.

I remembered then the words Charlie had babbled in the garden while we played croquet. *"Resist the devil."* He had been quoting these verses. Or at least the one from James.

I glanced at Max, wondering if he understood any of this better than I did. He scowled down at the paper, before allowing his gaze to drift back to the harmonica.

"What does it mean?"

He shook his head in bafflement. "I don't know. Except . . ." He paused. "Except that one of the men who were convicted of desertion was always playing one. It irritated some of the men to no end."

His eyes lifted to meet mine in silent comprehension. Maybe our previous discussions about the possibility that someone had framed two men for desertion and then killed at least one more, possibly two, to keep that truth from coming out had merely been speculation, but this seemed like a confirmation. Perhaps it wasn't proof that it was true, but it was certainly evidence that someone else believed it was.

Max's mouth firmed with resolve. "Come on. We need to telephone the authorities." His voice lowered so that I almost couldn't hear him. "Before someone else is killed."

Regrettably, while the vestry did indeed have a telephone, it was not connecting any better than those at the castle. Max struggled in vain to make it work, testing the cords and tapping the switchhook repeatedly, but the connection remained dead.

Since there was nothing we could do about it in the storm, we hastened back to the lorry. Max cautiously reversed down the narrow lane between the two stone walls and turned us around at the crossroad to drive us back to Umbersea Castle. Sometime while we were inside the church, the storm had begun to worsen again. Winds buffeted the lorry, driving the rain nearly sideways. I gripped the seat beneath me as Max painstakingly inched us forward.

He drove the lorry into the carriage house a trifle too fast, almost slamming the bonnet into the back wall as the tires slid on the dirt. Pulling the hood of my mackintosh up over my head, I climbed out to dash across the small yard toward the conservatory door with Max following at my heels.

I was half-afraid we would find it locked, but it swung inward easily, allowing us to escape from the tempestuous weather. Even so, the parts of me not covered by my mackintosh were thoroughly soaked, and I was certain my hair looked a frightful mess. However, we did not dally taking inventory of our appearances, but strode off through the glass-encased room toward the interior of the castle.

We didn't attempt to speak, seeming to already be in accord with what must be done. In any case, we would never have been able to hear each other over the deafening drumming of the rain against the glass surrounding us.

Returning to the corridor outside the conservatory, I turned left as Max turned right, skirting around the more public rooms lest I alarm any of the ladies with my bedraggled state. My shoes squelched against the polished floors, drawing the attention of a passing footman, whom I asked to stop. His eyes widened as I drew nearer, directing him to find his employer and tell him he was needed in his study immediately.

Then I retraced my steps to join Max there myself. He tapped furiously at the switchhook, asking if anyone could hear him through the mouthpiece. With an exasperated sigh, he slammed the earpiece down.

"No luck?"

He turned to face me, pushing his fingers through his damp hair. "Not a dashed bit. The storm appears to have knocked out all of the connections."

A sharp gust of rain whipped against the house as if to assert its power.

I frowned at the window. "And it would be nothing short of suicide to attempt to take a boat out in this wind."

"Agreed." His expression was grim. "Which means we shall have no outside help until the morning or this bloody storm abates, whichever comes first."

My chest tightened in apprehension, but I forced a breath past it, unwilling to give in to my fears no matter how much I disliked being effectively trapped on this island.

"Verity, dear, do not tell me you mean to attempt to leave in this weather. I'm sure the ladies are sorry . . ." Walter's words faltered as he drew up short at the sight of me and Max dripping all over his rug. His eyebrows lifted in astonishment as he glanced between us, trying to make sense of the sight before him.

It was Sam who managed to voice the question he must be thinking. "What's happened?" he gasped, staring at us over Walter's shoulder.

"Maybe we should all sit down," Max suggested as Felix and Tom also crowded into the room, though perhaps "staggered" would have been a better word.

Both men had clearly consumed large quantities of liquor, for they could barely remain upright. Neither of them would be the least bit helpful, and I wanted nothing so much but to order them to go to bed. But I also knew that neither would be budged until they were told what all the excitement was about.

"Have the ladies retired?" I asked, as the men arranged themselves about the room, leaving the chair nearest to the fire for me.

"Yes." Walter's face was pale, but whether that was because he knew what was coming or only suspected, I didn't know.

I watched him and the others closely as Max leaned back

against the table that held the telephone, and delivered our news.

"Charlie is dead."

Sam's reaction was hardly notable, as his eyes merely widened in what appeared to be genuine shock. But the others' proved more interesting. Walter flinched as if someone had jabbed him with the fireplace poker, draining the last vestiges of color from his face. For a moment, I thought he might faint. Felix, on the other hand, seemed more disgruntled than surprised. His brow lowered in a ferocious scowl that he turned on Tom as my childhood friend began to guffaw.

"Dead? You must be joking," Tom wheezed between chortles.

"I'm afraid we're quite serious," Max replied, his voice tight with disapproval.

"But how would such a thing—"

"Was it another suicide?" Walter interrupted.

Max met his incredulous gaze, answering him with certainty. "No."

Tom's laughter abruptly stopped as he seemed to choke on it.

"Wait." Felix sat forward. "Another suicide?!"

Max's fingers tapped against the edge of the table beneath him as he turned to address Tom and Felix. "Jimmy was found earlier this morning. It appeared he had hung himself." His gaze shifted to Walter. "Now we're not so sure."

Walter recoiled under the force of Max's stare, but any words he might have wished to say were drowned out by the angry protests of Felix and Tom, who were both affronted they hadn't been told.

"It was decided . . ." Max raised his voice even louder to be heard over the tumult. "IT WAS DECIDED that it would be best not to alarm the remainder of the guests with such dismal news. At least, not until the authorities had a chance to investigate." He tipped his head at Walter. "What did they have to say about it?"

He shifted uncomfortably in his seat and glowered at his desk blotter. "Oh, er . . . well. Said it appeared rather open-and-shut."

"Well, they may change their minds once we inform them of Charlie's murder."

"How did he die?" Sam ventured to ask.

Max paused, as if not wanting to say the words. "Shot through the chest. Looked to be close range."

The men seemed to absorb this information with varying degrees of acceptance. Their having all served in the war, I supposed none of them was greatly impacted by the idea of someone being killed by a bullet. There were certainly worse ways to go, and they had witnessed them. Which only made reading their reactions all the more difficult.

"Shall I telephone the police then?" Walter asked, starting to rise from his chair.

Max shook his head. "Already tried. The connections are down. Because of the storm, I suspect." He glanced over his shoulder at the telephone perched on the table behind him. "I tried to place a call earlier, and the lines were already dead. That's why your butler suggested I try the one at the church, that it might still be operational." He nodded his head in the direction of the center of the island. "That's how we stumbled across Charlie. Dead in the middle of the nave." His eyes flicked toward me. "If we hadn't gone to try the telephone there, he wouldn't have been found until tomorrow."

"Then the matter will have to wait until the morning," Walter said. His eyes gleamed with resolve. "And if the telephone connections are still not working, then we'll fetch the police from the mainland ourselves in one of the boats."

"It's lucky you haven't converted the entire castle to electricity yet, or we might be without lights as well," Max remarked, his gaze narrowing on the steadily burning gas lamp on the desk.

"Yes, well, that's part of the renovation plans, but costs a pretty penny, even with the cables already having been run for the telephones."

"What of the ladies?" I murmured, speaking up for the first time. "Shouldn't they be informed? After all . . ." I hesitated to say the words we were all thinking but must be said. "Someone is murdering our fellow guests. And it stands to reason, it could be one of us." The others glanced at each other suspiciously as I persisted. "Don't we want them to be on guard?"

Walter was the first to protest. "I . . . I don't think that's a good idea. And not just to spare Helen's feelings," he hastened to add.

"I don't either," Tom added in a dull voice, lifting his head from his hands. Our news seemed to have had the effect of a cold dunking, breaking through the jovial haze of his drunkenness. "If Nellie knew . . ." He sank his head back in his hands, as if unable to finish the thought.

Walter looked to Sam. "Mabel might be able to handle it. She was a nurse, after all. And heaven knows, she undoubtedly saw far worse things in the field hospital. But the other ladies would dissolve into hysterics."

I frowned, thinking they gave the women far less credit than they deserved. Yes, I suspected Nellie would cause a scene, but only because she wanted the attention, not because she couldn't handle the news. We had all lost loved ones in the war. We had all learned to bury our grief—admittedly some more than others—and carry on the best we could. The soldiers weren't the only ones who'd suffered through the war. We all carried burdens and scars of some kind.

But their minds appeared to be made up, so I stewed in silence, deciding that if the situation became critical I would ignore their ridiculous sensibilities on the matter. I was certain Mabel would agree with me.

However, as annoying as their insistence on treating the other women with kid leather gloves was, that wasn't the only thing that disturbed me. I couldn't help but note they seemed to prefer to ignore the fact that one of us could be the killer. That, in fact, it was more than likely someone in this very room.

I'd swept their appearances when they entered the room, and I did so again now, but I could not tell whether any of them had been out in the pouring rain earlier. Of course, some time had passed since the murder must have taken place. They could have easily snuck back into the castle, changed clothes, dried their hair, and rejoined the others.

But maybe someone's absence had been noted. Maybe there was a way to trace everyone's movements through the house after I'd stormed out of the parlor.

My gaze met Sam's across the expanse of Walter's desk, and he nodded almost imperceptibly, seeming to know without my saying a word what I was asking. Of the four men who had remained behind in the castle when Max and I ventured out, he was the one I most trusted to be able to give us straight responses.

So when we dispersed from Walter's study, all casting wary glances at one another, I gravitated to Sam's side. Max followed us wordlessly as we meandered toward the base of the right staircase, waiting for Felix and Tom to disappear out of hearing range. Walter had remained behind his desk, his shoulders slumped and his hands spread wide on the blotter, as if somehow they held answers for him.

"I know what you're going to ask me," Sam said in a hushed voice, darting one last glance over his shoulder to be sure we were alone. "But I'm afraid I don't have any easy answers for you. I didn't notice anyone acting guilty or even uneasy. They behaved more or less as I expected after that ridiculous bit of table-turning."

"What of their whereabouts? Was anyone missing for a long period of time?" I asked.

He considered the matter and shook his head in frustration. "I don't know. Everyone was coming and going. Several of the women retired soon after you left. First Tom's wife and then a short time later Helen and Mabel. Though Mabel did pop back down after a bit to ask after you. I think she assumed you would be in your room."

"What of the others?" Max pressed.

He frowned. "They all came and went at different intervals. I . . . I think Felix left before Helen and Mabel. Though Tom also disappeared for a time. And when Mabel pulled me aside,

I wasn't there to note who was coming and going. All I know is that when I returned to the parlor, Felix and Tom were there chatting with Helen's two friends, but Walter had stepped out." He huffed in frustration. "I'm sorry. This is no help at all, is it? I think the only people I can safely vouch for are Mabel and Helen's young friends. None of them was gone long enough to fit the time when you suspect Charlie was murdered." He paused to search our gazes. "You *do* think it happened sometime after the séance, correct?"

"I don't know when else the killer would have had the opportunity," Max replied. "Verity and I were with Charlie until about a quarter of an hour before dinner, and then we were all essentially together until Verity and I left the parlor."

Except for Max, I couldn't help but silently add.

While Sam and I were enduring Helen's table-turning in order to keep everyone occupied, Max was supposed to be using the telephone. But he had been gone a rather long time. I wasn't certain it had been long enough that he could have feasibly driven down to the church, murdered Charlie, and rushed back to change his clothes before rejoining us. The timing would have been awfully close, but it might have been just possible.

I glanced sideways up at Max as a cold lump settled in my stomach. I wanted to dismiss the idea as preposterous. If Max was the killer, I would have noticed something odd in his demeanor. Not to mention the fact that he need not have ever mentioned the other telephone at the church or his desire to see if it was working. He could have simply told me the connections to the telephones at the castle were down and left it at that. I would have been none the wiser. Why drag me out into the weather to stumble across Charlie's body? It made no sense.

"What of their appearance?" Max was quizzing Sam. "Did anyone's hair look damp? Did you notice if anyone had changed their clothes?"

Sam's head turned to the side as he thought back on the evening. "Not that I can recall." He inhaled swiftly. "Wait. Elsie did spill her drink on Tom's coat at one point." His face fell. "But he never left the room to change it."

I smothered a sigh. So we were no nearer to answers than we were before. My gaze strayed toward the tall windows at the front of the foyer looking out on the sea. And from the sound of the wind, the storm was only intensifying.

Tired and chilled to the bone—both mentally and physically, as I'd yet to change from my wet garments—I hauled myself up the stairs toward my room. Max trailed along beside me, pressing a warm, reassuring hand to my back. Perhaps I shouldn't have allowed him to escort me to my chamber, but under the circumstances, I was grateful for his steadying presence.

In any case, it turned out I had nothing to be wary of. I should have known Max would never presume anything except that I did not wish to traverse the shadowy corridors alone. At my door, I turned to thank him, but the misery etched in his eyes stopped my words.

Unable to help myself, I reached up to cup his cheek in my hand. The faint stubble that had begun to show at this late hour rasped my skin. "This is not your fault. This is not a battlefield, and you are not failing your men."

His mouth creased into a humorless smile. "I wish I could believe that." Then he withdrew my hand gently from his face, squeezing it. "Good night, Verity."

He backed away a step, still gazing at me before turning to stride down the hall in the direction we had come. I couldn't help wondering what it was exactly that he wished. That this wasn't a battlefield, or that he wasn't failing his men. Perhaps both.

Feeling the weight of the day and my restless sleep the night before, I pushed my door shut behind me and sagged against it. One of the maids had pulled the drapes and turned down the bed, leaving a single lamp on the writing desk burning. It was a welcoming sight after fumbling about in the dark at the church. Reaching up, I unbuttoned my mackintosh and allowed it to fall from my shoulders, grateful to be free of its confines, even though I missed its warmth. Chill air stole over my torso, making me shiver. I began to step away from the door, but then as an afterthought, reached back to turn the key, locking myself in.

Dragging my coat along behind me, I crossed toward the bed. But before I could take more than three steps, a pair of hands seized me from behind, hauling me back against a hard body.

CHAPTER 15

One hand pressed against my mouth, cutting off any chance of my screaming for help, while the other locked across my chest, trapping my arms like a vise. However, my assailant was clearly unaware that I had spent enough time in the Secret Service to know how to break free of such a hold without the use of my upper limbs.

I lifted my foot, bringing my heel crashing down on his instep. As he cursed and his grip slackened just that little bit, I leaned forward and then thrust my head back and upward into his chin. I would have preferred to hit something softer, but he was much too tall.

His hold broke as he cursed roundly. "Dash it, Verity! Are you trying to break my teeth?"

I whirled around and then backed away, staring wide-eyed, unable to accept what I was seeing.

I knew that voice. That face. They had haunted my nights and every waking hour since I'd received that cursed telegram. Since before that. Since he marched off to the front, leaving me to fret and worry over what was happening to him. Wondering whether he was alive and safe and warm and well-fed.

My legs gave out and I fell backward onto my bottom, still clambering, until my back came up against the footboard of the bed.

For a wild moment, I wondered if Helen had been right. Had we let his spirit out? Had he come to haunt me?

But then he lowered his hands from his mouth and moved slowly toward me, and I realized this was no spirit. He was real flesh and blood.

"How . . . You . . ." I stammered, unable to find my words as my husband kneeled before me repeating my name over and over again, like a benediction.

I scoured his face, studying each turn and crevice. The heaviness of his brow, the height of his cheekbones, the fullness of his lips. I lifted a trembling hand to touch his cheek, feeling its warmth, its suppleness.

"You . . . you're alive?" I finally managed to gasp in bewilderment.

His deep blue eyes smiled down at me tenderly. "Yes."

"You're alive," I said more assertively, lifting my other hand to feel the coarseness of the dark stubble framing his jaw.

"Yes," he repeated before leaning in to kiss me.

A swell of emotion rushed through me at the touch of his lips after believing I would never again feel his mouth on mine— caressing, tasting—and I choked on a sob. His scent surrounded me, at once invigorating and familiar, and yet somehow more earthy. I inhaled sharply, light-headed at all the sensations that filled me, and I gave myself over to them, unable to contain them. My body arched forward to touch every fiber of his, needing to know he was truly with me, needing to accept this wasn't a dream.

"Oh, darling," he murmured, brushing his thumbs against the tears that spilled down my cheeks. His voice was rougher than I remembered, but still the same tone that strummed across my nerves like a favorite melody.

"Sidney," I said, pronouncing his name for the first time. "Is this real?"

"Yes, darling."

That stubborn lock of dark curling hair had fallen over his brow, as it always insisted on doing, though this time it was much longer than usual. All of his hair was longer than usual. The dark brown wavy locks, which he kept trimmed and neatly combed, spilled down over his ears almost to his jaw. Had I been dreaming of him or even just imagining him, I never would have pictured him this way.

That realization jolted me out of my wondering stupor.

"You're alive," I repeated again.

His lips curled into a smile. "Yes, darling. We've already established that."

I pushed against his chest, moving him off of me where we lay tangled on the floor, frantic to be free. The light in his eyes began to dim.

"Then why . . . why have I been led to believe you were *dead* for the last fifteen months?" I demanded, pushing up into a seated position against the baseboard and tugging my skirt back over my legs. "There was a telegram. And . . . and the casualty list in the newspapers."

"Verity," he began soothingly.

"Where have you been?!"

He held up his hands in a defensive gesture. "You have every right to be angry. But *please* let me explain."

"You'd better," I snapped, grabbing the bed to help me rise to my feet. I was not going to hold this conversation while seated on the floor in this unfamiliar bedchamber. I glanced about me, raising my hands in exasperation. "And for that matter, what am I doing here? Is this *your* doing? Did you send me that letter and leave the book?" I sucked in a harsh breath as another thought occurred to me. "Did you kill Jimmy and Charlie?"

Sidney scowled. "For heaven's sake, Verity. Do you not know me at all?"

I refused to be chastised. "It seems not. Or else I wouldn't have been *grieving* over your sorry hide for the last year and more. What a waste." I whirled away, moving around to the side of the bed to sit on it.

He slowly followed. "I'm sorry, Ver."

He began to sit on the bed next to me, but I pointed a furious finger toward the chair in front of the writing desk. He hesitated a moment, but obeyed my unspoken order.

I missed his warmth and scent almost immediately, but I squashed the longing that welled up inside me. After all, I'd been missing them for a year and half. I could do without it for a bit longer.

The truth was, I was worried that if he sat beside me, if he put his arm around me and started to kiss me again, I would never want him to stop. I would forgive him anything, even if it was more horrible than the things I was already imagining.

He reached into the pocket of his worn trousers and extracted a battered, silver cigarette case. The one he'd taken with him to war that I'd had made special for him. I could still see the faint outline of his initials on the cover, and inside I knew it bore the message, *Love always, Verity.*

"Do you mind?" he asked, already removing one of the Turkish cigarettes he favored. He grimaced. "This is rather a long tale to tell."

I nodded once.

His hands were steady and his bearing calm. There was nothing to indicate he was at all unnerved by this situation. Though, to be fair, he hadn't just suffered from a great shock. But I still resented it. That cool confidence that had initially drawn me to him could also be infuriating. Just the tiniest indication that he was in any way flustered would have made me feel a little better.

From this vantage, I could see he wasn't dressed in the clothing of a gentleman, but more of a laborer. His skin was bronzed from the sun, and his hands rough, the knuckles on one hand scraped.

He exhaled a long stream of smoke, fixing his midnight blue eyes on me. "I truly am sorry, Verity. I never intended for any of this to happen. But once it did, well, there was no turning back. There's nothing I would have rather done than come home to you, but I assure you, the deception was necessary. For your safety and mine."

"Quit talking in riddles," I said, already feeling my heart soften toward him without knowing the barest of facts.

He nodded, reaching behind him to tip a fall of ash into the tray at the corner of the desk. "The first thing you should know is that I *was* wounded." He pressed a hand to the left side of his chest. "Just as it was reported. Would have been fatal, too, if it hadn't been for two things. The shooter's aim was off. The bullet missed my heart by less than an inch."

My hands fisted in my skirt as an image of Sidney lying wounded in the red sucking mud of the Somme flashed before my eyes. It wasn't difficult to imagine, seeing as I'd been staring down at Charlie's blood-soaked chest only a short time ago. It was all I could do not to leap up and rush over to press my hand over his heart to reassure myself it was still beating.

"But the shot wasn't taken by a German." His eyes turned hard. "It was a British soldier from my own battalion. An officer, from the brief glimpse I got of his uniform."

I forced myself to take a steadying breath, but otherwise didn't react, having already been presented with this possibility twice that evening. "You don't know who it was?"

"No, I didn't see his face." His eyes lifted from where they had been glaring a hole into the floor. "You don't sound very surprised."

"Max and I already figured this much out."

"Hmm. Max, is it?"

I frowned at the animosity in Sidney's voice. "Yes, Helen insisted we call each other by our given names," I retorted in exasperation. "So then what happened? Obviously you weren't taken to the casualty clearing station or on to the field hospital. Where did you go?"

"Sam helped me retreat from the front."

My eyebrows rose at this bit of news. "Sam knows you're alive?"

"Yes." He paused, but I could tell he had more to say as he lifted his cigarette to take another drag. "As does Mabel."

I pressed a hand to my forehead, feeling hurt and bewildered. "Anybody else?"

He shook his head. "Only them. And only because they saved my life."

I supposed I could hardly begrudge them knowing after that. And it was undoubtedly at Sidney's behest that they'd remained silent on the matter, though I still felt aggravated that they'd helped keep this from me. "Do they know that you're here?"

"Yes."

I smothered a sigh. "Go on."

"We were in retreat, even the casualty clearing stations, so it wasn't difficult for us to get lost in all the disorder. Sam found a place to hide me and went for help. By that point I had lost so much blood, I was fading in and out of consciousness." His brow furrowed as if it was painful just to remember. "But when I finally came to a few days later, I realized he'd convinced Mabel to care for my wounds. And between the two of them, they'd given me enough blood to survive."

"Why didn't you just go to the field hospital and tell them what happened?" I asked in confusion.

His eyes snapped to mine. "Because I knew whoever shot me would be looking for me there. That I couldn't even stay conscious, let alone defend myself should the need arise. I simply couldn't risk it. Not in such chaos. I didn't know who exactly had tried to kill me, or if I would even be believed."

I thought I understood. The safeguards that normally would have been in place in such a situation would have been ineffectual at best, if not completely broken down. He couldn't rely on the nurses to be able to watch over him, and Sam couldn't remain at his side. He would have been expected to report to his battalion directly, taking over Sidney's command.

"Walter reported you had been killed," I told him.

His mouth tightened into a thin line. "I know. And that definitely makes him a suspect. But the fact of the matter is, my shooter and I weren't the last men in the trench. There were others about. So Walter might have seen me lying there after the fact, but not pulled the trigger."

"But you were still breathing?" I argued.

"Yes, but he would have been able to see where my wound was, that I would almost surely be dead in a matter of minutes." His gaze turned stark. "Sometimes as officers we had to make the tough call about who was worth trying to save and who was beyond assistance. If that was the case, I don't hold that against him."

I wasn't certain I viewed it the same way he did, but I wasn't about to disagree. Not when it was evident he was also living with the guilt of having made those sorts of choices.

"Then what about after?" I said, kicking off my shoes and sliding back on the bed to fold my knees up beside me. "Why didn't you return once your wounds were healed enough and report what had happened? Surely they wouldn't have held that against you."

His face was doubtful. "Maybe. But Sam and Mabel would have faced some serious consequences for assisting me the way they did, and I couldn't allow that to happen. Not after everything they'd done." He stubbed out his cigarette in the dish a trifle harder than necessary. "In any case, I could hardly accuse an officer in my regiment of attempting to kill me without knowing who shot at me, or having proof of their intentions."

"Then what did you do? Don't tell me you've been laying low in France all this time."

"No, I went in search of evidence to prove what I suspected got me targeted for death." His gaze sharpened. "That one of the officers in my battalion was committing treason."

I stiffened in shock, not having suspected this, and he nodded.

"I figured out that the two men in our battalion who had been tried and executed for desertion had been framed. That in actuality they had been delivering messages for one of the officers to a nearby town."

"Just like Sam's brother, Ben, thought."

"Yes, Ben was the one who brought the matter to my attention. He'd discovered that on more than one occasion, these men had delivered messages, which were supposedly love letters, to the French mistress of one of the officers in a nearby town."

"But they weren't love letters?"

His eyes brightened in approval. "No, they were coded missives to a German informant. And when that informant was arrested by the French on suspicion of aiding the enemy, the traitor, whoever he is, realized he needed to silence his messengers before they talked."

"But why weren't these messages disguised as love letters ever mentioned at the court-martial?" I protested, recalling what

Max had said about their not being transcribed in the trial notes he'd seen. "Or if they were, why wasn't a bigger deal made of them? Surely the soldiers on trial would have used them in their defense."

Sidney shook his head. "I don't know. Except . . . I have to believe the officer who gave them such an assignment had promised he would safeguard them. That's how it was supposed to work, you know. As officers, we were supposed to look after our men, to protect them as best we could and deal with them fairly. That was our charge, our duty. And in exchange, our men gave us their loyalty and devotion."

"Noblesse oblige," I said, referring to the concept that nobility, at its best, was supposed to encapsulate. That those born with entitlements and privileges also had the responsibility to care for those less fortunate, be it their servants, tenants, subjects, or, in this case, the soldiers under their command. It was a matter of honor.

"At its heart, yes."

"And yet this officer did no such thing. Effectively, he let them take the fall for him."

His jaw was tight with anger. "Yes, which is also why I suspect he contrived to stay away from the trial. He wouldn't have wanted to testify, to face these men or risk their turning on him once they realized he wasn't going to help them. He would have tried to barter for their silence until it was much too late for them to do anything about it."

I was aghast. It was the worst sort of betrayal. No wonder Ben and later Sidney had become so invested in uncovering the truth. And then for Sidney to stumble upon the fact it all came down to treason.

I frowned. "But Sam didn't know anything about the treason or the German informant posing as a French mistress." I thought of how discouraged he'd seemed earlier when speaking with me and Max. "Between him, and Max, and me, we were able to piece together much of the rest. And Charlie mentioned something about a letter. But not the treason or the informant."

Sidney's brow creased. "Getting cozy, were the three of you?"

I glowered.

His gaze dropped to the arm of his chair, where his fingers plucked at the leather edge. "Yes, well, I figured it was better if Sam didn't know all the details I uncovered later, lest he slip up."

"So he doesn't know the real reason they killed his brother? To keep him from uncovering the treason?"

He looked up at me through his lashes. "No."

I looked away from him, having trouble reconciling this cold, unkempt man with the gentleman who was my husband. "May I presume you found this informant, then? Is *that* where you went on your last leave when you didn't come home?"

When he didn't answer, I turned to find him studying me, though infuriatingly I couldn't tell what he was thinking. I reached a hand up self-consciously to try to smooth out the wild kinks in my hair.

"Not then, though I did try," he replied, making no apology for his actions, or for the pain it had caused me to find out about this leave from someone else. "But after I had recovered from my gunshot wound, after I was able to travel about the country disguised as a lame peddler, then I was able to track down the woman. Though it wasn't easy. She'd done quite a thorough job of covering her trail once she was released from custody."

He swiveled his chair so that while he still faced me, he could also fiddle with the items on my desk—shifting papers and picking up books to examine the titles. "Fortunately, she was more than forthcoming with what she knew." He flicked a glance at me. "She was still rather irate at him that she'd been left to fend for herself when she was detained by the French. She insisted she'd never known his name, or not his real one, in any case, and that she'd only met him twice briefly. But she was able to describe him as being tall and dark haired, handsome, but not *très ravissant*."

"But that could describe half the men at this house party," I pointed out.

"So I noticed. Though perhaps even more frustrating is that

she told me it was obvious to her that the man was only a messenger himself. A lackey. That he received the information from someone else to pass along."

"So there's another traitor? One higher up the food chain, so to speak?"

"From everything else I've learned, I would have to agree with her."

He opened one of the desk drawers and began to rustle through its contents. I started to protest, but his next comments explained what he was looking for.

"However, she did hold in her possession one last coded missive she was never able to deliver before she was detained. Apparently, she'd hidden it well from the French authorities—a precaution against future trouble. But she agreed to give it to me."

I arched a single eyebrow in disdain. "And I suppose that's the coded missive you left tucked inside your copy of *The Pilgrim's Progress* for me to find. The one you implied was proof of the treason you alleged that *you* had committed in the anonymous letter you wrote to me in order to drag me here."

He looked up at me, pausing for a moment to note my scorn before carrying on without the slightest hint of remorse. "Yes. Where is it?"

I pressed my lips together, holding in all of the invectives I wanted to hurl at him. "Did you honestly think I would be stupid enough to leave it in plain sight?"

He sank back in his chair staring at me, and after a moment I realized he wasn't forming a reply, but still waiting for me to answer. Well, I wasn't about to give him one without his answering my questions first.

"Why did you send it to me? Was this some sort of sick game? A test?"

"I need your help to break it."

"Why? Didn't your informant provide you with the key to the cipher?" I sneered.

His jaw hardened as if he was grinding his teeth together. "No, she swore she never knew it. That it was safer that way."

Plainly her partners had been right, as she'd sung like a canary under Sidney's questioning. But that still didn't explain why he believed I could break the code for him.

Sitting up straighter, I glanced at the window, where I could still hear the rain pounding against the glass, and then back to Sidney, finally daring to voice my next question. "How did you know I worked for the Secret Service?"

It was Sidney's turn to look uncomfortable, the first real sign of uneasiness I'd witnessed in him all night. "Calvin Applegate told me he saw you outside Ypres. Said it was from a distance and he didn't talk to you, but that he swore it was you, regardless."

I struggled not to stiffen, searching my brain for the date in question. I'd been near Ypres several times during the war. And though I'd always known it was a danger someone at the front—a soldier or a nurse or a volunteer—would recognize me, I'd believed I'd managed to dodge that particular land mine. Apparently not.

"I told him he was hallucinating. That the gas must have affected his eyesight more than he realized. But then"—his brow furrowed—"I began to wonder. After all, there was that time I arrived in London for leave and you weren't there. When you returned the next day, you said you'd just gone to visit a friend in Cornwall, but, Verity, you'd looked exhausted."

I looked down at my lap, not wanting to confront the concern tightening his features.

"And . . . there was this look in your eyes. It was an expression I'd never seen in a civilian, but confronted every day at the front. A wide-eyed mien those of us who had seen the truth couldn't hide. So I followed you."

I lifted my head in surprise.

"The next time you reported to your job, I followed you. To Whitehall. *Not* Vauxhall Bridge Road, where you said you worked." He pulled his cigarette case from his pocket again. "And I had the rather great fortune to see an old acquaintance of mine from Oxford exiting the building. I knew then there was no way you worked at a shipping company. A few pints of ale got me most of the rest of my answers."

I frowned, angry that one of my colleagues had so easily been coerced into sharing classified information. "Who was this acquaintance?"

He flicked a glance at me over the fag he was lighting. "Does it matter? I know for a fact he doesn't work there now any more than you do."

I pursed my lips in irritation, but let that one slide. "And you've decided this means I know how to break your code?"

"It seemed a safe bet." He exhaled a plume of smoke. "You always have been dashed clever, Ver." His head tilted to the side. "Are you telling me you can't?"

I studied the medallion pattern of the carpet. "I honestly don't know. Codebreaking was never my expertise." It felt odd admitting all of this to him when I'd kept it hidden for so long. The words felt wrong on my lips. "But what I do know was taught to me by the best." I caught myself before I glanced at the wardrobe, giving away the location of the book and the encrypted missive. "However, this code is not anything I've ever seen. It doesn't follow any of the standard ciphers." I looked up at him. "But I suspect you already know that."

He grimaced, staring at his cigarette. "Yes, I tried my hand at breaking it, and evidently failed." His gaze flicked upward to meet mine. "That's why I decided to draw you into this wretched mess, despite the dangers, despite the risks." He leaned forward over his knees toward me. "I'm so close to ending this, Verity. I can feel it. But I *need* to know what's coded in that missive. Will you help me?"

His eyes were dark in the dim light of that single lamp, the pupils nearly swallowing the deep blue of his irises. They were pleading with me in a way I knew I was helpless to deny. Not when my husband had just been returned to me from the grave. Despite what he might have done, despite how he had hurt me, I knew I couldn't walk away when he needed me.

But that didn't mean I was going to make it easy for him.

"Why did you wait so long to inform me you were alive? Why did you leave me to grieve for so long?" My voice broke on the last, and I lifted my chin, forbidding the tears burning at the back of my eyes from surfacing.

A line formed between Sidney's brows as he slowly sat up. "I was afraid I would be placing you in danger," he admitted. "If the traitor who attempted to murder me found out I was alive, and that I'd come to see you, I knew they would assume I'd revealed all to you. Not to mention the fact that if the authorities discovered I was alive, I would be arrested for desertion. And without the proof I've been seeking, at the very least, I would be imprisoned. Sam and Mabel would face similar consequences. I just couldn't risk it."

He blew a stream of smoke at the ceiling, watching it as it dissipated. "I also admit, knowing you worked for the Secret Service, I was a bit hesitant to contact you because I couldn't be absolutely certain where your loyalties would lie. Whether I would be placing you in the untenable position of having to choose between betraying your husband or your country."

I felt stung by his admission, despite its truth. It would have been a terrible situation to be put in. But I was wounded that he assumed I would choose my loyalty to Britain over him, especially after hearing what he'd told me about his treasonous fellow officer.

"I sent you that note suggesting I might have committed treason because I needed you to come to this house party. And because I knew you would never allow such an accusation against me to go unchallenged." His lips curled upward in a humorless smile. "I knew it would eat at you, Verity. That you wouldn't be able to rest until you knew the truth, no matter what it was. That was something I was certain I could count on."

I hated that he knew me so well in that regard, and yet had not felt he could trust me with the truth long before now. I hated that he'd left me to mourn for him, to suffer so much pain over his loss. But I suspected I hated myself more for not sensing somehow that he was still alive, and for being weak enough to let myself fall into such disreputable habits. Even now, even having him seated before me, returned to life, I wanted to numb the ache in my chest with a glass of gin or champagne.

What should have been a joy was instead an agony. For it was evident Sidney didn't know how I had been spending my time since his reported death, and how could I tell him? How could I divulge such a thing?

So instead I turned the matter back on him.

"It was you who sent the notes, and the burnt cork and harmonica to Jimmy and Charlie," I accused him.

He didn't attempt to deny it. "Yes, I thought if I could prod their consciences, then maybe they would confess their parts in the plot and everything they knew about the others. For it's certain that whoever the actual traitor is, he had help, whether willingly given or coerced."

"Did you kill them?" I asked, insisting he give me a straight answer to the question that terrified me most.

Sidney's scowl turned black. "No." He opened his mouth to say something, but then seemed to reconsider it, exhaling in frustration before he continued to explain. "Whether you believe me or not, I needed them alive. They were the two most likely to share what they knew. I'd hoped that by gathering all the men I suspected, together with Sam and you, their guilt would eat at them and convince one of them to talk. The notes were just meant to be an extra nudge."

"Yes, and how on earth did you manage that? Convincing Helen and Walter to invite all of us."

He swiveled to stub out his second cigarette, before answering obliquely. "You'll have to ask Sam that one."

I frowned. "And what of you? Isn't it rather reckless of you to be here?"

He shrugged. "I've been here for several weeks making preparations, posing as a gardener."

I could hardly believe his audacity. "Aren't you afraid Walter or one of the others will recognize you?"

He arched his eyebrows scornfully. "People rarely notice the help, Verity. And if they do, they only see what they want to see. A scruffy young man with a strong back, pruning their bushes."

I supposed that explained those times I'd felt like I was being watched. I had been. On at least one instance, I *had* noted the gardeners, but I'd never looked close enough to see that one of them was Sidney. Though I was certain he'd done a good job of hiding himself from me.

And what about at the church tonight?

I looked up to find him watching me, as if he'd known where my musings had led. "Were you at St. Mary's when we found Charlie's body?"

"No, but I arrived soon after to find you and Ryde seated rather cozily in one of the pews."

"Yes, as you can imagine, I was quite distressed at having found a second dead body," I bit out, refusing to apologize for my actions. I narrowed my eyes as another thought occurred to me. "If you were responsible for sending the rest of those notes, then I assume you also sent Max the letter that drew him here as well."

His gaze sharpened and his voice became insistent. "You didn't tell him you'd received a letter accusing me of treason, did you?"

I crossed my arms over my chest, irritated that this was the point on which he should become so agitated. "No, I did admit I'd received a letter, but said it only told me the correspondent had information to share about your death."

He settled back in his seat, but the glower marring his brow did not disappear. "I told you not to trust anyone."

"And I haven't. Though I don't understand why you're warning me away from Max. He had nothing to do with those messengers who were executed for desertion, nor was he in the trenches the night Ben was killed. *And* he doesn't have dark hair. Beside, *you* lured him here. Why?"

"I wasn't sure how he played into the matter, but I knew Ben had confided in him, and that he might hold other information that was important. However, I'm still not certain of his innocence. There is also a mastermind to uncover, remember. Someone lurking behind the scenes who directed the entire plot. He could very well be Ryde."

I hadn't considered that. Max had been ideally situated for such a role. But I didn't wish to admit as much to Sidney, not after the insinuations he'd just made about my relationship with Max.

In any case, I *hadn't* trusted Max. Not completely. And neither, for that matter, did I fully trust Sidney, even though I desperately wanted to. He was my husband, after all. But he had allowed me to believe he was dead for fifteen long months. I could not forget or forgive that so easily.

Even if everything he'd told me *was* true, even if there was a traitor at work, that didn't mean this traitor was the same person killing the men on this island. Perhaps the traitor was silencing those who could expose him, or perhaps someone else was exacting revenge. I didn't know for certain, and until I did, I had to agree he was right about one thing. I couldn't trust anyone.

Sidney rose from his chair suddenly and moved to stand before me. It took everything within me not to shrink backward at the look in his eyes.

"You cannot tell Ryde I'm alive."

"I know," I replied crossly.

His eyes searched my face, as if uncertain of my compliance. Whatever he saw there must have made him believe me, for he relented. His shoulders relaxed and he spoke to me in a more subdued voice. "Will you help me, Verity? Will you break the code?" When I didn't answer, he lowered himself to one knee and took my hand. "Please. It might be the proof I need."

I stared down into his glittering eyes, wishing he would speak to me on another subject so fervently. It hadn't escaped my notice that he hadn't said the words I most longed to hear. *I love you. I missed you. I wish I could have been with you.* But even after being separated from me for almost a year and a half, his thoughts appeared solely focused on this quest of his.

I nodded, knowing I could do nothing else but agree. Because despite what Sidney might or might not feel about me, I knew I was still in love with him. I had been fooling myself to think I had buried any of that affection.

I had my doubts about this plan of his, doubts that the decrypted missive would contain the proof he needed, but I would do all I could to help it succeed. To help him unmask the traitor and uncover the evidence required to convict them and clear Sidney's name. I only prayed that if proof could not be found, he could be persuaded to let the matter go, to move forward in a different direction. For if he didn't, I could see no future for us.

I might understand his need for vengeance and reprisal, but I didn't know if I would ever be able to forgive him for it if the cost became too high. It already seemed almost insurmountable.

"Yes, I'll help you," I whispered, wishing I could keep the heartache from my voice, but I knew it was evident for anyone to hear.

He lifted his hand to gently cup my cheek. "Thank you, Verity. I knew I could count on you. I wish . . ." He broke off, shaking his head. His expression hardened with resolve. "I'm staying in one of the outbuildings at the farm, should you urgently need me. Otherwise, it's best if I come to you."

He leaned forward and kissed me, swift and deep. But before I became weak enough to beg him to stay, he was gone.

I stared at the door through which he'd vanished, feeling the emptiness of the room, the emptiness of my bed, the emptiness of my arms. And I wept.

CHAPTER 16

When I woke early the next morning, bleary-eyed and swollen faced, I could still hear the howling wind beating the rain against the side of the castle. I stared up at the ceiling, as memories from the evening before filtered through my brain, like a dream I'd almost forgotten. It would have been all too easy to believe I'd imagined it all, except for the fact that I could still smell the smoke from Sidney's cigarettes lingering in the air, still feel the gentle abrasions around my lips from the rasp of his stubble.

Rising from bed, I picked up the ashtray and dumped the remnants of his cigarettes into the still-smoldering hearth before stirring up the ashes to cover them. It certainly wouldn't do to leave behind any evidence that someone else had been in my room last night, even though I knew what the others would assume. After all, no one would think twice if a young widow like myself decided to quietly indulge in a dalliance. It was almost cliché.

Many of my friends, both widowed and single, regularly took lovers—oftentimes because they wanted to, but sometimes because they simply couldn't bear *not* to. I'd watched their exploits, their maddened pursuit, but quickly learned that sex when one was merely desperate was never good. It never filled the void, but only left you even emptier than you were before.

At any rate, I was more worried that someone would remember how Sidney had preferred this particular type of Turkish cigarettes and begin asking questions than that they would think I'd taken one of the male guests to my bed. It wouldn't do to raise anyone's alarm, not when two men had already been killed and a traitor, or two, possibly lurked in our midst.

Though curious to discover whether the telephones were yet working, I decided to leave that problem to the men for the moment and instead focus on the coded missive. It had not escaped my notice that if the storm broke and the authorities were called in, Sidney might very well be in danger of being found out. For surely they would question the staff, especially those who lived at the farm, only a short distance from the church. Most of the guests were also scheduled to leave today, including myself, and if we were able to depart before Sidney uncovered his proof, I wasn't certain how he would react.

In truth, that was one of the aspects that troubled me most—Sidney's unpredictability. He could not have failed to note that time was slipping away from him. In fact, I was certain that had figured rather prominently in his decision to reveal himself to me the night before. What might he do, or have already done, to prevent his suspects from leaving?

Pushing the dark misgivings from my mind, I turned on the lamp at my desk to peel back the gloom and redoubled my efforts to break the code. Now knowing that Sidney had not written the missive, I could discard the possibility that it was a book cipher connected to *The Pilgrim's Progress* and concentrate on the other methods. However, the key to unraveling it remained elusive. I continued to labor over the variations of the transposition cipher I had been trained in, but the harder I tried to concentrate, the more difficult it became to keep my mind focused. No doubt my raw nerves and lack of sleep were not helping matters.

At least in this matter, Sidney's resurrection was proving more of a hindrance than a help, for I could not banish him from my thoughts. How could I? Not eight hours ago, my husband had still been dead, and now he was alive. The thing I had wanted most in the world—for him to return to me, alive and whole—had happened, and yet I had let him go. Let him leave me and traipse back through the storm to his lodgings at the farm.

And worst of all, I had been so angry and cold toward him. Not that my fury and bewilderment weren't justified. They were. But perhaps if I hadn't retreated into such icy reserve, perhaps if I'd shown him a bit more welcome and sympathy, maybe then he wouldn't have behaved so indifferently. Maybe then he would have stayed.

Or maybe it hadn't mattered what I did. After all, it was obvious he was obsessed with finding this traitor and bringing him to justice. He was determined to pursue the truth to the exclusion of all else. Including me.

I rubbed my temples, trying to blunt the pain of an oncoming headache. Sitting here in the chilly gloom of dawn while I berated and tortured myself wasn't getting me anywhere, be it with the code, this investigation, or in comprehending my shattered marriage. It was past time I emerged from my room to discover what else the night had wrought and to seek some sustenance.

I washed and dressed myself in a blouse of white voile with a pale green collar and cuffs, and a navy blue botany serge skirt before making my way to the breakfast room. However, before I could cross to the sideboard, Helen rose from her seat in a swirl of pale yellow chiffon and pulled me to the side with a gentle hand on my elbow.

"Dearest Verity, I simply *must* apologize for our abominable behavior last evening." Her eyes were bright with contrition. "I have been positively racked with guilt all night. Had I known Gladys intended to do such a cruel thing as to pretend to summon your dearly departed husband, I would *never* have let her touch the planchette."

I pressed a staying hand to the arm that still gripped mine. "All is well," I told her, aware of the curious gazes of the others gathered in the room. The last thing I wanted was to create another scene. "I was upset—"

"Understandably," she hastened to say.

I offered her a strained smile. "But a night of sleep has set me to rights. In any case, I know you had nothing to do with it. And Gladys's actions, while not well thought out, were not malicious in intent."

Nellie, on the other hand, had been nothing but spiteful. A quick glance about the room relieved me that she was not at the moment present.

"You are kindness itself," Helen gushed. "I was so afraid we'd offended you unforgivably, and yet here you are, offering me a sunny pardon on such a miserable day." Her gaze strayed toward the large windows, their drapes pulled back to reveal the storm-lashed garden.

"Think nothing of it," I assured her, prying myself loose of her grip to serve myself breakfast from the warming dishes.

The number of guests gathered in the room was small, consisting only of Max, Sam, Mabel, and Tom. My childhood friend looked as if he belonged in bed instead of slumped in his chair, grimacing down at the cup of black coffee he was forcing himself to drink. His face held a green cast that made me worry he would need to run from the room at a moment's notice. So I elected to sit next to Max, despite the discomfort inching along my skin at being so near to him now that I knew my husband was alive.

We had done nothing wrong. Neither of us had behaved inappropriately given what we'd believed to be true until Sidney appeared in my room the night before. But I still felt a pale wash of color suffusing my cheeks and the vague stirrings of shame in my gut.

Having delivered her apology, Helen had vanished from the room, making me suspect she had been lying in wait for me here. That she had been so anxious to make amends only made me more disposed to like her. I hoped, for her sake, Walter was not the traitor or murderer Sidney and I were looking for.

"Good morning," I murmured, exchanging greetings with everyone around the table. "Did anyone sleep well?" I couldn't help asking ironically.

Most of them mustered a weak smile at my jest, but it was Sam who answered with a heavy sigh. "Not bloody likely."

His eyes met Mabel's and I could tell from the look they exchanged that he had disobeyed Walter's orders and told her about Charlie's death. Having already known she could handle the shock of such news, even before I'd learned how she had helped save Sidney's life, I was only too glad he'd trusted her with this latest development.

Naturally, I saw Sam and Mabel with new eyes this morning. It would have been difficult *not* to knowing now what I did. It colored all of our past interactions in a new light, and I couldn't help but wonder how comfortable they were with the position Sidney had placed them in. Namely lying to his wife by continuing to pretend he was dead. I had seen something in Mabel's eyes as we interacted, and I thought I could safely say she was not happy about it. I liked her, and sensed she liked me in return. How awful it must be to keep such a secret.

Sam was more difficult to decipher. But then, having served alongside Sidney in the trenches, it was only natural that his loyalty should be to him. Especially since Sidney was also trying to avenge his brother's death. I pondered how he would feel if he knew Sidney had not shared everything he'd learned about Ben's death with him, or that he'd been the one to use his brother's memory in such a shocking manner on that Field Service Postcard he'd sent Jimmy.

"The telephones are still not working," Max told me before I had to ask. His expression turned grim. "And there have been some interesting developments."

I sat taller. "What do you mean?"

He nodded at Sam and Tom. "There was a short lull in the weather earlier this morning, so the three of us along with Walter tried to take the boat across the harbor to the mainland. But the motor wouldn't start, and the winds were much too ferocious for us to attempt to use the sails, even had Walter's normal crew remained on the island instead of returning to their homes in Poole yesterday afternoon. It would be suicide."

I stiffened in alarm, my tea cup poised before my lips. "Then the servants haven't returned?"

He shook his head. "Only those who live here on the island—

a skeleton crew here at the castle and some of the farm workers and gardeners."

Knowing that Sidney was one of those gardeners, it took a great deal of effort not to look at Sam and Mabel.

I set down my cup and sat forward. "But there must be other boats? Surely Walter's yacht isn't the only vessel on the island."

"Yes. But according to Walter, they're all stored on the other end of the quay or the opposite side of the island. And once the storm kicked up again, it was too late to try to take them out even if we could reach them. The seas are just too choppy."

I nodded my understanding. It would not do us any good if the boat that set out to summon help then capsized and killed its crew.

"Then I guess we'll have to wait for better weather." I glanced toward the windows, out across the lawn to where the boughs of the elm trees were nearly bent sideways by the force of the wind. But how long would that be?

"I suppose that means none of us will be leaving today, as we originally intended," I added, feeling a prickle of unease run down my spine. For all intents and purposes, we were trapped here, and I didn't like it. I didn't like it at all.

Not that the killer could have predicted such a thing, or caused it to happen. But he, or she, could be taking advantage of it all the same.

Tom looked across the table at me for the first time since I'd sat down, almost as if rousing himself from a stupor. I could see that he was deeply troubled. "Nellie isn't going to be happy. In fact, I think she's going to be downright impossible." He leaned forward, lowering his voice. "She's desperate to get off this island."

The almost frantic light in his eyes startled me. "I think a lot of us are," I replied calmly.

He shook his head even as his eyes strayed toward the door. "Yes, but she said the cards told her something terrible was going to happen. Something none of us would ever be able to forget."

I frowned. The cards? Was he saying that Nellie, of all people, consulted tarot cards? I couldn't believe it. It didn't seem possible.

"Did you tell her about Jimmy and Charlie?" Sam wanted to know, echoing my own curiosity.

"No!" he gasped. "And she can't *ever* know, or else I will hang myself from listening to her drone on about it."

I stared after Tom as he rose from his seat and limped from the room, startled by his last statement. He knew how Jimmy had died, and yet he'd made that comment without a hint of irony. As for the rest, I couldn't make heads or tails of his comments. They seemed far too dire and morbid for the Tom I knew, or even Nellie. Perhaps Tom had been more primed from the spirits he'd consumed the night before than he'd first seemed.

Or maybe he was under the influence of something far stronger. He wouldn't have been the first soldier to use morphia to dull the pain of his injuries and his memories.

I glanced at Mabel, curious what she thought of his wild pronouncements, and then at Sam and Max, who as former soldiers must also be battling recollections from the war the murders had dredged up that they would rather not revisit. I could read the strain in all of their features, just as I suspected they could see the tension in mine.

Sam and Mabel soon excused themselves from the room, but Max remained behind, sipping his coffee while I nibbled at my toast. It was difficult to summon much of an appetite under the circumstances, and my awareness of Max's proximity and our being alone only made it worse.

"There's something else you should know," he said, staring straight ahead of him at the painting on the far wall. "Walter told me that a second boat should have been anchored at his pier." His gaze shifted to meet mine. "But this morning it was nowhere to be found."

"You mean it's missing?"

He nodded. "We decided it was best not to tell the others. Not yet anyway. In case Walter was mistaken and had forgotten what his crew's captain had told him he was going to do with it. But I thought you should know."

I studied his taut features, working through the implications of what he'd just told me. "Do . . . do you think someone is trying to prevent us from getting off the island? From getting help?"

His mouth pursed in consideration before he answered. "I think it's too early to say for sure. But let's just say, my suspicions are aroused."

I picked up my teacup, hoping to hide my agitation behind the fine china. For I couldn't help but wonder whether Sidney might have had anything to do with the missing boat and the stalled motor. After all, he seemed to have the most to lose from us all leaving the island.

Unless the killer wasn't finished. Unless there were more guests to be silenced or punished, depending on his motives.

I wished I could be more certain of my husband, of anything on this forsaken island.

Unsurprisingly, the mood of the gathering could only be described as going precipitously downhill. Everyone was tense, and more than half of the party was also suffering from hangovers. So even though we all tried to occupy ourselves with playing cards, reading, and even a bit of light dancing, it was obvious no one's hearts were in it. All of the joviality of the past few days—false though it may have been—had fled in the face of the storm, and tempers flared as more than a few sharp words were exchanged between guests.

Gladys and Elsie, who had always seemed to be bosom friends, persisted to snipe at each other about the littlest of things—from the volume of the gramophone to whether or not Elsie had borrowed Gladys's favorite pair of shoes and scuffed the leather. While Sam and Mabel, who had seemed in perfect accord at breakfast, proceeded to sit on opposite sides of the parlor and shoot daggers at each other from time to time. Sometime just before midday, Nellie deemed to join us, sitting herself in the corner to whine and bemoan the weather and her being trapped on the island away from her beloved son. Even Helen seemed on edge, flitting in and out of the room, refusing to coddle Nellie or either of her friends in their ridiculous complaining. I suspected her patience had simply run out.

But Walter and Felix seemed to be the most cutting toward one another. In fact, I was surprised neither of them had actually drawn blood with their barbed comments, many of which I didn't always understand. However, I couldn't help but note the brief glances exchanged by Max and Sam, making me suspect it had something to do with the war.

The most unusual exchange occurred during the men's discussion about how to fix the motor on Walter's yacht. Apparently, his farm laborer who'd also had quite a knack for mechanical things—tractors, threshing machines, motorcars, motorboats—had left his employ not a week earlier. With his yacht crew on the mainland, that left only the men present to try to repair the engine.

"Do you think you'll be able to fix it?" Max asked our host, phrasing in the politest terms possible the dubious confidence I suspected many of us felt in Walter's mechanical competence. Even Helen, who after fluttering here and there had finally settled on the opposite end of the Weston sofa from me, had peered up at him through her lashes with a look that could only be described as doubtful.

"I suspect I'll be able to manage just fine," Walter replied, seeming oblivious to our misgivings.

Felix scoffed. "Yes, because you've always managed *just fine* in the past."

Walter frowned. "I have no doubt I can make do. I'll cobble something together, if necessary."

"Are you sure you wouldn't rather leave the matter to someone else? After all, that seems your forte." Felix's eyes had narrowed rather nastily to glare at him across the room from where he slouched in one of the bergère chairs near the windows, puffing on a cigarette.

For a moment, no one said anything, instead watching the air crackle between the two gentlemen.

It was Gladys who spoke first, rousing herself from her

lounged stupor before the hearth. "Is it really so urgent we leave the island today?"

"I agree," Nellie interjected, sitting taller in her own seat. "As anxious as you all know I am to return to my son, wouldn't it be better to wait for the crew to return? Surely they'll come directly here once the storm breaks."

I turned to Walter, who glanced wide-eyed in turn at each of us who knew about Charlie's death. I'd wondered why he had introduced such a topic of conversation in front of the others in the first place. Wouldn't it have been better not to inform the other women that the motor on his boat wouldn't start?

"Well, one can hope," he spluttered. "But who knows how long this storm will last? And I would prefer my boat have a working engine." He paused before adding hastily, "Just in case it's needed, you understand."

"Oh, too true," Nellie, subsided, nodded in agreement before lifting a hand to her brow. "I was so light-headed this morning, I thought I might have to be carried downstairs. At first, I wondered if I might have come down with whatever dreadful illness Charlie and Jimmy have contracted. But fortunately, I rallied. As I always do." This was said in such a long-suffering manner that I almost rolled my eyes.

"As does Walter," Felix remarked.

Walter's scowl darkened. "As does *any* good Englishman." He flicked a glance at Nellie. "Or Englishwoman."

"Is that what it is? Rallying for King and country." Felix took a long drag on his cigarette before retorting under his breath, though it was loud enough for all of us to hear. "I thought it was retreat and panic."

Walter rose from his chair and charged from the room, or rather hobbled, as the weather seemed to have aggravated his leg wound as well.

Nellie glowered at Felix, clearly uncertain whether she'd just been insulted. But before she could speak, Tom rose from his chair, and in a rare display of husbandly subdual, placed a hand on her shoulder to halt her words. Then he crossed to the sideboard to pour himself a drink from the selection of decanters. It was rather early to begin imbibing, but given the circumstances I could hardly blame him. Especially as I was craving something with a bit more kick than the tea myself.

"Do you know what that was all about?" I couldn't help but turn to Helen and ask.

Her gaze was still on the doorway through which Walter had vanished. "The war, I suppose," she murmured in distraction. She closed the book she held in her lap, not bothering to mark her page. Though, in truth, she'd seemed to be more lost in her own thoughts than reading, even before Walter and Felix's tiff. "Would you excuse me?" she said, and rose to her feet to follow her fiancé.

I didn't bother to reply, for she didn't seem to need one.

Returning my attention to the scratch paper in my hands, I continued to sketch flowers along the border as I tried to focus on the first two lines of the code I'd penciled across the middle. Perhaps it was a bit reckless to set the lines I'd memorized to paper in such company, but it was easier to concentrate when the letters were before me and not just in my head. Besides, I couldn't very well keep track of the others' movements if I locked myself away in my room all day. Thus far no one had asked me what I was doing, though Max had fastened his inquisitive gaze on me more than once. When the butler called us all into luncheon a short time later, I folded the papers and tucked them into the pocket of my skirt before following the others from the room.

Sometime during the midst of the meal, there was a sudden lull in the din. I'd grown so accustomed to it that I glanced around at the others in confusion until I realized it was the rain. Precipitation had ceased to be driven against the windows.

Tom rose from his chair to peer through the drapes, before turning back to confirm what I'd suspected. "The rain has stopped. Or, at least, it's not coming down in such a deluge. But the wind is still gusting like the devil."

This pronouncement lightened the mood of the gathering

somewhat, though I felt a tightening around my ribcage, wondering what Sidney's reaction would be.

When luncheon was over, Max waylaid me outside of the dining room. "Shall we try the telephone?"

"Yes," I answered enthusiastically. Anything for a respite from the others, at least for a short time.

But when we reached the study, it seemed Walter had already had a similar idea. He stood tapping the switchhook, but to no avail. Pulling the earpiece away from his head, he offered it to Max. "It's still not working."

Max tried speaking into the mouthpiece and fiddling with the switchhook as well, but it only ended with him shaking his head.

"Shall I try the telephone in the butler's rooms?" Walter asked.

"Yes. Yes, do," Max replied.

Walter nodded and limped from the room, but Max's eyes remained narrowed in speculation on the study's telephone. I wasn't certain what he was thinking, but I knew it wasn't pleasant. I watched as he lifted the telephone's cord and traced it to its plug in the socket on the wall. Everything seemed in order, and yet I began to follow his implicit line of reasoning.

Crossing toward the window, I lifted aside the drape to gaze out over the windswept sea. Spurts of rain periodically dashed against the glass.

"It does seem rather odd that the telephones stopped operating so soon after the storm began." I sensed Max's solid presence as he moved to stand behind me. "Aren't most telephone cables laid on the seabed, under the water?"

"Yes," he murmured, and I could hear the same speculation in his voice.

"Then, how . . ."

But before I could finish my thought, Max turned toward the door. "Come with me."

Perhaps dashing off alone with him should have given me greater pause, but given the fact that I had a strong suspicion where we were headed, I didn't even hesitate. I followed him through the green baize door and down the stairs into the servants' domain. A maid carrying a stack of linens stumbled to a stop at the sight of us, nearly dropping her towering stack. However, Max strode on past her without a backward glance, headed for the servants' exterior entrance at the end of the long corridor.

A blast of chill air hit us as he opened the door. I wrapped my arms around me and braced my head against the wind as we climbed the shallow steps up into the outer yard. In such weather, it was deserted. Max glanced right and then left, before pacing around the exterior of the building toward the left.

A short distance along the stone wall, hidden by a shrub, he found what he was looking for. I leaned over his shoulder to watch as he knelt to examine the telephone wires where they entered the house.

Or where they should have. For these wires had been neatly severed.

CHAPTER 17

The telephone wires were not frayed or tattered, but had been deliberately cut with a knife or an ax.

A sinking feeling began in my gut and spread outward. Someone had wanted to prevent us from using the telephone. Someone had wanted to hinder our ability to contact the mainland. Which made sabotage of the yacht's motor and the intentional disappearance of the second boat seem even more likely.

Even though I could feel Max's gaze on me, I couldn't stop my eyes from straying toward the west, where I knew the farm and its outbuildings stood. Had Sidney done this? Could he have been so determined to keep us all here until he found the proof he sought and confronted the traitor and the man who'd attempted to kill him, whom I expected were one and the same, that he'd effectively trapped us here?

I didn't want to believe it. I didn't want to think it was even possible he would do such a thing. But I had seen the look in his eyes the night before—the ruthless resolve—and it had chilled me. As the lashing wind and those severed telephone wires chilled me now.

Max's head turned to follow my gaze. "I don't think we need to trace the wire to the telephone at the church to know it's also been cut."

I blinked at him as he rose to his feet, at first too lost in my own worries to follow what he was saying. Then I nodded, grateful the church lay in the same direction as the farm, and that he'd misinterpreted my concern.

"Let's go back inside," he prodded.

Shivering in the wind, I didn't need to be told twice. Max trailed me into the servants' level and up the stairs to the main floor. But when I would have hurried toward the drawing room and its warm hearth, he took hold of my arm to halt me.

"Our only way of getting help now is to get off this island," he said. "Which means I think we must inform the others. Or at least Walter. Because I haven't the slightest idea how to fix an engine."

"But what if Walter is the one doing all this," I whispered, glancing around to be certain we weren't overheard. "He owns this house. He invited us all here. And he easily could have been the officer who arranged to have those men framed for desertion, as well as Ben and Sidney killed." I choked on the last, hating that I had to maintain this ruse that my husband was dead, especially with Max. But I knew it was necessary.

"Then he already knows the lines are cut. And it will only look suspicious if he finds out we were outside examining them and yet didn't tell him what we'd discovered. Any number of servants saw us. We weren't exactly furtive."

I pressed a hand to my temple, having to concede his point. In any case, we couldn't very well keep this to ourselves if we wanted to have any hope of getting someone over to the mainland to fetch the authorities before the wind let up. The servants and yacht crew *might* attempt to return, but the later the hour grew, the less likely that became. After all, Walter had sent them home early the day before out of concern for their safety. Or so he said. It seemed only natural the servants would assume their employer expected the same of them today, and that they would receive a telephone call summoning them to the island if anything had changed. They couldn't know we were effectively stranded.

"Let's see if he's returned to his study," Max suggested.

However, we did not find him alone. We exchanged a look at the sound of raised voices within. One was Walter's, and the other we quickly learned belonged to Felix, as he snapped back a sneering retort.

"Well, it's evident, as usual, that you have no grasp of what's going on. And no control over it either."

I reached out to halt Max a few steps from the open doorway, curious to hear Walter's reply, but it was already too late. Felix had whirled toward the door, catching sight of us. He didn't bother to hide the glittering derision in his eyes.

"We've news," Max remarked, explaining our presence. "And I think you'll both want to hear it."

I studied Felix's face for any sign of uneasiness, but contempt seemed to have settled permanently over his features.

Walter, on the other hand, gripped the edge of his desk, as if bracing for a blow. "Not another body?"

Max's mouth flattened. "No, but the telephone lines running into the house have been cut. And I suspect those at the church have also."

Walter's brow furrowed. "Cut? Do you mean a tree limb or something has fallen on them?"

"No, this was definitely deliberate," Max assured him.

I was so focused on Walter's puzzled reaction that I almost missed Felix's. He rolled his eyes as if Max and I were a pair of old pensioners complaining about the price of tea instead of two perfectly rational people informing of something for which he should be truly alarmed. Someone had *purposely* severed those lines, cutting off our ability to contact the mainland, and yet he didn't seem the least concerned. Was that because he had already known about it because *he* was the saboteur? Or was he truly unconcerned for his safety? If so, how could he be so certain he was safe?

Walter stared down at his desk, his eyes clouded with worry, but not shock. "I suppose Tom and Sam should be informed."

"And the women?"

The three men glanced up at me blankly.

I frowned in annoyance. "Don't you think it's time to tell them?"

"No!" Walter replied with such force that I drew back. He flushed. "That is"—he cleared his throat—"definitely not."

"I agree," Felix said, scowling at our host in displeasure.

"You know how women can be." His eyes flicked to me as he added disingenuously, "Present company excluded, of course. They'll only imagine the worst. And I don't know about you, but I would rather not have to deal with a lot of female hysterics."

I arched my eyebrows in reproof. "Actually, in my experience, most women are rather better at keeping their heads than many of the men I know. But regardless, it seems to me that matters have progressed far beyond the point where we can continue to hide all of this from them. One of them is bound to start asking questions about why Jimmy and Charlie have not seen fit to join the rest of us downstairs. And what if they wish to use the telephone? Honestly, I'm surprised one of them hasn't already tried to do so. Are you going to continue to blame the weather?"

"Yes," Walter replied, as if there was no question about what we should do. "And . . . and we'll continue to explain that Jimmy and Charlie are ill."

"But ill with what?"

"We needn't be specific. None of us are doctors, after all."

"But Mabel—"

"Already knows about Jimmy, and I'm sure Sam has told her about Charlie."

I was somewhat surprised Walter had deduced this, but then again he'd known Sam and Mabel longer than I had.

"And what if the other women start asking her questions about this illness, what then?" I persisted. "You can't expect her to lie for the lot of you."

"We'll cross that bridge when we have to."

"Yes, when Nellie suddenly takes it into her head that both men have contracted the dreaded Spanish flu and we're keeping it from her," I retorted. After all, the last outbreak of the deadly virus, which had killed hundreds of thousands of British since it first appeared a year ago, had only just subsided in late April. Everyone was still bracing for its possible return for a fourth round.

"Well, don't give her any ideas," Walter protested.

I glared at him, frustrated by the men's refusal to listen to me. The women had as much a right to know what was going on as the rest of us. The men's insistence on keeping them in the dark was both offensive and dangerous.

What was Walter really so anxious to hide? He *was* the person each time who had been most insistent we keep the matter quiet. Why? Who was he apprehensive about discovering the truth? His fiancée? She seemed the obvious choice, but I supposed it could be one of the other women.

"Well, what's to be done?" Max asked, dismissing the matter of informing the women. He leaned his hip against the corner of Walter's desk. "Do you think you can repair your boat's motor?"

Walter's brow crinkled in affront. "I'll just have to now, won't I?" He opened a drawer in his desk and extracted what looked to be a key before slamming it shut again. "I'll work late into the night if I have to," he muttered, hobbling angrily around his desk to the door. "Tell Helen where I've gone if I don't appear for dinner."

We all stood silently, listening as his uneven footsteps receded down the hall.

Then Max turned to Felix. "In the meantime, I think we should find Sam and Tom, and pair up to search the island for any other boats that might be scattered about the place."

Felix's nose wrinkled. "I don't want to go out in this." He nodded in the direction our host had retreated. "Let Walter fix his cursed boat."

"And if he can't?" Max demanded, losing his patience. "No, it's best if we search while we still have daylight. And I need all of the men to help. Including you. We'll recruit whatever male servants we can find to our effort as well."

Max's tone brooked no argument and Felix relented, though not graciously.

"Fine. I'll just go change then, shall I?" he jeered, exiting the room.

Watching him disappear from sight, I remembered how Max and I had seen him returning from the pier late the afternoon before, just as the rain was beginning. He'd told us he'd merely wanted a bit of fresh air, but Felix had never struck me as the type to take constitutionals. It had seemed a flimsy excuse at the time, and now I had to wonder what he'd really been doing at the pier. Damaging Walter's boat engine, perhaps?

I turned to Max, who had finally deigned to shift his glance to me. Though I would have liked to discuss my theory with him, I was still too aggravated at him. So instead I arched a single eyebrow mockingly. "And I'll just stay here, shall I? Along with the other womenfolk."

He frowned as I brushed past him and out of the room. I had better things to do than to go traipsing about the island in this biting wind looking for a boat anyway. But that didn't mean I wasn't furious he hadn't spoken up to agree with me that the other women should be told. I'd supposed he had more common sense than that.

Undoubtedly, the best thing I could do to help us all was to break the code on that missive Sidney had given me. If the winds persisted and Walter couldn't get his yacht engine working or the other men couldn't locate another boat, then we were going to be stuck on this island for another night. Too much could go wrong between now and tomorrow morning. Too much I didn't want to contemplate.

That meant I needed to double down on my efforts to crack this cipher. Besides, something one of the men had said in the parlor had triggered something in my brain. It had been wiggling around in my neurons for the past few hours, and I thought I might be on to something.

I opened the door to my room, eager to set my notions to paper, and halted in my tracks.

My chamber had been ransacked. The sheets and counterpane had nearly been ripped from the bed, and the mattress was askew. Half of the clothes in my wardrobe had been pulled from their hangers, and the contents of the drawers had either been rifled through or discarded on the floor. The papers from the drawers in my desk had been unceremoniously dumped on top, and even the cushions had been yanked from their chairs.

For a moment, all I could do was stand there staring at it all, such was my shock. But surprise gradually gave rise to anger and trepidation. Whoever had done this had obviously been looking for something. And I had a very good idea what it was.

I began to rush forward, but then whirled around to lock my door. It wouldn't do for the perpetrator or anyone else to surprise me. Then I hurried over to the wardrobe, ignoring the rest of the mess, and shifted the remainder of the clothes cascading from the drawers so that I could close the top one and open the bottom. I thrust a hand past the back of the drawer, scraping my knuckles in my haste, and felt around behind it until my hand closed around a book.

Extracting it, I breathed a sigh of relief as the now-familiar cover of *The Pilgrim's Progress* met my gaze. I flipped through the pages, grateful to discover nothing was missing. Sidney's letter drawing me here, the coded missive, and the papers I'd scrawled with my previous attempts to decipher the code were all accounted for. Thank heavens I'd hidden them well.

Pressing the book and its extra pages to my chest, I glanced about me at the disarray, contemplating for the first time who might have done such a thing. As far as I knew, no one knew they existed except for me and Sidney.

I considered for a moment that my husband might have done this. After all, I'd refused to tell him where I'd hidden them the night before. But that made no sense. Sidney had lured me here for the sole purpose of decrypting this missive. Why would he then steal it back from me?

Unless he'd found the key to the code.

No, that still didn't seem right. If he'd needed the missive back, he could have sent me another letter through the butler as he had his warning not to trust anyone. Or at the very least he could have left me a note here in my room after he'd failed to find what he was looking for.

Rising to my feet, I searched through the papers scattered about the desk and on the floor, but none contained any writing.

So that meant the culprit was someone else. Someone who was also aware that I possessed this coded missive. My breath tightened in my chest at the thought, and I glanced toward the locked door.

It only made sense for that person to also be the traitor Sidney was so desperate to expose. For who else would even be cognizant of the missive's existence and what it meant? How they knew I had it, I didn't know, but I was all of a sudden very conscious of the danger I was in. If the traitor and killer were one and the same, as I felt they must be, then they had already killed twice to keep their secrets. What would stop them from doing so again?

Inhaling deeply, I struggled to settle my nerves, and push my worries and fears aside. Nothing had changed. I still needed to decrypt this code. And I couldn't do that if I couldn't concentrate.

Tidying the stationery on the top of my desk as I wanted to tidy my mind, I pushed it to the corner and sat down to set to work.

It was Felix who I believed had uttered the words "retreat and panic," and though I was certain he hadn't been referencing a cipher at the time, it had prompted something in my brain nonetheless. My friend George, the decryption expert, had mentioned more than one transposition cipher I had never had cause to use. One of which had been called a *route cipher*.

When creating a route cipher, the plaintext was written out in columns of a given dimension and then converted to code using a predetermined pattern. The pattern could be as simple or elaborate as one wished, and depending on the complexity, make the algorithm challenging to decipher. With so much text, I could spend months searching for the right configuration, but there was something about the lettering near the middle of the missive that made me suspect some sort of spiral pattern had been used. And not just any spiral pattern, but a backward one. Probably more than one, dividing the missive into sections.

Setting pencil to paper, I began to try to translate it back to plaintext. It took me several faulty starts, but my heart quickened as I realized I'd finally stumbled onto the correct pattern. I worked as rapidly as I could at the painstaking work, though it still took me the better part of an hour to finish the task.

But when at last I could sit back and read the missive in its entirety, my elation swiftly faded to confusion and alarm. The information contained within didn't merely talk of troop movements or the position of artillery. It referenced events in London. Political policy, propaganda efforts, and broad, sweeping battle strategies. This data could have only come from a prominent politician of some standing, or someone close to him.

My deliberations immediately turned to Max. His father had been a great political force, a member of the Prime Minister's inner circle, and a man whom many believed would one day be Prime Minister himself until his sudden death seven months earlier. Could Max have been sharing with the enemy secrets his father had revealed to him? Was he the traitor?

I didn't want to consider such a thing was possible. Not Max. But I had to face the facts.

However, that didn't mean that I wasn't also going to explore other options. Helen's father had also been a politician, though not one of nearly as great a standing as the former Earl of Ryde. I wasn't certain he would have been privy to some of the information contained in this missive. As for the others, I knew Tom and Nellie's backgrounds and families fairly well, but I was almost completely unfamiliar with some of the others'. I would have to remedy that.

Glancing at the clock on the mantel, I decided it was time I sought out Sidney while I still had the chance. The skies were still leaden, so night would fall fast, and it was only a matter of time before the men searching for another boat would return, if they hadn't already.

I grabbed my Donegal tweed coat and its matching forest green Torin-style side cap, and made my way as stealthily as possible down to the conservatory and out the French doors Max and I had used the night before. There I could skirt along the perimeter of the house and into the gardens, hopefully without being seen from any of the windows that looked out on the terrace. The ground was saturated and muddy in spots, but I decided I had less of a chance of being seen on the garden paths than on the roads. I figured there must be a trail that cut away from the gardens to the west and the farm beyond, and was pleased when after only a few wrong turns, I was able to find it.

The wind whipped at me fiercely as I stumbled downhill across an open field toward the buildings I could see in the distance. After the labyrinth of shrubberies in the garden, I felt horribly exposed with nothing but tufts of grass and heath for cover. To the north, a stone wall tangled with overgrowth stretched along the perimeter of the meadow, separating it from the main road. I only hoped no one traveling that lane looked south and caught sight of me.

I inched cautiously around to the front of the first row of buildings, relieved to see that the gravel yard beyond was empty. At this time of day, I supposed most of the gardeners and laborers would be at their duties, even with the wind and damp hindering them. Sidney had told me his lodgings were the farthest to the left when facing the front of the building, so I glided as silently as I could around the corner and down to the first door.

As I'd suspected, it was locked. But I was prepared for just such an eventuality. Pulling my set of lock picks from my pocket, I set to work and had managed to open the rather rudimentary lock within a minute and a half. The smell of Sidney's Turkish cigarettes washed over me as I entered the room, and I knew I had the correct chamber. I closed the door behind me and reached out to twitch the simple curtains covering the room's lone window aside just far enough to provide me with a sufficient amount of light to see.

The space was tiny, no larger than a ten-by-ten square. In one corner stood a sink next to a low cupboard and a small table with two chairs. In the opposite corner sat a narrow bed, scarcely more than a cot, and a two-drawer dresser. The floors were swept clean, the bedding pulled tight. Everything seemed to be in its precise place. Even the rag draped over the sink's edge was positioned just so. Except for the papers scattered across the surface of the small table next to a typewriter.

I moved closer, curiosity outweighing any consideration I might have felt about invading Sidney's privacy. Some of the papers were organized in crude stacks—though I could not immediately discern the order—while others were spread open and jumbled together at the center of the work space. There were pages of notes; letters from varied correspondents—some addressed to him, some not—maps; charts; newspaper clippings; even photographs of people and places both familiar and unknown to me.

There was too much to make sense of it all—not in such a short time—apart from the fact that Sidney seemed obsessed. I wanted to call it mere determination, a firm resolve to right the wrong and justify his desertion, but this had clearly become the sole purpose of his existence. There was nothing else in the room, save the spare necessities. Not a book, or a deck of cards, or a chessboard, or a memento from his past was stored in any of the drawers, or cupboards, or tucked up under the thin mattress. Nothing but the small photograph of me and the button from my wedding dress I'd forgotten he'd taken with him to the front as a sort of amulet, which I found rolled up in one of his shirts.

I stared down at the picture, trying to remember what it had been like to be that naïve, hopeful girl. But five years separated me from her. Five years of war, and pain, and struggle, and loneliness, and loss, and horrors I could never unsee, actions I could never undo, words I could never take back. Part of me hated that young, fresh-faced girl, while the other part of me wished I could turn back the clock and do so many things differently.

I didn't hear him until the door swung open and he stood half in front of and half behind the door frame. In the gloomy light of the stormy afternoon it was difficult to see at first that it was, in fact, my husband, but my other senses seemed to have known it before my eyes, for I did not cower or reach for a weapon. And a good thing, too. For as Sidney entered the room, shutting the door behind him, I could see he gripped a pistol. One I was certain he wouldn't have hesitated to use if necessary.

CHAPTER 18

"How did you get in?" Sidney demanded.

"Do you really need to ask that?" I responded wearily.

His gaze flicked down at the picture in my hands and then back to my face.

"You kept it," I remarked lightly, before leaning forward to set it and the button back in his drawer.

"Of course." He spoke as if such a comment on my part was inane, as if holding on to my picture and the button was the most natural thing in the word. And maybe for him, it was. But in light of everything, it was quite a different matter for me.

"I see you've been gathering your evidence diligently." I nodded toward his table strewn with papers, wishing he had pursued me even a fraction as persistently.

He ignored my remark, moving deeper into the room. "Why are you here?" His dark eyes searched my face. "Have you broken the cipher?"

I stood so that I could be at a more even level with him, even though he towered more than a foot over me, and arched a single eyebrow. "Why else would I have troubled you?"

He hesitated a moment, perhaps realizing how wounding his gruffness was to our already fragile relationship, perhaps doubting the veracity of my statement. Whatever the truth, he wasted no time in homing in on what he'd made very clear was most important to him.

"You've done it."

My mouth flattened into a thin line, wanting to deny it, but I knew something more important than me or my feelings was at stake. "Yes. Though, I'm not sure how pleased you'll be." Reaching into my coat pocket, I extracted the translated text.

He eagerly took it from my hands and moved toward the window, where he pushed the curtains wider to let in the murky daylight. His brow furrowed in concentration as he read through the document, and I watched as dawning comprehension and its accompanying frustration suffused his features. He turned the paper over, obviously hopeful there was more, and I was sorry to disappoint him.

"This is all of it?" He gestured with the paper. "There isn't another part to decode?"

"That's all of it."

He swiped a hand back through his thick hair and lowered the paper to his side. "I thought *surely* there would be some clear indication who the traitor was. There would be a name, or a distinguishing remark, or some sort of conclusive proof."

"People writing coded messages are rarely stupid enough to sign their names to them," I told him, not ungently.

He stared at me blankly and then nodded. "Yes, I suppose you're right." He sank down on the edge of the bed.

I gazed down at his lowered head, hating to see how dejected he was. His cold, single-minded pursuit of the truth was easier to take than this. My heart clenched, wishing I could do something to ease his pain. Wishing I could sweep away all of this madness and take him home to our flat in Berkeley Square. But nothing was ever as simple as it should be.

I sat down beside him, taking the decrypted letter from his loose fingers. "It's not entirely useless," I pointed out. "It does tell us that whoever the traitor is, he had powerful connections in London. That the treason being committed was far higher reaching than we even suspected." I glanced at Sidney. "Or at least, higher than I suspected."

He exhaled sharply. "Yes, but it does not name names. I need *proof,* Verity." He flipped his hand toward the table covered in papers. "I have evidence that treason was being committed, but no confirmation who was doing it. The War Office isn't just going to want a lot of theories and suppositions that something was going on. They're going to want names. Hard facts. And I won't destroy a bunch of men's reputations without sound evidence of who truly *is* the culprit."

"So what do you wish to do?" I asked, struggling to hold on to my own temper.

"There's nothing else *to* do," he muttered. "I'll just have to keep searching."

"For how long?"

"For as long as it takes." He glanced sideways at me, bristling with aggravation. "What choice do I have?"

"And what am I to do?" I bit out. "Return home to wait for you? Continue to pretend you're dead?"

His demeanor softened, as if finally grasping what a difficult situation he'd placed me in, and how very close I was to losing my composure. "I know it's a lot to ask of you."

"It's an *intolerable* thing to ask of me." I pushed to my feet, needing distance from him, and went to stare down at the detritus of the last fifteen months of his life scattered across the table.

He heaved an aggrieved sigh. "*This* is exactly why I didn't contact you before. I knew it would be impossible to make you understand."

I whirled around to face him in furious disbelief. "What I can't understand is why you must do this alone. I realize you wish to protect the men who were your fellow officers and closest allies through nearly four hellish years of war, but isn't it the War Office's job to figure out who is guilty and who is innocent? Haven't you sacrificed enough? Haven't I?" I inhaled a shaky breath. "Or don't I count for anything in all of this?"

He jumped to his feet. "Don't count for anything?" he snapped, then cursed roundly as he strode forward to grip my waist. "Why do you think I'm so desperate to solve this? To come home to *you*."

I stared up into his glimmering eyes and reached up to grasp his square jaw firmly between my hands. "Then end this. Take the evidence you have to the authorities and let *them* figure out who is behind it all."

"And if they don't believe me?"

I stiffened. "What do you mean? Why wouldn't they believe you?"

He squeezed my waist in emphasis. "I'm a deserter, Verity. If I had been caught during the war I would have faced a firing squad."

I dropped my hands from his face to his shoulders. "Yes, but clearly you had a reason—"

"And what if they think it's all a lie? What if they think *I'm* the traitor?"

My brain stumbled over my response. "But your evidence—"

"*You* believed it."

I frowned. "I did not believe it. Or not truly. I wanted to know how the letter writer had known I was in the Secret Service and why they were making up such ludicrous nonsense about my husband."

"And when you found the coded missive tucked inside my book?" he pressed, unwilling to let the matter go. "What then?"

I wanted to lie. To tell him that I'd not doubted him for a second. But I could already tell he knew the answer. "I . . . I didn't know what to think. But *you* were the one who tucked it into the spine of your copy of *The Pilgrim's Progress,* not the traitor."

"Ah, but you have only my word on that."

I paused, startled by what he was suggesting.

"Are you going to lie about where you found it, about the other things that happened this weekend when you're questioned?"

His gaze was sharp, already knowing the answers. I wouldn't lie, I couldn't, not even for Sidney.

"You do realize that Scotland Yard as a whole is not a very imaginative bunch. Who do you think they're going to decide murdered Tufton and Montague once they discover I'm here? I'm supposed to be dead, but here I am. Pretending to be a gardener, hiding in the wings, waiting to exact revenge for something I believe to be true, whether it is or not."

I shook my head, trying to pull away, but he held fast, making me stare up at him as he pressed on ruthlessly.

"Maybe one of them shot me. Maybe one of them is a traitor. Or maybe I made it all up in my head. Just another sorry case of shell shock. A man who can't leave the war behind. A man who's lost his mind."

"It's not true," I protested.

"Are you certain?" His eyes had lost their luster. "I know you saw it during my last leave in London."

I stilled, staring up at him in horror.

"You never said anything, but I could see it in your eyes. The worry, the uncertainty, the reticence."

I opened my mouth to deny it, but he cut me off.

"Don't." His voice was stark with pain. "Denying it won't make it better."

I swallowed against the answering lump in my throat, managing to choke out just a few words. "I'm sorry."

He inhaled raggedly, leaning forward to press his forehead to mine as I fought back tears. "I know, Verity. Please. Don't apologize." He rolled his head back and forth against mine. "I'm not . . . blaming you. I'm merely making the point that Scotland Yard and the War Office will." He lifted his head to look down at me. "And no matter how hard you might try to deny it means anything, they will see it differently." His lips curled into a tight grimace devoid of humor. "After all, you're just my wife."

I understood what he meant. None of them would know of my work with the Secret Service, and I was forbidden from speaking of it. I was just a simple society wife who knew nothing of the war or what the men who had fought in it had gone through.

"Then I'll contact C," I replied, unwilling to go down without a fight.

But it was Sidney's turn to shake his head. "If you mean your chief, I doubt he will take much of an interest in the matter."

"Of course, he will. This is treason we're talking about. And besides, he rather liked me. He was gruff and difficult at times, but I overheard him say that while most of the men who worked for him were blackguards, I had a remarkably keen intellect. How else do you think I was ever allowed to do any fieldwork?"

A genuine smile lit his eyes. "I'm sure that's so, but it still won't serve." He reached up to brush a stray curl back from my cheek. "Calling in the Secret Service, blowing your cover, and possibly being brought up on charges because of it won't clear me of blame."

I studied his face while my brain worked feverishly, trying to figure out a way he could be reasoned with, but ultimately I knew he was right. I had seen firsthand how our government agencies often handled things. They preferred to have someone to blame rather than no one, and Sidney would so easily fit the bill.

"Then what do we do?" I asked.

"We find the culprit. Preferably *before* anyone gets off this island."

Given all our setbacks, I pondered whether that was even possible. "And if we don't?"

"Then I'd better depart before the authorities arrive."

I followed his gaze toward the window, where the light was already beginning to fade.

"The men were searching the island for any other functional boats, and Walter was trying to fix the motor on his," I informed him, then tilted my head in suspicion. "Were you the one who sabotaged it?"

His mind was somewhere else, for he answered me almost absently. "No, I've been wondering if that was a bit of mischief on someone's part." His brow furrowed. "I wonder why . . . Oh, but wait. Toby left the island about a week ago."

"The laborer who was good with mechanical things?"

His gaze dipped to meet mine. "Yes."

"Do you know where he went?"

"No, I didn't even see him leave." His eyes searched mine. "It does seem awfully coincidental, doesn't it?"

I arched my eyebrows. "That Walter's boat engine should break so soon after he left? Quite." Leaning back, I watched his face for a reaction. "Did you know the telephone lines have also been deliberately cut?"

The corners of his eyes crinkled as he muttered dryly. "Searching me for signs of guilt, are we, Verity? Yes, I discovered the line at the church had been cut, and surmised the one at the house must have been also."

I wanted to believe he'd had nothing to do with the matter, but his amusement over my suspicion made it difficult to tell. That is, until he spoke next.

"Did *you* know that Tufton's body has been moved to the church to be laid out beside Montague's?"

My eyes widened in alarm. "You mean Walter never contacted the authorities yesterday?"

Sidney shook his head.

"But he told us he had. Max even asked what they had said about Jimmy's apparent suicide, whether they had agreed. Why would Walter have lied?"

He didn't have to answer that, for I already knew. Either he was the murderer, or he was covering for someone who was.

But Sidney had latched on to another part of my statement. "Didn't Ryde think it was odd that the authorities never questioned him?"

I shifted my gaze from where I had been staring over Sidney's shoulder to meet his scrutiny.

"I mean, I assume you didn't expect to be questioned because men tend to shield women from such matters, thinking they're too delicate. But Ryde should have known he would be quizzed on the matter. And yet he didn't say anything when Walter lied."

My head was spinning at the implications, trying to recall exactly what Max had said. "Well, neither did Sam."

"Yes, but that's because he knows he's supposed to try to stand back and observe, as much as it's possible for him to do so, without interfering."

Part of me wanted to defend Max, to deny that he could possibly be playing a part in all of this. After all, he had become, at the very least, a friend. Someone I felt to some extent I could rely on, particularly with things being so strange between me and my newly resurrected husband. But I knew that doing so would be foolish. After all, I had already begun to harbor suspicions about him after decoding that missive. This was but one more reason to be wary.

However, Sidney seemed to think my frown indicated something else, for his jaw hardened. "Is that how it is, then?"

"How what is?"

He scoffed. "You've been a widow for all of fifteen months. I'm sure it's been lonely."

I gasped at the pain his horrid words caused me. It was as if he'd thrust a blade into my heart and twisted. Especially knowing the secret I harbored from him. The secret that had racked me with guilt even before I'd known he was still alive.

I pushed away from him, trying to break free of his grasp, but Sidney only pulled me closer, wrapping his arms around me.

"Let me go," I gulped, desperate to be free.

"Verity, wait," he pleaded. "I'm sorry. That was uncalled for."

"It . . . it was . . . monstrous!" I retorted, still trying to pull away.

"I know, I know. Please, Verity, stop. Please."

I could have called on my training to force him to let me go, but I didn't want to hurt him. Not when I could hear the genuine remorse in his voice. It worked quite effectively in breaking down my defenses, and I fell against his chest, sobbing.

He gathered me close, running his hands through my hair as he murmured apologies and self-recriminations. But I only wished he would stop talking. For with each expression of regret, each insult he heaped on himself, he thrust the knife deeper.

"Stop," I hiccuped. "Just stop."

When he didn't, whether because he couldn't hear me or he didn't believe that's what I really wanted, I lurched up on my tiptoes and pressed my lips to his. It took only a split second for him to respond, and when he did it was like it had always been between us, like a flame to tinder, sweeping me away until I didn't know where one breath started and the next began.

How much time had passed exactly, I wasn't sure, but I did know it was Sidney who tore his mouth away from mine first. Our breathing was ragged. Our chests rose and fell rapidly against each other. And I found I had been backed up against the table, practically seated on it, with my husband pressed between my legs. I physically ached for him to continue, but my mind had begun to clear, even with his face buried in the sensitive curve between my shoulder and my neck.

Now was not the time for this. No matter how much I might think I wanted it, once the haze of passion dissipated I would regret it. There were too many things unresolved between us. Too many things left to be said.

For one thing, I wasn't entirely certain I trusted him. Not after everything that had happened. And for another, what if I were to become pregnant from this clandestine encounter? After all, it had happened once before, during his second to last leave he'd spent in London. But before I could write to tell him, it had been over. At the time, I'd been glad I'd kept it to myself and wouldn't have to snatch back such happy news through a letter. I'd planned to tell him all during his next leave, but then he'd seemed so distracted, so haunted, I simply couldn't bring it up and add to his pain. So I'd remained silent, never again having the chance to tell him. Until now, though it was hardly the time.

If I were to become pregnant again, it would be weeks before I knew it, and what if in that time we were unable to find proof of who the traitor was and Sidney insisted on disappearing again? What would I do then?

No. It was better this way. Better to keep our heads about us than add to the guilt and remorse already heaped between us. When . . . *If* I ever slept with Sidney again, I didn't want there to be any doubts between us. Or at least not a mountain of them.

I pushed him away from me, and though at first he resisted, a moment later he retreated. His deep blue eyes didn't even hold a question. He already understood.

Grateful not to have to explain, I lifted a trembling hand to my hair, brushing it back from my temple as I stepped to the side and readjusted my skirt with my other hand. When I felt I could speak without my voice shaking, I turned back to face him.

"I should go."

He looked up from where his gaze had been trained on the floor as if to stare a hole in it.

"I'll . . . I'll see what I can find out about the others' pasts. Try to ascertain who might have had the right political connections to obtain the information contained in that coded missive." I nodded at where the paper containing the letter's plaintext translation lay wrinkled on the bed. "And whether they utilized those connections. Even Max," I added at the last, wanting to reassure Sidney that I could be impartial.

"There's something else you should know," he said.

I could tell by the wariness in his eyes it was something I wasn't going to like hearing.

He shifted his feet so that he could face me more fully, but backed up to lean against the wall at the foot of the bed, crossing his arms over his chest. I wondered if he was trying to put as much distance between us as possible because he was afraid of what I would do, or what he would do.

"The informant who gave me that missive, the traitor's liaison in France, she also suggested I speak to the officer stationed as the town major. The man handling logistics and translation between the locals and the British Army," he began to explain as if I didn't understand what that meant.

I raised a hand to forestall him. "I know what a town major is."

He pressed his lips together, as if holding back a question or a comment, and then dipped his head in acknowledgment. "Of course. Well, she suspected this officer was bribed for his silence on the matter, as she was never caught until after the man was injured and replaced."

A worrying thought entered my mind. "What village was this?"

My nerves tightened when he didn't immediately answer.

"Suzanne," he murmured.

I pressed a hand to my abdomen in astonishment. "Are you telling me Tom Ashley may be mixed up in this mess as well?" I'd assumed that of all the guests at this house party, all the male ones in any case, my childhood friend was the only one I could safely exclude from the matter.

"I'm afraid so. Though it might not be as bad as all that," Sidney hastened to assure me. "I was never able to find proof that Ashley was ever bribed. No suspicious income or expenditures. In fact, he's far more in debt than he ever was. *Unlike* Walter and Halbert, who both received hefty influxes of cash during the war and just after."

I didn't ask how he'd uncovered all of that when he'd supposedly remained safely distant from London all these months. I didn't want to know just then.

"However, Tom Ashley still might know something," he said. "Something he doesn't even realize is important, that could help us uncover who the traitor is."

"And you want me to question him?"

"Him or his wife. Whoever you think will talk to you. Perhaps he shared something with her or revealed something in his letters." Seeing my sour expression and misinterpreting it, he frowned. "What? I thought you wished to help?"

I shook my head, brushing it aside. "I'll speak to Tom."

It was obvious he wanted to ask more, but he kept his queries to himself. "Good."

I moved toward the door, but he stopped me with a hand on my arm.

"And, Verity? Remember, don't—"

"Don't trust anyone," I spoke with him. "I got it the first time."

He nodded, releasing my arm.

I studied his carefully neutral expression. "What are *you* going to do?" I could tell he didn't want to answer, for he broke eye contact.

"Me? I'm going to find Walter."

My eyes widened in alarm.

"Perhaps a more direct approach is called for."

His voice was hard, brooking no argument, but I ventured one anyway. "Is that wise?"

"Maybe not. But we've run out of time, and I'm tired of wondering if Walter is still my friend or a foe."

I pressed my lips together to keep from begging him to reconsider. His mind was already made up. "Well, be careful," I said as my chest squeezed in dread.

"I always am." I opened the door, almost missing the last statement he muttered under his breath. "Little good it's done me."

CHAPTER 19

Upon my return to the castle, I was frustrated to find I couldn't locate Tom in any of the public rooms. Felix and Sam were slumped before the hearth in the library, their search for another boat having been fruitless. A small rowboat had been located in a shed behind the old customs house, but a hole they discovered in the bottom of it rendered it less than useless. They told me that Max and Tom's search had also proved futile, but they had no idea where either man had taken themselves off to since then.

Flustered and restless, I stood at the bottom of one of the staircases, considering my options. It was possible Tom had retreated to his bedchamber. If so, I could ask a servant to deliver him a message, but that might draw more attention to my eagerness to speak with him than I wished. Despite the urgency, I thought it best not to make my quest too obvious.

I was debating my next step when Nellie emerged at the top of the stairs. Catching sight of me at the bottom, she hesitated a moment before lifting her chin and descending.

Despite my anger toward the woman, I had no desire to quarrel with her. In fact, I would have preferred not to speak with her at all. But there was too much at stake. So, I pasted on a pleasant expression. "Good afternoon, Nellie. Do you know where I might find Tom?"

She halted a few steps above me, forcing me to crane my neck backward to look up at her, and narrowed her eyes. "Why? You wrecked your own marriage, so now you feel you need to wreck mine?"

I inhaled a sharp breath, astonished by her accusation. But my shock swiftly gave way to fury. It swept through my veins— hot and fierce. I climbed the steps to stand even with her. "I have had enough from you, Nellie May Sutton Ashley. What is your problem? Why are you being so wretchedly cruel?"

"I've seen the way you dangle after Tom," she sniffed. "Clinging to his arm, hanging on his every word. Oh, I knew I should never have come here! The cards told me this would happen."

"You *must* be joking," I scoffed.

"I have two eyes."

"Then you must be blind. Tom?! For heaven's sake, Nellie. I haven't the slightest interest in your husband that way. It would be like carrying on with one of my brothers." My face contorted at the thought. "What on earth sort of nonsense is this?" And why was she consulting tarot?

"Well, maybe you aren't interested in Tom," she grudgingly conceded. "But he's certainly interested in you."

"Oh, Nellie, no, he's not," I replied wearily.

"He is," she insisted. "You should hear how he talks about you. About how brave and resilient you are. How he knows any number of chaps who would marry you in a heartbeat. How any man would be lucky to have you, so they'd better act fast before you take a fancy to someone else."

I stared at her in disbelief. "*Tom* said all this?"

"Yes."

"Was he drunk?" I asked baldy, having difficulty imagining him uttering any of those words, especially to his green with envy wife. Was he *trying* to infuriate her?

Her nostrils flared. "That doesn't signify. He still said it."

I wanted to howl with frustration. Of course, it signified. "But you *do* understand none of that means he has any interest in me? Besides, he's already married. To *you*," I pointed out needlessly.

Her mouth tightened into that little moue I hated, indicating she was biting back whatever beastly retort was stewing in her malicious little mind.

I sighed, turning to retreat to the parlor. "This is ridiculous."

"It's not ridiculous," she snapped. "But you wouldn't understand, would you? Your husband died a hero before you could ever wonder if he would grow tired of you."

I swung back around, my patience at an end. "Yes, Nellie. You got your wish, didn't you?" I retorted, harking back to those horrid words she'd shrieked at me days before my wedding to Sidney. "He never returned to me. Aren't you happy?" It didn't matter that the outcome was no longer true, that my husband was alive. It was the vindictiveness of her words that counted, and the fact she'd never apologized for uttering them. For all she knew, they *had* come true. Just as I'd believed until eighteen hours ago.

"Well, at least that wasn't by choice!" she fired back, then turned aside, as if she could no longer face me.

I stared up at her in dawning comprehension, lowering my voice. "You mean . . ."

"Tom wants a divorce." Her words were clipped and brittle like ice.

I didn't know how to respond. The part of me that could still recall our earlier friendship with any warmth wanted to wrap her up in my arms, while the rest of me wanted to chide her for her petty, manipulative behavior, which had helped put her into this situation in the first place. But it was none of my affair, and in any case, Nellie would never listen to my advice. She was merely following her mother's example.

I'd watched Mrs. Sutton wheedle and harass her husband for years. Mr. Sutton largely ignored his wife or retreated into his study, but Tom had never been so complacent. And with divorce now becoming more and more acceptable, especially with the large number of soldiers returning to wives they'd hastily wed before being shipped off to the front and now barely knew, I would have been surprised had Tom not considered it. But I *was* sorry it had come to this, and I told Nellie so.

She turned aside. "Yes, well, it's my fault, isn't it?"

I was astounded to hear her admit any blame. Maybe she *was* aware of her own part in the matter. Not that Tom was perfect. I was certain he held a fair share of the responsibility.

But then she spoke again.

"I should have known better than to fall for an Ashley's charms. Or be stupid enough to think he would know the meaning of the word *loyalty*." With a twitch of her skirt, she whirled around and marched back up the steps.

I sighed and shook my head. Even if I wanted to help, there was nothing I could do. Not if she didn't want to listen. And she'd made it abundantly clear I was the last person she wished advice from.

"What was that about?"

I turned to see Tom striding toward me, his hands tucked in his pockets, watching his wife disappear around the corner above.

"You don't want to know," I told him, refusing to step into the middle of Nellie and Tom's conjugal difficulties. I had enough problems to deal with, including my own marital issues. "But I do need to speak with you."

Tom's eyebrows lifted. "Oh?"

I gestured for him to follow me down the hall to the left, away from the parlor, and into a shallow alcove. It was private, but also quite proper, as we were visible to anyone coming or going through this part of the castle, as they were to us.

He sat next to me on the mahogany bench nestled in the niche with a jaunty grin. "Why all the secrecy, Pip?"

"I need to ask you about the time you spent serving in the village of Suzanne on the Somme as a town major."

He straightened in surprise, but otherwise did not seem particularly wary. "What do you wish to know?"

I hesitated to lay my cards out on the table, but I didn't quite know how else to approach the matter. "Were you aware that a woman in that village was arrested on suspicion of being a German informant not long after you were injured?"

He frowned. "No, but I suppose that's not entirely unexpected. There were a number of instances when soldiers . . . *meeting* with the local women were not as circumspect as they should have been. It was a common problem."

"Well, in this instance, I'm afraid she was more of a . . . regular friend. One of our soldiers was passing coded missives to her to be carried on to the enemy."

Tom blinked at me in bewilderment. "You're quite serious."

"I'm afraid so."

His gaze drifted to the floor and his hand lowered to his leg. He began to rub almost subconsciously the place where the bullet must have hit him. "Well, I didn't know anything about it," he glanced up again to say. "How do you?"

I ignored his query in favor of asking my own. "Did you notice whether any of our men had a particular association with any of the women in the village? Someone who visited often, or sent messages to a woman there? This man would likely have been an officer? Maybe even someone attending this very house party?"

He had been searching the floor at his feet as if it could somehow give him answers, but at this last question, his head snapped up in alarm, and I could tell he'd thought of something. However, he pressed his lips together, as if unwilling to admit it.

"Tom," I coaxed. "You know this is important, or I would never ask it of you."

His eyes were dark with shadows, but he relented with a nod. He swallowed, as if working up the courage to speak. "Walter. I always suspected he had a lover in town. A French mistress. He visited her a few times, and she seemed to regularly receive love letters and packages from him. I even joked with him about it once, and he led me to believe . . ." He shook his head. "Exactly what I wanted to." He cursed. "I can't believe it." He glanced sideways at me. "You're sure?"

I nodded and he cursed again, sinking his head back against the wall behind us.

"So you didn't suspect the truth about her?" I asked calmly, though my heart beat faster at his confirmation of Sidney's and my suspicions.

He lifted his head to look at me with wild eyes. "No. Jeez! You don't honestly think I would have knowingly allowed such a thing to happen?"

I pressed a staying hand to his arm. "I don't. And I'm sorry, but the question had to be asked."

His face was tight with insult. "How do you know all this?" he demanded. "If someone else had suggested such a thing, I would have called them cracked. But I know you, Verity. You would never make such outlandish, defamatory accusations without good reason. What I don't understand is how you could have obtained such information."

His belief in me was bolstering, but it was obvious he also expected answers, and I couldn't give those to him. "You're right. I do have good reason. But I can't reveal all to you. Not yet. However, I promise I won't do anything to slander anyone's reputation without proof. That's why you must keep this conversation to yourself for now."

His eyes narrowed in misgiving, but he reluctantly acceded. "For now."

"Thank you," I replied, then opened my mouth to press him for more information.

Until the door at the end of the hall opened behind me, letting in a blast of cool air from outside. I turned to see Max staggering inside, carrying Walter.

"I could use . . . some help," he panted between breaths.

Tom and I rushed forward.

"What happened?" I demanded as Tom took part of Walter's weight from Max. The pair of them formed a sort of sling between their arms, which afforded me my first clear view of our host.

I pressed my hand to my mouth in shock at the sight of his face distended and contorted, and covered in red hives. He appeared to be unconscious, though it was difficult to tell with his eyes almost swollen shut. His breath wheezed in and out of him in agonized gasps.

"I don't know," Max replied. "He appears to be suffering from some sort of reaction."

"Bee stings," I deduced. "Helen told us he's deathly allergic to them. Take him to his bedchamber. I'll find Mabel."

I dashed down the hall toward the parlor, praying Mabel was still there, as she had been twenty minutes prior. Not finding her seated by the hearth reading as I expected, I swung my gaze around the room.

Helen sat forward in her seat, reading the alarm on my face. "Verity?"

I located my quarry standing next to the drapes, looking out the window at the wind-swept garden. "Mabel, you're needed." My gaze flicked back toward Helen. "I believe Walter has suffered a bee sting. Maybe several. He's having difficulty breathing."

"A bee sting?!" Helen squeaked, rising to her feet. "In this weather?"

I didn't try to answer her, having wondered the very same thing. Instead I turned my steps toward the hall, leading Mabel and Helen from the room. "Max and Tom are carrying him up to his bedchamber," I explained as we lifted our skirts to mount the stairs.

"I'll just fetch my medical kit," Mabel explained, hurrying ahead of us as I let Helen overtake me to lead the way to the master bedchamber.

We reached the room just as Max and Tom were laying Walter back against the pillows and loosening his necktie. Helen rushed to his side, but I hung back near the door, knowing there was little I could do. I would only be in the way. Less than half a minute passed before Mabel hastened past me with her small case of supplies. Upon her arrival, Max and Tom withdrew to join me in the hall just outside the door.

"How is he?" I asked.

"Worse," Max replied succinctly, his face drawn with worry.

"What the devil happened?" Tom demanded to know, echoing my thoughts.

Max turned to us, shaking his head. "I don't know. I found

him crumpled next to the path leading up from the quay." His jaw hardened as he lifted his hand to examine a small red welt rising next to his knuckle. "But your suggestion that it was a bee sting was a good one. For there was a box of honeycomb swarming with bees kicked over next to him."

I shook my head at the impossibility of it. "But why? That makes no sense. Unless . . ." I paused as the implications struck me.

"Someone put it there on purpose," Max finished my thought.

How many people knew that Walter was allergic to bee stings? Helen hadn't exactly been secretive about the fact. She'd had no reason to be. And how many of us had known he was down at the pier, attempting to fix the engine on his yacht? That circumstance hadn't been private information either. Any one of us could have seized the opportunity.

Max glanced back toward where Walter lay struggling to catch his breath. "Depending on the number of stings he received and the severity of his reaction, this could prove the death of him."

I felt sickened. Especially when I remembered what Sidney had intended to do after I left him less than an hour before. When he'd said he wanted to confront Walter, surely he meant to talk to him, not to trigger a deadly reaction. That would make no sense. If Walter was dead, how could he find out the truth and prove it?

Unless his macabre jests about his going barmy from shell shock were not jests at all.

I shook the worrying thought aside to focus on the facts in front of us. If someone had placed that honeycomb swarming with bees in Walter's path—and it seemed impossible to believe it was not intentional—then they'd either wanted to do one of two things: kill him or send him a warning. It was conceivable that the perpetrator hadn't known how severe his reaction would be, so this could be a matter of intimidation rather than attempted murder. But given Jimmy's and Charlie's deaths, homicide seemed more probable.

Then if murder was the intent, I could only assume the motive was also the same as those previous deaths. Someone was trying to silence Walter or enact his revenge. If it was the former, then we were running out of men who could enlighten us as to what precisely had happened in the Thirtieth battalion.

A man who proved to be Walter's valet approached us, and Max filled him in on what had happened and sent him into the room to assist Mabel and Helen in whatever way he could. Then Max, Tom, and I withdrew ourselves from the doorway, turning toward the stairs.

"Whatever your previous feelings on the matter, I think it's *now* time to inform the other ladies what has been going on here," I said firmly. "We cannot keep this from them any longer."

Max exchanged a grim look with Tom over my head. "You're right. Let's gather everyone in the main parlor, save Mabel and Helen, of course."

Relieved not to have to argue with them, I split off to the right at the base of the stairs, headed toward the breakfast room and the conservatory to round up anyone who had strayed toward that part of the house. I stepped into the breakfast parlor just long enough to glance around, and finding it empty began to turn to leave again. But someone grabbed me from behind and pushed me deeper into the room.

CHAPTER 20

I whirled around and struck out at my assailant, only to have my blow blocked by Sidney's arm. My forearm stung from the impact.

"You have to stop doing that!" I hissed at him, rubbing the spot where a bruise was certainly forming.

"Do you think I relish having my wife try to maim me," he growled, glancing toward the door. "Unless you know of a better way for me to get your attention without drawing anyone else's, I'm afraid this is it."

I scowled up at him, lowering my voice to match his. "What do you want?"

He grabbed my shoulder, guiding me deeper into the corner, away from the door. "What happened to Walter? I saw Ryde carrying him into the house."

"Did he see you?" I asked, searching Sidney's face for any sign of dissembling. He seemed genuinely ignorant of the source of Walter's injuries, but I couldn't be sure.

"No," he snapped. "Was Walter shot? I didn't see any blood."

"Someone placed a box filled with honeycomb swarming with bees in his path so that he would kick it over. Or, at least, we presume that's what happened. That's how Max said he found him."

Sidney's eyes hardened. "And Walter is allergic."

"Yes." I didn't ask how he knew. They had been friends since boyhood. It only made sense that he was aware of Walter's sensitivity.

He cursed, turning his head to stare out the window. "Is Mabel with him?"

"Yes."

"Does she think he'll survive?"

"I don't know," I admitted hesitantly, feeling my throat tighten in answer to the distress stamped across my husband's face. Despite the fact that he'd accepted that Walter might very well be a traitor who had tried to kill him, he still evidently cared for him. It was difficult to dismiss decades of attachment, no matter the cause.

He didn't speak, but I could see the pain carving grooves between his eyebrows as he struggled to master his emotions.

"There's something else you should know," I said, then told him the information Tom had shared with me about Walter's French "mistress" in the village of Suzanne.

"Could he describe the woman?"

"I didn't get a chance to ask. Max stumbled in the door carrying Walter."

Sidney's face was like stone—harsh and rigid. As was his voice, when he next spoke. "So it appears Walter was the traitor, after all. Unless more than one man was visiting this woman and sending her letters."

We both knew that wasn't likely given all the facts we knew.

"Then who is killing all the men from the Thirtieth?" I asked in consternation. "Walter's spy chief? Another accomplice—maybe Felix?"

"It could be," Sidney replied, but I could tell another thought had occurred to him and I didn't like it.

If Walter died, if he took whatever secrets he held to the grave, would we ever learn the truth? Would we ever find the proof to justify Sidney's decision not to return to the ranks after his recovery from his gunshot wound? Had his last chance to return to his old life a free man just slipped through our fingers?

Pushed past my endurance, I reached out to grip his shirt in my hands. "Forget this. Forget it all," I pleaded. "We'll . . . we'll run away together. I'll go wherever you wish to go. To Europe?

To America? Just name it. We can start our lives over there. No one here ever need know you're alive."

His hands came up to clasp my shoulders. "Verity, I could never ask that of you."

"You're not. I'm the one suggesting it, remember? Not you."

"Yes, but think of your family, your friends, the life you've built for yourself."

"What life?" I scoffed.

He smiled sadly. "You might very well never see them again. And you would have to lie to them, never telling them the truth. Could you really do that?"

"I . . . I know it wouldn't be easy," I stammered, faltering. "But we would have each other." I stared up at him. "That counts for a lot."

I could see that he was conflicted. His deep blue eyes swam with doubts and uncertainties.

"Please, Sidney," I implored him, putting all of my heartache into my words. "Give this up. For me."

He stood stiffly in indecision for one more moment and then shook his head, shattering what little hopes I still had of salvaging our marriage after the revelations of the past day, along with my heart.

"I can't, Verity," he replied, as I backed out of his arms. "Not when I'm so close to the truth. I can't quit this until I've found proof. I *need* to do this—for myself, for the other men."

I nodded, crossing my arms over my chest as I turned to stare out the window.

"You do understand, don't you, Verity?"

"Of course," I replied bitterly.

What I understood was that justice and revenge had become all-important to him. He was determined to pursue them to the exclusion of all else, and nothing and no one would be allowed to stand in the way. After all, hadn't he already proven that by being willing to sacrifice me and our marriage?

Everything was now about his drive, his *obsession* with catching this traitor. Even his decision to first lure me here to this house party and then later expose that he was alive had nothing to do with his desire to see me and everything to do with the fact that he needed my presence to play on the conscience of the members of the Thirtieth battalion, as well as my skills to decrypt the coded missive. Otherwise, I had no doubt I would still be completely ignorant of his survival. For if something didn't serve his current purposes, it didn't matter.

"This isn't just about me," he protested as I withdrew further into myself. "Think of those messengers and Ben Gerard, and all the hundreds or thousands more men who lost their lives because of this traitor's actions."

I didn't respond, knowing he wanted to believe that. But if this was really about the others he would have already turned over what evidence he had to the authorities, despite the risks to himself. He would have turned himself in and let the other people who had grown suspicious and witnessed worrying things, like Sam and Max and Mabel, help him. Yes, Sam and Mabel might face some difficulties of their own for the part they played, but surely the War Office would have to listen if so many people expressed their misgivings.

Now, Sidney had painted himself neatly into a corner.

Even so, I knew the resources the Secret Service could summon up when needed, and regardless of Sidney's doubts, I felt certain they would take great interest in a matter such as treason, even if the war was now over. Or almost so. The treaties had yet to be signed.

I wanted to find the traitor, too, but I wasn't willing to sacrifice everything else to it. Not my husband, or my marriage, or my life!

But Sidney seemed to think otherwise.

"Don't think I don't know you well enough to know you'll never be able to let this go either," he muttered in frustration. "Maybe for a short time you'll convince yourself it doesn't matter. That you can live with the injustice. But it will always haunt you. It will always haunt us."

Inside I squirmed, uncomfortable with his words. "That's not the point," I replied.

"It is if you're insisting we run away together, away from all of this," he persisted.

How could he be so obtuse?

"It isn't about running away!" I snapped, shooting him a venomous look before turning back to glare outside the window. "It's about much more than that. And if you can't already see it . . . then I don't know if I want to bother to explain."

Sidney drew breath to speak, but at that moment we both became aware of the sound of footsteps in the hall just outside the door, signaling we were no longer alone. He drew back deeper into the corner, concealing his body from the sight of anyone entering the room behind a tall hutch while I pivoted to face whoever approached.

"Verity?" Max asked, glancing about the room. "Were you just speaking with someone?"

I took a few steps closer to keep Max from moving deeper into the breakfast room. "No, I . . . I was just talking to myself," I admitted in feigned embarrassment. "I do that sometimes." I flicked a glance over my shoulder at the windows, checking to be certain my husband remained hidden. "After everything that's happened. Well, I needed a few moments to myself."

I could tell that Max wasn't completely convinced. "I could have sworn I heard voices. And you sounded quite angry."

"Well, who wouldn't be? Two men are dead and another is clinging to life." I stiffened in alarm. "Unless . . . ?"

He shook his head. "We've had no report yet. But I'm sure if he had succumbed, someone would have let us know."

"Are the others gathered in the parlor?"

"Yes." He paused, as if unsure whether to say anything more. "When you didn't join us, I worried something . . . unpleasant might have waylaid you."

Out of the corner of my eye, I could see Sidney's face tighten in irritation.

"No, I'm well. I just needed a few minutes to . . . clear my thoughts. But I realize now I'm better off staying with the rest of you."

I could feel Sidney's gaze boring into mine and turned as if to glance out the window one last time at the weather, allowing my eyes to meet his briefly as they slid past. They burned with resentment and frustration, and the clear desire to shake some sense into me. But they began to soften as I looked away, perhaps in answer to the sorrow and longing I couldn't seem to hide.

"I'll join you now," I told Max, moving toward the door. Sidney disappeared from my peripheral vision.

Max's eyes searched mine and I offered him a tight smile, hoping he would assume my distress was due to the murders. He pressed a warm hand to the small of my back and escorted me from the room.

When we reached the parlor, I was surprised to find everyone in an uproar. Apparently, Sam and Tom had taken it upon themselves to inform the other ladies of Jimmy's and Charlie's deaths, as well as Walter's precarious situation. Gladys and Elsie were furious, and not a little frantic. They wanted to know if they were in danger, and demanded to know why they hadn't been told sooner.

"Of course, you're not in danger," Tom replied, glancing to Sam and then Felix, who sat slumped in one of the chairs near the pianoforte, refusing to assist with the difficult conversation.

At my and Max's entrance, Tom looked up hopefully, perhaps thinking we could offer the ladies some reassurance. But given the fact we didn't know precisely *who* was responsible, it was difficult to declare that any of us were safe.

Gladys rounded to face us, her eyes wide with what I recognized to be fear, though she masked it well behind her strident tone. "Did you both know about this? Did *you*, Verity?"

There was no need to answer, for it seemed obvious from our calm demeanors that we were already cognizant of the problem.

"And you didn't tell us?" she shrieked at me, rather unfairly placing the blame on my shoulders. Though I was sure I would have done the same. As a woman, I would have expected her to take my part.

"I told them they were idiots to keep it from you," I replied, sparing the men none of my scorn. "But it was five against one. I hadn't much of a chance of driving the point into their thick skulls."

I turned to cast a disdainful look at Max, and was stunned to see Nellie seated rigidly in a chair near the door. Her eyes were troubled and her brow furrowed, but otherwise she gave no indication of upset. And yet Tom had been so certain she would fly up into the boughs.

I scowled at Tom and he shrugged.

"But how can you be certain we aren't in any danger?" Gladys pressed.

"He can't," I replied. The men turned to glare at me, but I ignored them. We'd just revealed the truth of our situation, and I wasn't about to start sugarcoating it to placate the men and their sensibilities about what the ladies should or should not know. "But we can say with some certainty that whoever is behind these incidents appears to be targeting the men," I explained to Gladys, whose shoulders had relaxed, seeming grateful I was leveling with her. "So I would venture to say the ladies are probably safe."

"Probably?" squeaked Elsie.

"Don't worry," Tom murmured. "We'll do everything in our power to keep you safe."

Elsie's expression was doubtful. "Yes. But who will keep *you* safe?"

This seemed to stun Tom into silence.

"And more to the point," Gladys pressed. "*Who* is doing this?"

"We're attempting to figure that out," Max said.

I wished we had some news of Walter's condition. How bad off was he? Might he recover enough to be able to tell us what had happened? And who he suspected of doing this to him?

"Was Walter able to fix the motor on his yacht?" I asked, noting the failing light outside the windows. Soon it would be dark, and any attempt to reach the mainland in this wind would become even more treacherous.

"Not if the number of tools still scattered about the engine area of the boat were any indication," Max replied. "I went to offer him what little assistance I could, and when he wasn't there, went to see if he'd returned to the castle. That's when I found him lying next to the path."

I nodded grimly, wondering how else we might reach help. Or would we be forced to spend another night here, stranded on this island? Perhaps a signal fire. Surely if we placed it near the end of the main quay it could be seen from Poole Harbor. But in these strong winds? We were likely to burn the entire island down, if we could even manage to light it.

Max raised his voice to be heard over the others' discussion. "Given the circumstances, I think it would be wise if, for everyone's safety, we all agreed that no one should leave the castle until the morning when the servants from the mainland are certain to return."

The others glanced around the room at each other, and most of them nodded or murmured in agreement.

"How is that going to keep us safe if the killer is inside the castle with us?" Felix argued disparagingly, speaking up for the first time since we'd entered the room.

Max frowned. "Because it makes it more difficult for them to isolate us. Jimmy, Charlie, and Walter were all harmed in locations away from the castle, where they would not have expected to find any assistance if they needed it. At least, inside the castle someone might hear you if you called for help. Not to mention the fact it might give the killer pause before acting, out of fear of being caught."

It seemed sound logic to me, and the others seemed to agree, but Felix rolled his eyes. I couldn't help but wonder if his disapproval of Max's suggestion was solely because Max had made it, or if he had another reason to wish the others would venture away from the castle.

Max leaned down to murmur in my ear. "I would like to take Felix aside and question him. After all, he is the last officer of his battalion involved with both of the messengers executed for desertion and the deaths of Ben Gerard and Sidney who is not currently clinging to life."

He had a point.

"Would you like to join me? He *might* be more civil with a lady present."

I highly doubted that, but I did want to hear what Felix had to say for himself. I was still wary of Max and how much he might be involved, but in this instance his presence might be beneficial, for Felix plainly did not like him. Maybe he would let something slip that could tell me if the two men happened to be working together.

"Yes. Shall we adjourn to the library?"

Max dipped his head in assent and strolled over to corral our suspect.

I had half expected Felix to refuse to speak with us given his extreme dislike of Max, but I should have known better. What better opportunity to mock and insult his former commanding officer than by agreeing to be interviewed and then belligerently refusing to cooperate. As usual, he was smartly dressed in another slim pin-striped suit, with his dark hair slicked back into place. He seemed determined to be at ease, staring back at us with mocking eyes as Max tried to draw him out. Realizing that he was prepared to endure this for hours without giving anything away just for the pleasure of holding such sway over us, I rose to my feet and began to pace behind the settee Max now occupied alone. Felix's gaze flickered with confusion, and I knew I'd pegged his motives correctly.

"Felix, where are you from?" I asked almost indifferently, interrupting Max. From the corner of my eye, I could see that both men were looking at me in confusion. "I can't seem to recall if anyone has mentioned it." I knew this would be a blow to his ego that I should not remember something pertaining to him, and as such was not surprised when he answered.

"Watford."

I frowned in contrived contemplation. "Is that near London?"

"Yes, northwest of the city."

"Near Harrow?"

"Yes."

"Then I suppose that's where you attended school."

Felix scowled, and for good reason, for I distinctly recalled the conversation where he had talked about being part of the rowing team at Radley. "No, I attended Radley."

"And then Cambridge?" I guessed, correctly recalling this bit of information. It wouldn't do to appear as if I'd paid attention to nothing, or he might grow suspicious.

"Yes."

I could feel Max watching me over the back of the settee, wondering what on earth I was doing, but he allowed me to continue.

"So you weren't at Oxford with Sidney and Walter and Max."

"No," Felix replied, exasperation growing in his voice.

"Hmmm." I hummed, needling him. "Any MPs in your family?"

"No," he bit out. "But what does that have to do with anything? I thought you were asking me about the attack on Walter."

I halted my steps and finally turned to look at him. "So you admit you attacked him."

"No!" he protested, sitting forward. "I don't admit any such thing."

I arched my eyebrows in doubt.

"I was in the billiard room with Gladys and Elsie for at least an hour before Tom demanded we join everyone in the parlor. So I couldn't have planted those bees."

Except we didn't know how long that package had been lying at the bend in the path, waiting for Walter to trip over it. However, the fact that Felix was at least denying his involvement was a step forward from his stubborn refusal to answer.

He scowled as if realizing this, but plunged onward. "And I didn't kill Jimmy or Charlie either, though I'm not going to pretend I'm heartbroken over their deaths."

"But you *did* sabotage Walter's yacht," I insisted.

"I did no such thing!"

Ah, but if I were a betting woman, and I had been a rather avid poker player at one time—a good one, too, until I watched a friend be ruined by her predilection for the card game and decided to bow out while I was ahead. But if I were still that woman, I would have bet all-in that Felix was lying about Walter's boat. So I decided to press my advantage.

"What about those men you helped frame for desertion?"

He opened his mouth to hotly retort, then snapped it shut, realizing too late that he'd just displayed he knew exactly whom we were talking about. He studied each of us in turn as we waited for his reply, and a sharp glint entered his eyes. A glint I didn't like one bit.

"That wasn't my doing," he claimed, sinking back in his seat. "Nor my fault."

"But you admit to knowing those men were wrongly accused?" Max pressed.

Felix shrugged. "I don't know anything about that. All I did was give my testimony *exactly* as I witnessed it."

"And phrase it in the worst possible light," Max argued, knowing the details of the case better than I did.

"I never lied."

I could almost hear Max's teeth grinding at this slimy bit of semantics.

"But who asked you to testify? Who accused those men of desertion in the first place?" I interjected, tired of Felix's games.

Nevertheless, he wasn't finished, for he feigned shock, even as his eyes still shone with cutting glee. "Why, don't you know? It was your husband."

CHAPTER 21

I stiffened at this pronouncement, but before I could so much as blink, Max leapt in to berate Felix.

"That's a lie. And a rotten, shameful one, too. I've read the reports. I know it was Charlie Montague who issued the complaint."

"Yes, but at Sidney Kent's urging," Felix sneered, as if Max was stupid. His gaze flicked toward where I stood gripping the back of the settee with white knuckles. "Sidney had a lover, some French woman he'd set up in the next town. He utilized some of the younger privates we would sometimes send back and forth with communications to HQ when a runner couldn't be found as his own private messengers to hand-deliver his love letters for him when he couldn't get away."

He flipped open his cigarette case and extracted a fag as if he hadn't a care in the world, though his words were ripping a hole in mine.

"I'm not sure how he discovered it," he drawled. "But somehow he found out that two of the men he used most often, the two who were always most eager, were actually committing treason. Said they were sharing information with some German spy, but he couldn't get the evidence he needed to prove it." He blew out a long plume of smoke. "So several of us officers agreed it would be better to see them shot for a charge we *could* prove, namely desertion, than let them go on betraying the lot of us."

Unable to maintain my silence one more second through this ridiculous recitation of balderdash, I leaned forward, stabbing a finger at him. "That's a lie! A bloody, filthy lie. Sidney would *never* have done such a thing." I stood taller, inhaling an angry breath. "Besides, Tom already told me which officer had a French lover, and it wasn't Sidney."

Far from being daunted, Felix merely fixed me with a negligent stare. "Well, he wouldn't want to admit such a thing to the man's widow and his childhood friend, now would he?"

I wanted to launch myself over the chair and force Felix to take back his words, but I made myself turn away with a furious huff instead.

"Halbert, this is low even for you," Max scolded. "You know this is all a lot of nonsense. Kent was the best of us. We all knew it. Just as we all knew you were a scheming little weasel. And you couldn't stand the fact that Kent was the first to figure it out."

Felix's eyes narrowed in loathing. "Just as you were a cowardly little mouse, hiding behind your father's title." He rose to his feet, flicking the remainder of his cigarette into the hearth. "We're done here."

I glared at his retreating back, despising the fact that he had been able to upset me, hating that he had so adroitly stirred up my worst fears.

"You cannot be taking any of that drivel seriously," Max objected, standing to face me over the back of the settee. "He's obviously lying about Sidney's part in the matter, though some of the rest may be true," he conceded. "If Sidney was, in fact, the officer behind it all, why would they have killed him to keep him quiet?"

I wrapped my arms across my torso, clutching my elbows. "Perhaps he wasn't shot to keep him quiet, but to stop him."

Max's gaze scoured my face as I struggled not to let my extreme apprehension show. "Very well, then," he declared, perching on the padded arm of the settee. "For the sake of argument, let's say that's true. Why would they need to stop him? If the other officers believed his assertions that those two messengers were committing treason and colluded with him to frame them for desertion . . . *which,* by the way, I find nigh impossible, as Sidney is not mentioned even once in connection with that affair, and I don't for one minute think that would have been conceivable had he been the ringleader of their demise. But *if* he was, then what reason would they possibly have had to stop him?"

Hearing it phrased like that did make it seem preposterous. I inhaled deeply, feeling the fear that had gripped me loosen its hold. "Well, he then would have arranged to have Ben Gerard killed, to keep their secret," I hypothesized, willing to play devil's advocate if it would help me understand better. "So maybe they were worried they were next?"

"But why would Sidney then request to have Ben's brother Sam assigned to his command?"

"Maybe he was worried that Ben had shared something with him."

"But Sam already told us he hadn't. Sam didn't suspect anything was wrong with his brother's death until Sidney revealed his misgivings."

I nibbled on my thumbnail, considering the matter, wondering how close I should prod to the truth as I knew it. "What if . . . what if the messengers weren't the ones committing treason?"

I looked up to find I'd arrested Max's attention. The firelight threw his shadow across the floor, making him appear even larger and more brooding than usual.

"What if Sidney was the traitor and he was using those two young soldiers to deliver his messages to his informant."

"And then something went wrong and he decided he needed to cover his tracks, having the messengers discredited and silenced," Max surmised, filling in the rest of the blanks. His brow furrowed as he contemplated the scenario in silence.

I watched his face closely, trying to tell what he might have already known, whether he was merely startled by the suggestion or alarmed that I had figured it out. Had he been part of the plot or not?

My intuition was telling me that this was the first time he'd even considered the possibility that treason was the motive behind it all, but I also knew I *wanted* him to be innocent. Irrespective of any attraction I might feel for him, I liked Max. He was kind, intelligent, and steady. And that was more than I could say for a lot of people. He seemed like someone on whom I could rely.

But these perceptions were also tempered by the fact that I still wanted to trust my husband, to believe he was good and honest and true, even though he had cruelly abused that trust by allowing me to believe he had been dead for more than a year. Even though he had placed his resolve to catch this traitor over all else, including me.

"I suppose it's possible," Max replied, interrupting my tormented thoughts. "But I would have thought Sidney the least likely officer in that battalion to indulge in such a perfidious deception. And it still doesn't explain why he would have requested that Sam join his company and then told him his suspicions about Ben's death."

He looked up from his study of the rug to find me watching him. I could see the questions forming in his eyes, his curiosity about how I had developed such a theory. So before he spoke, before he forced me to lie, I chose retreat.

"I'm going up to check on Walter," I said, moving toward the door. "If he's conscious and able to speak, perhaps he'll be able to tell us something useful." Not wanting him to follow me, I glanced back and added, "Maybe you should check on the others."

And with that feeble attempt at diversion, I swept from the room.

"How is he?" I whispered when Walter's valet answered my knock on the master bedchamber's door. His face looked drawn and I could hear weeping coming from inside the room behind him.

He shook his head. "Not good, I'm afraid." He glanced over his shoulder, affording me a view of Helen seated in a chair next to the bed. She had crumpled forward, sobbing into the counter-pane. "Miss Lorraine has gone to mix up some sort of remedy she hopes might help Mr. Ponsonby, and I need to go fetch some more provisions. However, I hesitate to leave Miss Crawford alone." He looked distinctly uncomfortable, but I knew what request he was trying to make of me.

"I'll sit with her," I said, saving him from having to voice the entreaty.

He nodded gratefully. "If you have need of me, ring the bell. I'll return as swiftly as I can."

He closed the door softly behind him and I inched toward the bed, unsure whether Helen would welcome my presence. After all, I knew quite well that sometimes one preferred to cry alone. She sniffed into the silence and lifted her head to look back at me. Her eyes were red and puffy, and her cheeks streaked with tears. Her countenance was so miserable and frightened, I couldn't hold back.

"Oh, Helen, dear," I crooned, hastening forward to offer her what consolation I could.

She let me lead her away from the bed where Walter lay laboring to breathe. His face was even more swollen and ruddy than before, all but swallowing his eyes except for two slits. However, she refused to leave the room when I suggested a bit of distance might help her settle herself. I couldn't blame her for wanting to remain by his side, so I didn't press the matter, instead sitting beside her on a gold settee a short distance from the foot of the bed.

She buried her face in my shoulder, sobbing into her handkerchief while I rubbed her back and offered what comfort I could. After a few minutes, she began to take hold of herself, lifting her head as she dabbed at her eyes.

"I'm sorry," she sniffed. "It's just so . . . so terrible."

"I know," I said, patting her hand in her lap.

"Of all the nasty luck. He lives through the war and that horrid injury, and then has to suffer this." Her gaze crumpled as she glanced at the bed, but she managed to inhale and steady herself.

"What does Mabel think? Has she much hope this remedy she's preparing will work?"

Helen shook her head. "I don't know. She won't tell me much. I think because it's not good." She dropped the hand clutching her handkerchief into her lap with a snap that rattled the bracelets on her wrists. "If only the telephones were working and we could reach one of the hospitals on the mainland. I'm certain they must have something they could give him."

I smiled in commiseration. Yes, the killer seemed to have thought of everything.

"This cursed weather," she grumbled, glaring at the window over my shoulder. Even through the thick walls of the castle we could still hear the wind battering at the glass, stone, and wood.

I remembered then that she did not know about Jimmy's and Charlie's deaths, or that the bee stings her fiancé had suffered had not been by accident. But now did not seem like the time to tell her.

"Shall I pour you a drink?" I asked, wondering if that might help brace her.

"Yes, please."

I crossed the room toward the table where the glasses and decanters stood, taking a moment to observe Walter again. He truly did look in a bad way. His breathing was tortured, scraping against my ears as he dragged it into his constricted airway. I could only pray Mabel returned soon, and this preparation of hers helped.

I returned to Helen and passed her a glass of brandy, which she sipped. Sinking her head back against the cushions, she sighed wearily and closed her eyes. I couldn't help but note how pretty she still looked even blotchy-faced from crying. Though the luster and vivaciousness that I suspected had first drawn Walter's interest had decidedly faded.

"Perhaps this house party wasn't such a good idea," she surprised me by murmuring as I settled down beside her.

"What do you mean?"

She peered through her eyelashes up at me. "Everyone has

been quarreling and bickering, two of the men have fallen ill, and now . . . and now this." She gestured toward the bed.

I waited as she took another swallow of brandy, smothering the emotion welling up inside her.

"Walter didn't want it, you know. The house party. He thought we should just host a small affair at his London town-house. But I insisted." Her face screwed up in self-recrimination. "I didn't even consult him on the guest list, wanting to surprise him. That was a mistake."

"So it was your idea to invite all of the surviving officers from his former battalion?" I asked, curious exactly how the matter had played out.

"Well, no. I suppose Sam was the first to suggest it. But I thought it was a capital idea. And it only seemed right to invite you, too, for I knew how close Walter had been to Sidney." Her eyes grew troubled. "He used to talk about him, especially when he first returned from the front. He would mutter about him in his sleep or when the pain became so bad the nurses had to dose him with more morphine." She glanced over at me. "I could tell how much Sidney's death affected him."

I smiled tightly, not certain I wanted to hear all that. "But Sam believed your surprise was a good idea? And Mabel?"

Sidney had said that, at his instigation, Sam had encouraged Helen to invite the officers of the Thirtieth, but I couldn't help wondering if there might have been more to it than that.

"Oh, yes. He said Walter would be shocked, but grateful to see his old war chums again." She tilted her head in consideration. "Mabel was a bit more hesitant at first, but she came around to the notion easily enough."

I studied her profile as she sat gazing across the room toward the bed, wondering again at her curious mix of naïveté and worldliness. It seemed obvious to me that a gathering of the men one had so recently fought alongside would not be welcomed by most soldiers. Not so soon after the war, when they were all still trying to recover from the horror of those four years, and certainly not in mixed company. But, then, I had seen far more than the average British citizen. I had some grasp of what they were coming home from, even if I could never completely understand. I suspected several of my female friends would not have had the sensibility either to recognize the impending disaster of such a gathering. At least, no more than Helen had.

But Sam had known what he was doing. Supposedly the plan was all Sidney's doing, but what if Sam had decided to use it to further his own agenda? Perhaps he had decided to exact his own revenge for his brother's death, killing the men one by one.

It didn't seem any more preposterous than any of the other theories I'd considered. After all, what did I really know about Sam? Next to nothing. And all of that had been vetted by Sidney or Mabel, who could be blinded to his true purpose here.

If I were in Sam's shoes, suddenly presented with the men who had played a part in my brother's death, whether directly or indirectly, wouldn't I be tempted to take matters into my own hands? Any loyalty he owed Sidney he'd more than reciprocated by saving his life and keeping his secrets. What was to stop him from doing just what he pleased now that the stage had been set?

I needed to speak with Sam, to gauge for myself just what he might be capable of.

Mabel returned to the room then, carrying a bowl of some sort of liquid. At the sight of me, she gave a tiny nod and crossed the chamber to set her remedy down on the table next to Walter's bed.

"I shall need Baxter's assistance," she informed us, glancing over her shoulder toward the door to see if the valet had arrived. "He should be along in a moment."

"Do you think it will work?" Helen asked anxiously, rising to her feet with me.

Mabel's gaze rested on Walter, her expression carefully blank. "We can hope."

Helen moved closer to smooth the covers surrounding Walter, and I beckoned Mabel toward the door.

"Something important has just come to my attention, and I

must leave to take care of it," I told her, lowering my voice so Helen couldn't hear me.

Mabel's eyes sharpened, grasping what I was implying.

"I need you to watch over Walter. Do not leave him alone. With *anyone*."

She stiffened in alarm and I nodded.

"I suspect he may be safe with Helen and Baxter, but I can't be certain. So take no chances. None," I emphasized. "If we're to ever have the chance to hear what he knows, he must be kept alive."

Mabel might be Sam's sweetheart and Helen's cousin, but I trusted that her training as a nurse and a healer would override any loyalty she felt. Walter was in her charge, and she would see him through, if it was remotely possible.

She swallowed before stating firmly, "Don't worry. I'll see to it."

"I knew you would," I replied, squeezing her arm.

Hastening downstairs, I swept through all of the public rooms, my sense of urgency growing when I discovered Sam wasn't there. At least, not in any of the obvious places. And neither was Felix.

An uneasy premonition swept over me, and I quickened my steps, anxious to locate at least one of them. It was because of this haste that I turned a corner and almost bowled straight into Max.

"Verity," he exclaimed, grabbing hold of my arms to keep me from stumbling to the ground.

"My apologies," I gasped. "I wasn't looking where I was going."

Once we'd righted ourselves, he stared down into my face in concern. "What is it? What's wrong?"

I opened my mouth to fob him off, but then I realized two people could search much faster than one. Not to mention the fact that, as a man, he could go into places I reasonably could not. I wasn't certain yet whether I *should* trust him, but I made the decision to do so anyway.

"I can't find Sam or Felix."

Max needed no further explanation, deducing the reason for my alarm. "I'll help you search. Tell me where you've already looked."

We divided the house into quadrants and each set out to search them. I made certain to give Max the bedrooms, while I took the section of the house nearest to the gardens, thinking that if I was to have any chance of encountering Sidney it would be there. But though I made no effort to hide my progress through the chambers, my husband did not make himself known to me, and I didn't locate Sam or Felix.

Max shook his head when we regrouped in the foyer some time later. "No sign of them anywhere."

I glanced toward the windows out into the dark, wind-swept night. "At least, not in the castle."

Max followed my gaze, his brow tightening as he came to the same conclusion I had. "We have to find them. Before . . ."

I nodded, not needing him to finish that sentence. "Yes."

His expression was grim. "I'll fetch my coat."

I dashed up the stairs beside him, peeling away from him toward the corridor where my bedchamber was located. All the way to my room and back, I couldn't help searching the shadows for Sidney, wishing for once he *would* grab me and startle me. But he remained obstinately absent. Having no way of knowing precisely where he was, and no time to warn him, I hurried to meet Max.

CHAPTER 22

Max and I bumped along the main road cutting through the heart of the island in the castle's lorry with the trees lashing each other overhead. The night was dark, illuminated only by the snatches of moonlight that managed to penetrate through the heavy clouds billowing across the sky, and the dim swathe cut by the lorry's headlamps. More than a few limbs had fallen in the lane, making us swerve around them, but so far nothing large enough to block the single-track entirely.

Max paused at the church, dashing inside with the electric torch to see if anyone was inside. Returning to the lorry, he shook his head in frustration and set off down the road again. If he'd noted the presence of Jimmy's body laid out next to Charlie's in the chill sanctuary, he chose not to speak of it, and I didn't dare bring it up. Doing so would mean I would have to explain how I knew that Walter had deceived us, that the authorities had never visited the island the day before, and I didn't particularly relish lying to him. Not now.

· The island was not overly large, and there weren't many dwellings, but there were still plenty of places Sam and Felix could have disappeared to. The question was where? I'd considered suggesting we explore the farm's outbuildings, wondering if Sam had gone in search of Sidney, but that would put my husband at risk of discovery. So instead I let Max choose the direction we should go, first to the church, and then on to the abandoned village near the old pottery works where Jimmy had been found.

We drove along at what I thought to be a spanking pace, considering the blustery weather and the state of the roads. Max hunched over the driving wheel, his eyes narrowed to peer through the darkness, while I gripped the seat beneath me. That's when we saw a man dart across the road, out of the glare of the headlamps, and into the forest.

Max slammed on the brakes, skidding the lorry through the mud. I lifted my hands just in time to stop myself from crashing headlong into the dashboard.

"Stay with the lorry," Max ordered as he threw open his door and catapulted out of the vehicle. He raced across the road in front of the lamps and plunged into the trees after the man.

A narrow trail seemed to lead off into the woods to my left, only to be swallowed by overgrown foliage and the dark of the night. I hadn't gotten a good look at the man who had run out of the road and into the forest, so I didn't know whether it was Sam, Felix, or Sidney. I only hoped that if it was the latter, he managed to evade Max. Otherwise he was going to have some awkward explaining to do.

And if it was one of the former? Well, I hoped Max could handle him on his own, because there was no way I could catch up with them at this point. The fact that the man had run did not bode well for his willingness to cooperate, or for his reasons for being out here on such a night.

The lorry's engine suddenly sputtered to a stop, and I inhaled a breath through the tightness in my chest, recognizing how alone and vulnerable I was. I glanced about me, trying to get my bearings. However, the acetylene headlamps still burned bright at the front of the lorry and proved more harmful than helpful, blinding me to anything beyond their glow.

Pulling my tweed coat tighter around me, I climbed out of the lorry into the wind and moved toward the bonnet, studying the bulk of the building several yards in front of me lit by the beam of the lamps. We were at the edge of the abandoned village, near the western tip of the island. Not being able to see much more, and fearful of what anyone beyond the beams could see of me, I switched off the lamps.

I blinked several times, trying to adjust my eyes to the piercing darkness that settled around me. The trees and shrubberies rustled in the wind at the verges of the road, but at the front of the lorry I could sense the forest clearing created by those who'd originally built the village. There was a softening to the blackness above me, and a hazy sense of movement, no doubt created by the fast-moving cloud banks.

The breeze felt sharp against my cheeks and carried very little scent except for the damp of the earth and the forest, and a slight tinge of the salty sea beyond. As my night vision improved, I began to make out the shapes of the other abandoned buildings—a cottage here and another one there. A round stone well stood to my left, its wooden winch hunched over it like a protective ogre.

I turned to the left, trying to peer down the path Max and his quarry had fled. There was no way of telling exactly where the trail led, or how long Max would choose to pursue the man. So I elected to stay where I was, sheltered in the deep shadow cast by the lorry as I listened for any sound of their approach.

Several minutes ticked by, marked only by the wind and the pounding of my heart, and yet there was still no sign of either man. I began to worry something bad had befallen Max, for surely he would have come to his senses and halted the chase if he had not caught up to the other fellow within a few dozen yards. He had not struck me as a man who took unnecessary risks, particularly with a female to protect. But I had been wrong about such things before.

I glanced at the lorry and then toward the village, considering my options. Now that my sight was improved, I noticed there seemed to be a faint, wavering glow in the distance. It was very weak, probably because it was being blocked by several of the buildings, but there was definitely something there. I hesitated a moment longer and then ventured forward, stepping as softly as I could on the damp, leaves-strewn ground so as to avoid making noise.

The closer I moved toward it, the brighter the glow became, though it was still more of a hazy wash of gray than an actual light. I had reached the first pair of old dwellings when a sudden noise behind me to the left made me race forward to conceal myself behind the closest building. My heart beat fast inside my chest, and I took a moment to catch my breath before peering around the corner.

Two men had emerged from the tangled overgrowth of the forest, striding past the well into the village. However, this was far from a leisurely stroll, as the man in the rear was holding the other at gunpoint. I couldn't see well enough to say for certain who the man wielding the pistol was, but from the manner in which the captured man tossed a glance in the direction of the lorry, earning a prod from the other man's gun, I suspected the captive was Max.

I watched as they disappeared behind the far building toward the center of the village and then sank my head against the wall before me, trying to think. I couldn't just abandon Max to whatever fate the other man intended for him, for it obviously would not be pleasant. If only I knew what and who I was facing.

Fearing I had already tarried too long, I retraced my steps to the lorry. The click of the door latch opening sounded overloud to my ears and I cringed before climbing up inside to search its contents for some sort of weapon. The glove compartment sat empty, but there was a wealth of detritus on the floor, under which I found a tire iron. Knowing that time might literally be of the essence, I snatched up the iron rod and set off after the men.

My pursuit was slow, necessitated not only by my desire to remain undetected, but also the crumbling piles of masonry, tree roots, and low-lying shrubs that had sprung up between the deserted cottages. I could no longer see the men, but I had already guessed they were headed toward whatever the source of that light was. As I crept closer I could hear the sound of voices, the first of which was sharp and mocking, while the second was raised in anger. I nearly stumbled when a third voice joined the conversation, for by now I had recognized the mocking man to be Felix and the angry one to be Max. The third voice, which I realized must be Sam, for it certainly wasn't Sidney, sounded almost listless, making me wonder just what had happened to him.

The soft, wavering glow proved to be a lantern shining through the openings of a building near the village pier. I paused to survey the area around the building and then dipped low to skitter across the ground toward the window on the side nearest me. Remaining hunched over, I waited to hear if my approach had been noticed, but the conversation inside continued without interruption.

Slowly rising up on my toes, I peered over the ledge through a hole in the corner of the broken glass. Felix stood with his back to the door, his eyes hard and his mouth curled into a nasty sneer while he aimed a pistol across the room at Max. But far from being cowed, Max appeared furious. He glared at his captor as if daring him to pull the trigger. I tightened my grip on the tire iron, fearful Felix might just do it.

Beyond Max, crumpled in the far corner, sat Sam. His hands were bound, and blood poured from a cut over his eye down the right side of his face. Or at least, at one point it had. Now it seemed, as I looked harder, that most of it had dried.

"How did you do it?" Max demanded to know. "How did you convince Jimmy to kill Ben on that night raid?"

Felix's smirk widened. "I didn't have to convince him of anything. He understood what had to be done."

"But he couldn't live with it."

"Some men are weaker than others."

Max's jaw tightened. "Some men have more of a conscience than others."

Felix shrugged one shoulder. "Conscience, cowardice—it's all the same."

"And what of Sidney? I suppose that was your doing, too."

"It wasn't exactly my 'doing,' but I exerted the right pressure to make it happen."

My blood surged indignantly at the insinuation in his voice, the utter lack of remorse. Felix might not have pulled the trigger, but he had just as assuredly been behind the attempt on my husband's life. I wondered idly if Walter, Jimmy, or Charlie had been the one forced to do the deed, as I focused my thoughts on the open doorway behind Felix.

If I could sneak up on him, catch him by surprise, I might be able to land a blow to his head or at least knock the gun from his hands. The difficulty would be in crossing those five feet between the doorway and where Felix stood without making a noise or Max and Sam giving me away.

I frowned, wondering if I had time to find Sidney, but then just as swiftly discarded the idea. I had no idea where on the island he was, and Felix could shoot and kill Max and Sam in the matter of a moment. I was alone in this. Just as I was in so many other things.

Taking a firmer grip on the tire iron, I began to back away from the window, but Max's next words arrested me in place.

"Why did you decide to frame those men for desertion? As I understand it they were only messengers." He lowered his voice. "Or was it because they were at risk of exposing you for treason?"

There was a beat of silence followed by the snap of Felix's voice. "How the devil did you know that?"

I cursed Max and his rash decision to push for answers. As annoying as Felix was when he was behaving so blasé and scornful, it was far preferable to the irate and panicked version. An infuriated Felix was more likely to fire that pistol, whether he intended to or not. There was no time to lose.

But as I shifted position to slink down the wall toward the doorway, I heard the crunch of a foot shifting in the debris behind me. Before I could turn to face them, or even lift my hand, I felt the cold press of metal against the back of my neck. I inhaled sharply, recognizing the round object for what it was— the nozzle of a gun.

"Drop the weapon."

My senses froze in shock as I let the tire iron drop from my numb fingers, for I knew that voice. I had listened to it sob into my shoulder such a short time ago. She was quite the accomplished actress, it seemed.

"Now move," she ordered, prodding me toward the doorway with her other hand.

As I stepped to the left, the kiss of the metal lifted from my now-icy skin, but I knew without looking that she kept it trained on my back. The center of my spine tingled as if aware that it had transformed into a bull's-eye. When we reached the doorway, I could see that Max and Sam remained in their previous positions, while Felix had pivoted so that he could see who approached.

"Over there. In the corner with the others," she instructed me in a cold voice.

I did as I was told, moving close to Max's side as I turned to get my first glimpse of Helen. Her eyes sparkled with malice, though the rest of her remained chillingly composed, never wavering as she lowered her gun to her side.

"Well, now, isn't this a charming tête-à-tête," she proclaimed.

I was tempted to correct her French and remind her that a tête-à-tête was between two people, not five, but then I would be no better than Max prodding Felix. We needed one of them to remain calm, no matter how their contemptuous countenances irked me. It would have been nice if she could have at least looked bedraggled and swollen from all of her fake crying earlier, but she seemed perfectly coifed and dewy fresh. Even her feet were shod in a pair of darling kid leather half boots.

"But before we continue, *Verity*," she drawled my name mockingly. "I really must insist you bind his lordship's hands. After all, we don't want Max to force me to shoot him prematurely."

My hands curled into fists, revolting against the idea of doing her bidding.

"Go on," she coaxed with an arch smile. "I'm sure he won't mind."

I glanced at Max, whose entire body vibrated with rage. He nodded once and I knelt to pick up the rope Felix tossed at my feet. As I did so, I spared a glance at Sam, who seemed to be struggling to remain conscious. His eyes were bleary and his skin pale. I wondered if he'd suffered more than that nasty blow to the head.

Rising to my feet, I turned so that my back was to Helen and Felix, but she would have none of it.

"Ah, ah, ah," she scolded in singsong. "So that we can watch you, please. And no slipshod knots either. I would so hate to punish him for your lazy handiwork."

I glanced up at Max through my eyelashes, and we pivoted as one to obey her directives. His eyes softened a fraction, telling me he understood I had no choice. He even gripped my right wrist, the hand farthest from their view, trying to offer me some sort of reassurance.

Inhaling deeply, I performed the task before me while concentrating on figuring out a way to get us out of this precarious situation. Helen and Felix each had at least one gun. Sam and Max both had their hands bound, and Sam seemed barely cognizant of what was happening around him. If we were going to escape with our lives, it was going to have to be a matter of brains, not brawn.

Once I'd finished, I turned back to face them, expecting Helen to send Felix closer to check the bindings, but she was too shrewd for that. Instead she ordered Max to lift his hands and then attempt to maneuver them in several ways. Max's scowl darkened at his being treated like he was some sort of trained monkey.

Sensing this, Helen's pink lips curled into an amused smile. "Excellent. Now"—her gaze shifted to meet mine—"if Verity would be so good as to tell us where she's hidden that coded missive."

I could feel Max's eyes on me in confusion, but ignored him. "It was you," I stated somewhat unnecessarily. "*You* were the one who searched my room."

"I was already suspicious of you, but once I saw you scribbling on that scratch paper in the parlor earlier, I realized you and Sam must have found something." Her eyes narrowed, considering Sam where he sat hunched beside a pile of crumbled masonry. "Maybe he found it in your dear husband's belongings or maybe your husband mailed it to you himself." She shrugged. "It doesn't matter now, does it?" Her voice turned cold. "But I *want* that letter."

She arched her eyebrows expectantly as if I wouldn't dare defy her. It was evident she had grown accustomed to being obeyed in her every whim. I flicked a glance toward Felix, where he stood several steps to her right, his gun dangling at his side, at the ready. He had allowed her to do all the talking, but I could tell from his scowl he was not best pleased by it. What she held over him, I didn't know, but it must be significant.

Unwilling to lose my best, and possibly only, bargaining chip, I lifted my chin in defiance. "I'll tell you what you want to know *if* you explain why you decided to betray your country. *Why* a young woman like you, with every advantage in the world, would choose to sell secrets to its enemies? And how on earth you convinced Walter and the other men to help you?" I gestured toward Felix, recalling his earlier statement about Jimmy, and hoping to spark his temper. "I mean, clearly they're weak."

His nostrils flared and he took a step toward me, but Helen lifted a hand, stopping him with just one icy look.

"But *how* did you do it?" I continued, not just stalling for time now, but genuinely wanting to know. I studied her flawless, innocent appearance. "It must be eating you alive that no one knows the truth about how clever you are."

Far from being goaded, Helen's eyes only laughed at me. "Oh, Verity. Perhaps the men you've interrogated in the past have fallen for such an obvious ploy, but *I* am not so dumb." Her good humor vanished at the implication that I had just insulted her intelligence. "The only thing I will tell you is that it had nothing to do with money. And though you may hedge all you like, by the end, you *will* talk."

The cruel certainty behind her words made my chest tighten in dread.

"Now, your lordship," she taunted, turning to Max and all but dismissing me. "It seems you have a decision to make." She began to pace a tiny circle before the doorway, for all the world as if she didn't care what his answer would be. I wouldn't have been surprised if she lifted her hand to examine her manicure, such was the amount of interest she showed. "How would you prefer to die? As the hero or the victim?"

CHAPTER 23

Unlike me, Max did not react to this startling question, not by the quiver of a single muscle. He just continued to stare Helen down with a tightly restrained fury that didn't seem to bother her one iota.

"Either way, I'm afraid Sam is going to have to take the fall for Jimmy's and Charlie's deaths, and Walter's attempted murder." She tsked. "Such a sad case of shell shock. He'd deluded himself into believing all those men had arranged for his brother to die, and that he needed to avenge him."

Her words sickened me. Even more so because I had entertained a similar suspicion such a short time ago, minus the taint of shell shock. It didn't take any great leap to imagine the authorities would believe it as well. Even Sam seemed to accept such a thing, allowing his head to sink back against the wall behind him. Or perhaps he was merely overcome by his injuries.

I wished they would allow me to examine him, but I already knew without asking that such a request was foolish. They intended for him to die, for *all* of us to die. What did it matter if it happened a bit sooner than they planned?

"The real question is whether Verity helped him."

My gaze snapped back around to meet hers, seeing that she'd enjoyed shocking me.

"Either she confronted Sam about his actions, forcing him to kill her. In which case, Max, you then killed Sam, receiving a fatal gunshot wound in the process and dying before you could reach help. Such a heroic act," she murmured in breathless mockery. "*Or* Verity and Sam killed you because you knew too much and then fled the island together. Though, in actuality, they'll be sunk in the lagoon, never to be seen from again. All of our problems tied up in a nice, neat bow."

Except Helen didn't realize Mabel was also privy to part of the truth. Or that Sidney was alive.

I glanced toward the door and then the window, wishing my maddeningly tardy husband would appear. Surely he would notice that all of the key players save Walter were absent from the castle. Surely he would sense something was wrong. But would he reach us in time? He had just been returned to me, and now I might be snatched away before we'd ever had the chance to really reconcile. Before I could tell him I still loved him.

Both of the scenarios Helen laid out were horrifying. If Max chose the first one, then I would be the first to die, but it would give Max more time to find a way to break free. However, if he chose the second one, then he would die first and bargain that Sam or I could find a way out of this mess.

"So which is it?" Helen asked brusquely, her patience growing thin. "Are you a saint or sap?"

I already knew which one Max would choose, and I couldn't let him do it. "Don't choose, Max," I interrupted.

But he was already informing her of his decision. "Sap."

I stared up into his eyes, furious that he was sacrificing himself for me, and also touched beyond belief. I shook my head in denial, in disbelief. "Max."

His expression was resolute and unruffled by the choice he'd made.

Helen glanced between us, the gleam in her eyes telling me she was enjoying our torment. "I suspected as much. Couldn't resist the dashing, young widow, could you?" Her mouth twisted in malicious approval. "Well done, Verity."

Her comment stung, as I'd known she'd intended it to.

Helen sighed. "Then I suppose we should adjourn this little gathering to the pier, where Max will be shot trying to stop the two young murderers from fleeing."

I darted a surprised look up at Max, realizing he'd expected this move. Evidently he'd been thinking farther ahead than I had. He had been playing for more time for all of us all along, trying to get us out of the close confines of this building and its lantern light. At this point, the darkness was our best ally.

"On your feet," she ordered Sam.

He looked up at her dazedly, and I wondered if he could even comprehend what she was saying. However, when Felix lifted his pistol to level it at him once again, Sam blinked blearily and tried to push himself upright. His first attempt was not successful, and neither was his second.

Helen huffed in exasperation. "Verity, if you would." She gestured toward Sam with her gun.

I quickly moved to help him, less from fear of what Helen and Felix would do and more from compassion. "Easy does it, Sam," I murmured, so the others couldn't hear.

He looked up into my eyes, and I offered him a smile of encouragement. The right side of his face was obscured by dried blood, even crusting over his eyelid.

I looped my arm underneath his and coaxed him to bend his knees beneath him. "Are you hurt anywhere else?" I took the opportunity to ask, unable to tell in the dim lighting against his dark clothing.

"My side," he croaked. "Took a jab to the kidney."

Taking most of his weight on my shoulders, I was able to hoist him to his feet, though I wished I could have left him where he was. His low groan was agonizing.

Had he ruptured a kidney or possibly his spleen? Or was he just badly bruised and reeling from a concussion? Either way, he needed medical attention sooner, not later.

I was encouraged when he staggered forward a few steps and then seemed to regain his balance to walk on his own, clutching his left side. With a gentle nudge, he lifted his arm from around my shoulders.

"I can make it now," he told me gamely.

I wanted to argue, but it was clear he was trying to give me the best possible opportunity to escape, and attempting to do so while being hindered by an injured man was undoubtedly not it. That drove home the haunting realization that even if Max and I could somehow evade Helen and Felix and dart off into the darkness, we would have to leave Sam behind. In his current state, his ability to defend himself was limited. They would almost certainly kill him, but he seemed resigned to such a fate. I wanted to beg him not to surrender so easily, but Helen had had enough of our commiseration.

"Max, why don't you lead our merry parade," she said, nodding to Felix to follow him. "Then you, Sam. And last, but not least, Verity."

I fell in line behind Sam, keeping a worried eye on his trudging form and another on my surroundings as we exited the old cottage. Helen bent to pick up the lantern, bringing it with us, but I was certain she also held her gun in the other hand pointed at my back. All we needed was some sort of opening, some sort of distraction to break their concentration long enough to keep Felix and Helen from shooting us before we could scramble into the relative safety of the dark night. Preferably placing a building or two between us and those bullets as well.

I considered lashing out at Helen, but all of my experience had taught me to be patient, to never presume even a witless opponent would not get off a lucky shot. Helen was far from witless, and she seemed quite comfortable holding that pistol, but was she pretending or was she more skilled than I'd presumed? I wasn't certain I wanted to test that notion. I'd already been proven wrong in my other assumptions about Walter's pretty little fiancée.

As if aware where my thoughts had turned, Helen laughed delightedly. "Poor Verity. Didn't expect any of this of someone like me, did you? I could see it in your eyes, you know. When you first arrived and even this afternoon. You were worried I was too young and naïve for Walter. You never guessed."

I didn't dignify this with a response, and she didn't seem to require one.

"And now you're about to watch a man who obviously cares

for you be killed in cold blood," she continued mercilessly. "How painful that must be."

I bit down on my tongue, tasting blood in my effort to restrain myself from lashing out, just as I was certain she would love for me to do. She couldn't have known how sharply her words stung my conscience, for I never should have taken Max into my confidence. Had I known my husband was still alive, I would never have allowed myself to get so close to him, and maybe he would not have ended up in this predicament.

Or maybe he would have. Maybe his own conscience, his own guilt over his failure to protect his men at the front would have driven him to investigate with or without my assistance. It was useless to speculate. Not when I should be focusing on how to extricate us from this with our lives.

I scowled, furious with myself that I'd allowed Helen to distract me. The world beyond the lantern's glow was still steeped in darkness, and the wind howled strong enough to make the gas lamp flicker. It whipped my hair about my face and cooled my heated cheeks. I could hear the lapping of the sea against the rocky shore, then out of the inky blackness to our right appeared the pier.

At that moment, there was a temporary break in the clouds, and I spied the brilliant white decking of a small motorboat tied up at the bend in the pier. Where it had come from and how they'd managed to keep it concealed from the others during their search, I didn't know, but there was definitely one bobbing on the waves slapping the warped wood of the dock now. I stiffened in alarm, understanding now that was how they intended to transport me and Sam to the lagoon at the opposite end of the island, where we would be sunk. But not before killing Max first.

We had run out of time.

Where are you, Sidney? I wondered desperately, scanning our surroundings for any sign of movement.

And then, almost as if my plea had conjured him out of thin air, he appeared.

At first, I thought maybe I was deluding myself when a figure detached itself from the shadows clinging to the rickety remains of the boathouse at the end of the pier. That is, until Felix uttered a foul curse and yanked Max to a stunned stop.

"Halt right there or I'll shoot," Felix yelled.

But the figure did not obey, and somehow I knew without yet being able to really see him that it was Sidney. Perhaps it was a simple matter of deduction, for who else could it be? Or perhaps it was the cocksure walk. Regardless, it vibrated through me with a certainty I couldn't deny. His silhouette, his stride, his arrogant disregard for Felix's threat—they all shouted my husband's name.

"Halt!" Felix yelled again, swinging his gun around to aim it at him.

I wanted to scream at Sidney to stop, to not be a blasted fool and take cover. But I swallowed the panicked words, not wanting to distract him.

When he was near enough for the moon's glow to illuminate his features, I felt the collective impact of everyone's shock—the gasps, the startled steps backward as if they'd been struck.

Felix inhaled a strangled breath, rather like he'd swallowed his tongue. "It can't be," he protested, finding his words. "Y-You can't be here. You're dead!" He jabbed his gun in the air toward Sidney. "Stop! You're dead."

But Sidney kept coming, raising his own arm in front of him so that the moonlight glinted off the cold metal of his weapon.

Max seized the opportunity Sidney's sudden appearance afforded us and lowered his shoulder to slam into Felix, knocking him to the ground. As he did so, I recalled myself in time to note that Helen's concentration and aim had also wavered. I darted around the barrel of her gun, backing up to drive an elbow into her gut while grabbing the pistol with my other hand.

But, unfortunately, although she staggered under the blow, she did not loosen her grip on the weapon. We grappled for it. I pushed it over our heads, trying to land another blow to her midsection with my knee, but Helen proved not to be a weak flower. She twisted her torso to block my knee and swung her elbow inward, striking me in the cheek. I stumbled to the right, maintaining my grip on the gun, and managed to hook my foot around her ankle, nearly taking us both down. We lurched to the right, but somehow remained upright.

All things considered, we were quite evenly matched. We traded a series of blows, and I was certain I would have eventually bested her if it hadn't been for the stray stone that had fallen off one of the buildings which rolled my ankle, crumpling my leg beneath me. I dropped to my knee, losing my grip on the pistol, and Helen took full advantage of my blunder.

Grasping a hunk of hair in one hand and wrenching my head back, she pressed the pistol to my temple with the other. I sucked in a harsh breath.

"Stop!" she shouted. "Stop or I'll put a bullet in her brain."

I blinked through a haze of pained tears to see that Sidney stood less than three steps away. His face was a mask of fury. I could almost feel the heat of his anger radiating off him as he glared down his own pistol at Helen.

"Drop your gun," she ordered him.

He hesitated, and I thought for a moment he wasn't going to do it. That he was going to shoot Helen and ignore the consequences if his bullet didn't kill her before she could pull the trigger on her own gun.

"Do it!" she shrieked, pulling my hair harder.

I tried not to make a sound, but a whimper must have escaped, for I opened my eyes to find him staring down at me. His fingers slowly loosened and he allowed his weapon to fall from his grasp.

"You too," she snapped, and I realized she must be speaking to Max.

I heard the thud of something hitting the ground and the irate grunt of someone rising to their feet, but my eyes remained locked with Sidney's. I couldn't tell what he was thinking, whether he was furious with me or merely disappointed. After all, because of me he was about to watch the traitors he'd been searching for, that he'd sacrificed nearly everything to find, slip through his fingers. If I could, I would've told him I was furious with myself, too. That I hadn't been quicker, stronger, that I'd underestimated Helen's capability, her viciousness.

"Sidney Kent, I presume," she said in interest. "Well, well, this is a revelation I admit I didn't see coming. And you are rather splendid, aren't you? It's only too bad we never had the chance to meet outside these circumstances."

Sidney's expression did not waver from its hardened glare, even at this last insulting statement.

Then her voice lost all of its mockery. "Kick the gun toward me. But not too hard now," she warned.

He glanced down at his feet and did as she instructed.

"I suppose it's too much to hope you didn't take anyone else into your confidence about your being here?" she asked consideringly, and although Sidney didn't react, her mind was still quick. "Ah, yes. Mabel. Of course. You would have needed someone to nurse you back to health after Walter shot you."

Sidney's expression blanched in the light of the lantern Helen had dropped at our feet. After tonight's events, I had presumed it was Felix, but then I realized that was too neat and tidy for the messiness of this entire affair. My heart squeezed, knowing how much it must pain Sidney to know his friend had pulled the trigger.

If, in fact, he had. Maybe now that Helen's plans had been foiled she intended to burn everyone's bridges to the ground.

"Well, I suppose we can't kill everyone at this party," she declared almost begrudgingly. "That would simply be too, too suspicious. So I guess that means we'll have to resort to an alternative plan."

Releasing her grip on my hair, she slowly lowered herself to pick up Sidney's gun, never removing her pistol's muzzle from my temple. She pocketed the weapon.

"Stand up," she told me before addressing the men. "And you three, back up toward the village. Felix, make sure no one tries anything. I should so hate to ruin Verity's very pretty head."

Once the men had moved several yards away, she ordered Felix to start the boat's engine. Then gripping my upper arm, the gun still aimed at my head, she marched me forward, pausing only long enough to deliver one last parting quip. "Now, be good boys and stay off the pier until we're safely away, or I shall have to do something rather drastic. And none of us wants that now, do we?"

I ground my teeth together, wanting more than anything to silence her tart tongue, but I had no choice but to do as I was bid. We picked our way across the warped and splintered wood toward the motorboat. The sound of its engine roaring to life made my stomach dip. Felix hurried over to meet us, taking my hand roughly in his to pull me aboard before shoving me down onto the decking.

Before I could recover myself, Helen was standing above me and Felix had thrown off the moorings and returned to the controls. As we sped off into the inky night, all I caught was a brief glimpse of Sidney, Max, and Sam standing at the far edge of the pier.

I hoisted myself up into one of the seats lining the ship, but Helen demanded I move no farther. When I didn't voice a protest, she carefully staggered forward to confer with Felix where he stood driving the boat.

I glanced around me, unable to see much in the darkness, for there were few habitations on the western rim of Poole Harbor. All I could tell was that Felix had pointed the boat in the direction of the harbor opening. In the distance in front of me, I could see lights shining through the windows of one tall structure, which I decided must be Umbersea Castle. It was evident they intended to escape into the English Channel and then beyond to heavens knew where.

I was no fool. I knew better than to trust that either of them would have much use for me once we reached the open water of the sea. As soon as they had fled far enough to avoid any pursuit, it would only be a matter of time before they decided their hostage was no longer needed. Which meant they would either kill me outright or simply dump me overboard to meet my inevitable demise in the icy, blustery waters of the English Channel.

The waves within the harbor were choppy enough, stirred up by the recent storm and the lashing winds. The boat skimmed over them, jarring us with each rolling strike against the bow. How much worse they would be out on the open sea without the harbor's breakwaters to minimize them.

I slumped in my seat, hoping I appeared defeated, and waited for my opportunity to fight back. At the very least, I would pitch myself over the side of the boat before we reached the mouth of the harbor, to give myself a fighting chance of making it back to land. I only wished I had a better sense of exactly where we were. The night was so dark and the rough seas were making me slightly disoriented as the wind whipped my hair about my pounding head. Only the motorboat's headlamps pierced the darkness.

That is, until two dim lights appeared over the water in the distance behind us. At first, I thought I was imagining them, but they continued to grow brighter and closer. It was then that I realized it was another boat, and it was gaining on us. I bit my lip, hoping Felix and Helen would remain too distracted to notice, but the sound of the other boat's motor, its throttle fully opened, put paid to that wish.

Helen glanced behind her and shrieked, striking Felix on the shoulder. "Go faster, you fool!"

"I can't," he howled. "Not unless you want me to run aground on one of the sunken sand banks and tiny islands and kill us all!"

My heart surged in my chest. There was only one man I knew of who would drive that recklessly, one man whose single-mindedness could push him to behave so rashly.

Sidney.

I stared across the dark water trying to see beyond the lights that continued to grow nearer into the boat behind them, but it was impossible. I only hoped he could see us.

"I don't care how dangerous it is!" Helen snapped. "If that boat catches us and rams us, we might already be sunk." With two angry strides, she moved to stand before me at the back of the boat, raising her pistol to fire at the boat following us.

Fortunately for me, Felix chose that moment to oblige her, increasing the boat's speed with a sudden jolt from the engine.

Helen lost her balance and I seized my chance, diving forward to knock her into the opposite bench. This time I was not going to let her best me, whatever it took.

We grappled for the gun, and I slid my finger into the trigger alongside hers, pulling down on her digit to fire it. Felix cursed, screaming at us to stop, but I could spare none of my attention for him. Helen was determined to play dirty, struggling against me with all her might, and even going so far as to release one hand's grip on the gun to reach down and choke me as she rolled us over to straddle me. I bucked beneath her, trying to throw her off me, but she was too heavy; the angle was too great.

Just when I was starting to worry I would black out before I could escape, Felix unwittingly aided me a second time by making a sharp turn. Allowing the momentum of the vessel to assist me, I managed to roll her off me, wrenching the gun from her grasp in the process. However, the force was too great for my slackened grip, sending the pistol skittering down the deck and out of sight.

I gulped the sweet air, filling my lungs, and then elected to use what advantage I had while I still could. Pulling myself up, I toppled overboard into the glacially cold water.

CHAPTER 24

I surfaced with a gasp. Icy needles pricked every inch of my skin as I treaded the dark water, trying to keep my head above the waves. I could hear the sounds of the boats receding into the distance toward my left, leaving me alone in the black of night. So I turned to search for any indication of land.

Having no way of knowing how close we were to the harbor entrance, I nonetheless decided to strike out in the direction in front of me, hoping it was approximately south-southeast. At the speed we'd been traveling, I could only surmise we were closer to the Studland Peninsula at the south of the harbor than Umbersea Island. In any case, I could no longer see the lights of the castle, and if I was to have any chance of surviving this frigid dip and these pummeling waves I needed to reach land soon, even if all I could do was float there.

It was then that I heard at least one of the boats returning. Its motor had slowed, and I could see its headlamps cutting across the water. At first, I worried it might be Helen and Felix circling back to make sure they'd finished me off. Perhaps that made little sense with Sidney in hot pursuit, but the idea of my husband giving up his quarry when he was so close to catching them was almost as unfathomable. Until I could be sure, I elected to remain quiet and still, avoiding the glow of the boat's lights.

But then Sidney called my name, his frantic voice barely carrying over the sound of the wind.

I almost choked on the sob of my own reply. "Here! I'm here!"

Drawing on my last reserves of energy, I swam toward the boat, repeating his name over and over as loudly as I could manage.

He gave a shout as he caught sight of me. The boat turned in my direction, pulling up alongside me, and soon strong arms were lifting me into the vessel.

I crumpled to the floor, shivering and too exhausted to speak. I lay panting for breath while he scrambled about me. Then urgent hands peeled my sodden coat off my shoulders and wrapped a blanket around me.

Inhaling the familiar scent of Sidney's skin, I burrowed into the crook of his neck and shoulder as he pulled me close. His hands rubbed vigorously up and down my arms and back to warm me, while he seemed to completely ignore the fact that some of the chill water from my hair and clothing must be soaking through into his own clothing. Some minutes passed before I could find my voice, and even then it was not much louder than a whisper.

"You came back."

Sidney craned his neck, trying to see my face, and I lifted my head to look up at him.

"You . . . you let Helen and Felix get away, and you came back for me."

He lifted his hand, smoothing my damp hair back from my brow. "Yes, well, I can always pick up their trail later." His deep blue eyes met mine. "But I can never replace you."

I arched up to kiss him, tasting the salt of the sea that had dried on my lips and the heat of his mouth. I'm not certain how long we drifted along that way, locked in each other's embrace, but in due course I pulled back, recalling I had more to tell him.

"Well, I don't think their trail will be hard to find."

Sidney's eyes gleamed quizzically. "Oh?"

"When Helen and I were fighting for the gun, I managed to shoot the petrol tank." I smiled at the surprise radiating across his features. "I suspect they'll be running out of fuel soon."

I laughed as he planted another emphatic kiss to my mouth and then proceeded to rain kisses down over my cheeks.

"Well, then, my darling girl, what do you say we fetch the

authorities? It's high time we dragged them into this scandalous muddle."

I rose to my feet, clutching the blanket around me, and followed him toward the ship's wheel. Pulling me close to his side, he turned us toward the direction I trusted we needed to go to reach Poole.

"By the way, where on earth did you get a boat?" I asked. "I was astonished enough to discover Helen and Felix had one waiting for them after the men had already searched the island for a working craft."

His eyes twinkled down at me. "You didn't think I would strand myself on that island under an assumed identity without having some means of escape if I needed to, now did you?"

"Yes, but . . ." I began to argue and then stopped. It was useless to point out how we could have used his boat earlier today to leave the island and reach the authorities. He must have known this, and not wanted it to happen. Not until he'd gotten his answers.

I only hoped Sam hadn't paid dearly for his delay. I was too vexed with Walter after learning he'd been the one who attempted to kill my husband to spare him much sympathy.

It was early the following afternoon before all the necessary players could be gathered at Walter's bedside to hear his confession. Though the policemen from Poole had done their best to deal with the strange and alarming situation that greeted them when they arrived on Umbersea Island, it had become necessary to call in the more experienced Scotland Yard. A Detective Inspector Furnam had been summoned from his bed in London to take the earliest train down to Poole, crossing over to the island by boat around midmorning. He was a neat and tidy man with salt and pepper hair and a well-moderated voice. Had his origins been of a higher social standing I suspected he would have made an excellent barrister.

He had listened to the tales Sidney, Max, and I had to tell with a minimum of fuss, but there were still a number of holes to fill in, and only Walter could do that. Fortunately, Mabel's ministrations and Walter's own hearty disposition had saved him from what at one point had seemed certain death. He lounged in his bed, propped up by pillows, with his covers folded over his lap. His face was still puffy and his skin red, but his eyes were bright and open, and his tongue only slightly clumsy in his speech, telling me the swelling had not entirely gone down.

I settled on the settee between Sidney and Max—the place only a short time ago where I had coddled and comforted a murderess. Meanwhile, the detective inspector took the chair nearest Walter's bed, pulling out his notebook to record the facts and his observations. By all rights, Mabel and Sam should have also been present, but she had gone with him to the hospital when he was transferred there in the early morning hours. We had since received the heartening news that, thanks to Max's swift actions in returning him to Mabel's competent care at the castle the night before, he would soon make a full recovery.

I was furious at Walter and wanted to lash out at him. But seeing him in such a poor state, his brow heavy with the knowledge of all his misdeeds, cooled some of my temper and allowed me to sit calmly through our interview.

"Now, Mr. Ponsonby, if you would, please," Furnam said. "Tell us how all of this began."

"Well, I can't tell you exactly how it began, but I can tell you straight that the entire affair was Helen's invention." His eyes lowered to where his hands rested against the royal blue counterpane, looking ruddy and distended. "She was heartbroken and angry that her father, Sir Randolph Crawford, had arranged to have her stepfather, a German citizen living in London, arrested under suspicion of espionage at the beginning of the war. I'm not aware of all the specifics, but I gather her parents' marriage was not a pleasant one, and their divorce proceedings even nastier. When her mother then chose to marry a German, Sir Randolph was livid and tried to keep Helen away from them. However, Helen adored her mother, and grew to love her stepfather equally." His lips quirked humorlessly. "Said he was the only real father she ever had.

"So when Sir Randolph had her stepfather accused of espionage, you can imagine how distressed she was. She begged her father to get him set free, insisting he was innocent, but whatever the charges were exactly, they stuck. And he was executed." He inhaled a breath to steady himself. "And if all that wasn't bad enough, her mother was soon after declared insane and institutionalized. Helen says, to keep her quiet about what she knew, how Sir Randolph had arranged the entire matter."

"I've never heard any of this," I said, thinking of all the time I'd spent in London and even inside the enigmatic walls of the Secret Service, and yet I'd never caught a whiff of any such thing.

"Well, given Sir Randolph's position in the government, the matter was, of course, kept hush-hush." Walter tugged his covers higher, a nervous gesture. "I do know for a fact Helen's stepfather was executed and that her mother was institutionalized. I looked into it. But I can't tell you whether any of the rest of it is true."

"It's possible," Max admitted.

I glanced over to meet his eyes, seeing the weight of all his memories of his own father, and the manipulations he was capable of, reflected there. If anyone knew what a politician might or might not be able to arrange, it was Max.

"In the end, it doesn't really matter, does it?" Walter persisted. "Helen believed it was the truth, and so she decided she would undermine and injure her father however she could. Namely by doing everything her beloved stepfather had been framed for—sharing secrets with the enemy."

"And how did she obtain these secrets?" Furnam asked doubtfully.

His mouth twisted as if the detective inspector's skepticism proved his next point. "She said it was all too easy. That her father never worried about concealing sensitive documents from his silly daughter, so it was simple to learn the names of suspected German spies and collude with them to share information, as well as assist them in evading the authorities." He lifted his gaze to meet Max's. "She also used her father's political friends to the same ends, flirting and offering favors to them."

He paused before choking out the last. "I suspect she slept with a number of them as well."

The detective inspector tilted his head, studying Walter with his keen, dark eyes. "And how did she bring you into all of this?"

He nodded at us. "I suspect they've already told you about the Lonely Soldier columns I posted in the periodicals as a sort of a lark. She responded to one with her picture and a rather . . . provocative letter." His eyes dipped to the coverlet. "I admit I became rather fascinated with her, and we exchanged a number of letters and packages." He cleared his throat. "And then when I returned to London for my next leave, I . . . I visited her."

The rest he could leave to our imaginations, as Helen had already implied what those visitations had been about when she first told us the story at dinner that first night. Though Sidney and Furnam had not been present, I didn't think they needed us to spell it out for them.

"I discovered later, she had done her research, long before she ever contacted me," Walter said. "She knew how deeply I was in debt, how I was in danger of losing everything my father and grandfather had built." His mouth flattened in chagrin. "It was all too easy for her to convince me to deliver a few messages for her. Especially after she'd coerced some of my creditors into sending my bills to her father's solicitor in *her* name."

"And what were these messages?" Furnam asked doggedly.

I found his attention to detail tiresome, for he already knew from talking to us what the messages were. But I also understood he needed to hear the confession directly from the perpetrator's mouth, without coercion. Otherwise Walter and his barrister could later argue he hadn't known what they were talking about.

"Letters to a woman living in the village of Suzanne on the Somme, not far from where I was stationed. She insisted the post was unreliable, and as at first, they were largely conversant, with only small details that nagged at my conscience, I figured I couldn't complain. Not since she'd done so much for me. Besides, I never dreamed a flighty, giddy girl like Helen could be capable of such deception. I thought she must not realize she was sharing anything wrong." He stared bitterly at the wall to his right, indulging in a bit of self-pity.

"And then?" Furnam prodded.

"And then the details she was sharing were not so small. They were not so easy to dismiss. By the time I returned to London on my next leave, I realized it was too late. I couldn't back out." He scoffed at himself. "I'm not sure I wanted to. Not then. Not when her bribes were becoming larger, and I was watching my debt dwindle and disappear. I figured, what harm was it really doing?" He shook his head in disgust. "I wanted to believe that, so I did."

As relieved as I was to listen to him claim responsibility for his actions, I was just as appalled to even have to hear it. I couldn't help but think of the pain and anger Sidney and Max must be feeling, knowing they had somewhat miraculously lived through his betrayal. That they intimately knew those who had not. There was nothing I could do for the hurt etched across Max's brow, but I stole my hand into Sidney's, where it rested on the cushion next to me. He squeezed it, but did not spare me a glance, his glare too fixed on the man who had been one of his closest friends.

Furnam tapped his pencil against his notebook. "How long did this go on?"

"The better part of three years," Walter replied without emotion.

"Three years?!" the inspector gasped. "And you were never caught?"

"The censors rarely read letters from home. After all, who suspects love letters from a soldier's sweetheart of containing treasonous information."

His tongue stumbled on the last words, and he reached toward his bedside table for the glass of water. Furnam leaned forward to pass it to him.

Walter drank from it before lowering it to his lap. "The material that was particularly sensitive was always written in code between sentences that suggested it might be a tad . . . improper. So if the coded parts were ever questioned, they could easily be explained away. But they never were. And then I would transfer the data into another code Helen taught me, before passing it on to her informant in the village.

"It was all going according to plan, until the informant was arrested." He glanced up at Max and Sidney before his eyes darted away again. "Then I began to worry that the soldiers I had been using as messengers would realize they hadn't been delivering love letters to my French paramour, but rather something much more serious. I . . . I suppose you could say I panicked. I decided I should strike before they could, so I . . ." He broke off, taking another drink of his water and then inhaled raggedly. "I convinced Captain Tufton, Lieutenant Halbert, and Second Lieutenant Montague that Privates Arthur and Cortachy, m-my messengers, had been committing treason. But that I had no proof that would stand up to scrutiny. So we needed to take matters into our own hands to have them convicted of the lesser crime of desertion."

"Lesser crime, maybe," Max retorted angrily. "But it still resulted in them facing a firing squad."

"Yes," Walter admitted, sinking lower into his pillows either under the weight of his own guilt or to escape the intensity of Max's and Sidney's glares.

"When did you decide to kill"—Furnam consulted his notes—"Captain Ben Gerard?"

Walter swallowed. "A few months later. I found out he was asking questions about Arthur and Cortachy. I started to worry he might stumble onto the truth. So I convinced Tufton and Halbert that he needed to disappear. That he was making trouble for all of us."

"Disappear? On that night raid?" the inspector clarified.

"Yes."

"So they killed him?"

"Yes."

"At *your* behest?"

He swallowed again before forcing the word out. "Yes."

Furnam flicked a glance at Sidney. "And Captain Kent?"

Sidney sat stiffly beside me, his posture ramrod straight, waiting for Walter's answer.

"When . . . when I realized he'd become suspicious, too, about the deaths of the deserters and Gerard, I . . . I knew he also had to be silenced."

"And how did you attempt to do that?"

I spared a look at Furnam's expression, which could no longer hide his disapproval. I appreciated the fact that he was forcing Walter to state the bald truth, to face what he had done, but I wasn't certain how Sidney would survive it. I brushed my thumb over my husband's knuckles and waited for Walter's reply.

His voice lowered to almost a whisper. "I shot him during the retreat during the Battle of St. Quentin."

"And reported him dead—killed by enemy fire?"

"Yes."

We all sat in silence, letting the enormity of this confession wash over us. I wanted to scream at Walter to at least apologize. Wasn't that the very least he could do? But he remained mute, even closing his eyes as if to block us from his sight. He had been white-faced with shock when Sidney suddenly walked into his room—whole and alive—but now it was as if he wanted to deny his presence.

If I could have, I would have marched across the room and slapped Walter, but I knew that wouldn't make anything better. It wouldn't take away his actions or this rage and agony I felt on my and Sidney's behalf. It would only make my palm sting and force Detective Inspector Furnam to remove me from the room.

So I stayed where I was and instead gripped the black serge of my skirt between my fingers and clasped Sidney's hand tighter.

"Explain how you ended up engaged to Helen Crawford," Furnam said, breaking the silence. "And why you planned this house party?"

Walter set his empty glass of water on the bedside table and clasped his hands before him. "When I was invalided home from the front with my injury, Helen continued to come see me. It was evident she didn't trust me to keep quiet about our secrets, but she was also rather sweet and caring when I had almost no one else. I'm sure it was a charade, but it was quite a believable one. And so I let her convince me we should marry. After all, her father had died, and she had inherited a great deal of money. It didn't seem a bad bargain. At first."

"Her father's death," Furnam interrupted. "What do you know of it?"

He shook his head. "She never said a word to me about it, and I didn't ask. If she had anything to do with it, I'm afraid I can't tell you how. But . . . but I wouldn't be surprised."

Furnam nodded, I supposed trusting that if Walter was being honest with us about everything else, then he wouldn't lie about that. "Go on. What changed?"

"Well, she had always been a bit unnerved by the fact that Sam Gerard, Ben's brother, was stepping out with her cousin Mabel. I told her it meant nothing. That Sam couldn't possibly suspect anything. But then he came to her and suggested it would be a brilliant idea if she invited all of the surviving officers from my battalion, as well as Sidney Kent's widow, to our engagement party. We'd been planning to host a grand house party here on the island, like in my father's days before the war. But as soon as Sam proposed this scheme, she couldn't let it go. She decided he *must* have learned some part of the truth, and that Verity must have, too."

At this, his eyes finally lifted from the point at the end of the bed where he had been staring for most of this interrogation and locked with mine. Why he should choose to plead with me, I didn't know, except that, despite my animosity, I wasn't entirely unmoved.

"I tried to convince her to forget it, to ignore his suggestion, invite the guests she wished, and plan the party she'd originally intended to. I wanted her to just leave the matter alone. But she became *obsessed* with discovering whether the other men I'd involved in our sordid mess could be trusted to keep quiet. So she invited them and Verity, along with a few of her friends to round out the numbers." His eyes darted to the side as Furnam scratched something in his notebook. "I have to say, I was relieved when Verity initially declined her invitation, thinking maybe that would calm some of Helen's paranoia. And it did. Until Verity telephoned to say she'd had a change in plans and would be delighted to join us. Then Helen became more unreasonable than ever."

I arched my eyebrows. "So somehow the rest is my fault for accepting your invitation?"

He shook his head. "No. No, that's not what I'm saying at all. I'm just . . ." His hands fell open in futility. "I'm just trying to explain."

I could see that Walter was tiring, that despite his improved appearance he was still laboring harder than normal to breathe. So I decided to jump straight to one of the questions we hadn't been able to answer.

"Why did Helen attack you? Why did she set that box of honeycomb and bees in your path?" It didn't seem to make any sense. Though, as sickening as all the other revelations had been, I supposed nothing should seem irrational.

He rested his head back against his pillows and shut his eyes for a moment before answering. "Because I ordered her to stop." He looked between me and Max. "I knew when you came to tell me you'd found Jimmy's body that his death was probably not a suicide, but Helen's doing. And then you found Charlie, and there was no longer any doubt. I told her I knew she'd killed them to keep them quiet, and that if she didn't allow me to deliver everyone else back to the mainland safely that I would go to the authorities myself."

"So she decided she needed to silence you, too," Max guessed. "Or, at least, give you a strong warning."

I was suddenly very glad I'd asked Mabel to keep watch over him. There was no way of knowing whether Helen had only meant to threaten him or if she would have finished him off the moment she was alone with him, before he could talk. If she'd succeeded, we might never have found all the answers we sought.

I glanced at my husband. And Sidney's name might never have been satisfactorily cleared.

"What of Felix Halbert?" Furnam asked. "Wasn't she concerned with silencing him, too?"

Walter's eyes hardened. "Felix knew, or at least guessed, most of what had happened during the war, and he somehow divined Helen was involved, for he has been blackmailing us for some time. You would have thought that would make him an even bigger target for Helen, but his willingness to be bought off actually pleased her. I think she felt that meant that, in a way, we owned him. And she collected on that balance by forcing him to assist her this weekend. How involved he was, I don't know. But I suspect he was the one to cut the telephone lines. Among other things. You would need to ask them who exactly did what. If you ever manage to catch them, I'm sure Felix could be convinced to squeal."

The detective inspector exhaled, closing his notebook with a snap. "I suspect you're right, for Halbert was already agreeing to talk in exchange for leniency when they were taken into custody last night." His sharp eyes fixed on me, a gleam of humor shining in their depths. "Stranded in the Channel, I hear. Out of petrol."

I couldn't withhold a smile of my own. "Imagine that."

CHAPTER 25

The house was unsettlingly quiet when I descended the stairs after packing my bags. Most of the guests had scrambled to leave the island the moment the authorities had said they could, taking the yacht back to the mainland. As such, I had expected to find the majority of the castle empty, but turning the corner I discovered that Tom and Nellie were still struggling to make it out the door.

Tom paused at the threshold and said something to Nellie before hurrying back toward me. I could tell she was none too happy about the delay.

"Is it true?" he asked. "Is Sidney really alive?"

"Yes."

He scraped a hand back through his hair in amazement. "Well, confound it all. That's astonishing." Offering me his hand, he summoned a smile. "And wonderful. I'm glad for you, Pip."

"Thank you," I replied softly, still feeling rather uncertain about it all. It *was* wonderful, and also confusing.

"I suppose he'll see you safely home then."

"Yes. Yes, I suppose."

He grinned broadly, as if I'd said something funny. Or perhaps he found my perplexity amusing. Regardless, he began to back away and take his leave.

"Wait."

He arched his eyebrows in question.

"Tom," I began, then hesitated, unsure if I should say something. But then I thought of Sidney, and I realized I must. "Tom, before you do anything rash . . . take Nellie away for a few days. Just the two of you. *Talk* to her. You . . . you might be surprised."

His eyes darkened with the knowledge I was aware of his marital difficulties. I half expected him to tell me to mind my own business. After all, I had no right to interfere. But instead he simply nodded and set off back down the hall toward Nellie at a jog.

I didn't wait to watch them leave, but instead turned away toward the terrace. The sun shone brightly down on the garden, illuminating the damage the storm had wrought and sparkling off the standing pools of water along the pathways. Max leaned against the balustrade while he smoked a fag and studied the leaves and twigs strewn across the lawn. Knowing Sidney was still discussing matters with the detective inspector, I pushed open the door to join him.

At first, Max didn't acknowledge my presence, but merely continued to stare out across the garden, lost in thought. It wasn't until I approached the balustrade that he glanced up at me with an almost distracted smile.

"It's been quite an extraordinary few days, hasn't it?" he remarked.

"Yes, though I'm not certain I'd use that exact adjective."

He grunted. "Quite."

In the distance, I could hear the sound of an ax striking wood and the rustle of branches, no doubt from the gardeners clearing the paths. I wondered idly what Sidney's former coworkers had thought of the revelation that he wasn't actually of the laboring class, but the wealthy young scion of a noble house. For I was certain that if the other guests had learned of Sidney's survival, then the servants belowstairs had also discovered who he was.

I glanced sideways at Max, wondering how he felt about the revelation. There hadn't been time to observe his reaction when Sidney stepped out of the shadows next to the boathouse the night before, and since then I'd not had the opportunity to speak with him alone.

"Thank you for all of your assistance over the last few days," I murmured, examining my scraped knuckles where my hands rested against the stone. My words felt rather clumsy and inadequate, but something had to be said. "I'm not sure I could have discovered all I had without you, and I know I would have been in much graver danger."

"Of course."

I could feel his soft gray eyes on me, but I couldn't turn to meet them. Not yet. "And I wanted to apologize for not being able to tell you everything I knew sooner. I . . . I didn't really know whom I could trust. So even though I wanted to trust you, even though my . . . instincts told me I could, I just couldn't risk it." I lifted my eyes. "Not even after I discovered Sidney was alive."

There was no hurt or recrimination in his gaze, only tenderness and curiosity. "So you didn't know your husband was alive when you came here?"

I shook my head.

"I thought not."

"He . . . revealed himself to me that night after we found Charlie."

He tossed his cigarette aside. "That explains the change I sensed in you." He smiled sheepishly. "I wondered if maybe you had decided I was the guilty party."

"Well . . . yes and no." I sighed. "I didn't know what to think."

"That's understandable. And discovering your husband was alive and well on this island must have been quite a shock."

"To say the least."

Given the circumstances, he was being remarkably kind and forbearing. Had our situations been reversed, I'm not sure I would have been so forgiving.

I pushed a stray lock of hair behind my ear and stared down at the rain-trampled flower beds below us. The alstroemeria were bent nearly sideways, their petals touching the ground.

"I suppose you intend to try to make things work with your husband then," Max murmured cautiously, as if uncertain of my reaction to such a prying question.

But after all we'd been through, all we'd shared with each other and the emotions we'd stirred, he more than deserved an answer.

"Yes, I do." My words were stilted, perhaps exposing my insecurity. "I . . . I think I have to at least try."

He nodded, turning away. The Adam's apple bobbed in his throat as he swallowed. "Well, Sidney is a good man. I've known few finer." He spread his hands wide on the sun-warmed stone. "I think, perhaps, he just became blinded for a time by his own need for justice," he remarked, all too perceptibly. His mouth twisted. "And who can blame him after all we'd seen. I suspect, had I known everything he did, I might have done the same." His gaze met mine. "But he came to his senses in the end. Chose the more important pursuit." He tilted his head, his eyes gently trailing over my features. "I think that's what matters."

I felt a lump rise into my throat, not having realized how much I'd needed to hear those words. And coming from Max, they were doubly touching.

I nodded, too overcome to speak.

"But," he added at the last. "If you should ever change your mind, or . . . need a friend, feel free to look me up." His face softened. "I would be very happy to see you."

I smiled tightly, unsure how I should answer him, or if I even should.

That was how Sidney found us when the door behind us suddenly opened and he strode out onto the terrace. There was nothing improper in our postures or attitudes. We stood a perfectly respectable distance apart. And yet I found myself flushing as if I'd done something wrong. If Sidney noticed it, he chose the gentlemanly course of action and ignored it, stepping forward to take Max's hand.

"Thank you, Ryde. I'm not sure I can adequately express how much I appreciate all you've done for me, for my men"—his eyes locked with mine—"and for my wife."

Max shook his hand. "It's the least I could do considering you've caught us a couple of traitors and brought justice to several men who deserved it. After all, they were my men, too." He tucked his hand into the pocket of his navy worsted suit. "And don't worry about anything at the War Office. I'll smooth things over and make sure any question of desertion charges are dropped, as I'm certain they'll agree they should be. I'll also make certain Sam Gerard and Mabel Lorraine suffer no unpleasant consequences either. Though, I'm sure you'll all be called in, simply as a formality, to have you report the details firsthand. But they shouldn't give you any trouble."

"They do love their paperwork," Sidney quipped.

Ryde's lips quirked. "That they do."

Sidney reached over to wrap his arm around my waist, as casually as if he'd been doing so for years, as if the war and his feigned death had never separated us. "I hear you spend most of your time at your estate on Wight, but the next time you're in London, be sure to look us up."

Max's eyes locked with mine where I stood at Sidney's side. "I will."

I glanced over my shoulder at Max as he walked away, then offered Sidney a strained smile. I could tell he sensed my discomfort, my uncertainty, and I thought it might make him angry, but he only twisted his head to look out over the lawn and the gardens beyond.

"Will you walk with me?" he asked.

I nodded and he took my hand lightly in his, guiding me toward the steps and down onto the paths leading away from the castle. I'd expected him to take me toward the flower gardens, but instead he guided me around the left perimeter of the house toward the sea. We paused at the steps that would have led us down onto the beach, now strewn with the flotsam of the storm.

The sea today was a calm, cool blue, its waves rolling gently up onto the sand. Boats darted to and fro over its surface, most heading toward Poole or out into the Channel, but a few seemed to lazily chart their own course. Above, the skies were a brilliant azure, and only the wispiest of clouds remained.

We didn't talk for some time, just stood hand in hand, listening to the soft cadence of the sea and watching the light glisten off the water. I began to wonder if he expected me to speak first, but then he lifted his face to the sky and closed his eyes.

"I'd almost forgotten what it was like."

He didn't elaborate, and I was just about to ask him to explain when he opened his eyes and looked at me.

"To stand beside you, to feel your hand in mine, and to not worry what the next week, the next day, the next moment will bring." His gaze strayed back toward the water. "It's . . ."

He couldn't seem to find the word, so I tried to finish it for him. "Heartbreaking?"

His head snapped back around, seeing the pain it caused me to think of how bleak his life must have been over the last five years.

"I was going to say remarkable." He pivoted to face me, taking both of my hands in his. "*You* are remarkable." He stared at my fingers, at the wedding band that still gleamed back up at him. The one I'd never removed. "Verity, I'm sorry I hurt you. If I could have seen another way, one where I could return to you sooner, I would have taken it in a heartbeat. I can't tell you how many times I lay awake at night aching for you, wishing I could let it all go and just hold you in my arms again."

Hot tears welled in my eyes and spilled down my cheeks.

"I want to be with you. I've never stopped." His eyebrows arched. "And while I think Ryde is a capital fellow, I have to tell you I have absolutely no intention of giving you up. At least, not without a fight." He leaned closer, staring intently into my eyes. "Will you let me try? Will you return to London with me?"

I sniffed and pulled one of my hands from his grasp, swiping at the tears that continued to course down my cheeks. "Yes. Yes, I will," I replied through the emotion clogging my throat. "But . . ." I inhaled a ragged breath. "You must know it's not going to be so simple. We've both done things we regret. We've both made mistakes and kept secrets. And some of those secrets I know we're still guarding."

His eyes dropped from mine, as if acknowledging the truth of what I was saying. Except I had been referring to my own secrets. What was he still hiding from me?

Gathering my composure, I pressed on and squeezed his hands in emphasis. "I want to make it work. I hope we can. But it will take some time, and patience, and understanding, I think, on both our parts."

"You're right. I realize that. I accept it." He pulled me closer. "But as long as you still care for me the way I care for you, then I think we can see it through." His eyes clouded with worry, and I couldn't believe he didn't already know, that he couldn't tell the moment he looked in my eyes.

"Sidney," I murmured. "Of course I love you. You know I never stopped."

His eyes lit with an exultant gleam, and he captured my mouth in a kiss that almost made me forget myself and where we stood for all of Poole Harbor to see. Almost.

Some time later, he pulled back to look into my flushed face. "What do you say you let me take you home?"

"I would like that," I replied.

He took hold of my hand to lead me back up the path toward the castle. "I suppose Chumley will know the local train schedule, and when we can catch the next one to London."

"Perhaps." I pulled my hand from his, walking ahead of him. "But I didn't take the train down from London."

"You didn't?"

I clasped my hands behind my back and pivoted to walk backward, biting back a smile. "I drove your Pierce-Arrow. It's waiting for me at the Poole quay."

His eyes brightened and I could almost see the excitement humming through him at the prospect of getting behind the wheel of his beloved motorcar again.

"But don't think I'm going to let you drive," I teased, turning away. "You're a bit out of practice, and besides, I've grown rather accustomed to motoring myself."

"Have you?" His voice warmed, catching on to my game.

"Yes, I suspect you'll find I've grown quite independent."

"I see. As troublesome as always, then?"

I narrowed my eyes at him over my shoulder, catching the twinkle in his eyes. "Well, you know what they say. Once a hoyden, always a hoyden."

"And thank heavens for that," he quipped, capturing me about the waist and swinging me around.

I laughed and set about proving how very troublesome I was, indeed.

Connect with Us

Visit us online at
KensingtonBooks.com
to read more from your favorite authors, see books
by series, view reading group guides, and more.

for sneak peeks, chances to win books and prize packs,
and to share your thoughts with other readers.

facebook.com/kensingtonpublishing
twitter.com/kensingtonbooks

Tell us what you think!

To share your thoughts, submit a review,
or sign up for our eNewsletters, please visit:
KensingtonBooks.com/TellUs.